ANTIETAM

The Civil War Battles Series
by James Reasoner

Manassas
Shiloh

ANTIETAM

James Reasoner

CUMBERLAND HOUSE
NASHVILLE, TENNESSEE

Published by
Cumberland House Publishing, Inc.
431 Harding Industrial Drive
Nashville, Tennessee 37211

Cover design by Bob Bubkis, Nashville, Tennessee

Library of Congress Cataloging-in-Publication Data

Reasoner, James.
   Antietam / James Reasoner.
      p.   cm. — (The Civil War battles series ; bk. 3)
   ISBN 1-58182-084-4 (alk. paper)
   1. Antietam, Battle of, Md., 1862—Fiction. 2. Maryland—History—Civil War, 1861–1865—Fiction. 3. Virginia—History—Civil War, 1861–1865—Fiction. 4. Culpeper (Va.)—History—Fiction.
I. Title.
PS3568.E2685 A82 2000
813'.54—dc21

                                   00-022578

Printed in the United States of America
1 2 3 4 5 6 7 8—04 03 02 01 00

For Shayna,
Birthday Girl,
and Joanna,
Little Kahuna

Chapter One

MAC BRANNON HEARD THE shrill sound of the train whistle in the distance but didn't look up from what he was doing. After a long moment of studying the checkerboard with a solemn frown on his face, he reached out and moved one of the checkers.

Michael Davis, sitting opposite Mac on the other side of the cracker barrel serving as a table, let out a laugh and gleefully jumped one of his checkers over several of Mac's. Mac winced as the storekeeper said, "You must not have your mind on the game, Mac. You were never so easy to beat before."

Mac nodded. "Yep. I've got a lot of things on my mind, all right."

Like the war, and the fact that I'm not in it . . .

The two men were sitting on three-legged stools near the long main counter in the rear of Davis's general merchandise emporium in Culpeper, Virginia. It was late on a Saturday afternoon, so the traditional rush of people coming in from the farms in the surrounding area to do their weekly shopping was mostly over. Davis's clerks could easily handle the few remaining customers in the store, which had led Davis to challenge Mac Brannon to a game of checkers.

Outside, the sky was gray and overcast, and a blustery March wind blew, making it chilly enough so that the warmth coming from the black cast-iron stove at the end of the counter felt good. Despite the clouds and the wind, it hadn't rained in Culpeper County for over a week, and the roads were beginning to dry out after spending most of the winter of 1861–62 as quagmires.

Mac looked at the checkerboard and gave a slight shake of his head, uncertain what move to make next. He was saved from having to make that decision by the sound of the train

9

whistle blowing again, much closer this time, followed by a series of excited shouts from outside.

Mac glanced up as his younger brother Henry stuck his head in the door of the general store and called urgently, "Mac! Come on! You've got to see this!"

"What in blazes?" Davis reacted.

Mac came to his feet, a tall, lean man in his late twenties with a shock of brown hair. "Sorry, Mr. Davis," he noted dryly. "I reckon we'll have to call the game a draw."

"A draw!" exclaimed Davis. "But I was beatin' you!"

From the doorway, Henry urged, "Mac, hurry up!" The other customers in the store were already starting toward the door, drawn by Henry's excitement and agitation.

Mac joined them, stepping out onto the high, broad porch. Wagons were pulled up next to it so that they could be loaded with supplies. Earlier in the day they had been lined up three deep. Wooden steps at the end of the porch led down to the dusty street.

Mac, Henry, and the other people were standing where they could look along the street to the depot of the Orange and Alexandria Railroad. A locomotive had rolled into the station from the north, pulling behind it a long train of flatbed cars and freight cars with their doors thrown open. The flatbeds were stacked high with an assortment of trunks, crates, and small cannon. The freight cars were bulging with men in gray uniforms. The Confederate soldiers had begun to jump down out of the cars as soon as the train shuddered and jolted to a halt, and they were still disembarking, a gray tide on a gray day.

"What in the world?" Mac inquired.

"It looks like the whole Confederate army's come to Culpeper," Henry observed.

He was shorter and stockier than his brother and a decade younger. His hair was dark brown, almost black. His eyes shone with excitement as he watched the soldiers climbing off the train.

The arrival of the troops had drawn plenty of attention. People were emerging from buildings on both sides of Culpeper's main street and were looking toward the depot. They all knew that the Orange and Alexandria ran northeast to the town of Manassas, where it joined with the Manassas Railroad coming in from the west. Near Manassas was the farming community of Centreville, and in the countryside not far away was the meandering creek known as Bull Run, where the Confederacy had met the first thrust of the invading Union armies and won a decisive victory, throwing back the Yankees and sending them running home to Washington in a rout.

Since then, the bulk of the Confederate forces in Virginia had remained headquartered in Manassas and Centreville, under the command of Gen. Joseph E. Johnston. Gen. P. G. T. Beauregard, widely regarded as one of the heroes of the opening battle, had been sent west to Tennessee to help counter Union advances there.

Mac heard another train whistle from the northeast. Something had definitely changed, he thought. If this second train was bearing as many men and supplies as the first one, the only logical conclusion was that the Confederate army was pulling back. And from the looks of the way the gray-clad soldiers were beginning to unload the flatcars, they intended to stay in Culpeper for a while.

It looked to Mac very much like his hometown had just become the new Confederate headquarters.

And maybe, he thought with rising excitement, just maybe that meant he would soon see his older brother Will again.

WILL BRANNON hunkered on his heels and leaned his shoulder against the rough trunk of a pine tree. He had taken off his campaign hat and placed it on the ground next to him. Now he lifted a pair of field glasses to his eyes and intently studied the scene before him.

The slope of the hillside fell away steeply from the spot where Will was crouched. Below him, a half mile away, were scattered the buildings of Winchester, Virginia, a town Will knew quite well. Gen. Thomas J. Jackson's Stonewall Brigade, of which Will was a part, had been headquartered there for a time the previous autumn. Over the winter Jackson's forces had withdrawn to the vicinity of Romney, and the Yankees had taken over Winchester.

Like rats moving into an abandoned house, thought Will as his eyes followed the blue-clad figures moving around the town.

Cpl. Darcy Bennett knelt beside Will and asked in a low, rumbling voice, "What do you see, Cap'n?"

"The scouts were right," Will murmured without lowering the field glasses. "It looks like the Yankees are getting ready to move out."

He could see the railroad station in Winchester and the boxes of supplies that were being loaded onto wagons and carried to the depot. A train waited there, occasional puffs of smoke issuing from the octagonal stack of the locomotive to indicate that it already had steam up. More Yankee soldiers were waiting at the station to load the boxes onto the train.

So far, it seemed to be only supplies that the Yankees were moving. The troops were still in Winchester. Evidently they would be the last to go. But with those supplies being moved out, it was inevitable that the Union soldiers would follow them.

Will had a pretty good idea where they would be going, too: across the Blue Ridge Mountains to the Piedmont.

The Blue Ridge itself loomed in the distance to the east, beyond the Shenandoah River that had formed this great valley. Will had spent his childhood looking at the Blue Ridge from the other side, as he grew up on the Brannon family farm near Culpeper. Lowering the field glasses, he glanced toward the mountains and couldn't help but wonder how his family was doing. His mother, Abigail, his brothers Mac and Titus and Henry, his sister Cordelia—except for his wandering brother Cory, off somewhere to the west in Missouri—they were all he had left in the world. Even though his mother had disowned him, had turned him out from the bosom of his family, Will knew that she could never really break the ties that bound them all. He was a Brannon and always would be.

But right now he was also a captain in the Confederate army, commanding this detail on a vital reconnaissance mission. Rebel scouts had brought word to Jackson that the Yankees were getting ready to pull out of Winchester, out of the Shenandoah Valley entirely, more than likely. Will and his men had been sent to confirm or deny that speculation.

They had spent a couple of chilly days marching along muddy roads until they reached this range of hills just west of Winchester. Taking to the brush then, so that they wouldn't be as likely to be discovered by Union patrols, they had moved through the hills to this vantage point. Now they were so close to the Yankees that they could hear the shouts of men giving orders from below them and could smell the wood smoke from the many fires in the Union camp.

Will let drop the field glasses suspended from a rawhide thong around his neck. He picked up his hat and straightened from his crouch. A glance over his shoulder showed him the eight men who had accompanied him and Corporal Bennett on this mission. They were kneeling, using trees and brush for cover, their rifles held ready in their hands. To a man, their lean faces and hollow eyes showed the effects of the harsh winter just past. And spring was not yet here.

"The Yankees are getting ready to pull out," Will told them in a quiet voice. "Remember that. It's important."

They all understood what he meant. If anything happened to the group on the way back to Confederate headquarters, if some of them didn't make it . . . well, then, it would be up to the survivors to carry the word to Jackson. At least one member of this detail *had* to make it back to Mount Jackson, which had carried its name long before the famous general had located his headquarters there.

God willing, all of them will make it back, thought Will as he motioned for the men to pull back. The Yankees in the town were all occupied and hadn't spotted the Confederates on the hillside. In a matter of moments, Will and his men had withdrawn up the brushy slope until they were no longer visible from Winchester. All they had to do now was avoid any Union patrols in the area.

Darcy took the lead. Like Will, he had grown up in Culpeper County. He had been more of a hunter and a woodsman than a farmer, although he had worked a patch of ground before the war came along. When he was sober, that is. Darcy had had a fondness for getting liquored up and brawling that had caused his path to cross that of Sheriff Will Brannon several times, always with unpleasant consequences. The war had made both Will and Darcy put any hard feelings behind them, however. It was difficult to hold a grudge against a comrade in arms.

The Confederates wove through the rugged countryside and had put a couple of miles behind them when they reached a road. Darcy lifted a hand in a signal to stop. The enlisted men went down in a crouch as Will moved alongside the burly corporal.

"Somethin' comin', Cap'n," Darcy hissed.

Will heard it, too. The noise was the creaking of wagon wheels, he decided, accompanied by soft thuds that were probably from the hooves of horses or mules hitting the still-soft surface of the road. He glanced over his shoulder and saw that his men were well concealed. He figured he and Darcy should follow their example and indicated as much with a jerk of his head. The two men faded back into the brush to wait.

They didn't have to do so for very long. Within a matter of minutes, three wagons came into view, rolling around a bend in the road to the north. The wagons were piled high with household goods. A middle-aged woman with strong features under her bonnet was driving the first vehicle. An elderly man was beside her on the seat. The team of mules pulling the second wagon was being handled by a boy around twelve. A younger girl was sitting beside him. The driver of the third wagon, a young woman who was maybe twenty years old, was alone on that seat. Will found his attention drawn most to her. Blonde curls hung out from under her bonnet, and she was quite pretty. She also looked too delicate to be handling a team of mules, but from what Will could see of it, she was doing a good job.

"Well, I'll swan," Darcy whispered from beside Will as they knelt behind some brush. "Where do you reckon they're goin'?"

Will just shook his head in silence. He thought he saw a resemblance between all five of the pilgrims. The old man might be the woman's father. The three youngsters were likely her children. Like Darcy, he wondered where the family was headed.

More hoofbeats sounded before the wagons could roll out of sight. These came from the south, and they were much more rapid. A dozen men on horseback swept into view, cantering along the road toward the wagons. They wore the short blue jackets and black caps of a Yankee cavalry patrol. The man in the lead reined in and called an order for his men to stop. Then he barked, "You there in the wagons! Halt!"

Will's jaw tightened grimly. He didn't much like the looks of this. From the sound of the low, rumbling growl that issued from Darcy's throat, neither did the corporal. Will motioned for him to be quiet and wait to see what was going to happen.

"Whoa there! Whoa, I say!" the woman called to her mules as she hauled back on the reins. The wagon came to a stop, as did the other two vehicles. The woman asked in unfriendly tones, "What is it you want?"

The officer in charge of the patrol, a lieutenant, lifted a hand to his cap and tugged respectfully on the brim. "Begging your pardon, ma'am," he said, "but civilians aren't supposed to be traveling on these roads."

"And why not?" demanded the old man in a high-pitched, irritated voice. "These are our roads, ain't they? They sure as shootin' don't belong to you Yankees." The last word sounded as if it tasted bad in the old man's mouth.

The Union lieutenant kept his patience, and Will couldn't help but admire that about the man. He explained, "General Shields has ordered the roads closed so that aid cannot be sent to the Rebel forces west of here."

The old man cackled. "We ain't goin' west, sonny. We're goin' south. Can't you see that? Or are you Yankees so damn dumb you don't know which way's which?"

"Hush up, Pap," the woman directed, confirming Will's suspicion that the old man was her father. She must have seen the way the Union troops bristled at his scathing words. Will had certainly noted the soldiers' reaction. The woman looked at the lieutenant and went on, "We're just poor folks moving from one place to another, mister. We're not giving aid to anybody. Just trying to look out for ourselves."

"Where are you from, and where are you bound?" asked the lieutenant.

"We used to live up in Martinsburg, but we couldn't make a go of our farm with my husband and our three oldest boys gone."

One of the cavalrymen laughed and said, "Gone off to war is what she means."

The woman ignored the interruption and continued, "We got kinfolk down in Fisher's Hill. We plan to stay with them awhile. Everything we got left to our name is on these wagons, mister. We just want to go find a home."

The lieutenant hesitated, clearly torn. His orders were clear, but it was obvious the woman was telling the truth and that this family of pilgrims did not represent a threat to the Union forces. Will watched the young officer intently, reading the struggle that played out on the man's face.

Then the soldier part of him won, and he shook his head and said, "I'm sorry, ma'am, but you'll have to turn those wagons around and come with us into Winchester. If General Shields says it's all right, you can go on your way then."

Several of the troopers had edged their horses forward, and one of them prodded his mount into a trot that carried it alongside the third wagon, the one driven by the pretty young woman. The Yankee looked her over boldly, causing her face to flush with embarrassment.

The lieutenant snapped, "Higgins, get back here."

"Yes sir, Lieutenant," the cavalryman responded. "Right away." But he took his time turning his horse around, and his eyes lingered on the woman while he was doing it.

Will's teeth ground together in frustration. He would have liked to smash a fist into Higgins's grinning face, but he and his men had to stay out of this if at all possible. He glanced around at the others, saw the anger shining in their eyes, and knew they were anxious to intervene, even though it would jeopardize their mission.

The lieutenant seemed to be a humane sort, but he was going to follow his orders anyway and take these people into Winchester as virtual prisoners. Once again, the Yankees were going to run roughshod over the people whose homeland they had invaded.

The Union soldiers didn't seem to have any idea that they were being watched by a group of Confederates, crack shots each and every one of them. It would be so easy to teach these Yankees a lesson. One volley would knock most of them out of their saddles . . .

Will drew in a deep breath, the air hissing between his clenched teeth. Again he motioned for Darcy and the other men to wait.

Slowly and awkwardly, the wagons were turned around and pointed north. They rolled off into the distance, toward a crossroad that would take them into Winchester. Will didn't motion for his men to leave their hiding places until the pilgrims and the Union cavalrymen were well out of sight.

As the Confederate soldiers emerged from the brush, Darcy Bennett looked at Will and asked angrily, "How come we didn't put a stop to that, Cap'n? Them Yankees didn't hardly outnumber us, and they didn't know we were here. We could've taken 'em."

Mutters of agreement came from the other troopers in gray.

Will knew that everything Darcy said was true, but he snapped, "A fight would have meant that some of us might be killed, and that would hurt our chances of getting back to General Jackson. The shots could have drawn more Yankees, too."

"I never knew you to be scared of Yankees, Cap'n." Darcy's voice was low, but it held a definite challenge.

Will had to fight down the impulse to take off his cap and holster and saber and settle this with fists. As fond as he had grown of Darcy, he wasn't going to let any man call him a coward.

But even though he had never considered himself much of a soldier and had become an officer by chance as much as anything else, Will had learned something of military discipline during his time in the army. He ordered tautly, "That's enough, Corporal. In my judgment, the need to help those civilians did not outweigh the need to finish our mission. That's the only explanation you're going to get from me. And by God, it's more than you would have gotten from most officers." Will became aware that both of his hands were clenched into hard fists.

Darcy regarded him for a moment, then nodded. "Will Brannon ain't like most officers," he noted. Then he jerked his head toward the other men and ordered, "Let's go."

The patrol moved out, some of them still sullen but others seeming to understand Will's decision now. Darcy took the lead, as usual, as they resumed making their way southwest toward Jackson's headquarters.

Will didn't remind them of it, but he knew that if what they wanted was to kill Yankees, they would surely get another chance to do that, probably sooner rather than later.

Chapter Two

CORDELIA BRANNON SANK HER fingers into the biscuit dough and lightly kneaded it while her mother, Abigail, built a fire in the stove. Abigail was frowning and muttering about how Titus should have tended to the stove, instead of disappearing out into the barn.

But Titus wasn't much good for anything these days, Cordelia thought, except for drinking. No sooner had the thought gone through her head than she experienced a flash of guilt for feeling like that. Titus was her brother, after all, and she had to be a loyal sister and love him and give him the benefit of the doubt, even when it appeared that he had temporarily lost his way.

And all over a . . . a trollop such as Polly Ebersole.

Cordelia dug her fingers harder into the dough. Thinking that about Polly only made her feel worse. She had no right to condemn Polly just because the girl was the daughter of one of the richest men in Culpeper County, maybe in all of Virginia, or because Polly had always gotten pretty much whatever she wanted and didn't really care if anybody was in her way or not. To tell the truth, Cordelia reminded herself, Polly had never taken anything away from Cordelia, not one thing.

Except for maybe Titus.

Cordelia was the only one of the Brannon children to have inherited her father's red hair. They had all gotten a touch of John Brannon's Irish temper, though, and right now Cordelia was mad. Her mother was right. Titus had been moping around and neglecting his chores for months now, ever since Duncan Ebersole had sent his daughter to live with relatives in Richmond. Cordelia knew he was drinking a lot, and so did Mac and Henry. Only Abigail seemed to be blind to what was going on, and that came as something of a surprise to Cordelia. She would have thought that her mother's hard-shell Baptist nose would have sniffed out the reek of whiskey that seemed to hang around Titus most of the time these days. But all Abigail seemed to know was that her middle son had become a layabout.

Abigail stepped back from the stove and brushed her hands together. "There," she remarked. "Are you about done with that biscuit dough, Cordelia? If you work them too hard they'll be tough."

"Yes, Mama," Cordelia replied. She took the dough out of the bowl and placed it on a floured board. Quickly she rolled it out with a rolling pin and started cutting out the biscuits with a glass that she first dipped in flour. As each biscuit came off the glass, Cordelia placed it on the flat pan that would go on top of the stove.

"Your brothers should have been back from town by now," Abigail reflected as she turned toward the front of the farm-house. "As cloudy as it is, it'll be getting dark early. I hope they get home before night."

Since her mother's back was turned, Cordelia shook her head. Abigail still seemed to think of her children as little and helpless at times. Cordelia was the baby of the family, and she was eighteen, a full-grown woman. Why, most of the girls her age in the county were already married.

Yes, and their husbands had gone off to fight in the war, Cordelia reminded herself. With war raging across the country-side, maybe being unmarried wasn't such a bad thing after all.

But Mac and Henry were perfectly capable of taking care of themselves, even after dark. Mac wouldn't have any trouble with the horses—Mac never had any trouble with any animals—and Henry had taken along his rifle. Henry was a good shot. Not as good as Titus, of course, but nobody around here was as good with a rifle as Titus was, at least when he was sober.

As Cordelia was putting the biscuits on the stove to cook, Abigail announced, "Well, here they are now." Cordelia heard the front door open, and a moment later Mac and Henry walked through the dining room and into the kitchen. Henry had a sack of flour slung over his shoulder, and Mac was carrying a couple of boxes in which Mr. Davis's clerks had packed the supplies they'd bought.

"Put those boxes on the table," Abigail told Mac, "and Henry, you take that flour out to the pantry."

"Yes'm," Henry said. His face was flushed, and he seemed to be excited about something. With the sack of flour still on his shoulder, he went on, "You won't believe what happened in Culpeper this afternoon."

"Go put up that flour like I said," Abigail ordered crisply.

Henry hesitated, clearly not wanting to displease his mother but full of excitement at the news he had. He finally headed for the pantry, his boots clumping on the planks of the kitchen floor. As Henry went out into the narrow pantry built onto the back of the house, Abigail turned to Mac, who had placed the boxes on the table, and asked, "Now what's all this about something happening in Culpeper?"

"The army's pulled out of Manassas and Centreville, and they're going to make their headquarters here for a while," Mac answered.

Henry came out of the pantry in time to hear the last part of Mac's reply, and he explained, "Aw, Mac! You said I could tell 'em."

"Ma asked," Mac said, as if that explained everything, and truth to tell, in the Brannon household, it pretty much did.

"They came by train," Henry added quickly, determined to deliver some of the big news himself. "Three or four trains, one right after another. I never saw such. Never saw so many soldiers, either. They were everywhere, and they looked mighty fine in those gray uniforms." His voice held a trace of wistfulness.

Cordelia knew that Henry wished he could enlist in the army and help drive the invading Yankees back where they came from. She knew if she were a young man she would feel the same way.

But when her oldest brother, Will, had gone off to war, he had extracted promises from Mac and Titus and Henry that they would stay and keep the farm going. At the time, it had seemed a reasonable enough request. No one had expected the war to last more than a few weeks. The general feeling was that once the Yankees had been whipped a time or two, they would sue for peace. And when the battle of Manassas had ended with a rousing Confederate victory, that feeling was reinforced. It would be only a matter of days and all the young men would be coming home.

But it hadn't worked out that way. Months had passed, and still the North stubbornly insisted on prolonging the conflict. More and more men had enlisted, until nearly every able-bodied young man in Culpeper County was wearing the gray. Except for Cordelia's friend Nathan Hatcher, the studious young law clerk for Judge Darden, and the remaining Brannon boys. Nathan had come in for a lot of ragging by the citizens of the county, but nobody said much of anything about Mac and Titus and Henry still being civilians. That was probably because nobody doubted their courage—and nobody wanted to get Titus mad at them.

Still, Henry must have seen the looks that were sometimes cast his way whenever he was in town, the looks that said *Why isn't he in the fight?*

"There were cannons, too," Henry was going on, "and horses and guns and—"

"It all sounds like quite a spectacle," Abigail cut in. "I hope those soldiers don't eat up all the food that's left in the county."

That could be a real worry, Cordelia realized. With winter just now getting over with and spring coming on, folks were living on what they had put away the year before. They were getting ready to put in their crops, but it would be months before any of them made.

Henry turned to Cordelia. "I saw your beau Nathan in town. He looked a mite sick when he saw all those soldiers."

Cordelia felt her temper ignite. "He's not my beau," she snapped. "He's just a friend of mine. And you'd better just hush up, Henry Brannon. You don't have any room to talk about folks not wearing the uniform."

Henry flinched as her words struck him, and for just an instant, Cordelia felt sorry for him. But then she pushed that impulse away. All she'd done was tell the truth. Henry *didn't* have any room to talk. And Nathan *wasn't* her beau. She just enjoyed talking to him about books and such, since he read a lot. Whenever she ran into him in town, she liked walking along the street with him and hearing him talk about things. It didn't really matter what they discussed, Cordelia enjoyed listening to him anyway. She had found herself wishing a time or two that he would reach over and take hold of her hand while they were walking . . .

But that didn't make him her beau, for goodness' sake!

"You two quit fussing," Abigail demanded. "Cordelia, those biscuits are going to burn if you don't tend to them."

"Yes, Mama," Cordelia replied as she turned toward the oven.

"Mac, you'd better go find your brother," Abigail went on. "I swear, Titus is so absent-minded these days, he could get lost between the barn and the house."

Mac nodded. "I'll go get him." He turned to leave the room.

"I think he's in the barn," Abigail called after him, and Mac waved to show that he had heard.

Absent-minded didn't start to describe how Titus was these days, Cordelia thought as she swathed her hand in a thick leather potholder and grasped the handle of the biscuit pan to take it off the stove. It was sometimes an almighty trial for a girl to have to live with a bunch of brothers, she told herself.

Especially when they were like the Brannon boys.

———

"You're a big bastard, aren't you?" Titus muttered as he leaned on the stall door. In the gloom of the unlighted barn, the horse inside the stall did indeed seem massive. Seen in the light of day, the silver gray stallion was one of the most impressive pieces of horseflesh around. Titus took another swig from the flask in his hand and thought about what it would be like to ride up to Mountain Laurel on a horse like that. Old Man Ebersole wouldn't be so quick to dismiss him then as one of Polly's suitors, he told himself. A man who could ride that stallion was a man to be reckoned with.

Titus put the cap on the flask and said aloud, "By God, I'm going to do it." He slipped the flask into the inner pocket of his vest and reached for a halter hanging on the wall of the barn. He put his hand on the latch, ready to open the stall door. The stallion shifted around and blew air through its nostrils. That horse didn't much like him, Titus knew, but he didn't care. It was about time the dumb animal learned who was boss around here.

"Titus!" Mac's voice rang sharply from the big double doors that stood open at the front of the barn. "What do you think you're doing?"

Titus started guiltily, and no sooner had that reaction passed than he felt angry about it. "What are you doin', sneakin' up on a fella like that?" he demanded as he swung around toward Mac, the harness still dangling from his left hand.

"I didn't sneak up on anybody," Mac contended as he strode into the barn, coming along the hard-packed dirt floor of the wide center aisle toward Titus. He came to a stop and gestured toward the harness. "Getting ready to take a ride?"

"What if I am?" Titus challenged.

Mac shook his head. "Not on the stallion. You know better. You'd just get hurt."

"Not if I took a quirt and lashed some sense into him."

Mac tensed, and for a second Titus thought his older brother was going to take a swing at him. Then, with a visible effort, Mac forced himself to relax and said, "That horse wouldn't let you get near him with a quirt, and you know it."

Titus didn't argue with that. He declared sullenly, "You think you're so high and mighty. You think you're the only one who can ride that horse."

"So far that seems to be true," Mac pointed out.

Titus couldn't argue with that, either, he realized. Mac could handle the silver gray stallion, but anybody else was risking life and limb by going near the horse when Mac wasn't around.

That horse had been Mac Brannon's obsession for a year, mysteriously appearing and disappearing around the farm, seemingly taunting Mac with its speed and intelligence. Finally, though, a couple of months ago, Mac had caught the beast. Not only caught it, but tamed it. It was as if the horse had merely been waiting for Mac to prove himself worthy of it. Now that he had, the stallion was willing to surrender itself to whatever Mac wanted.

Titus knew all that, but that didn't mean he had to like it. As far as he was concerned, Mac's ownership of the stallion was just one more way his big brother liked to lord it over him. After all, Will had left Mac in charge on the farm when he went off to war, and everybody knew that Mac was soft, a dreamer, not the sort to be in charge of anything.

"I just thought I'd see if he'd let me ride him," Titus protested now, still sullen. He wished Mac wasn't here so he could get his flask out and take another drink.

"Well, you can't," Mac announced flatly. "Besides, supper's nearly ready. Ma wants you to come inside, so put that halter up and come on."

Titus hung the halter on the hook where he had gotten it and fell in step beside Mac. As they emerged from the barn, Mac said, "You know, Ma's going to smell that liquor on you one of these days, and then there'll be hell to pay."

"It won't be you who has to pay it," snapped Titus. "Mind your own business, Mac."

"You're my brother," Mac insisted. "It is my business when I see what you're doing to yourself, Titus."

Titus stopped short, forcing Mac to do likewise. In the shadowy dusk that was falling, Titus's face was haggard as he asked, "What would you do, Mac, if somebody took that horse away from you?"

"I told you," Mac began, "if you try to ride the stallion, you'll get hurt—"

"That's not what I'm talking about," Titus cut in. "Suppose somebody showed up and said that horse was his and took it away."

"Well . . . I suppose I wouldn't like it. I worked long and hard to catch that stallion. And there's something special between us." Mac's voice was hesitant, as if he were unsure about revealing just how deep the connection was between him and the magnificent silver gray horse.

"Just like there was something special between me and Polly." Titus saw his brother was about to speak and rushed on so that Mac couldn't interrupt him. "I kissed her, Mac, out there in the garden at her pa's house. You remember, the night of that party."

"I remember Ebersole had his men thrash you within an inch of your life," Mac recalled.

Titus threw his head back and laughed, taking Mac by surprise. "You just don't understand, do you?" Titus contended. "I didn't mind the beatin' all that much. If that was the price I had to pay to hold Polly in my arms and dance with her and kiss her, well, then, so be it. And it was worth it, big brother, worth every punch and kick, because I already knew there was something special between Polly and me. I felt it." Titus swallowed, but he couldn't get rid of the bitter taste that filled his mouth. "And then . . . Ebersole took her away from me. And I feel just like you would if somebody took that horse away from you."

For a long moment, Mac didn't say anything. Then, in a quiet voice, he said, "I'm sorry, Titus. I didn't know you were hurting that bad." He paused, then added, "But staying drunk half the time isn't going to make things any better."

Again, Titus laughed, but this time it had a more hollow sound. "Just couldn't stand it, could you, Mac? Couldn't say you were sorry and let it go at that. You had to play the big brother and tell me what to do and what not to do." Suddenly, Titus poked Mac in the chest with a stiff finger. "Well, you know what you can do, big brother? You can go and—"

The front door of the farm house opened, and Cordelia called, "Mac? Titus? What are you doing just standing out there? It's mighty chilly, and supper's ready."

Mac and Titus looked at each other, and Mac declared quietly, "This isn't over."

"That's where you're wrong, big brother," decreed Titus. "Everything's over, and you just don't know it yet."

<hr />

HENRY DIDN'T know what had gone on between Mac and Titus, but he was sure there had been some sort of argument. Probably over Titus's drinking, Henry thought. He knew better than anybody how much liquor his brother was putting away these days; he shared a room with Titus, after all, and had for his entire life.

He didn't think much about that, however, as he lay in bed that night and listened to Titus snoring next to him. Instead, Henry's thoughts were on the soldiers he had seen disembarking from the trains in Culpeper that afternoon. He had never seen a more dashing bunch in his life.

Truth be told, Henry supposed they weren't all *that* dashing. It had been a harsh winter, and the soldiers had looked rather cold and hungry as they climbed down from the freight cars. Their uniforms showed some wear, too. Cuffs had begun to fray, and more than one knee or elbow had a crude patch on it.

But Henry had seen all that without really seeing it. What he had noticed was how the brass insignia on the campaign caps seemed to gleam even on an overcast day, and how the sabers carried by the officers rattled, and how the bayonets attached to the barrels of the rifles looked so sharp and deadly. He would have given almost anything to be able to carry one of those rifles and use it to send the Yankees packing. They'd think twice about invading the sovereign homeland of honorable people after meeting up with Henry Brannon, yes sir.

Henry smiled in the darkness of the bedroom and pulled the blankets a little tighter around him. He could almost hear the glorious song of the trumpets blowing the charge as he drifted off to sleep.

———❦———

ABIGAIL CLOSED her Bible and placed it carefully on the little bedside table, then she leaned over to blow out the candle. After she had said her nightly prayers, she had read a bit of the Lord's Holy Word before going to sleep, as was her custom. Only a few verses tonight, though. She was tired, and the candle didn't seem to give off as much light as it used to, so she couldn't see the words as clearly as she once had.

Not that there was anything wrong with her eyesight. She could still see sinfulness and wickedness just as good as ever.

Titus thought he was fooling all of them, but Abigail knew he was going out and indulging in the Devil's brew. He was probably committing all sorts of other sins of the flesh, too. Abigail had pondered long and hard on the matter, and she had asked the Lord about it, but so far she hadn't been able to decide what to do.

Once it would have been simple enough. If she had discovered her children committing the sins that Titus was committing, she would have told them to begone. She would have told the transgressor the same thing that Jesus had told the Devil when He was tempted in the wilderness: "Get thee behind me, Satan."

But that was before she had cast her oldest son out of the family. Right or wrong, Abigail didn't think she could stand the pain of banishing another of her children, no matter what the provocation.

She rolled onto her side, shivering slightly. *Oh, John. You were a terrible, awful, infuriating man. But why did you have to go and leave me? I don't know what to do. I just don't know what to do . . . this terrible war, and the children, and . . . and nothing will ever be the same . . .*

If John Brannon had been there, he would have listened to her and then laughed and kissed her and said, "Aw, Abbie, me darlin', you worry too much. Life's goin' to do what it will. Time and tide, darlin', time and tide."

Abigail wished her husband were here with her again, so she could tell him one more time to hush his nonsense and one more time could feel the touch of his hand.

Chapter Three

THE WINTER OF 1861–62 HAD not been good to the South. February had been a disastrous month in the West, with Forts Henry and Donelson in Tennessee falling to Union forces under the command of Gen. Ulysses S. Grant. Those forts had been erected to protect Nashville, and with their loss, Tennessee's capital was in danger.

March had not begun any better. At Hampton Roads, Virginia, the Confederate ironclad *Virginia*—fashioned from the wreckage of the Union frigate *Merrimac*—had attacked several of the Northern ships trying to enforce the blockade of the South, only to find itself opposed by the Union ironclad *Monitor*. The duel between the two vessels had been fierce but inconclusive. However, in the end, the *Virginia* had been forced to withdraw, leaving Hampton Roads under the control of the Yankees.

All of those defeats were bitter pills for the Confederates to swallow, so Will Brannon wasn't surprised to overhear some of the men grumbling about them as he approached the house in the village of Mount Jackson where Gen. Thomas J. Jackson had made his headquarters after withdrawing from the area around Romney. On the porch several officers were talking animatedly, including Capt. Yancy Lattimer, and as Will came up the steps, the tall, lean, aristocratic Southerner greeted him with a friendly smile.

"There you are," said Yancy. "There are big doings afoot, Will. I was afraid you were going to miss them."

Will took off his hat and slapped it against his leg. "Not likely. I reckon what I've got to tell the general is part of what's got you boys so worked up."

One of the other officers, a man in his thirties with thick brown hair and a prominent beard, nodded to Will and said in

35

a soft-spoken voice, "I hear you've been doing some scouting, too, Brannon."

"That's right, Colonel Ashby. I just got back from taking a patrol up to Winchester."

Col. Turner Ashby smiled. "I suppose you found the same thing I did—the Yankees are preparing to move out."

"Yes sir," nodded Will. "That's the impression I got."

"If you'd seen the roads east of there, it would be more than an impression. General Shields is sending supplies and men out of there every day."

Will knew that to have seen what was going on east of Winchester, Ashby and his cavalry patrols would have had to penetrate behind enemy lines. That would be nothing unusual for Ashby, who despite his seemingly mild manner had a reputation for personal bravery unequaled in the Confederacy.

Jackson stepped out onto the porch, bringing the gathered officers to attention. He returned their salutes. With his rumpled uniform, thinning dark hair, and tangled beard, he did not look like one of the heroes of the South, but he was. He addressed them succinctly, "Come inside, gentlemen. We have much to discuss."

Some commanders would have sent an aide-de-camp to summon his subordinates to a meeting. Not Stonewall Jackson. He was a direct, plainspoken man. He led the officers into what had been a dining room before maps had been tacked up all over the walls. Pausing in front of one of them, the general prodded it with a finger and declared, "There lurks the viper poised to strike at our bosom, gentlemen. And that viper's name is McClellan."

Will looked more closely at the map and saw that Jackson was indicating Fort Monroe, a Union-held installation at the very tip of the peninsula that extended between the wide mouths of the York and the James Rivers on the Virginia coastline. Northwest of that peninsula, within easy striking distance, was the Confederate capital of Richmond.

Jackson continued, "I have received word that McClellan is transporting his men to the peninsula and landing them in the vicinity of Fort Monroe. What do you think this massing of Yankee troops on Virginia's soil portends, gentlemen?" There was a pedantic tone to Jackson's voice, reminiscent of his days as an instructor at the Virginia Military Institute. Those days, really, were not long in the past.

"McClellan intends to invade the peninsula and march on Richmond," Yancy Lattimer said, putting into words what was obvious to every man in the room.

And that realization carried with it a chill that went all the way to the bone.

Jackson nodded and clasped his hands together behind his back. "Exactly."

"Are we going to withdraw from the Valley and reinforce our positions around Richmond, General?" asked Brig. Gen. Gilbert S. Meem.

"Not at present," Jackson replied, and while Will would have expected him to be somewhat disappointed by that situation, Jackson really didn't seem displeased. "We've been given an important task to carry out here in the Shenandoah." Jackson turned to Will. "I believe you have a report for me, Captain Brannon."

All eyes were on Will now, and he found the scrutiny slightly uncomfortable. Although he tried not to let it bother him, he was unable to completely forget that many of these men were graduates of West Point and former officers in the U.S. Army, while others had been wealthy planters in civilian life. He, on the other hand, had never been anything except a farmer and a lawman. Still, his hesitation was very brief before he answered, "Yes sir. The Yankees are getting ready to pull out of Winchester. I agree with what Colonel Ashby has already told you."

"If they're leaving the Valley, where do you think they're going, Captain?"

"To attack Richmond from the northwest, so that the capital will be caught between two forces." Will hadn't really thought about it until now because he hadn't known about McClellan's massing of troops on the Virginia Peninsula, but it certainly made sense that the Yankees would like to catch the Confederate capital in a crossfire if they could.

"That's my feeling, too," Jackson agreed. Suddenly, he smacked one fist into the palm of the other hand. "So we're going to stop them!"

"How, sir?" one of the colonels asked.

"The Federals in these parts can't go gallivanting off to Richmond when their own capital is threatened, now can they?"

The wheels of Will's brain were turning over quickly. He saw what Jackson meant. If the Union army withdrew from northern Virginia, then a quick dash across the Blue Ridge and along the Potomac by an unopposed Confederate army would have the Southerners on Lincoln's doorstep in a matter of days. Unfortunately, they had fewer than five thousand men, and that wasn't enough to capture Washington.

But the Yankees didn't have to know that, Will thought with the beginnings of a slow smile of understanding.

"Call in all your troops, gentlemen," ordered Jackson. "We will be marching on Winchester as soon as possible to demonstrate to the enemy that we are still a force to be reckoned with."

"Yes sir!" The chorus of agreement rang from all the officers.

"You're dismissed." Jackson rubbed his hands together lightly in anticipation. "Let's get to work."

The officers filed out of the house, some of them talking excitedly, others grimly intent on the mission that lay before them. The heart of the Confederacy was in danger, and while they would not be participating directly in its defense, what they did here in the Shenandoah Valley might turn out to be of the utmost importance in the survival of their new nation.

"I'm ready for some action," Yancy announced as he and Will strode toward their company camps. "Those skirmishes we had with the Yankees when we moved up around Romney didn't amount to much."

Will had taken part in some of those "skirmishes," as Yancy called them, which had been designed to harry the Yankees by destroying several railroad bridges and dams. None of those thrusts had been particularly successful, but that hadn't made them any less dangerous for the men involved. Will had come through them without any fresh wounds, for which he was grateful since he still limped occasionally from a deep bullet graze on his thigh suffered in a fight with a Union patrol a couple of months earlier.

"You're just like the men," he told Yancy. "Can't wait to tussle with the Yankees some more."

"Well, that's what we're here for, isn't it?"

Will couldn't argue with that.

He and Yancy were fortunate to have a cabin that they shared. The slave called Roman, who had come along to war with Yancy as a personal servant, was waiting for them outside. The young man stood up hurriedly from the stool where he had been perched, a whittling knife in one hand and a piece of wood in the other. Roman folded up the knife and slid it into the pocket of his threadbare trousers along with the piece of wood.

"I'm afraid you'll have to pack us up again, Roman," Yancy told him with a grin. "We're going to go chase Yankees."

"Yes suh," Roman replied quietly. "I be ready when you be, suh."

Yancy went on into the cabin, but Will paused. "What are you working on?" he asked Roman. "Another chess piece?" He had seen evidence of the young man's skill at whittling.

"Naw," Roman grinned. "It's a cannon." He took the piece of wood from his pocket and held it up so that Will could see that indeed it had been carved into the shape of a cannon. Roman was even carving one end to look like the wheeled limbers on which such weapons rode. "Ain't quite done yet."

"That's good work." Will took the wooden cannon, studied it for a moment, and then handed it back. "I'll bet after the war you can carve things and sell them."

Roman frowned slightly. "Sell 'em? Me? You mean Marse Yancy, don't you?"

"Well, yes, I suppose so." For a moment, Will hadn't considered that Roman was a slave. Of course anything he might make, whatever it might be, would belong to Yancy. "But you should give it some thought. You've got a wonderful talent."

"Got to make it through the war fust."

Will had forgotten about that, too, forgotten that it was impossible to make any sort of plan for after the war, when no man had any assurance he would live to see that day.

"That's right," he admitted, unable to stop a grim edge from creeping into his voice. "We've all got to make it through the war."

THE NEXT morning was a Saturday. The weather had cleared somewhat, and the breeze was not as chilly as it had been for the past few days. When the soldiers formed ranks and began to move out, marching to the northeast, a spirit of anticipation could be felt in the air. After the long, dreary winter, the Southerners were once again ready to defend their homeland.

Will rode the rangy lineback dun that had been his mount ever since he had joined the army. He moved up and down the line of marching men, making sure that none of his company fell out. The advance guard set a fast pace. Ashby's cavalry was moving even faster; Will knew that Jackson had sent the horsemen ahead as skirmishers to probe the area around Winchester and weigh the strength of the town's defenses.

All day long the troops marched, and the enthusiasm of the morning's departure wore off, to be replaced with weariness. Some of the men had to stop and rest, but Will was glad to see that none of his troops did so. They marched relentlessly on, with Darcy Bennett at their head leading the way. By evening the army had reached the village of Strasburg, and the order was passed for the men to halt and make camp.

The soldiers were grateful for the opportunity to rest. Will, Yancy, and the other officers still had work to do, however, and they gathered around Jackson as he sat on a stool under the bare, spreading branches of a tree by the side of the road. A lantern hung from one of the lower limbs.

During the late afternoon Will had heard the rumble of artillery fire in the distance to the north, and he learned the cause of it as Col. Turner Ashby joined the gathering of officers. After saluting Jackson, Ashby swept off his hat wearily and ran his fingers through his beard.

"It was just as we suspected, General. My men and I were able to penetrate to within a mile of Winchester before we encountered Yankee pickets. We attacked and forced them to retreat into the town. The Yankees then sent out an infantry brigade and a couple of batteries of artillery to oppose us."

"So you faced superior numbers," Jackson summarized.

Ashby smiled faintly. "Yes sir, but we gave a good account of ourselves before falling back to Kernstown."

Will could imagine what that "good account" had been. Ashby's cavalrymen were splendid fighters. They might have been forced to retreat, but Will was sure they had done a considerable amount of damage to the enemy along the way.

"I left my men camped there," Ashby continued, referring to the village of Kernstown, which was only a few miles south of Winchester on the Strasburg road. "The Yankees showed no signs of pursuing us once night fell, so I thought it best to carry this information to you personally, General."

Jackson nodded. "You did the right thing, Colonel. Could you tell how many of the Yankees are left in Winchester?"

"I would estimate no more than four regiments of infantry." Ashby shrugged. "Some cannon and cavalry are left, as well, but certainly not an overpowering number of either."

Jackson leaned to one side and raised his arm on the other side, a habit of his. "The rest of the enemy have set off for Manassas," he declared. "We'll have to draw them back." He looked around the circle of officers. "Tomorrow, gentlemen, we will march to Kernstown and join Colonel Ashby's cavalry. I trust you will have your men ready to move out at first light."

"Yes sir." The chorus of agreement came from the officers, including Will.

The meeting broke up, and Will returned to the area where his company had made camp. Darcy greeted him with a cup of coffee and a biscuit with a piece of salt pork in it. Will ate and drank gratefully as he passed along the orders for the next day's march to Darcy and the company's other sergeants.

By first light, Jackson meant the first shadings of gray that crept into the dark mantle of night. The Confederates were on the move long before actual dawn the next morning. It was Sunday, Will realized, but he doubted if any of them would make it to church today.

As the sky to the east reddened, Will heard the crackle of small arms fire. That meant Ashby's cavalry, which would be going ahead as the leading edge of the Confederate advance, was once more encountering resistance from the Union forces. As dawn arrived, the boom of cannon fire was added to the sounds that drifted through the early morning air. The Yankees had been unwilling to bring their artillery batteries into play until it was light enough for them to see what they were shooting at.

All morning long the sporadic sounds of battle in the distance provided a grim accompaniment to the tramp of marching feet. Listening to the explosions made Will anxious to reach the scene, but he resisted the impulse to spur on ahead of his men. Instead, he, like the other company commanders, stayed with his troops.

It was almost midday, with the sun high overhead and the temperature warm, when the Confederate forces reached Kernstown. The village was small, little more than a hamlet, with a scattering of houses on either side of the road. A ridge dotted with trees ran west of Kernstown, extending both north and south of the settlement for a considerable distance in both directions. The flat ground between the ridge and the town was blue with the uniforms of massed Yankee troops. To the northwest rose a wooded hill, and as the Confederate troops came to a halt, Will raised his field glasses and studied the hilltop. A glance confirmed what he thought he had spotted with the naked eye: a cloud of powder smoke hung over the summit of the hill. As cannons roared, more smoke billowed up. The Yankees had an artillery battery up there, in perfect position to shell either the road or the ridge.

Will didn't completely understand the significance of that, however, until Jackson gathered his officers and commanded, "Colonel Burks, I want you to take your brigade and reinforce Colonel Ashby. Between the two of you, you'll have to hold the road. General Garnett, Colonel Fulkerson, the two of you will take the ridge and move along it to flank the Yankees."

Both men nodded their understanding of the orders. Garnett commanded the Stonewall Brigade, of which the Thirty-third Virginia—and Will's company—were a part.

Will didn't say anything, but he glanced with a frown at the hilltop where the Yankee cannons were parked. Taking the ridge wouldn't be easy if those big guns were turned toward them. But maybe Ashby and Burks could distract the Union artillerymen enough to give the rest of the Southern forces a chance.

Colonel Burks's brigade moved smartly to reinforce Ashby's cavalry as the Confederate artillery was brought up and began to fire at the Union troops coming from the village. Fulkerson's men took the left flank and advanced toward the ridge, while Garnett's Stonewall Brigade occupied the center and the artillery formed the right side of the Confederate line.

Will drew his saber, using it to wave his men forward as he shouted, "Charge!" The air, never quiet during the morning's march, was now filled with the roar of cannon, the whistle of shells, the rattle of musketry, and Rebel yells that howled from the throats of the soldiers as they ran forward. Will heeled his mount into a gallop that carried him into the forefront of the gray-clad mass surging toward the ridge.

As the dun started up the slope, Will spotted a rock fence along the crest of the ridge. It would provide excellent cover if he could get his men behind it, he thought.

But from the corner of his eye he saw that the Federals were charging, too, angling up the ridge from farther north along its base. Their objective had to be to block the Confederate charge and prevent them from reaching the fence. If that happened, the Union soldiers would have solid cover and a devastating field of fire down the slope. The Confederates couldn't afford to let them get there first.

Will twisted in the saddle and yelled, "Darcy! The fence!"

The burly sergeant gave a curt nod, indicating that he understood what Will meant. He stopped and fired his musket across the face of the ridge toward the Yankees, then resumed his charge toward the fence, bellowing over his shoulders, "Come on, you sons o' bitches! Follow me!"

An artillery shell slammed into the ground to Will's right, throwing dirt and smoke into the air and leaving a gaping crater where it had struck. Another shell screamed over Will's head and exploded in front of him, causing the dun to shy violently. Will sawed the reins and brought the horse under control. The dun was steady nerved and used to combat, but Will couldn't blame it for reacting as it had. The explosion had been close enough so that flying clods of dirt had pelted both Will and the horse.

He urged the animal on. The moment required to bring the dun under control had allowed some of the leading infantrymen to catch up to him, so now he had soldiers racing along on both sides of him. Among them was Darcy Bennett, who turned a grimy but grinning face toward Will. There was nothing Darcy liked better than a good scrap.

He was getting one here today, Will thought. They were only a handful of yards from the crest of the ridge now. He could see that there were no Union troops on the other side of the fence. Some Federal commander had missed an opportunity. If Union riflemen had ensconced themselves behind that fence during the morning while Jackson was still on the way from Strasburg, the Confederate forces wouldn't have had a chance of taking the ridge.

As it was, Will hauled back on the reins and shouted to his horse as he urged the dun into a leap that carried it over the fence and onto the other side. The horse's hooves slammed into the ground, and Will reined in sharply, bringing the dun to a skidding halt. He kicked his feet out of the stirrups and leaped to the ground, turning to see his men coming over the fence, some of them bounding over it easily, others clambering more awkwardly. But how they got there didn't matter. What was important was that now they had a barricade between them and the hail of Yankee lead that whistled along the ridge.

Will's company had reached the fence first. He slid his saber back into its scabbard and jerked his pistol from its holster. As he ran to the fence, he saw that the Yankees were close, well within pistol range. Will's company was among the first to reach the top of the ridge, so now they had to blunt the Federals' charge and give the other Confederate troops time to get there.

"Pour it into 'em, men!" Will shouted as he opened fire on the Yankees. The pistol bucked in his hand as he emptied the cylinder. A volley roared out from the Confederates crouched behind the stone fence, the lead slicing lethally into the Union ranks. The charge broke, and some of the Yankees began to retreat down the ridge while others sought what little cover there was and hung on stubbornly.

Will dropped into a crouch behind the fence, reloaded his pistol, and then rose up again to fire. About a hundred yards along the ridge to the southwest, a Union shell filled with grapeshot exploded, sending its deadly load ripping through the ranks of the Confederates clustered there. The screams of wounded and dying men were added to the havoc. Grimly, Will ignored them and concentrated on the enemy, picking his targets and firing more slowly and carefully now. It might be his turn to die in the next heartbeat, but until then he was going to do everything he could to defeat the Yankees.

The Union forces that had charged the ridge were falling back now, but as Will peered through the smoke-hazed air toward Kernstown, he saw still more waves of blue-clad troops coming from the village. Ashby must have been mistaken about the number of Federals in the area, he thought. He could see more Union soldiers than were supposed to have been left in Winchester. As the ranks of blue continued to swell, Will estimated their numbers would soon be more than double those of the Confederates.

Numbers didn't matter, he told himself. The Stonewall Brigade held the ridge, and they would throw back anything the Yankees wanted to send at them.

Yet the part of him that was becoming more and more familiar with military strategy realized that numbers *did* matter. And the Confederates were not only outnumbered, they were tired from marching that morning and all the previous day. The excitement of the charge had given them a momentary boost of energy, but sooner or later their weariness would begin to play a part. The blue-clad troops were undoubtedly fresher.

Will dropped down behind the fence and turned so that he could rest his back against it as he reloaded the pistol again. Beside him, Darcy hunkered on his heels and reloaded his rifle. "What now, Cap'n?" he asked.

"We hold the ridge," replied Will. Beyond that, he didn't know what to do. Jackson's plan had been to send Fulkerson's brigade on a flanking move to the north, so that they could cut off the Yankees in Kernstown.

A fresh surge of firing from below gave warning that there wouldn't be any time for such maneuvers. Will turned and lifted himself, his tired muscles protesting as he did so, and looked over the top of the stone fence to see that the Federals were charging the ridge again. As long as the Confederates were kept busy defending this position they had gained, there would be no chance for them to attempt any sort of encirclement.

Will's mouth was a taut line as he began to fire again. The Yankees had charged the ridge with a considerable number of troops before, but now several times that many Union soldiers were streaming across the field and starting up the slope in the face of the Confederate fire. At the same time the ridge was under heavy bombardment. Clearly, Ashby and Burks hadn't been able to distract all the Union gunners.

Where was Jackson? Will wondered.

He didn't have time to ponder the question. The tide of blue sweeping up the ridge reached the crest in places, and the fighting was suddenly hand to hand, with bayonets, knives, sabers, and rifle butts. Will emptied his pistol for the third time, jammed the gun back in its holster, and whipped his saber out of its scabbard in time to thrust it into the belly of a Union solder who came leaping over the stone fence, yelling at the top of his lungs. His shout turned into a gurgle of pain as Will's steel ripped into his guts. He fell heavily against Will, and both of them toppled to the ground. The Yankee's eyes were wide with agony, but as he sprawled on top of Will, his hand fumbled for Will's throat. Will thrust hard against the man, rolling him off and ripping the blade of the saber to the side as he did so. Blood and intestines spilled into Will's lap.

He fought down the feeling of nausea that rose in him and shoved the dying man aside. As he scrambled back to his feet he saw another Union soldier and pivoted that way, slashing with the saber at the man's neck. Blood spurted, and the Yankee stumbled and went down.

A few feet away, Darcy Bennett rammed his bayonet into the belly of a Yankee, pinning the Union soldier against the fence for a second before the sergeant ripped the blade free and let the mortally wounded man fall. Darcy twisted and brought his rifle up and around, slamming the butt against the jaw of another Yankee and breaking the bone. The man fell forward on his shattered face, and Darcy jabbed the bayonet in the middle of his back.

Will looked around for more opponents, but no more Federals were close by. They were retreating again, he saw. Some of them had not reached the fence, and those troops were falling back down the slope. Most of the ones who had made it over had been killed or wounded so badly they were out of the fight, and the others had to battle their way clear and flee as best they could. Many of them were shot down as they ran.

Will dropped to a knee and took a deep breath, leaning on his saber as he did so. The stench of spilled blood and entrails filled his nose, so he began breathing through his mouth instead as he drew air into his oxygen-starved lungs. Darcy came up beside him and said, "You all right, Cap'n?"

Will straightened. "How many casualties did we take?"

"Just a handful. The Yankees won't try that again anytime soon."

Unfortunately, he was wrong about that.

———◦◦◦———

ALL AFTERNOON long, the Union commanders sent charge after charge against the ridge. At a hastily called conference of officers, General Garnett exclaimed bitterly, "There weren't supposed to be that many of them in the whole Shenandoah Valley!"

Yancy Lattimer, whose face was grimy from powder smoke and streaked with blood from a cut on his cheek, said, "My men are running low on ammunition, General. We weren't prepared to fight a battle that lasted this long."

"I know," Garnett replied. "Any word of Ashby?"

One of the other officers said, "He and Burks have been skirmishing up and down the road, but they've had to gradually fall back. They're not occupying enough of the Federals to allow us to do anything else."

Garnett glanced at Fulkerson. "How are your men fixed for ammunition, Colonel?"

"Our supplies are limited," he answered. "And the men are exhausted, General."

Turning his attention to Will, Garnett said, "Your men have been at the center of the fighting, Captain. Can we hold?"

"Are those our orders, sir?" Will asked. "Because if they are, we'll do our best to follow them." He didn't say anything else.

After a moment, Garnett's mouth twitched, but Will couldn't tell if the reaction was a grimace or a humorless smile. The general said, "I understand, Captain." He took a deep breath and went on, "In the absence of orders to the contrary and the necessary support to do otherwise, we shall move to the rear, gentlemen. With all due dispatch."

The officers exchanged a glance. Garnett was ordering a retreat. None of the men liked it, but none of them argued the matter. Like it or not, the outnumbered Southern forces had done their best here at Kernstown, and it had not been enough.

The gathering broke up quickly, and within a matter of minutes, the retreat was underway. Company by company, the Confederates moved along the ridge out of range of the Union rifles and began heading back toward the road they had marched up that morning. The Yankee artillery fell silent. The commanders of the batteries must have seen that the Confederates were retreating and decided to allow them to do so unmolested.

Just as Will's company had been one of the first to the top of the ridge, it was one of the last to leave. Will found his dun on the far side of the hill and swung up into the saddle, then he paused to look over the bodies scattered along the line of the stone fence. There were plenty of blue-clad figures sprawled

there, but Will had to admit that the bodies of fallen Confederates outnumbered them.

It was the only way they had outdone the Yankees all day,
he thought bleakly.

Then he heeled the horse into a trot and followed his men
away from the scene of their defeat. The battle of Kernstown
was over.

Chapter Four

E ARLIER IN MARCH, THE invasion of Virginia alluded to by Jackson in his briefing had begun to take place. To the Federal navy fell the task of transporting the Army of the Potomac from Washington down the Potomac River, through Chesapeake Bay, to Fort Monroe at the tip of the Virginia Peninsula.

This had not been McClellan's original plan. That had called for the army to be ferried up the Rappahannock River to the town of Urbanna, where it would disembark and begin an overland march against Richmond. This plan had fallen apart due to a variety of factors, chief among them what McClellan considered to be meddling in military matters by Lincoln and a series of behind-the-scenes manipulations by Secretary of War Stanton, a one-time friend of McClellan but no longer a believer in his abilities. The Confederate ironclad *Virginia*, following its battle with the *Monitor*, was also patrolling the Rappahannock and might easily wreak havoc during any effort to land troops at Urbanna, giving the Yankees another reason to abandon that scheme.

Despite these difficulties, McClellan soldiered on, and once the peninsula plan had been agreed upon, he began to implement it as efficiently as possible. In the space of only three weeks, the fleet landed more than 120,000 troops at Fort Monroe, along with dozens of artillery batteries and thousands of horses, mules, and wagons. It was the largest invasion force assembled during the country's relatively short history.

And it was poised to strike at the heart of an even younger nation: the Confederate States of America.

ALMOST OVERNIGHT, Culpeper had been transformed from a sleepy country town into an armed camp. All the open fields on the edge of town were covered with tents, and the streets of the settlement itself were thick with soldiers, horses, and wagons. Johnston's withdrawal from Manassas had been hasty, and many of his supplies had been left behind. So at first the army's descent on Culpeper had been a boon to merchants like Michael Davis, who found that the soldiers were eager to purchase anything and everything on his shelves. Davis's coffers were soon overflowing with Confederate scrip.

Replacing the goods that were sold proved to be difficult, however, and by the middle of April Davis's emporium had been stripped bare. The storekeeper sat disconsolately in the middle of the empty store on a keg that a few weeks earlier had been full of flour, shaking his head as he said to Mac Brannon, "I don't know what I'll do. They've taken it all."

"You were paid, weren't you?" asked Mac.

Davis laughed hollowly. "I've got a money bag full of scrip, but what can I buy with it? The army has cleaned out all of northern Virginia."

"Surely there are still goods to be bought in Richmond," Mac suggested.

"The businesses in Richmond want to hang on to their supplies," Davis replied with a shake of his head. "There are forces being gathered there, too, for the defense of the capital, and the stores have plenty of ready customers. No, Mac, it looks like I'll have to close my doors. Look around you. I've nothing left to sell."

"I'll be sorry to see you close up, Mr. Davis. It seems like you've always had a store here in Culpeper. As far back as I can remember, anyway."

Davis just shook his head again and smiled ruefully.

Mac had ridden into town to pick up the mail at the post office and had stopped by the emporium just to say hello. From the looks of things, the Brannon farm might have to be pretty much self-sufficient for a while, he thought. Picking up supplies in town was going to be difficult.

He said good-bye to Davis, leaving the merchant sitting in the empty store, then went out and unhitched his horse from the post in front of the building. He had ridden in on a slow but strong roan mare, an animal that Cordelia sometimes rode. For a moment that morning he had thought about saddling up the silver-gray stallion and riding it to town, then he decided against the idea. The stallion had settled down to the point that Mac could ride it all over the farm now, but he was still leery about having the horse around a lot of people.

As Mac turned toward the post office, a soldier leading several horses came around the corner and started toward the blacksmith shop in the next block. The animals were skittish, and one of them suddenly broke away, jerking its reins out of the man's hand. As the horse bolted down the street, the soldier yelled, "Hey! Come back here, you nag!"

Mac dropped the mare's reins, knowing that it wouldn't go anywhere, and stepped out into the street. Instinctively holding up his hands, he called out several whoas to the runaway horse. The animal shied away from him at first and then suddenly stopped and reared up on its hind legs to paw at the air angrily.

"Settle down," Mac said calmly. "Nobody's going to hurt you." From the corner of his eye he saw the soldier who was in charge of the horses coming toward him, and he held up his other hand to motion the man back.

The runaway came back down on all fours and eyed Mac warily, but it didn't run as he stepped closer to it.

"That's a good boy," Mac told the horse. "Just stay calm." He came within reach of the dangling reins. Moving smoothly, he reached out and took hold of them, gradually tightening his grip and coming close enough to pat the animal's shoulder. "Easy, big fella."

The horse's handler came closer and announced loudly, "Thanks, mister. I'll take him now."

The jittery horse jerked at the reins. Mac coached the soldier, "If you'll speak in a quieter voice, this horse will respond
better. He doesn't like loud noises."

"Well, then, he's not goin' be much of a cavalry horse, is he?"

"Maybe not, but you can't make him something he isn't."
Mac handed over the reins. "Talk softly to him and see if he
doesn't cooperate."

The trooper looked impatient but did as Mac suggested
and quietly said to the horse, "Come on, now. We got to get
new shoes for you."

To the man's obvious surprise, the horse came along easily
as he led it along with the others to the blacksmith shop.

Mac turned back toward his mare and stopped as he saw several men on horseback riding out from a cross street while others
were walking their mounts along the main road. They were all
cavalrymen, and the man in the lead was as striking a figure as
Mac had ever seen. Tall and erect in the saddle, he sported a full
brown beard with a hint of auburn in it. He wore the uniform of
a general, but its trappings set it apart from the usual garb of an
officer: a bright yellow sash was around the man's waist, a gray
cloak with a brilliant red lining was fastened around his shoulders, and an ostrich plume at least a foot long adorned his soft
gray hat that was pinned up on the right side.

The other riders were dressed similarly but not quite as
flamboyantly. One of them was a colonel, also bearded, but
slightly younger and with a rounder face than the leader. He
glanced over and saw Mac watching the group, and seemingly
on impulse he turned his horse in that direction. Mac stood
there, frozen with surprise, as the officer cantered up to him
and reined to a halt.

"Good morning," the colonel said. He touched a finger to
the brim of his hat. "I saw the skill with which you handled
that horse. Good work."

"Thank you, sir," Mac said, a little overwhelmed that the
officer had approached him.

"I also notice that you seem to be watching us."

"I meant no offense," Mac said quickly. "It's just that — "

"I know," the colonel interrupted with a chuckle. "You caught your first glimpse of Beauty there, and you couldn't help but stare."

"Beauty?" Mac repeated, confused by this encounter.

The colonel leaned his head toward his companions, who were riding slowly on up the street. "General Stuart. Everyone called him Beauty when we were cadets together at West Point because he was so plain-looking. The beard helps, don't you think? Makes him look rather dashing."

Mac couldn't argue with that. General Stuart had certainly looked dashing.

"You're part of the cavalry, aren't you?" Mac asked, then instantly regretted the question because it sounded so foolish. What else would these men be, wearing their bright uniforms and mounted on such fine horses?

"That's right," replied the colonel. "We've been posted up at Warrenton Junction to serve as General Johnston's eyes and ears. We're down here today for a meeting with him."

"I've thought . . . ," Mac wasn't quite sure where the words were coming from, but they bubbled out of him anyway. "I've thought that I might join the cavalry."

The colonel's eyes went to the stolid-looking mare. "I can see why," he said in a mocking drawl.

Mac felt himself flushing in a mixture of embarrassment and anger. The colonel had no reason to make fun of him. "I have another horse," he said stiffly.

"A good one?"

Mac thought about the silver-gray stallion. "I believe so."

"From the way you handled that runaway, you've some experience with animals. Ride on up to Warrenton, then, if you like, and let us have a look at this horse of yours."

Mac forgot about being angry as excitement coursed through him. "Do you mean it?"

"Of course. We can always use another good man—and another good horse."

"I'll do it," Mac began, but he was interrupted by a shout.

"Fitz!" called Stuart. "Are you coming or not?"

"I'll be right there, General," the colonel replied, lazily touching the brim of his hat again and said, "Don't forget the invitation."

"I won't," Mac promised as the officer turned and heeled his horse into a trot that rapidly caught up with the others. Mac stood there and watched them ride toward the house in which Johnston had established his headquarters.

For a long moment, Mac couldn't think of anything else except the fact that he had been invited to join the cavalry. Despite the fact that the colonel had been unimpressed with the mare, the invitation had seemed genuine. And Mac was certain that once the officers saw the stallion, they would be more than happy to have both him and the magnificent horse among their number.

Finally, Mac started toward the post office again. He tied the mare outside the little building and went in to call for the Brannon family's mail at the window. The postmaster, a spare, elderly man with crisp white hair, passed over a single piece of mail. Mac recognized the scrawled writing on it immediately. The letter was from his brother Cory.

Cory, the wandering Brannon! Mac grinned at the thought. Coriolanus Troilus Brannon, like all the other children in the family named after characters from Shakespeare's plays—except for Will, who'd been named for the playwright himself—had left home to make his fortune in the world, or so he said. Mac suspected that Cory was just restless, like their father had been. The last the family had heard from him, he had been in Missouri, working at the New Madrid docks and doing quite well for himself.

Mac fought the temptation to break the seal on the letter and read it. It was addressed to Mrs. Abigail Brannon and family, however, and Mac knew he should take it home so that everyone could gather 'round and hear it read aloud. He tucked it into his coat pocket and thanked the postmaster, then went outside, unhitched the mare, and swung into the saddle.

Mac headed for the farm, making his way through the crowded streets, pausing only to glance once more toward Johnston's headquarters. He could see the cavalrymen's horses tied in front of the house.

And in his mind's eye he could see himself on the stallion, dressed in gray with an ostrich plume streaming behind his hat as he rode into battle.

MAC PATTED the stallion's shoulder and the powerful muscles under the sleek, silver gray hide. Taking a deep breath he announced, "I was thinking he might make a pretty good cavalry horse."

"Cavalry horse?" Henry repeated excitedly. "You mean you're going to enlist?"

"Nonsense," Abigail declared from the doorway of the farmhouse. "I have two boys fighting those godless Yankees. That ought to be enough."

Cordelia came closer to the stallion and reached up to scratch his nose. The horse tolerated it, now that he was used to the other members of the Brannon family being around. Cordelia didn't say anything, but Mac thought she looked worried.

He had just been exercising the stallion, galloping it around the farm and thinking about whether or not he ought to accept that cavalry colonel's invitation to visit Stuart's camp. Although Mac had been leaning in that direction from the start, the letter the family had received from Cory a couple of days earlier had helped convince him that his proper place was helping to defend his homeland from the Yankees. In the letter Cory described his experiences at the battles of Forts Henry and Donelson and Shiloh. All those clashes had resulted in Southern defeats, but at least Cory had been there doing what he could to help the noble Southern cause. That was more than what Mac had been doing. And Will, of course, was fighting Yankees, too, probably still with Jackson.

Standing beside the stallion, Mac looked up at his mother on the porch. "I've given this a lot of thought. I talked to a colonel in town the other day. He invited me to join the cavalry."

That was stretching the truth, but only a mite. His acceptance into the cavalry probably would be determined by how the officers felt about the stallion.

But how could they refuse him once they got a look at this animal? Mac asked himself as he once more patted the horse's shoulder.

"I don't know . . . ," Abigail began dubiously.

"Ma, you were the one who wanted to see the Yankees beat so bad," Henry interjected. "You said they were all heathens and anarchists and had no right to interfere with the South."

"And that's all true, too," Abigail declared. "But we have a farm to run."

"You've got Titus and Henry and Cordelia for that," Mac pointed out. "It'd be harder, I know, but . . . but good Lord, Ma, nearly every other able-bodied man in the county has joined up!"

Abigail took a sharply indrawn breath. "You mind that tongue of yours, Mac Brannon. You've got no call to be speaking to your mother that way."

Mac's head dropped, and he nodded. "Yes ma'am, but that doesn't change anything." He looked up again. "I've made up my mind to go see General Stuart, anyway, and find out if he wants me."

Henry let out a whoop and punched the air with his fist. "I bet you'll be leadin' charges before the summer's over, Mac!"

Mac looked at Cordelia, aware that she still hadn't spoken. He knew she had taken it hard first when Cory and then when Will left home, and now yet another of her brothers was talking about riding away and maybe never coming back. He saw that she had caught her bottom lip between her teeth and was chewing on it.

"Cordelia?" he inquired. "What do you think about this?"

"What does it matter?" she burst out. "You'll do what you want to. Men always do." With that, she turned and went quickly up the porch steps and into the house. Abigail moved out of the doorway to let her daughter past.

"You've upset your sister," she admonished Mac sternly.

"I'm sorry," he said and meant it. "But I can't just stand back and let somebody else defend my home, not even if it's Will and Cory. If the cavalry will have me, I intend to enlist."

"Well," Abigail acknowledged. "There it is, then. You'll do as you please, as Cordelia said." She turned and stepped into the house, letting the door slam behind her.

"Don't listen to them, Mac," Henry blurted excitedly. "I think it's great! You'll have to promise to save a few Yankees for me to whip, though."

"*You're* not going anywhere," Mac said. "Didn't you hear me tell Mama that you and Titus would have to take care of the farm?"

Henry looked as if he wanted to argue, but suddenly he questioned, "Who'd be in charge?"

This took Mac by surprise. "Titus is older."

"He's also a drunk," Henry stated, pitching his voice lower so that Abigail couldn't hear him from the house.

Mac frowned. Henry had a point. The idea of leaving Titus in charge of anything was worrisome. But maybe having that responsibility thrust upon him would finally make Titus grow up and stop moping over Polly Ebersole. It could be good for him to be left in charge of the farm.

"I'll have a talk with Titus," Mac promised. "I'm sure he'll straighten up and do just fine."

"He won't, and you know it," insisted Henry. "You'd be better off leaving me in charge."

Mac glanced toward the house. "We both know who's really in charge around here," he said quietly.

Henry rolled his eyes, but then he sighed and nodded. "I reckon you're right." His enthusiasm returned as he went on, "When are you going to join up?"

Mac glanced at the sky. It wasn't noon yet. "I thought I'd ride up to Warrenton today. That's where the cavalry's camped."

"I wish I could go with you," Henry said earnestly. "You'll be back tonight?"

"I reckon so. Even if I go ahead and enlist, they'll let me come home and get my possibles together."

Henry stuck his hand out. "Good luck, Mac." He hesitated, then added as Mac shook his hand, "We'll sure miss you around here."

"I'll miss the place, and all of you, too," Mac conceded with a smile. "But remember, I'm not gone yet. I'll see you tonight."

───────

MAC DIDN'T have any trouble finding Stuart's camp. It was the place next to the Warrenton turnpike where men and horses were rushing around like bees smoked out of a hive.

It was midafternoon when Mac reached the cavalry encampment. He reined in and brought the stallion to a halt, then thumbed back his broad-brimmed hat as he looked around in astonishment. Tents were being struck, horses were being saddled, and there was an air of controlled confusion about the place. Mac wondered where the general was, wondered as well which of the busy cavalrymen he ought to ask. He realized he didn't even know the name of the other cavalry officer he had talked to, the colonel whom Stuart had called Fitz.

He was about to take a chance and stop one of the soldiers, when he heard someone call, "Hey! Culpeper!"

Mac turned his head and saw the colonel riding toward him. The officer lifted a hand in greeting as he came up beside Mac and pulled his horse to a stop.

"Hello, Colonel," Mac said. "My name's Brannon, not Culpeper. Mac Brannon."

"Well, you knew who I meant," countered the officer jovially, looking over the silver gray stallion. "This is that other horse?"

"That's right," Mac confirmed, unable to prevent a note of pride from creeping into his voice.

"He's certainly a fine-looking animal. If you're such a good judge of horseflesh, maybe you *would* make a good cavalryman."

"That's why I'm here, sir," Mac announced. "To see if you want me, and if I want to enlist."

"We could simply commandeer the horse . . . ," the colonel said, stroking his beard as if in deep thought.

Mac's eyes widened in surprise, and he instinctively tugged on the reins, backing the stallion up a step. "No sir," he decreed. "The stallion and me, we go together or we don't go at all."

The colonel let out a laugh. "I was just joshing you, Brannon. The Confederate cavalry isn't a bunch of horse thieves, you know, at least not Stuart's bunch. Beauty wouldn't stand for thievery." He started to turn his mount. "Come on. I'll take you to him."

"To General Stuart, you mean?"

"That's right. I'm sure he'll want to see this stallion for himself." The colonel added as he prodded his horse into a walk, "If you want to join us, you'll have to make up your mind in a hurry, though. We're pulling out."

"That's what it looked like to me," Mac said as he walked the stallion alongside the colonel's mount. "Where are you going?"

The officer's casual attitude was replaced by a solemn demeanor. "McClellan's got over a hundred thousand men sitting on the end of the Virginia Peninsula. It's obvious that he's going to march up the peninsula and try to take Richmond. General Johnston just got back from there today with orders straight from President Davis himself. We're going to meet McClellan on the peninsula and stop him."

Mac felt a thrill of excitement course through him. "The cavalry, too?"

"Of course!" exclaimed the colonel. "The army wouldn't have any idea where to go to fight if it wasn't for the cavalry telling them."

Mac hadn't realized that the cavalry played such an important part in strategy. But he had been a farmer all his life, he told himself, and knew very little about military matters. He rode with the officer up to a small knoll where several men mounted on horseback were monitoring the preparations for breaking camp.

One of them was Stuart. Mac recognized him instantly. The general turned a curious look toward the two newcomers. "Who's this, Fitz?" he asked.

"That farmer I talked to the other day in Culpeper," the colonel replied. "You remember, I told you about him, General."

"You told me you twitted him about joining the cavalry because he had a plowhorse with him," Stuart said with a twinkle in his eyes. "That doesn't look like a plowhorse to me, Fitz."

"No sir," the colonel admitted a little sheepishly. "This is a different horse."

Stuart looked at Mac and nodded pleasantly. "Gen. Jeb Stuart, sir, at your service," he said.

"I'm MacBeth Brannon, General Stuart."

"Named after the Bard's immortal play, no doubt. I've always considered *Hamlet* the man's masterpiece, myself, but the plays are all quite good."

"My father knew them by heart," Mac explained. He felt an instinctive liking for Stuart. The general sat upright in the saddle but not stiffly. His eyes shone with both wit and intelligence. Mac pushed on bravely, "If you'll have me, sir, I'd like to join your cavalry."

"Can you ride?" asked Stuart.

Mac hesitated. If there had been room, he could have demonstrated the stallion's—and his own—abilities, but this cluttered encampment didn't provide enough space for a true demonstration of either horse or rider.

"Yes sir. I can ride."

"You sound very positive."

"I've been riding since I was . . . well, since as far back as I can remember, General." Mac leaned forward to pat the stallion. "But never on a horse like this until lately."

"You bought this mount only recently?"

Mac shook his head. "Caught him. He was wild before that."

"A wild stallion? And you tamed him, sir?"

"You could say that. Really, he tamed himself, though. I could ride him right from the start." Mac hesitated to say what he had thought more than once: the stallion was much more intelligent than most horses, catching him had been a test of sorts, and once Mac had passed it, the horse had been happy to cooperate with him.

"Interesting," Stuart observed. "Mr. Brannon, I pride myself on being a good judge of both horses and men, and so far I don't find either of you wanting. If you wish to enlist in our cause, you'll be welcome. Are you prepared to ride with us today?"

"You mean join up and go with you now?" Mac hadn't expected things to move this quickly.

"That's right. Did Colonel Lee explain to you that we're bound for the Virginia Peninsula?"

"Yes sir, he did, but . . ."

Stuart waited silently.

Finally, Mac went on, "I'd planned on going back home to say good-bye to my family and gather up my gear."

"No need for that," Colonel Lee declared. "Our quartermaster will issue you a uniform, and you've already got a rifle and a saddle. You have everything you need to wage war on the Yankees, Private Brannon."

Private Brannon? He hadn't even sworn any sort of oath yet. Mac felt as if the world was starting to go a little crazy around him.

But that was what war did, he supposed.

"I'm afraid we don't have time to wait," Stuart said. "We'll be galloping within the hour. Are you with us or not, Mr. Brannon?"

Mac swallowed hard, then announced, "Private Brannon, sir. I reckon I'm reporting for duty."

Chapter Five

THE BATTLE OF KERNSTOWN might have been a defeat for the Confederacy, but it was not entirely fruitless. The evening following the battle, even as the exhausted Southerners were flinging themselves down to rest beside the road on which they had fled, messages were already flying back and forth among the Union commanders. General Shields, who had started most of his troops on the way to Manassas several days previously, hastily sent riders galloping after them to call them back to Winchester. He could not believe that Jackson would have attacked so boldly had he not had more troops in reserve. And if a Confederate force large enough to be so audacious was still at large in the Shenandoah Valley, then northern Virginia could hardly be abandoned to them. That would be like swinging open the doors of Washington City and inviting the Rebels in.

Jackson's bluff had worked.

In his mind, however, the advance at Kernstown had hardly been a bluff. He firmly believed that the South could have won the day had not Garnett decided to withdraw from the ridge. Some of his subordinates attempted to convince him that Garnett's men had been weary to the point of collapse, as well as being out of ammunition in many cases. That was true, but Jackson would not be swayed in his opinion. He removed Garnett from command.

"How can a man be a fool and a genius at the same time?" Yancy Lattimer grumbled as he sat down on a pile of fence poles several days later. The army was camped on Rude's Hill, a broad plateau overlooking the Shenandoah River near the town of Front Royal. Jackson had withdrawn his forces there during the days following the battle.

Will, sitting next to Yancy, inquired, "I reckon you're talking about Stonewall?"

"Of course. He's relieved Garnett. Can you imagine? Garnett wasn't to blame for what happened at Kernstown."

Will was a little surprised to hear Yancy talking that way. Yancy had been a staunch supporter of Jackson's decisions in the past.

"The general's just put out because he figured we could win the fight. Maybe he didn't go into it thinking we could, but somewhere along the way he convinced himself we might whip them even though they had us outnumbered and outgunned."

Yancy snorted. "We should have. The Yankees will never be able to outfight us."

"Now you sound like you're saying Jackson was right to blame getting beat on General Garnett."

Yancy shook his head ruefully. "I don't know what I'm saying, I suppose." He laughed. "War's not nearly as clear-cut as you'd think it would be, is it?"

"Most things aren't," Will conceded, glancing up at the overcast sky. "Going to rain again, maybe even snow."

"I'm afraid you're right," agreed Yancy. "Isn't this blasted winter ever going to end? It's April. It should be spring."

If the heavens heard what he said, they ignored it, because a few minutes later, a cold drizzle began to fall, and Yancy and Will headed for their tent to wait out the rain.

THE FIRST half of April was a time of waiting for both sides in the conflict, a time of rain and sleet and snow, of muddy roads, dwindling supplies, and uncertainty. But as so often occurs, once things began to happen, they happened fast.

This was true for Mac Brannon, beginning on the day in mid-April when he rode up to Warrenton Junction. Having accepted Stuart's offer of enlistment in the cavalry, all Mac had an opportunity to do was scribble a note on a piece of paper borrowed from the general's aide. In the note he explained that he wasn't going to have a chance to return home to say good-bye to everyone, that he was sorry things had worked out like this, and that he would be in touch as soon and as often as possible. When he had laboriously printed that out with a stub of pencil—also borrowed—he folded the paper, wrote his mother's name on the outside, and went in search of someone to deliver it. Luckily, he was able to find a farmer who promised to take the note to Culpeper the next time he was down that way. It was the best Mac could do, even though he knew his abrupt departure was going to hurt his mother and Cordelia.

He had barely finished doing that when the quartermaster thrust a bundled-up shirt and trousers into his hands. "There you go, private," the man said. He had a gray cap with a stiff black bill in his hand. He put it on top of the uniform.

Mac took off his hat and put the cap on. It fit, which surprised him slightly. He held up the uniform, saw the patched holes in the front and back of the shirt that were surrounded by faded brownish stains and decided not to ask about the previous owner. That was grimly obvious, he thought.

Going behind some brush he changed into the uniform, rolling his own shirt and trousers into a ball and stuffing them into his hat. As he emerged, Colonel Lee came riding by.

"Well, you're a soldier now, sure enough, Brannon," the colonel said with a grin. "Ready to ride?"

"Yes sir," Mac replied, trying to sound military-like. He wondered if he was supposed to salute.

"You'll be in Lieutenant Ramsey's company. He needs replacements since his bunch got shot up pretty bad in the last skirmish." Lee pointed to a group of riders forming up about fifty yards away. "That's them over there."

"Thank you, sir." Mac untied the stallion's reins from the bush where he had left the horse hitched and swung up into the saddle. He attempted a salute, holding his fingers stiff and touching them to the bill of the cap. Lee returned the salute, and for some reason that made Mac feel good.

He turned the stallion and rode over to join Ramsey's company. The lieutenant was a stocky, red-faced man who nodded when Mac introduced himself. "Glad to have you with us, Brannon," he greeted him. "That's a mighty nice horse you've got there."

"Thank you, sir," Mac said. "He's the main reason I decided to join the cavalry."

"I think we can put both of you to good use," the officer commented dryly.

Only a few minutes later, the cavalry was ready to move out. Mac watched the other men in his company and followed their example as they formed into rough ranks so that they rode four or five abreast. He spotted the general and several other officers, among them Colonel Lee, riding toward the front of the long line of men on horseback. When Stuart reached the point, he turned his horse so that he faced his men and swept his plumed hat off his head. "We ride to glory!" he shouted, his clear, ringing voice carrying easily over the ranks of the assembled cavalry. "We ride to victory, men!"

A huge cheer went up in response to the general's encouraging words. Stuart waved his hat over his head, signaling the troops into motion. Putting his horse to the gallop, he led the way, and the Confederate cavalry followed. Another shout rang out, blending with the rumble of hooves, and Mac yelled along with the other men.

He was on his way to war.

———◦◦◦———

STUART SET a fast pace, keeping the men in their saddles that first day until well after dark. The next day the horsemen were moving before the sun rose. The roads were still muddy in a lot of places, but they were beginning to dry after the recent rains.

The stallion proved to be tireless, loping along in a ground-eating trot. At times Mac even had to hold his steed back a little, so that he wouldn't find himself riding out in front of his company. That was the lieutenant's place, and Mac didn't think Ramsey would take kindly to being prodded.

Mac had ridden a great deal in his life and was at home in the saddle, but he had never spent so many hours on horseback in such a short period of time. By the end of the second day, he was sore. By the end of the third, he almost wished he had never caught the stallion, because then he likely never would have joined the cavalry.

On the fourth day, however, his muscles didn't protest quite as much, and besides, Stuart slowed down a little when the cavalry reached Richmond that afternoon. After a short halt outside of town so that the men could clean up and straighten their uniforms, the ranks of riders moved out again, following the road through the center of town. Evidently word of their coming had reached Richmond even before the cavalry itself did, because the street was lined with people who had turned out for this impromptu parade. Cheers rang out from their throats at the sight of the soldiers. Men brandished Confederate flags in the air, and women waved brightly colored scarves. Children pulled away from their parents and scampered alongside the horses.

Mac kept a tight grip on the stallion's reins. As far as he knew, this was the first time the horse had been in such commotion, and he worried that the stallion might get spooked by all the noise and people. After a few minutes, though, he realized he had no reason to be concerned. The stallion stepped along smartly, keeping pace with the other horses and never faltering despite the hoopla in the air around it.

The general was certainly enjoying the acclaim. Mac could see him at the head of the column, turning from side to side in the saddle so that he could wave at the onlookers on both sides of the street. He swept off his hat and bowed gallantly to a group of ladies in fine dresses who were shading themselves with parasols. Several of the ladies blew kisses at him, and he accepted the accolades graciously.

When their route passed in front of the capitol, Mac saw a large group of men standing on the steps of the impressive building. Some were in uniform, the others wore expensive suits. One of the troopers leaned over and hissed, "Gawd, that's ol' Jeff Davis hisself."

Mac spotted the tall, spare, patrician-looking president of the Confederacy, recognizing him from newspaper illustrations. Jefferson Davis stood bareheaded in the sunshine on the capitol steps, and next to him was an equally tall, erect soldier with a neatly trimmed white beard.

"Who's that with the president?" Mac asked.

"Reckon that must be Gen'ral Lee, Davis's military adviser. I've heard a heap about him, 'bout how he fought in Mexico. They say Lincoln wanted him to take over the Union army when the war came, but Gen'ral Lee warn't havin' none of that. When Virginia left the Union, so did he." The trooper pointed to the officers directly behind Stuart at the front of the column. "Colonel Lee's his nephew. We got the gen'ral's son ridin' with us, too, and his name's Fitzhugh, just like the colonel, but they call him Rooney, so I hear."

Mac nodded. He had heard of Robert E. Lee, but he hadn't connected him with Colonel Lee, who was at least partially responsible for Mac's being in Richmond today. As they rode past the capitol, Mac got a good look at the dignified General Lee and was impressed with what he saw. He seemed to be the very image of what a soldier should be, at least to Mac's way of thinking.

The cavalry moved on, basking in the cheers of the crowd, until they reached the edge of town. Then Stuart passed the order for the men to stop and make camp. There was still some daylight left, but after the past several days of hard riding, Mac and the other men were glad for the chance to rest.

Of course, rest wasn't all the men were interested in. Word quickly went around the camp that the troopers would be permitted to go back into town for the evening. The prospect of women and liquor set off a general exuberance among the cavalry. The red-light district of Richmond would do a booming business tonight.

Mac couldn't decide whether to go into town or not. After supper, he spent some time working on the stallion with a brush he borrowed from one of the other troopers. While Mac was brushing the horse, Colonel Lee rode by.

Lee reined in when he noticed Mac. "Not going into Richmond, Brannon?" he asked.

"I haven't decided, Colonel," Mac replied honestly. "I'm a mite tired after the past few days."

Lee chuckled. "Beauty pushes himself hard and expects equally as much from his men. But he believes in letting them have some fun, too. If you decide not to go into town, come over to the general's tent later. We'll be having a concert."

"A concert?" Mac repeated, puzzled.

"The general enjoys music." Lee lifted a gauntleted hand in farewell. "See you later, perhaps, Brannon."

With a frown, Mac watched the colonel ride off. He was surprised that he had been invited to the general's tent for the evening. Clearly, the separation between officers and enlisted men wasn't as great in the cavalry as Mac had expected it to be. Most of the officers, like Lee, seemed to be genuinely friendly. Mac suspected that attitude sprang from General Stuart himself. The general took his job seriously, but at the same time, something about him said that he was having the time of his life.

Mac finished brushing the stallion as darkness settled over the camp. Fires dotted the area, but the largest one was in front of the tent reserved for the general. It drew Mac's eyes, and after making sure the stallion was securely picketed, he began strolling in that direction.

He heard the music before he got there, and it was loud, raucous, and joyful. Several fiddles were being sawed on with great enthusiasm. Deep, rich voices lifted in song. As Mac came closer, he saw that the music had drawn quite a crowd around

Stuart's tent. Officers and enlisted men seemed to be mingling with little thought as to rank. Many of them were grinning and clapping their hands in time to the music.

From the edge of the crowd, Mac saw half a dozen black men standing in front of the general's tent. Four of them were playing fiddles while the other two sang. Mac didn't recognize the tune, but it was certainly catchy.

Suddenly, a man's voice bellowed, "Gimme some room, boys!" With whistles and cheers of encouragement, the crowd moved back, so that Mac could see a huge, broad-shouldered figure in the uniform of a cavalry corporal launching into a jig. The massive soldier tried to keep time with the music, but that seemed to be a lost cause. Still, he danced with such enthusiasm that it made up for his lack of rhythm. As the corporal spun around, Mac saw his face in the firelight, and it was a fearsome visage, covered with thick, stiff, black bristles so that he almost seemed more animal than man.

Someone nudged Mac in the side and asked, "What do you think of Corporal Hagen?"

Mac recognized the voice and looked over to see Colonel Lee standing beside him. The colonel was grinning and clapping along with the music. Mac leaned closer and said, "I think if I was a child and saw the corporal, I'd have nightmares for a month!"

Lee threw his head back and laughed. "Hagen's every bit as fierce as he looks—unless he likes you. Then you'd never have a better friend."

"Where did the musicians come from?" asked Mac. He thought about adding *sir*, then decided not to. The atmosphere here tonight was definitely informal, not military.

"They serve as couriers for the general. But they were selected for their musical ability as much as anything else. Like I told you earlier, Beauty enjoys a good serenade."

The minstrels had finished one song and started another, and Hagen was still dancing. Mac could see the general now, sitting on a stump near the entrance to the tent. He had his hat pushed back on his head and was clapping with the music like the other spectators. His attitude changed somewhat, however, as he glanced out at the crowd and spotted Lee. Stuart stood up, and the musicians suddenly fell silent until he motioned for them to go on. The general caught Lee's eye and angled his head toward the tent. The colonel started to move around the circle of men, but he stopped and looked over his shoulder.

"Come with me, Brannon."

"Sir?" Mac asked, startled.

"I said come with me. You strike me as an intelligent sort, and I am in need of an aide-de-camp."

"But . . . I'm in Lieutenant Ramsey's company."

"Ramsey can do without your services."

It occurred to Mac that maybe it wasn't a good idea to be arguing with an officer, especially the nephew of Robert E. Lee. Not knowing what he was getting into here, he answered, "Yes sir," and followed Lee toward the entrance of General Stuart's tent.

Several other officers were also converging on the tent. Mac held the tent flap open so that the other men could follow the general, then stepped inside himself, letting the canvas fall shut behind him.

A small lantern burned on a folding table that had been set up. One of Stuart's aides was spreading a map on the table next to the lantern. The general took his hat off and placed it on the tent's single cot. He tugged off his gauntlets and dropped them beside the hat, then turned to the assembled officers. Mac stood in the back of the group, trying to be inconspicuous.

He hadn't escaped Stuart's keen eyes, though. The general asked, "What are you doing here, Private? It's Brannon, isn't it?"

Before Mac could reply, Lee spoke up. "I asked the private to accompany me, General. Or perhaps I should say 'the corporal,' since I've just promoted him and selected him as my aide-de-camp."

Stuart grinned at Mac. "Corporal, eh? You've started your climb through the ranks quickly, my friend. Fitz, try not to get this one killed so fast, all right?"

"Of course, General," Lee replied with a grin of his own.

Mac's jaw dropped a little with Stuart's last comment, but he supposed it wouldn't be a good idea to inquire too much.

Stuart stepped over to the table and pointed at the map. "I was just waiting for Fitz to get here so I could tell you boys the news I've had from down the peninsula. The Army of the Potomac has left Fort Monroe and moved into position near Yorktown. As some of you may know, there are a great many battlements surrounding the town, most of them built by the British during the Revolution. Our boys have fortified those battlements and are holding them against McClellan's forces."

One of the officers asked, "How many men do we have there?"

"Not enough," the general acknowledged dryly. "But he doesn't seem to know that. Boldness is not his watchword. McClellan would rather sit and wait than move, and he seems to have settled down for a long siege, much like the siege of Sebastopol during the Crimean War."

Mac had heard vaguely of the Crimean War, but he didn't know anything about the siege of Sebastopol. The realization came to him that being around General Stuart might well be something of an education.

Lee spoke up, "Yorktown's on the river, and McClellan's got the whole peninsula to work with. Why doesn't he bypass the town and leave the defenders sitting behind the breastworks?"

"Perhaps he would if he could," replied Stuart, "but I'm told that the Warwick River is flooding, and it runs across the peninsula, blocking McClellan's path. There are several dams that cross the river, but we have all of them heavily guarded. A company of marksmen can hold one of those narrow dams, no matter how many men the Federals have on the other side of the river."

"So McClellan is stalled before Yorktown," Lee said. "What do we do, General?"

Stuart laughed. "The thing we do best, Colonel. We make life as miserable as we can for the Yankees."

Chapter Six

THE LAST TIME TITUS had seen his mother this angry had been a year earlier, when Will had gunned down Joe Fogarty in Davis's store, turning the hostility between the Brannons and the Fogartys into a blood feud that had threatened to wipe out the Brannon family. Will had forestalled that by joining the army and going off to war, but not until after Abigail had furiously disowned him and banished him from the farm.

Now another Brannon brother had gone off to war, and Titus had to admit he was a mite disgruntled about the situation himself. With Mac gone, there was going to be more work for everyone who was left, mainly for him and Henry.

And if his head hadn't hurt so bad from the hangover he had, Titus might have even been willing to admit that he would miss Mac. Mac was a self-righteous prig sometimes, but hell, he was still family, wasn't he?

"He had no right," Cordelia spoke brokenly as she stared at the piece of paper in her hand. She had taken it from her mother after Abigail had finished reading it out loud. "He didn't even say good-bye."

"We already knew something had happened to him," Abigail observed stiffly. Her weathered face was set in grim lines. "We knew when he didn't come back from Warrenton Junction last week."

Michael Davis had brought the note out to the Brannon farm from Culpeper. He still stood with his hat in his hands in the farmyard in front of the house, next to his buggy. He offered, "I don't reckon you have to worry about Mac, Mrs. Brannon. He can take care of himself. And that stallion of his is a mighty fine one, from what I hear. If a cavalryman has a good horse, he'll always be all right."

Titus wanted to ask the storekeeper what in blazes he knew about such things. He didn't, though, knowing they ought to be appreciative to Davis for bringing out the message that had been given to him by a farmer who'd come down to Culpeper to try to buy some supplies. The farmer had been out of luck—the army had cleaned out Culpeper just like it had Warrenton—but he had brought Mac's scrawled letter with him and given it to Davis, figuring that the storekeeper would be acquainted with the Brannons.

"Mac said he was going to join the cavalry," noted Henry. "He didn't waste any time, did he?"

Davis said, "I've heard that all the troops who were headquartered here are going to be pulled out and taken down to Richmond. They say the Yankees are going to try to come up the peninsula."

"Let 'em come," Henry stated fiercely. "We'll stop 'em."

Titus grunted. If the Yankees really were coming, and if they weren't stopped, the war would be over soon. If Richmond fell, that would be the end of it.

Surprisingly, the thought filled him with bitterness. He had believed that deep down he didn't really care that much one way or the other about the war, especially since he'd lost Polly. Whether the Federals or the Confederates were running things didn't matter to him. The Brannons didn't have any slaves, had never had any slaves. They wouldn't lose anything by the Yankees' winning.

But although he could see that logically, Titus still found himself burning with the desire to send the Northerners packing.

"We appreciate you bringing us the news about Mac, Mr. Davis," Abigail said politely. "Would you like to stay to supper?"

Davis put his hat on. "No, ma'am, but I thank you anyway. I've got to get back to town. My store may be empty, but I still don't like to leave it sitting there unattended for too long."

"This war will be over someday, Mr. Davis, and I'm certain that then your business will do just fine."

Davis grinned hollowly. "Obliged for the kind words, ma'am. I hope you're right." He stepped up into his buggy and took hold of the reins. "I had an offer to buy the place the other day."

"From who?" Henry asked.

"Duncan Ebersole. He's already bought several businesses in town that have gone under, paying dirt cheap prices. He stopped by to see me, him and his gal—"

"What did you say?" Titus's head snapped up sharply.

"I said, when Ebersole and his gal were in town the other day, he stopped to see me—"

Titus interrupted again, stepping forward to grab the harness of Davis's buggy horse. "Polly was with him? Speak up, you damned fool!"

"Titus!" Abigail's voice lashed out. "Don't speak that way to your elders, especially not to a guest." To the storekeeper, she appealed, "I apologize for my son's behavior, Mr. Davis. He's obviously out of his head."

"That's all right, ma'am," Davis answered. "I recollect now that Titus here was sweet on the Ebersole girl."

Titus took a deep breath, and his hand tightened on the harness as he made an effort to calm himself. Had the whole town known about his feelings for Polly? Had he been the subject of a lot of gossip?

Right now he didn't care. All he wanted was to know if he had heard Davis right.

"I'm sorry, Mr. Davis," he forced himself to say. "I didn't know Polly was back from Richmond."

Davis nodded and added, "Yep, Ebersole brought her back last week when he heard about how the Yankees might try to come up the peninsula. Reckon he must've decided she'd be safer at Mountain Laurel than off with the relatives."

Titus's pulse thundered in his head. Polly was back! He had been afraid that he wouldn't see her again until the war was over. Hell, he'd been afraid he would *never* see her again! All he could think of now was getting to her as fast as he could.

Letting go of the harness, Titus spun on his heel and started toward the barn. "Titus!" Abigail snapped. "Where are you going?"

"Mountain Laurel," Titus flung over his shoulder. He heard the rattle of buggy wheels as Davis drove out of the yard after delivering his second bombshell of the day, but he didn't look back.

Henry followed, catching up as Titus reached the barn. "Ma and Cordelia don't look happy about this, Titus," Henry cautioned. "In fact, Cordelia said you ought to stay as far away as you can from Polly Ebersole."

"Cordelia never liked Polly," Titus growled as he went into the tack room and gathered a saddle and bridle. He headed through the barn toward the corral. "She's just jealous 'cause Polly's so pretty. And Ma never liked any of the Ebersoles because they're Congregationalists and not Baptists. But I don't give a hang about that."

"Maybe not, but you know what happened the last time you went to Mountain Laurel."

Titus knew, all right: his last visit to the Ebersole plantation had ended with his getting thrashed by some of Ebersole's hired men. But as he swung open the corral gate, he blurted, "I don't care. I'm going anyway."

"Well, then, I'm going with you," Henry declared.

Titus swung around toward him. "No, you're not. I don't need any damned company."

"What if Ebersole sics his hounds on you?"

"He won't."

"How can you be sure of that?"

He couldn't be, Titus realized. He couldn't be certain what sort of reception he'd get from anyone on the Ebersole plantation.

But the one thing he knew was that Polly was there, and if Polly was there, he had to go to her. It was as simple as that.

"Just stay out of my way, little brother," he grated as he started saddling one of the horses.

For a moment, Henry didn't say anything. Then he stepped back and yielded angrily, "All right, if that's the way you want it."

"It ain't just the way I want it," Titus declared, drawing tight the saddle cinch. "It's the way it's got to be."

A couple of minutes later, he rode away from the farm. Abigail and Cordelia had already gone into the house, but that didn't matter. Titus didn't even glance in that direction.

His eyes were turned toward Mountain Laurel.

DUNCAN EBERSOLE'S teeth clenched an unlit cigar as he tried to make the scrawled numbers in the ledger book add up right. Try as he might, though, the numbers refused to tell any story other than the one he didn't want to hear, that his finances were failing and Mountain Laurel was in trouble.

No one would know that to look at the plantation, of course. The place was still well kept up. And the illusion of wealth extended beyond that. The carriage Ebersole rode into town was still the finest one in the county, pulled by the best team of horses. Ebersole's suits were as elegant as always. He already had a reputation for being thrifty in other matters, to the point that some called him a skinflint, so no one would wonder about the fact that he wasn't throwing money around.

In point of fact, Ebersole reflected as he took the cigar out of his mouth and reached for the glass of whiskey on the desk next to the ledger, he had actually been spending more than usual lately. With businesses failing in town, he had seen the opportunity to expand his holdings, and he had seized it. That was the smart thing to do. But it had aggravated his cash-poor situation, leaving him wondering if he would be able to keep Mountain Laurel afloat until the war was over. *Maybe I should have been more cautious*, he thought.

He leaned back in his chair and stretched his legs in front of him as he tossed down the whiskey. The liquor burned his throat but started a pleasant warmth in his belly. He used one hand to toy with the empty glass and the other to put the cigar back in his mouth.

Ebersole was a medium-sized man with thinning gray hair on top of his head but worn long in the back, falling to his shoulders. His closely trimmed beard was gray as well but it retained more of the reddish hue that had been its original color. He was a colonel in the Virginia State Militia—self-appointed, of course—but he wore his uniform only on special occasions. Ebersole had been born six years after his parents had immigrated to the United States from Scotland in 1809. By that time his father had become a contract farmer in the Virginia Piedmont, little better than a slave himself.

Things had changed mightily since that time, Ebersole reflected. The son of immigrants and a contract farmer had grown up to be the richest, most powerful man in this part of the country, the owner of a beautiful mansion and hundreds of slaves. His teeth clenched on the cigar again. He was damned if he was going to let it all slip away. He was going to hang on to what he had, no matter what it took.

The door of his study opened behind him, and Polly announced, "Father? Someone's here to see you."

There was something strange about her voice, a strained tautness that made Ebersole swing around in his swivel chair. Thank God for Polly, he thought as he saw his daughter standing in the doorway as lovely as ever, the very picture of how her mother had looked when Ebersole married her. He never would have made it through the bad times when his wife died if it hadn't been for Polly comforting him the way she had. He wasn't going to have anything upsetting her now.

"Who is it?" he asked as he came to his feet.

"A man from the army. He's got some other men with him."

Ebersole frowned. What did the army want with him? He had already been more than helpful to the Southern cause, organizing the local militia unit and leading the drive to recruit men into the regular army. Not that it had been difficult to do. Nearly all the young men in the county had been anxious to go fight the Yankees.

He patted Polly on the shoulder as he went past her into the hallway. "Dinna ye worry, lass. I'll see what they want."

The dogs were barking, Ebersole noticed as he walked toward the front of the house. If he hadn't been concentrating so hard on the financial plight facing him, he probably would have heard them, he thought. When he stepped out onto the mansion's vast front gallery, he saw the hounds capering around several skittish horses. The gray-uniformed riders had their hands full trying to keep their mounts under control.

"Here now!" Ebersole called sharply. "Get away from here, ye craven curs! Away, I say!"

The dogs obeyed, slinking off around the corner of the house. The soldiers calmed their horses, and their leader said, "Thank you, sir. Sorry for the disturbance."

Ebersole frowned as he looked at the man's campaign cap and the insignia on his uniform jacket. A sergeant? They had sent a *sergeant* out here to talk to him? Not even an officer? Ebersole felt his face growing warm with anger and resentment, but he kept his voice under control as he asked, "What can I do for ye, Sergeant?"

"The quartermaster sent us out here on a supply detail, Mr. Ebersole. He sends his apologies as well, but we need to commandeer a few things in the name of the Confederacy."

"What? I've already been more than generous wi' what I've got. I've provided horses for the cavalry, an' milk and eggs and cotton and—"

"The quartermaster sent us to bring in your livestock, sir. We need all your hogs and chickens. He said to leave you a milk cow, though."

The anger that was simmering inside Ebersole boiled up. "Ye mean t' steal my animals, is that it? What's next, takin' all my slaves? Usin' my house for a damned barracks?" Even as the words tumbled out of him, Ebersole thought that he ought not to be saying them, lest he give the soldiers ideas that hadn't already occurred to them, the damned scavengers.

"I'm sorry, sir," the sergeant offered. "But we have orders."

Ebersole took a deep breath. He knew he ought to comply without complaint. It was for the Confederacy, after all. Any sacrifice for that noble cause ought to be acceptable.

But at this moment, as frustrated as he was about the problems facing Mountain Laurel, he was in no mood to be cooperative. As the sergeant and the men with him started to turn their mounts away from the gallery, Ebersole's voice lashed out at them.

"Dinna ye lay a hand on my animals! Ye'll just have t' go back to Culpeper an' tell that quartermaster o' yers that ye won't be commandeerin' anything from Mountain Laurel today." In his anger, Ebersole's Scottish burr, which he had inherited even though he had been born in America, grew thicker.

The sergeant hesitated. "Sir, we have our orders . . ."

Without really thinking about what he was doing, Ebersole reached into his coat pocket and brought out the small pistol he carried there. It was only a single-shot weapon, but he trained it directly on the sergeant, who at the moment represented everything that was going wrong in Duncan Ebersole's life.

"I told ye not today," Ebersole grated. "Now, if ye dinna get out o' here mighty fast, I'll blow ye right out o' that saddle."

The sergeant paled, but he warned, "You don't want to do that, sir."

"The hell I don't."

Behind Ebersole, a footstep sounded. "Father, don't!" Polly gasped. Ebersole grimaced. He should have given her specific orders not to follow him out here, he thought.

"Polly, go back in the house!"

"No, I won't." She came up beside him, so that he could see her from the corner of his eye even though he kept his gaze fastened on the sergeant. "You have to put the gun down, Father. You can't fight these men."

"The hell I can't. This is my home, and I'll not let them come in here an' just take wha'ever they want."

The sergeant tried again to talk reason. "Mr. Ebersole, I know you're a strong believer in the Confederacy. You don't want to go against your own country."

Ebersole's frown deepened. It was true that he wanted to do everything he could to help the Confederacy, but at what cost? At what cost?

Then the sergeant made the mistake of saying, "Besides, if you shoot me, my men will gun you down."

Ebersole sharply drew in his breath, then said in an even angrier tone than before, "By God, I'll not be threatened on my own land! Now get off, damn ye!"

"I can't—"

A new voice crackled from the corner of the house. "Oh, yes, you can."

Ebersole glanced in the direction of the voice and saw Titus Brannon step around the corner, carrying the Sharps rifle he nearly always had with him. The stock of the big-bored weapon was snugged firmly against Titus's shoulder, and he was peering intently over the sights attached to the muzzle. He went on, "If you got the sergeant, Mr. Ebersole, I got two more of those soldier boys lined up so I can take 'em down with one bullet. This Sharps o' mine will put a .50 caliber slug all the way through one fella and into another with no trouble at all."

"Damn it!" exclaimed the sergeant. "This is treason."

"No, 'tisn't," Ebersole argued, thinking furiously, trying to come up with some way out of this mess. He continued, "All we're doin' is puttin' a stop to some thievery. Ye can't ride onto a man's land an' *tell* him yer takin' this an' takin' that, and expect him t' like it. Tell yer quartermaster t' come out here an' *ask* for what he wants, and we'll see about givin' it to him."

"I can't tell him that! I have my orders!"

"Well, then, sonny boy, yer only choice is t' get yerself killed, I reckon."

The sergeant glowered at Ebersole for a long moment. "All right. I'll tell him."

While Ebersole and Titus stood there tensely, the soldiers wheeled their horses around and trotted down the long lane bordered with mountain laurels, the trees that gave the plantation its name. Not until the soldiers were out of range did either man lower his weapon.

Then, as Titus let the barrel of the Sharps sag toward the ground, Polly started to rush toward him, crying, "Titus! Oh, where did you come from?"

"Polly!" Ebersole snapped. He saw the look of anticipation on Titus's face and knew that in another moment, the farmer would have his arms around his daughter. Grateful though he might be for Titus's help, Ebersole would not let that happen. As Polly stopped short, her father commanded, "Get on in the house, like I told ye before."

She looked back at him, her face still pale and drawn with the strain of the confrontation. "I want to say hello to Titus."

"I'm sure he heard ye. There's nothin' wrong with yer hearin', is there, Brannon?"

"No sir," Titus replied tightly.

Ebersole put his pistol away and jerked a thumb toward the door. "Go on, girl."

Reluctantly, Polly turned and went toward the door. She threw a glance over her shoulder at Titus, but Ebersole moved so that he was between the two of them. Titus started to step up onto the gallery.

"No need for that, Brannon."

"I helped you," Titus reminded him.

"Aye, and ye have my gratitude for that. But th' fact remains, ye were not invited here, Brannon. I think ye'd best go on back to yer farm."

"I came to see Polly, not you."

"Ye've seen her." Ebersole glanced at the door, which had closed behind his daughter. "She's not receivin' any callers right now."

"You . . . you arrogant old bastard!" Titus sputtered.

"I'll overlook yer impoliteness . . . this time," Ebersole said with a smug smile. "Now, if there's nothin' else I can do for ye—"

"You can let me call on your daughter!" Titus burst out.

Ebersole shook his head. "Not bloody likely. She's not for the likes o' you."

Titus was trembling with anger. "I should've let those soldiers shoot you."

"But ye didn't." Ebersole turned away, adding over his shoulder, "I'll be sendin' a servant for my overseer an' his men. Ye recall, I expect, what happened the last time ye saw them."

"I remember. You set them on me like they were a pack of hounds."

"I can call the hounds, too, if ye like," Ebersole sneered as he reached the doorway. "Best be goin' while ye still can. Good-bye, Brannon."

The door closed firmly behind him.

Ebersole knew that Titus's timely arrival had made the difference in the encounter with the soldiers. If they hadn't been faced with the threat of that Sharps rifle, they probably wouldn't have backed down. And Ebersole was truly grateful for that assistance. He might have even given Titus a coin or two, if Titus hadn't insisted on trying to talk to Polly.

The lad would never understand that he wasn't a fit suitor. His unwelcome attentions were one reason Ebersole had sent Polly to Richmond in the first place. Ebersole knew that Polly was attracted to the farmer, though only God knew why she would be. Of course, Polly could be a spiteful minx at times. She might have played up to Titus simply to annoy her father. She was capable of that, Ebersole had decided.

So now that she was back, and Titus had found out somehow that she had returned from Richmond, Ebersole knew he had another problem to deal with. Titus would simply have to learn to stay away from Polly.

And if the price of that knowledge was his life . . . well, then, so be it.

Chapter Seven

GEN. GEORGE B. MCCLELLAN had arrived at Fort Monroe on April 2, while his invasion force was still being assembled. He had studied all the maps and intended to move his army as quickly as possible to the town of West Point, where the Pamunkey and Mattapony Rivers flowed together to form the York and also to form the northeastern border of the Virginia Peninsula. Once the Army of the Potomac was established at West Point, that would serve as the staging area for the attack on Richmond, some fifty miles due west.

The road to West Point was not wide open, however. Yorktown, twenty miles up the river from Fort Monroe, had been heavily reinforced by the Confederates. Surrounded by battlements as it was, the town would be easy for the Southerners to defend. Also, across the river at Gloucester Point, artillery batteries had been set up so that any force attacking by either land or water would fall under their guns.

McClellan was counting on using naval gunboats to destroy the Confederate batteries, but that plan had to be abandoned when the navy refused to go along with it. The gunboats were needed elsewhere, Adm. Louis Goldsborough informed McClellan, primarily at Hampton Roads to keep the Confederate ironclad *Virginia* at bay.

Chagrined but determined to carry on anyway, McClellan began his advance up the peninsula with two columns even before all the troops bound for Fort Monroe had arrived. On the first day of the march, everything seemed to go his way: the weather was good, the men were eager, and what few Confederate outposts they encountered were quickly abandoned by fleeing Southerners.

The next day, however, McClellan's luck changed. Rain fell in buckets, making streams that were already swollen rise even more. And most of those streams, according to the Federal commander's maps, weren't even supposed to be there. Between the muddy roads and the arduous fording of flooded streams, the progress of the invading army was slowed dramatically. Still, the leading units were able to reach a stretch of marshy ground just south of Yorktown during the afternoon—where they promptly came under heavy bombardment from the Confederate artillery.

The Yankees had no choice except to dig in and wait. McClellan had been expecting strong Confederate resistance from the old colonial town; he was prepared to wait until his own artillery caught up and then slug it out at long range with the Rebels, confident that his second column, several miles to the west, would be able to bypass the town and continue on up the peninsula.

McClellan's maps had betrayed him again, however, as he discovered later that day when he received an urgent message from Gen. Erasmus Keyes, in command of the western column. A large river that had been shown on the maps as running parallel to the York actually cut across the peninsula, blocking the path of the Union advance. The only routes across the flooded river were narrow dams, and those dams were blocked by Confederate artillery and riflemen. Keyes's column was stalled, just like McClellan's at Yorktown.

Expecting reinforcements, McClellan was stymied again by a telegram from the War Department informing him that the men he was waiting for would be staying in Washington to protect the capital. Activity on the part of the Confederates in the Shenandoah Valley had convinced President Lincoln that Washington would be in imminent danger of attack from that direction if too many of the troops were sent to McClellan.

That left a seething McClellan bottled up on the peninsula below Yorktown and the flooded Warwick River. Even so, with almost sixty thousand men at his command, McClellan's forces outnumbered the Confederates by more than four to one. His choices were to push ahead and try to overrun Yorktown with his superior numbers or to wait and lay siege to the city.

McClellan, ever cautious, decided on the siege.

———

THE WEATHER this spring had alternated between being glorious and miserable. This was one of the glorious mornings, Mac thought as he rode beside Col. Fitzhugh Lee. There was not a cloud in the sky . . . although the constant roar of artillery could almost have been mistaken for thunder.

Stuart's cavalry had just arrived in the area, and already, despite the good weather, a sense of discouragement was spreading among the men. The area around Yorktown was not the sort of terrain where cavalry could be particularly effective. The ground was either wooded and marshy or scored with deep gullies. There was no room for saber charges or running battles. About the best the horsemen could do would be to serve as scouts and to harass the Yankees if they caught any of them venturing out from the siege lines.

The cavalry was approaching a large group of men gathered under a tree at the side of the road. As they came nearer, Mac studied the men and saw that many of them wore the insignia of high officers. One of them, a man with a short salt-and-pepper goatee, was a general, Mac noted.

Fitz Lee leaned toward Mac and said quietly, "That's General Johnston."

Mac looked at the colonel. "The commander of all the Confederate forces?"

"One and the same. Although that designation might be open to some dispute, especially from General Beauregard and my uncle. General Johnston is certainly in charge of the defense of the peninsula, however."

Mac nodded slowly as he looked at the group of officers. Although it had been Gen. Joseph E. Johnston who had ordered the Confederate withdrawal from Manassas and Centreville that

had resulted in the massive influx of troops at Culpeper, Mac
had never actually seen him in person until now. He wondered
if Johnston's presence here at Yorktown meant that the soldiers
had all left Culpeper.

General Stuart drew rein and dismounted to join the group
under the tree. Colonel Lee also swung down from the saddle
and moved toward the conference. As the colonel's aide-de-
camp, Mac figured that meant he should go along, too, even
though he would be careful to stay well back and not interrupt the discussion.

And it was a heated discussion, he realized as he came
closer, almost an argument. Words were flying back and forth
only among the junior officers, however. Generals Johnston
and Stuart merely stood and listened, obviously noting the
points that were being made. As far as Mac could tell, they
were arguing about whether to continue to defend Yorktown
or to retreat.

"McClellan's afraid to attack us directly," one of the
officers insisted. "When he sent that sortie out against Burnt
Chimneys a couple of days ago, he could have broken the Warwick River line. Some of the Yankees actually made it across
the dam and were on our side of the river. All McClellan had
to do was keep pouring them across. He didn't."

"That doesn't mean he's afraid," insisted another. "He's
simply cautious."

The first man snorted. "Cautious to the point of cowardice."

Johnston spoke up for the first time since Stuart and the
others had arrived. "That's enough," he declared. "I served
beside George McClellan in Mexico, and he is not a coward.
But he *is* too hesitant to act at times, and we should count ourselves fortunate that he is." Clearly, Johnston had made up his
mind about something. "Yorktown will become a death trap if
we stay here, despite its defenses. The Yankees have enough
artillery and ammunition to keep on pounding us until there's
not an earthwork left standing, nor a building, either."

"Then you intend to withdraw, sir?" one of the officers asked.

Almost imperceptibly, Johnston hesitated, then said, "Not yet. President Davis has ordered us to hold here. I intend to bring in as many reinforcements as I can, so that a direct assault by McClellan's forces will not be able to succeed."

From the sound of what he had heard, Mac thought it was pretty unlikely such a direct assault would come anytime soon. This fella McClellan sounded like the type who liked to sit back and wait.

Johnston turned to Stuart. "General, do you have any suggestions how we might make best use of your cavalry forces?"

Mac thought Stuart looked frustrated. "The cavalry was not invented for siege warfare, General."

"I am aware of that facet of military strategy, General," Johnston snapped.

"My apologies, General. I did not mean to sound pedantic. I meant simply that our particular skills will be of little use here." Stuart shrugged. "Perhaps we can patrol the area of the Warwick River, in case the Yankees attempt a crossing elsewhere than the dams."

"Unlikely," countered Johnston. "But not impossible, I suppose. Very well, General. I leave the arrangement of the patrols to you."

Stuart had taken off his gauntlets. He saluted Johnston, then began pulling them on again as he turned to leave the conference. Lee, Mac, and the other cavalry officers who had joined him followed Stuart back to their horses.

"Glorified pickets," Stuart muttered under his breath. He lifted his head, looked at the others, and predicted, "Never fear, boys. Our time shall come."

———

BUT NOT anytime soon, Mac discovered. As Stuart had prophesied, the cavalry acted merely as glorified pickets for the next two weeks, riding along the Warwick River from dam to dam, carrying messages between the defensive posts, and watching for any signs that the enemy might be attempting to bridge the river elsewhere. The Warwick, however, was so swollen and swift moving that it was impossible to cross except at the dams.

Then, early in May, word came that the Yankees were bringing up heavier guns than they had been using thus far. A scout who had been behind enemy lines claimed to have seen mortars so large that they must have weighed ten tons. He knew for certain that the guns were so heavy teams of one hundred horses were required to pull them over logs laid across the muddy roads; from his hiding place in the woods, he had counted the animals hauling one of the mortars.

This news told Johnston that McClellan would soon be ready to batter Yorktown into submission. Orders from the president or not, the Confederate army had no choice but to retreat or be destroyed.

After meeting with Johnston, Stuart summoned his officers. Mac went along with Lee.

"We're to function as the rear guard for General Johnston," Stuart explained. "But before that, we're going to be dashing about near the front lines so that the Yankees can see us. We don't want them to know that we're withdrawing."

"So we'll be serving as decoys, you mean," Fitz Lee commented with a grin. "What if the Yankees open up on us with those giant mortars we've heard so much about?"

"Ride faster," Stuart replied dryly, drawing a chuckle from the assembled officers.

Mac wiped the back of his hand across his mouth. Trying to dodge mortar shells fired from those massive weapons didn't sound like a pleasant prospect to him, but Stuart and the others seemed to be almost looking forward to it. He supposed if he survived and served with these men long enough, he might develop some of the same reckless, devil-may-care attitudes. Now, though, such a dashing demeanor went against the grain for him.

"Worried, Mac?" Fitz Lee asked as they left the meeting.

"No sir," Mac lied.

"Well, you should be," Lee countered, surprising him. "I've a feeling that sometime in the next few days, we'll be going into battle, and that means many of us—or all of us—could wind up dead."

"I don't plan to die."

"No soldier worth his salt does. While laughing in the face of death doesn't make the fear go away, sometimes it helps a little."

Mac nodded. "I'll remember that, sir."

The next day, May 4, was spent as Stuart had suggested, with the cavalry dashing back and forth along the defensive line as if they were carrying messages from post to post, when in fact most of the trenches behind the earthworks were empty. The troops had moved out with great stealth during the night and were now marching up the road toward Williamsburg.

The Union's big guns had not yet come into play, although they were still shelling the Southern fortifications with their smaller artillery. Except for Stuart's cavalry and a few Confederate gun crews that kept up token fire, the defenses at Yorktown had been abandoned. As night fell, Stuart and his men withdrew to the north of Yorktown, covering the retreat of the last of the soldiers who had held gallantly against the Federals for the past few weeks.

That evening, Stuart spread out a map in his tent and dispersed his forces. "Fitz, you'll take your regiment up here to Eltham's Landing," he directed, pointing at a spot at the junction of the Pamunkey and Mattapony Rivers. "General Johnston is sending some of the infantry up there in case General McClellan tries to slip some men past us by way of the rivers. Colonel Wickham, you'll take the Telegraph Road here"—Stuart traced a line between Yorktown and Williamsburg—"while I'll cover the Hampton Road here to the west. We'll join forces again here where the two roads converge south of

Williamsburg. That way we should be able to stymie the pursuit along both routes."

"Are you sure McClellan will send men by way of Eltham's Landing, General?" asked Colonel Lee.

Stuart shook his head. "It seems likely, but we can't know for certain, no."

"Then may I suggest, sir, that you send me and my men to cover one of these roads instead?" Lee pointed to the map.

Mac saw a smile tug at Stuart's mouth for a second before he said, "You want to make sure you get in on the action, eh, Fitz?"

Again, Stuart shook his head. "No, I want you at Eltham's Landing. Those are your orders, Colonel."

Lee nodded immediately. "Yes sir. Of course."

He was muttering under his breath as he and Mac left the meeting a short time later, however. "Beauty's keeping part of the rear guard action for himself," he noted. "If there *is* a fight, he doesn't want to be left out."

Mac ventured, "Couldn't the same thing be said of you, sir?"

Lee laughed. "You've come to know me well in a short time, Mac. You're right, of course. Well, we shall just have to hope that McClellan tries something daring—for a change."

Before dawn the next morning, Lee, Mac, and the members of the First Virginia Cavalry were galloping northwestward along the peninsula. They passed through a series of fortifications outside of Williamsburg. These earthen redoubts spanned nearly the entire width of the peninsula here where it narrowed slightly, and in the center was the largest earthwork in this defensive line, Fort Magruder. Lee pointed it out. "General Johnston's left some men behind to hold the Yankees here for a time before retreating. These delaying tactics are hell on a cavalryman, Mac, but I suppose they do serve a purpose. Some say that a battle postponed is a battle not yet lost. I prefer to think of it as a battle not yet won."

Leaving Williamsburg behind them, the group rode on and in the evening reached Eltham's Landing, on the western shore of the York at the spot where it forked into the Pamunkey and the Mattapony. Across the way, on the tip of land that extended between the two rivers, were the lights of the town of West Point. The infantry division that had been sent here by Johnston was already in place, although they were making a cold camp tonight. No fires burned to warn the Union army that a good number of troops were waiting here for them.

Gen. G. W. Smith, the commander of the infantry, came out to greet Colonel Lee, who swung down from his horse and saluted the general, then said, "General Stuart's compliments, sir. He sent us to assist you should the Yankees attempt to pass by this spot."

In the darkness, made deeper by the overcast sky, Mac could not see Smith's face, but he heard the general say, "Very well, Colonel. I expect we shall have work to do on the morrow."

Fitz Lee could not contain his enthusiasm. "I hope so, General," he declared. Smith just grunted.

The next day was still cloudy, but the rain had tapered off to nothing. Early in the morning, at Smith's request, Lee led a cavalry patrol along the river, downstream from the Confederate camp.

Mac felt the stallion pacing restlessly under him, and he knew the horse wanted to run. There was no place for that along these wooded shores, though. They had to be content with winding through the trees, trying to keep the river where they could see it while remaining out of sight themselves.

Suddenly, Lee signaled a halt. Mac was right behind him, so he had almost the same view as the colonel. As he leaned forward to peer through a gap in the trees and brush, Mac spotted movement on the river. Lee lifted his field glasses to his eyes and murmured, "Boats loaded with troops, escorted by gunboats. McClellan's trying to cut us off, all right, just as General Stuart thought he might."

"Do we take the word back to General Smith?" asked Mac.

Lee lowered the field glasses and motioned for the riders with him to turn around. "As quickly as possible," he replied. "We'll have a warm welcome waiting for those Yankees."

The cavalrymen made their way out of the trees, and as soon as they reached a road, they prodded their horses into a gallop. The stallion enjoyed stretching his legs, and Mac was soon out in front of all the others. He thought about pulling the horse in and slowing it down, but the sensation felt exhilarating. He was enjoying this as much as the stallion was. Still, he was worried about getting too far out in front, so he glanced over his shoulder at Lee. To Mac's surprise, the colonel waved him on with a grin on his face.

Mac took that to mean he should let the stallion have its head. He loosened his grip on the reins, and the horse surged on with a fresh burst of speed.

By the time Mac got back to Eltham's Landing, he was more than a mile ahead of the rest of the patrol. He headed straight for General Smith's tent and dismounted. At Mac's request, one of the sentries stuck his head in the tent and announced, "General? One of those cavalrymen is here to see you."

Smith stepped out and returned Mac's salute. "Yes, Corporal, what is it?"

"The Yankees are on their way upriver, sir," Mac reported. "I figure they'll be here in less than an hour."

Smith frowned. "Where is Colonel Lee?"

Mac waved back down the road. "The colonel sent me on ahead, sir." He rubbed the stallion's nose. "I reckon he thought I could make better time and get the news to you sooner."

Smith looked at the stallion, and his frown faded. "Yes, I can see why he would think that. Good work, Corporal. When Colonel Lee gets here, tell him I wish to see him."

"Yes sir."

Mac led the horse away, unsaddled it, and began rubbing it down. Sweat flecked the stallion's silver gray hide. By the time he had finished, Lee and the rest of the patrol were riding in.

Mac conveyed the general's message, and Lee nodded then remarked, "That horse of yours really likes to run, doesn't he?"

"Yes sir, he does."

"Ever race him?"

Mac thought about the races in Richmond in which he had ridden before the war and before he had captured the stallion. "No sir, I never got the chance. I hope to someday, though, when the war's over."

"I hope you get the chance. Let's visit the general."

Mac listened as Smith and Lee discussed the strategy for the impending battle. The general planned to greet the Federals with a barrage from his artillery, forcing them to come ashore here rather than heading upriver in an attempt to cut off Johnston's retreat.

"I don't want to engage them on the ground right away, however," Smith clarified. "I'd like to draw them onshore as far as possible first." There were several hundred yards between the Confederate camp and the riverbank.

Lee nodded. "Sounds like a good plan to me, General. What did you have in mind for me and my men?"

"I want to hold you in reserve," said Smith, and Mac saw the slight frown that appeared on Lee's face. Smith must have noticed the expression, too, because he chuckled. "Don't worry, Colonel. I'm just going to soften them up for you, and then you're going to push the Yankees back into the river."

That brought a grin from Lee. "Yes sir. We'll be ready."

All the Confederate forces were ready when the Union boats steamed around a bend in the river and came into view a short time later. The artillery batteries held their fire at first, waiting until the vessels were in the right position, then smoke and flame suddenly geysered from the mouths of the cannon. The roar of their fire filled the humid air.

Several of the Yankee gunboats guarding the troop transports were hit and crippled by the first Confederate volley. Knowing that they would be easy targets for the batteries if they stayed on the river, the Federals turned their vessels and made a run for shore, coming in under the Confederate guns. The batteries couldn't be aimed that steeply downward, but Rebel riflemen posted along the riverbank peppered the Northerners with lead.

From his position with the other cavalrymen at the rear of the Confederate lines, Mac couldn't really see what was going on along the river, but he heard the roar of the cannon and the crackling rattle of rifle fire. He leaned forward anxiously in the saddle, feeling a mixture of fear and anticipation coursing through him. He was ready to fight, he told himself. The revolver holstered on his hip, which had been issued to him when Lee had made him a corporal and his aide-de-camp, was fully loaded. The colonel, sitting his horse just in front of Mac, had already drawn his saber, even though the order for the cavalry to join the fight might not come for a while.

The Confederate skirmishers withdrew, pulling all the way back to the camp. After a short time, Mac saw men in blue uniforms beginning to mass in the distance. The enemy. The men who had invaded his homeland rather than accept that the Confederacy had a legal, constitutional right to secede from the Union.

Mac's mouth was dry. He swallowed, then licked his lips, but it didn't do much good. That was the enemy up yonder, he told himself again.

"Why don't they come?" Lee wondered aloud. "Why are they just sitting there?"

"Maybe they don't want to fight," Mac said.

Lee turned and looked at him. "How could they not want to fight?" he asked, and his tone made it clear that right now, such a thing was beyond his comprehension. The time for holding back was past.

General Smith must have felt the same way, because a short time later, orders were passed and the front ranks of the Confederate infantry launched an advance toward the Federals.

The firing grew louder, and the air was so thick with smoke that Mac couldn't even see the fighting. After what seemed like an interminable time, a gap in the Confederate ranks suddenly opened up, and Colonel Lee lifted his saber. "That's our signal," he cried excitedly. "Smith's men have pushed them back, and now it's up to us." The saber flashed down, and he shouted, "Charge!"

Rebel yells welled up the throats of most of the cavalrymen. Mac stayed silent, concentrating on guiding the stallion as he rode close on the heels of the colonel's horse. The cavalry thundered forward, across the field toward the river and through the gap in the infantry. Mac saw the bodies of men sprawled on the ground in front of them and realized to his horror that they would have to ride right over the dead and wounded men, Union and Confederate alike, in order to reach the retreating Yankees.

Forcing down the sickness that threatened to rise within him, Mac kept the stallion at the gallop and tried to ignore the awful thudding of hooves around him. In what seemed like the blink of an eye, the riders reached the blue-clad soldiers fleeing on foot. Mac lifted his pistol and tried to aim, only to discover that it was impossible to do so from the back of a running horse. He made sure the gun was pointed in the direction of the Yankees and began firing blindly, squeezing the trigger, pulling back the trigger to cock the weapon again, squeezing the trigger once more. He fired slowly and methodically until the pistol was empty, and he had no idea if any of his shots hit any of the Federals. His nose and eyes stung from the acrid smell of powder smoke that was whipped into his face.

The Yankee retreat was a rout now. They fled back to the river, sliding and tumbling down the steep bank. Lee called a halt and waved his men back. The Union soldiers had taken shelter behind a bluff at the very edge of the river, and they were firing sporadically, trying to keep the Confederates from pushing them all the way into the water.

A few riflemen came up to keep the Yankees occupied, while the rest of the Confederate forces fell back. As Mac and Lee jogged their horses alongside one another toward the camp, the colonel declared, "That'll slow them down enough for Johnston to get the rest of his men safely away. We did our job today, eh, Mac?"

"I suppose so, sir." Mac realized he was still holding his empty pistol. Now he slid the weapon back into its holster, still unloaded. That was probably the wrong thing to do, he thought, but he was slightly numb from the battle and didn't really care.

Mac realized Lee was still talking to him. "Sir?" he asked.

"I asked if you're all right. You're bleeding, you know."

Mac felt a trickle of something warm and sticky on his right cheek. He lifted his hand to his face and saw that the fingertips came away red. His cheek stung fiercely, now that he was aware of the wound.

"Looks like a bullet just grazed you," said Lee. He looked at Mac for a second, then continued, "You didn't even know it, did you?"

"No sir."

"I'm not surprised. In the heat of battle, we sometimes don't notice the little things."

Little things, Mac thought. A bullet had come within an inch of killing him, and the colonel considered it a little thing.

Well, maybe it was, he realized as he drew a deep breath. Despite the narrowness of his escape, he was still alive.

And that was the biggest thing of all.

Chapter Eight

THE CITIZENS OF CULPEPER County had mixed emotions as they watched the thousands of Confederate soldiers leaving the town. Unanswered questions nagged at the minds of many of the inhabitants of the county. Did the departure of the troops mean that the Federals now might come sweeping down from the north, ravaging the countryside as they came? Had this part of Virginia been deliberately abandoned to its fate by the Confederacy? No one wanted to believe that, but with the soldiers gone, there was no line of defense between the civilians and the Northern horde.

On the other hand, having so many troops in the area had been a serious drain on the county's resources. Food, ammunition, horses, other livestock . . . the army had taken just about all of those things it could, as well as other supplies. Now, with the soldiers leaving, the county might have a chance to recover a little—as long as the Yankees stayed away.

Then rumors began to circulate about how the Army of the Potomac was advancing up the Virginia Peninsula closer to its objective—the capture of Richmond. If the Northerners were successful in this effort, it would most likely mean the fall of the Confederacy. Once that was generally known, the citizens of Culpeper came to the correct conclusion that the troops were being moved up to defend the capital.

Not all the soldiers had left town yet on the late April Saturday when the Brannon family—those who were left in the county—came into Culpeper. Cordelia sat in the back of the wagon with Titus while Henry and Abigail were on the seat, with Henry handling the reins. A basket of eggs was beside Cordelia, the fragile cargo covered with a cloth. They had "donated" chickens and hogs to the cause, like the other farmers in the county, but they still had some good laying hens.

113

Abigail thought it would be kind to take a basket of eggs into town to share with some of those less fortunate, and her children had regarded the trip as a chance to break the monotony of farm life.

Cordelia glanced at Titus, who sat with his back against one of the wagon's sideboards. He looked as gloomy as ever, but at least he wasn't drunk today. He hadn't been drinking nearly as much in recent days, Cordelia reminded herself, and she wondered if that had anything to do with Polly Ebersole's coming back to her father's plantation. If Polly's return had the result of making Titus stop drinking, then Cordelia supposed she shouldn't be too resentful of the other young woman. But what ill effects Polly's presence might have on Titus were yet to be seen.

Men in gray uniforms were climbing onto flat cars lined up behind a locomotive that was puffing smoke and steam at the depot of the Orange and Alexandria Railroad. From Culpeper the troop train would proceed south to Gordonsville Junction, where it would be switched to the rails of the Virginia Centra,l which would carry it on to Richmond. At the rate the army was pulling out of Culpeper, Cordelia thought, they would all be gone in another few days. Then things could start getting back to normal.

Henry brought the wagon to a stop in front of the emporium, where Michael Davis stood on the high porch puffing on his pipe. Abigail greeted him, "Good morning, Mr. Davis. Could you use a few eggs?"

"Mornin', ma'am," replied Davis. "I could sure use the eggs, right enough, but I can't pay you for them."

"We don't want any pay," Abigail told him. "Cordelia, give Mr. Davis some eggs."

Cordelia stood up in the back of the wagon and lifted the cloth off the eggs, then extended the basket toward Davis. "Help yourself, Mr. Davis," she offered, managing to put a smile on her face.

The storekeeper reached out, hesitated, then took just one egg in each hand. "I'll only take a couple," he said, "but I'm much obliged, Miss Brannon. Much obliged to all of you."

"In times like these, we all have to do what we can for each other," Abigail reminded him. "It's our duty as Christians and Southerners."

Davis nodded. "Yes ma'am. If there's ever anything I can do for you—"

"You've been a good friend to us, and you've given us credit many a time when we needed it. As far as I'm concerned, this is just a little something toward paying off that debt." Abigail nodded to the young man on the seat beside her. "Let's go, Henry."

Cordelia sat down, covering the eggs again with the cloth, and the wagon rolled on. In the next block, Abigail motioned for Henry to stop as they passed a man striding along the street. "Excuse me, sir," Abigail called to him. "Could you perhaps use some eggs?"

The man turned toward the wagon, and Cordelia saw that he was a stranger. He was middle-aged, with a thick white mustache, but still powerfully built and wearing a dusty black suit. A black hat sat on thick white hair. He plucked it off and replied in a deep voice, "Good morning to you, ma'am, and the Lord's blessings on you."

"Why, the same to you, sir. Have we had the pleasure of making your acquaintance?"

"No, ma'am," said the stranger. His voice had what seemed to be a naturally booming quality to it. "I'm certain that I would remember if that was the case. My name is Benjamin Spanner. Reverend Benjamin Spanner."

"You're a man of God?"

"Yes ma'am. Just been called to pastor the First Baptist Church here in Culpeper."

Henry broke in, "The First Baptist Church? What happened to Reverend Crosley?"

"He's gone to Richmond to serve as a chaplain for the army."

"Gone?" Cordelia exclaimed, surprised that the long-time pastor would simply leave town like that. "But he never even said anything."

"Evidently Reverend Crosley had been wrestling with his conscience for quite some time without revealing his struggle to any of his flock here in Culpeper. At least that's what he indicated in the letter he wrote to me asking me to come here and take over his pulpit. I was one of his instructors at the seminary."

Cordelia hadn't known that, and she doubted if anyone in Culpeper had. Now that she thought about it, she realized that Josiah Crosley had been pretty much of a private individual, willingly listening to other folks' troubles but never revealing much about himself. He had been the Baptist pastor in Culpeper for almost as long as Cordelia could remember. As far as she was concerned, he had been a fixture there, just like the white-washed, steepled building itself.

But ministers were human, too, and clearly the Reverend Crosley had decided that he had to do his part for the Confederacy, not by taking up arms but by spreading the Word of God and comforting the soldiers as best he could.

"Josiah always tried to do what he thought was right," Abigail stated. "He's a good man. And I'm certain you are, too, Reverend Spanner, if Josiah trusted you to take over the church."

"I'll do my best," the burly preacher promised humbly.

"My name is Abigail Brannon, and these are my children: Henry and Titus and Cordelia."

"I recall Reverend Crosley speaking highly of you, ma'am," Spanner said. "I don't know of any higher compliment."

Cordelia looked at her mother and was surprised to see that Abigail was blushing. That had to be from the warmth of the sun, Cordelia thought; there was no other explanation.

After a moment, Abigail asked, "What about those eggs, Reverend? Would you like a few for your dinner?"

"You're distributing them free of charge?"

"Of course. We're fortunate enough to still have some chickens on our farm, and we believe we ought to share that good fortune."

"Well, in that case, I'll take one or two," Spanner said. He held out his hat, and Cordelia carefully placed two eggs in it. "Thank you, young lady." He looked at Abigail again. "I'll be seeing you at the services tomorrow morning?"

"Certainly," she replied without hesitation. "We'll be there."

"Good. Since I'll be giving my first sermon here in Culpeper, it'll be nice to have a friendly face in the congregation."

"Well then . . . good-bye."

"Ma'am." Spanner nodded to the others. "So long to you young folks, too."

Henry flapped the reins and got the team of mules moving again. "How about that," he said as the wagon rolled on. "A new preacher in town, and we didn't even know he was coming."

Abigail sniffed a little. "You'd think Reverend Crosley could have told somebody in the congregation what he was planning to do. We should have had a voice in selecting the new pastor."

"Don't you like Reverend Spanner, Mama?" Cordelia asked.

"He seems like a fine man, and I'm sure he'll do a good job. I just think Reverend Crosley should have told someone before he left."

Cordelia wasn't really interested in discussing either of the ministers anymore, because she had just noticed someone she knew sitting on a bench on the dead grass of the lawn in front of the courthouse. She thrust the basket of eggs into the hands of a surprised Titus.

"Can I get down from the wagon, Mama?" she asked. "I see someone I want to talk to."

Henry chuckled. "She just spotted Nathan Hatcher sitting over yonder by the courthouse."

Cordelia forced down the irritation she felt. Henry liked to talk about how she was sweet on Nathan, but that wasn't true at all. "I just want to talk to him for a few minutes," she said.

Abigail looked back over her shoulder, but Cordelia couldn't tell if her mother was looking at her or watching Reverend Spanner stroll on down the street. With a somewhat distracted expression on her face, Abigail replied, "All right. But you be around when we're ready to go back."

"Yes ma'am," Cordelia promised. Henry slowed the wagon, and she dropped off from the back of it. Behind her as she started toward the courthouse lawn, she heard Titus grumbling about having to hold the eggs.

Nathan looked up from his reading as she approached. Cordelia recognized the thick volume as one of the law books he spent a great deal of time studying. He clerked for Judge Darden and planned on being a lawyer himself. He was also one of the few young men in the county who had not enlisted.

Sitting bareheaded in the sun, the slender young man raked his fingers through his brown hair. He got to his feet, leaving a finger in the book to mark his place as he closed it. With a smile, he greeted her. "Good morning, Cordelia. What brings you to town?"

"We're passing out eggs," she explained, gesturing toward the wagon that held her mother and brothers. "And we just wanted to come to town, too. At least I know I did. There's no reason to come every Saturday anymore, since most of the stores closed down, and I sure miss seeing folks."

"Well, I'm glad you're here today." He indicated the bench. "Would you like to sit down?"

"Well . . . I thought we might go for a walk." Cordelia wasn't sure where those bold words had come from, but as soon as she had spoken them, she was glad she had.

"A walk," Nathan repeated. "That sounds nice, especially since the sun's shining for a change today. Indeed, why don't we go for a walk?"

They fell in step side by side, moving along the street to the corner. "Around the square?" Nathan suggested, and Cordelia nodded her agreement.

"You were studying again, weren't you?"

"I still hope to pass the bar. It may have to wait until the war is over, though."

"I hope that's soon," Cordelia declared fervently.

"So do I," agreed Nathan. "So do I."

After a moment of silence, she asked, "Have you met the new pastor?"

"Reverend Spanner? He introduced himself in the post office. Seems like a nice man, although a bit too hellfire-and-brimstone for my taste."

"You don't like a good sermon?"

"I've been having something of a . . . a crisis of faith recently, I suppose you could say."

Cordelia stopped short, shocked. "Nathan!" she exclaimed. "You mean you don't believe in God anymore?"

"That's not what I said," he replied. "Don't misunderstand me, Cordelia. I certainly believe in the Lord. But I'm having a bit of trouble these days understanding His methods."

"The Lord works in mysterious ways," she quoted.

With a rueful smile, Nathan nodded. "He surely does."

They resumed their pace, and Cordelia suggested, "I think you should come to church. If you're having problems with what you believe, that's the best place to work them out."

"You're probably right. I've just been so distracted, what with the trouble—" He stopped short, frowning as if he had said too much.

"What trouble?"

"You're the only one I'd tell this, Cordelia, so I'd appreciate it if you wouldn't say anything to anyone."

"I swear," she promised, a little breathlessly.

"Some men came to the boarding house a few evenings ago to see me. They told me that, as a Virginian, I should enlist in the army."

"Well . . . you can't blame people for feeling like that, Nathan. The Yankees have invaded our home, after all."

"Yes, but they did more than just urge me to do my duty as a Confederate. They said if I didn't join up, I'd be tarred and feathered and ridden out of town on a rail."

That brought Cordelia to an abrupt stop again. "Nathan! Surely not. Surely you misunderstood." She didn't want to believe that anyone from Culpeper could do such a thing.

Nathan's voice turned bitter. "It's hard to misunderstand when someone calls you a damned yellow-bellied coward."

Cordelia felt a surge of anger. "Who was it?" she demanded. "Who would say such a thing to you?"

He shrugged. "It doesn't matter. There were several of them there, older men who fought back in the Mexican War or even before that, against the British in 1812."

"You . . . you should report them to the law."

Even as she said that, Cordelia knew how futile that would be. Old Marcus Gilworth had taken over as sheriff for a while after Will left, but then he had passed away and authority in the county now rested with the militia. The head of the militia was Duncan Ebersole. Cordelia knew the planter wouldn't be sympathetic to Nathan's problem.

"It doesn't really matter," Nathan contended. "I'm not going to let anybody stampede me into doing something I don't want to do."

"But they *threatened* you. They might really do what they said."

"And if they did, no one would care."

"That's not true!" Cordelia exclaimed. "I . . . I would . . ."

Suddenly, without thinking about what she was doing, she stepped closer to him. She put her hands on his arms and came up on her toes and pressed her mouth to his. In the back of her mind, she was horrified by the idea that she was kissing a man in broad daylight on the street like this, but right now she didn't care what was proper and what wasn't. A vision of Nathan, covered with tar and feathers and tied to a rail, had burst into her mind, and the idea of his being forced to go through such an ordeal had made sympathy well up inside her.

But maybe that wasn't all it was. Maybe she liked the way his mouth tasted and the heat that suddenly flowed between them like lightning in a summer thunderstorm. Maybe she liked the feeling that was swelling within her until it felt like she was going to burst.

The law book slipped out of his hands and fell to the ground at their feet with a solid thump.

The noise broke the spell that had engulfed them. Cordelia gasped and practically sprang backward, putting some distance between them. She looked around as if she no longer had any idea where she was. She realized that they had come around on the back side of the courthouse, where at least there weren't as many people to witness her wanton behavior.

"Cordelia, I . . . I'm sorry," Nathan offered hurriedly, holding his hands out toward her as if he were imploring her for her forgiveness. "I shouldn't have—"

"Oh, hush. You didn't do a thing, Nathan Hatcher. I'm the one who kissed you." She gave a defiant toss of her red hair. "And I liked it, too, whether that shocks you or not. But I shouldn't have. I shouldn't have done it. I . . . I just couldn't stand the thought of anybody hurting you."

"Then why do you want me to go to war?" he asked quietly.

Cordelia stared at him. "I never said that!"

"But that's what you think, whether you've ever said it or not. That's what all the good Confederates around here think. And you're a good Confederate, aren't you, Cordelia?"

Cordelia didn't like the harsh, bitter tone that had crept into his voice. Of course he had reason to be angry about the way he had been treated, about the threats that had been made against him. But that didn't give him any right to take it out on her.

"I believe in the Confederacy," she flung back at him. "Don't you?"

"No," Nathan retorted. "As a matter of fact, I don't."

For a long moment, the implications of his words didn't fully penetrate her brain. But then, as his words soaked in, she felt a wave of horror and revulsion and nausea rising within her. "What . . . what did you say?" she managed to ask.

Nathan's voice was quiet now, all the anger and bitterness leached out of it by despair. "I said I don't believe in the Confederacy. I think Lincoln is right. About slavery, about secession, about all of it."

"Then . . . then you're a *Yankee?*" Cordelia couldn't keep the loathing out of her voice, even though she regretted it momentarily as she saw the flash of pain in Nathan's eyes.

"I'm a Virginian, born and bred. You know that. But Virginia is wrong, Cordelia. The Confederacy is wrong." He lifted a hand, as if he were about to reach out to her.

She took a quick step backward. "Stay away from me," she demanded, her voice wavering. "Don't you touch me."

"I won't," he promised. "I just want you to calm down—"

A humorless laugh burst from her. "Calm down? My . . . my best friend just tells me that everything I believe in is wrong, and you want me to calm down!"

"Best friend . . . ?"

"You could have been more than that to me. I didn't want to admit it, even to myself, but you could have been." A shudder went through her. "Oh, Nathan . . ."

He came toward her, and she turned and ran. Cordelia didn't know where she was going, didn't care who might see or what they might think. In a matter of moments, her entire world had been turned upside down twice, first by the kiss she had shared with Nathan, and then by the revelation he had made to her. She wished she had never gotten out of the wagon and gone to talk to him. She wished things could be like they were before, and she knew they never would be.

That was one of the lessons of war, and like the rest of the South, Cordelia Brannon was learning it.

Chapter Nine

IF HE NEVER SAW another drop of rain or another road that had turned into a quagmire of mud, it would be too soon, Will thought as his horse plodded along next to the marching men. Water dripped steadily, monotonously, from the brim of his hat. The mud of the road sucked at the hooves of the horses and the feet of the infantry, reluctantly releasing them at each step with a soft sucking sound.

For the past three days, the Confederate forces under the command of Gen. Thomas J. Jackson had been on the move. Departing from the town of Port Republic, where they had bivouacked after leaving Front Royal, they had struggled along in this heavy rain, following a road that led northeast along the Shenandoah River. The foothills of the Blue Ridge Mountains came almost all the way down to the river in this area, so there was nowhere to go except straight ahead.

Will had no idea what the general was planning. He suspected that few if any of the officers knew Jackson's strategy, because Jackson had grown more tightlipped in recent days. Will had heard how pleased the government in Richmond was with the bold thrust against the Yankees at Kernstown, despite the way it had turned into a Confederate withdrawal. He and Yancy and the other men had been expecting to launch another attack on the Union forces ever since then, but so far it had not come. Now they seemed to be heading away from the Federals, who were clustered around the town of McDowell to the southwest.

The heavy overcast meant that night fell earlier than usual, and the men were grateful for the chance to stop and rest after slogging through the mud all day. So were the horses and mules, which had been struggling to haul artillery over roads that had been turned into swamps by the steady rain.

Will pitched his tent, knowing that he was soaked to start with and that the tent wouldn't keep out all the rain, but he was still thankful for what little shelter it would provide. The men weren't even that lucky. They had to roll up in sodden blankets under the dripping branches of trees. It was almost impossible to build a fire under such circumstances, so supper consisted of jerked beef and stale biscuits, washed down with cold coffee.

Will had just choked down the unpalatable stuff when Yancy Lattimer crawled into his tent. "I hear that Jackson is considering changing his name to Noah," he commented as he hunkered on his heels.

"I didn't know Mount Ararat was one of the Blue Ridge Mountains," Will joked back wearily. The exchange wasn't very humorous, but anything that might keep their spirits up was worth a try.

"I suppose we'll be in Richmond in another few days." That was the rumor that was going around at the moment: the troops were being withdrawn from the Shenandoah Valley and sent to Richmond to help defend it from McClellan's advance up the Virginia Peninsula.

Will shook his head. "I'm not convinced of that. The Yankees have a lot of men here in the Shenandoah. I can't imagine us just turning our backs on them and leaving them here to do what they want."

"I don't know," Yancy said with a shrug. "The general is keeping his own counsel these days. All I know is that the men are worn out from tramping through all this mud. If we don't get where we're going soon, or if we don't get a break in the weather, they're going to be too tired to fight."

Will agreed with Yancy. Even good soldiers—and the men of the Stonewall Brigade were among the best, in Will's opinion—had limits.

Early the next morning, when Will rolled out of his damp blankets and pushed aside the tent flap, he was greeted with a brighter sky than usual. It was still before dawn, but as he crawled out of the tent and stood up stiffly, he saw that the sky to the east over the Blue Ridge was red with the approach of the sun. The clouds had finally broken.

The end of the rain lifted the spirits of the men immeasurably. The atmosphere as camp was broken was much better than it had been the day before. True, the road would still be muddy, but at least now they would have the warmth of the sun to dry their uniforms.

Not only that, but soon after the march was resumed, Jackson led the troops eastward, away from the river and toward Brown's Gap, which would take them over the Blue Ridge. The road became drier and harder as they climbed into the mountains, and the snail's pace of the previous three days soon was a thing of the past. The men marched briskly along, following the path that wound through the rugged terrain.

Will felt a tug on his heart when the column reached the gap itself and he was able to look down on the eastern side of the Blue Ridge. The Piedmont country swept away into the distance, the country where he had grown to manhood. Culpeper County was less than a day's ride away. It would be nice if he got a chance to see his family again.

That wasn't likely to happen, though, he knew. Now that the Confederate forces were on the east side of the Blue Ridge, it would be an easy march to one of the stations on the Virginia Central Railroad, and once they were loaded on trains, it would be on to Richmond. It certainly appeared that Yancy had been right about what Jackson was planning to do.

By evening, after a day of marching in beautiful weather, the army reached the tiny hamlet of Mechum's River. This was a settlement on the railroad line, and there were locomotives and empty cars waiting, just as Will had come to expect during the day. Despite the fact that it was no longer raining, an air of gloom began to settle once more over the men. Some of them, like Will, were from the Piedmont, but most of the soldiers were from the Shenandoah Valley, and it seemed to them as if they were abandoning their homes to the ravages of the Yankees.

A better night's sleep than they had had in almost a week did little to dispel the bad mood the next morning as the men began to climb into the railroad cars. All of them wanted to save Richmond, of course, but they wished there were some other way to do it. Will understood that feeling. He loaded his horse into one of the freight cars that would carry the officers' mounts, then jumped down to the ground, pulled off his gauntlets, and slapped them impatiently against his thigh. He was still thinking about the farm, about his mother and Mac and Titus and Henry and Cordelia. And Cory, too, wherever he was.

"Good morning, Captain Brannon," a voice said. "Ready to go?"

Will looked around and saw Jackson standing there. He saluted, then replied, "Yes sir, I suppose so."

"You don't sound too eager," the general observed.

"Well, sir," Will answered honestly, "I'm not sure we should leave the Shenandoah to the Yankees. That's bound to make them bolder." He paused, then added, "And I was thinking about my home, too. It's in Culpeper County."

"Not that far away, eh? I'm sorry, Captain, but there'll be no time for a visit. I wish it were otherwise."

"Yes sir, so do I. But I reckon we'll be getting on to Richmond as soon as we can." Will wasn't fishing for information; he was just talking. He had never really learned to be in awe of generals and keep his mouth shut around them.

"Richmond," Jackson repeated with a slight smile. "We shall see."

With that, the general moved off to check on something else along the line of railroad cars, and Will couldn't help but wonder what he had meant by that last comment. If they weren't going to Richmond, where in blazes *were* they going?

He got his answer as soon as everyone was loaded on the trains. The one Will had boarded got underway with only a slight lurch. He and the other officers were riding in a regular passenger car, rather than in a freight car or on an open flat car, and from the bench where he was sitting by a window, he watched the landscape roll past outside. It took him a moment to understand what he was seeing, but as soon as he did, he turned to Yancy, who was seated beside him, and exclaimed excitedly, "We're heading west!"

"What?" Yancy leaned forward to peer out the window. His eyes widened as he realized that Will was right. "By God, we *are* going west, back toward the Blue Ridge and the Shenandoah. What's old Stonewall up to?"

Will grinned. "I don't know, but if we don't have any idea, you can bet the Yankees don't, either!"

THE TRAINS stopped in Charlottesville, and to Will's surprise, he saw young men wearing uniforms that were unfamiliar to him boarding the cars. Yancy recognized them, however. "Those are cadets from the Virginia Military Institute," he explained. "General Jackson was a professor there, remember? He must have arranged with the superintendent to let the cadets observe."

"Observe what?" Will asked.

"It looks to me like the general is expecting a battle."

Will tended to agree, especially when the trains rolled on west, climbing into the mountains and crossing the Blue Ridge at Rockfish Gap. From there it was an easy trip into the town of Staunton. News of the troops' arrival spread like wildfire through the town, and it wasn't long before citizens were thronging the railroad station to watch the trains pull in. Cheers rang out as the gray-clad troops jumped down from the cars that had brought them here.

Will saw to it that his horse was unloaded, then found Darcy and the rest of his company. Darcy had mustered the men into a compact group instead of allowing them to wander around as some of the companies were doing. Will nodded his appreciation and said, "Good work, Sergeant."

"Thank you, sir," Darcy replied. "You know where we're goin' next?"

Will had given the matter quite a bit of thought during the journey across the mountains. He knew from scouts' reports that a goodly number of Federals were gathered at McDowell, not very many miles to the west. "I expect we'll be heading for McDowell," he told Darcy.

The sergeant's rugged face creased in a grin. "That'll mean fightin'. We'll be ready, Cap'n."

Will had no doubt of that.

Despite the easier time of it they'd had the past couple of days, the men were still tired from the long march in the mud, so for a day they tarried at Staunton, the Stonewall Brigade camping just to the east of the settlement, the other two brigades under Jackson's command camping to the west. On the morning of May 8, a Thursday, the now fresh and rested troops set out again, heading west along the Parkersburg turn-pike toward McDowell.

Will found that his company was toward the rear of the column, which he didn't particularly like. He would rather have been in the front, where the Confederate forces would probably encounter the Yankees first. Not that he was particu-larly hungry for battle, he told himself, but once a clash was underway, it was hard to tell what was going on from the rear.

The road climbed steeply onto a tableland known as Bull Pasture Mountain. The top of this plateau was dotted with more steep hills. When Will and his men reached the crest of the slope, he saw the leading edge of the Confederate advance approaching the largest of the hills in the distance. He turned to Darcy Bennett and told the sergeant, "Keep the men moving. I'm going to go see what's in store for us."

Darcy acknowledged the command with a salute, and Will heeled his horse into a fast trot that carried him alongside the column of marching men. He passed Yancy's company, and the aristocratic captain called, "Will! Where are you going?"

"To the front," Will replied, and Yancy spurred up alongside him.

"I'll go with you," he announced with a grin. "You're afraid the fighting's going to start while we're stuck back here in the rear, aren't you?"

"I just want to see what the situation is."

Will felt a twinge of guilt at abandoning his company, but he knew that Darcy and the other sergeants would keep the men moving, and it would take only a few minutes to gallop back and join them if the necessity arose. As he and Yancy rode toward the hill where the forefront of the army was gathering, Yancy commented, "This is Sitlington's Hill, if I remember the map correctly. Down below is the Bull Pasture River, and across the way is McDowell itself."

Will had already spotted smoke in the distance and had assumed it came from the settlement. Or perhaps from the campfires of the Yankees, he thought grimly.

The sides of Sitlington Hill were steep and heavily wooded at the base, with brush so thick that it would have been impossible for the troops to march through it. The top of the hill was bare of larger vegetation, however, and Will could see gray-clad figures on top of it. He pointed and said, "There's got to be a way up there."

"We'll find it," Yancy declared confidently.

A few minutes later, they came to a narrow ravine that cut into the side of the hill, rising steeply toward the top. The floor of the ravine was littered with boulders, so it was slow going as the horses picked their way up the slope. Eventually, the ravine came out on the top of the hill, which, like the larger Bull Pasture Mountain on which it sat, was flat and treeless.

Will saw a group of men on horseback gathered at the western edge of the hilltop. He and Yancy rode over to join them, recognizing Jackson, Gen. Edward Johnson, and several other high-ranking officers as they approached. Jackson turned his head and gave Will and Yancy a pleasant nod as the two captains joined the group.

"Gentlemen," Jackson began. "What do you think?"

The view was spectacular. Will could see the river far below and the roofs of the buildings in the town on the other side of the stream. He also saw the massed Federals on both sides of the river. A crackle of rifle fire drew his attention to the north. There was another hill, its summit about a mile away. The shots were coming from it, he realized after a moment.

"Are those Yankees over there?" he asked.

Jackson made a dismissive gesture. "Yes, but they're too far away to worry about. They've been shooting at us ever since we rode up here, but none of their shots can reach us."

Will frowned slightly. He didn't much like the idea of sharpshooters taking potshots at him, even if they were supposedly out of range. A Sharps rifle could throw a bullet a mile or more, and if there happened to be a marksman over there the equal of his brother Titus . . .

If that had been the case, then likely Jackson would have already been shot out of the saddle, Will told himself. He put thoughts of the Federal riflemen out of his mind and turned his attention to the situation in front of him.

"We have the high ground," he noted. "Looks to me like this would be a good place to meet the Yankees."

"I agree, General," Yancy said. "Make them come to us."

"That is exactly what we plan to do," declared Jackson. "You two are from the Thirty-third, is that correct?"

"Yes sir," Will and Yancy said together.

"You and the rest of the First Brigade will be held in reserve today. But you two gentlemen are welcome to observe from here, at least for the time being."

Yancy thanked the general. Will just nodded, feeling disappointed again that he and his men would not be involved in the battle until later, if at all.

He had a perfect vantage point, however, and watched intently as the Yankees launched an attack a short time later. Evidently they had only one battery in position, because only a few artillery shells came toward the Confederate lines. For their part, the Southern artillery was mostly silent. The terrain here was not suited to an artillery battle, or for cavalry work, either.

This left the bulk of the fighting up to the infantry of both armies, and from where he sat on his horse, Will watched the two sides come together, blue against gray, in a panorama blurred by powder smoke and punctuated by the crackling of rifle fire and the shouts of the struggling men.

The Federals were the attackers, the Confederates higher on the slopes the defenders. Wave after wave of blue-uniformed soldiers surged up the hillsides. The steepness of the slopes made accurate fire difficult for everyone. Bullets whined through the air, more often than not missing their targets, and the smoke grew thicker as more and more shots were fired. Inevitably, when rifle fire failed, the two sides came together in hand-to-hand combat. Rifle butts, bayonets, and knives did the bloody work instead of minié balls.

Will's jaw clamped tighter and tighter as he watched the men fighting and dying far below him. His horse must have picked up on his tension, because the animal became increasingly skittish and Will had to take a firmer grip on the reins to settle the animal down.

For the first time, he was experiencing war as an observer, and he didn't like it. He had been in the thick of the fighting at Manassas and Kernstown and countless other skirmishes. While being in the middle of a battle was a sometimes confusing mixture of fear and anger and courage, at least it was better than sitting and watching.

"Being a general has its peculiar challenges."

Will realized that someone was speaking and looked over to see Jackson on his horse. "Sir?" Will questioned.

134 • James Reasoner

"What I mean by that, Captain, is that while a general can sometimes lead his men into battle personally, all too often he is relegated to the role of an observer, as we are here today." Jackson nodded toward the battlefield. "Knowing that you have sent men to their deaths is more difficult than risking your own life. But it is a necessary evil, Captain, and we must all do what is required of us to win this war. That's something you may want to remember if you intend to make a career of the military."

"Yes sir," Will acknowledged, keeping to himself the thought that he had no intention of making a career out of the military. As soon as the war was over, assuming he lived through it, he planned to go home and resume his life there. By then, he thought, maybe his mother would have forgiven him for everything that had happened to drive a wedge between him and the rest of his family.

By evening, the Northerners were falling back in retreat. As they withdrew from McDowell and fled west toward Franklin, Jackson sent orders to Turner Ashby's cavalry to pursue them and make sure they didn't turn back for another attack. The rest of the Confederate forces moved forward, across the river and into the town of McDowell. The Stonewall Brigade had not been engaged in the battle at all, so the task of securing the town fell to them, since they were well rested. Will and Yancy rode in at the head of their respective companies to find that the enemy had withdrawn completely. The townspeople welcomed the Confederates eagerly.

One elderly man stepped out into the road and reached up to grasp Will's hand. "Thank you," the man said sincerely. "Thank you for runnin' those damn Yankees out of our home."

Will nodded to the old man, feeling a little embarrassed as he did so. *He* hadn't done anything to run the Federals out of McDowell. He hadn't done anything except watch.

"I hope they never come back, sir," Will said to the man.

"If they do, you boys'll just whip 'em again!"

Will smiled, sketched a salute to the brim of his hat, and rode on. That was one thing that was true about war, he thought: he might not have taken an active part in this battle, but there was always another one to come.

Chapter Ten

A NIGHT WIND MOVED GENTLY through the trees, swaying the branches that were now thick with leaves. Will sat in front of his tent, staring into the low-burning flames of the campfire, even though he knew he shouldn't be ruining his night vision that way. All the scouts reported that there were no Yankees nearby, so Will didn't think an attack very likely.

Two weeks had passed since the battle at McDowell. During that time, Jackson had split up his command, moved the various units around the Shenandoah Valley, reunited them, marched north, split his command again to send a column up either side of the Massanutten Mountains, and finally brought them back together a short distance south of Front Royal. While that had been going on, according to reports Jackson had received, the Union forces in northern and western Virginia had also been undergoing some fracturing. Those that had been under the command of Brig. Gen. James Shields had departed the Shenandoah Valley, leaving behind a smaller force under Maj. Gen. Nathaniel Banks at Strasburg, a short distance north of Front Royal. Jackson had fought both Banks and Shields at Kernstown, and he was eager for a rematch with Banks, Will knew. The engagement was sure to come soon, because Jackson's forces were moving steadily up the valley.

If he climbed one of the wooded hills around here, he could probably see the Yankee campfires, thought Will. They were that close. He had come to be able to sense things like that, and tonight all his instincts told him that it wouldn't be long before he was fighting again.

The sound of a horse walking somewhere nearby made him lift his head. His tent wasn't far from the edge of the Confederate camp, but there were plenty of pickets out in the woods. No one should have been moving around on horseback. Will came to his feet, his hand moving to the flap of his holster and unfastening it so that his fingers could wrap around the smooth walnut grips of the Colt Navy .36. A muscle in his leg twinged as he stood. That deep bullet graze in his thigh was going to plague him for the rest of his life, he thought.

Then he heard Darcy Bennett's challenge. "Who's there?"

The hoofbeats came to an abrupt halt. "I need to see General Jackson," a husky voice said. Some quality about it made Will frown. He strode toward the spot where Darcy had stopped the rider.

"Well, who the hell are you?" Darcy was demanding as Will walked up. "A fella can't just ride in here and ask to see the gen'ral."

"It's all right, Sergeant," Will said. He had drawn his Colt, and he held it beside his leg as he spoke. "I'll handle this."

Reluctantly, Darcy turned away from the visitor. "All right, Cap'n. If you're sure."

Will didn't say anything as Darcy walked away. After a moment, the stranger asked, "Can I get down from this horse?"

"Go ahead," Will granted. In the thick shadows under the trees, he couldn't see much except vague shapes, and the glow from the nearby fires didn't penetrate here very well. He waited until the stranger was in the act of dismounting, with the left foot still in the stirrup and the right leg swinging over the back of the horse, before he added, "ma'am."

He was rewarded with the sound of a sharply indrawn breath. The stranger hesitated, but only for a second, then finished stepping down from the saddle. She turned and asked in the husky voice, "How did you know?"

"I haven't forgotten what a woman sounds like, even when she's trying to talk like a man. Haven't been at war that long."

"Obviously not." The stranger abandoned the rasping attempt to disguise her tone. "I still need to see General Jackson."

"Not until I know who you are—and how you got through the picket lines."

That brought a laugh from the visitor. "Don't punish any of your sentries. I'm sure they'd give you plenty of warning if a bunch of Yankees tried to sneak up on you, but I've had a lot of practice at slipping through a picket line."

"You're a spy," Will guessed.

"Miss Belle Boyd, at your service, Captain."

The name made Will's eyes widen in surprise. He had heard of Belle Boyd, of course. Newspapers in both the North and the South sometimes referred to her as "La Belle Rebelle" and "That Secesh Cleopatra." She was young, not even twenty years old yet, but she had been passing messages and carrying information for Confederate officers almost since the beginning of the war. The Yankees knew what she was up to, but she still managed to worm information out of them. One of these days, Will thought, she is going to get shot for her trouble.

"So you're Belle Boyd," he probed.

She reached up and took off the cap she had been wearing. Thick masses of curly hair tumbled down around her shoulders, and Will wondered how she had been able to tuck all of it in the cap. She came closer to him, so that he could make out more details about her strong-featured but attractive face.

"I assure you I'm Belle Boyd. And you are . . . ?"

"Capt. Will Brannon," he introduced himself. Almost as an afterthought, he holstered his gun and snapped down the flap.

"Well, Captain Brannon, about General Jackson . . ."

"Follow me," Will told her. "I'll take you to him."

As they emerged from the trees into the light from the campfires, Will was acutely aware of the startled looks his companion drew from the men. There was more than surprise on many of their faces, too. Some of these men hadn't seen a woman close up for weeks, and certainly not one as compelling as Belle Boyd. Will saw awe, adoration, and outright lust in the eyes of many of the soldiers. He started to put a protective hand on the spy's arm, but then he saw how confidently she strode along and realized she wasn't bothered by the looks of the men.

She wore a loose-fitting homespun shirt, men's trousers, and high-topped black boots. She wasn't armed, as far as Will could tell. As they passed Yancy Lattimer's tent, Yancy sprang to his feet and exclaimed, "Belle?"

"Hello, Yancy," she answered.

"You two know each other?" asked Will.

"We met several times in Richmond, before the war," she explained. "How are you, Yancy?"

He fell in step beside her and Will. "Never better. I've read about your exploits, Belle, and hoped I'd run into you sooner or later." Yancy's tone became more solemn. "You're going to get yourself thrown into a Yankee prison, you know. Either that, or you'll find yourself in front of a firing squad."

Belle laughed. "The Yankees would never execute me, and you know it. And I'm not afraid of prison."

"Well, you should be," Yancy cautioned in a lecturing tone. "Why—"

"Here's the general's tent," Will cut in. To the corporal who was standing guard, he announced, "Miss Belle Boyd to see the general."

Before the sentry could open the tent flap, Jackson himself thrust back the canvas and stepped out. "Miss Boyd!" he said heartily. "What news have you for me?"

"Colonel Kenly is at Front Royal with a thousand men," Belle replied. "Banks stationed him there as an advance guard."

Front Royal, the bench of land overlooking the Shenandoah River where Jackson's men had camped following the battle of Kernstown, was not far away. And now Jackson had confirmation that Yankee troops were there, even though it was only a token force. "Excellent!" the general responded. "We shall move on the Federals first thing in the morning."

"General Banks still has a goodly number of men in Strasburg," Belle Boyd continued.

Jackson nodded. "We will deal with Banks when the time comes, as it soon shall. In the meantime, Miss Boyd, allow me to offer you the hospitality of our camp, such as it is. Is there anything we can do for you?"

Belle smiled. "I've had a long ride. I wouldn't mind something to eat and perhaps a cup of coffee. And someone needs to see to my horse."

Jackson looked at Will and Yancy. "I'm sure these two young gallants would be more than happy to attend to your needs, Miss Boyd."

"Captain Lattimer and I are old friends," Belle noted, still smiling. "And Captain Brannon and I are new friends, aren't we, Captain?"

"Uh, yes ma'am," Will answered. "I'll have someone tend to your horse."

"And you can come back to my tent with me for something to eat," Yancy offered. "You remember my boy Roman, of course?"

"Of course," Belle said.

"He still makes the best cup of coffee in Virginia." Yancy slipped his arm through hers. "Come along, my dear."

Will felt a pang of jealousy as he turned and watched Yancy and Belle stroll away. Behind him, the general chuckled. "Perhaps you should not have been so quick to volunteer to care for the lady's mount, Captain."

"That's all right, General," Will mumbled. "I reckon I know more about horses than I do about women, anyway."

———

FOR A day on which a battle was impending, there wasn't a particular sense of urgency in the air the next morning, Will thought as he and his men prepared to break camp. Jackson was in no hurry to launch the attack on Kenly's forces at Front Royal. The artillery had been lagging behind the infantry all during the push up the Valley, and the general wanted to wait for his cannon to catch up before departing. As the morning wore on, however, and the artillery still did not arrive, Jackson finally became impatient and passed the order for the men to get ready to move out.

Seeing that his company was in good shape, Will trotted his horse over to Yancy's company, where his friend sat on horseback and watched the preparations. Yancy smiled a greeting, and Will asked, "Where's Miss Boyd?"

"Well on her way back to Richmond by now, I expect," Yancy replied. "She left quite early this morning. I gave her the use of my tent last night, and she said she slept well."

"Where did you sleep?" Will asked bluntly.

Yancy laughed. "Good Lord, what sort of question is that? I took my bedroll and stayed with the men, of course. You shouldn't impugn a lady's honor even by implication, Will."

"I know," Will muttered. "Sorry."

"Don't worry, the next time I see Belle, I won't tell her what you said. But rest assured there's nothing romantic between her and me. We're just old friends, that's all." Grinning, Yancy shook his head. "I never thought I'd see the day when Will Brannon got his head turned around by a woman."

"Yeah, well . . . we've got a battle to fight." Will turned his horse and rode back to his company, well aware that Yancy was still chuckling behind him.

Will was glad the march got underway soon. It enabled him to get his mind off of Belle Boyd. With its customary speed, Jackson's army moved out, advancing toward Front Royal. Will remembered the area well from their previous bivouac here, so he knew when the leading edge of the Confederate force began to approach the bench overlooking the river. He wasn't surprised when he heard the crackle of rifle fire in the distance. Confederate skirmishers had encountered the Union pickets posted by Kenly.

One of Jackson's regiments surged forward, driving the pickets back, killing some, capturing others, forcing the rest to flee. Will saw Turner Ashby's cavalry split off from the main body of the attack and begin sweeping around Front Royal toward the Shenandoah River. There was a railroad bridge over the river, and a short distance to the west, another bridge spanned a smaller branch of the river. Ashby's orders were probably to secure those bridges so that the Federals couldn't retreat over them.

Meanwhile, the infantry continued its surge toward the Union position. Again, Will's company was not in the forefront of the battle, but at least he was closer to the action this time and could see the Confederate troops advancing steadily. The usual haze of smoke began to drift over the battlefield.

Suddenly, from a rocky ridge along the edge of Front Royal, a Union artillery battery opened up, slowing the Confederate advance. Will heard the whistle of shells in the air, followed by explosions as they burst and did their deadly work. After a few minutes, the barrage succeeded in bringing the attack to a shuddering halt.

Acting quickly in response to this setback, Jackson wheeled his horse and called for the cavalry units under the command of Flournoy to sweep around the Union left flank and come at them from the rear. Ashby's cavalry was already flanking the Yankees to their right. If Ashby and Flournoy were successful in their missions, the Federal forces would soon be surrounded.

Hearing a commotion in the rear, Will reined in and turned in his saddle to look behind him. He saw that the Confederate artillery had finally arrived and was being brought up so that it could return the fire from the Union batteries. Jackson had no intention of waiting for that to happen, however. Rallying his men, he sent them forward again. Will followed the general's lead, drawing his saber and waving it forward as he shouted to his company, "Charge! Charge!"

The troops surged ahead once more. Will found himself galloping up the slope toward the top of the bench with Darcy and the rest of the company running along behind him. At the top of the rise, some of the Yankees had rolled some fallen logs to form a barricade of sorts. Will saw blue-clad figures crouching behind the logs. Powder smoke spurted into the air as they fired their rifles at the onrushing Confederates. Will leaned forward over his horse's neck, making himself a smaller target. His pulse thundered in his head, seemingly as loud as the roar of the cannon and the beat of galloping hooves.

The log barricade loomed in front of him. He hauled up on the reins, and his mount leaped high in the air, clearing the barricade. The horse slammed into one of the Federals, sending the man spinning off his feet. Will slashed to the right and then to the left with the saber, cutting down two more men. One of the Yankees thrust a bayonet at him, but Will slammed the steel of his blade against it, turning aside the thrust at the last second. He pulled his foot from the stirrup and kicked the man in the chest, feeling ribs snap and collapse under the blow.

Then he was through the group of Northerners that had clustered behind the log barricade. He wheeled his horse and saw that Darcy and the others had reached the logs and were swarming over them. A moment of fierce, hand-to-hand fighting left all the Federals either dead or badly wounded. Will's company was in firm possession of this part of the battlefield. Will waved them on with his saber. If they kept going, they might be able to split the Union forces here on Front Royal.

They didn't have the chance. The Yankees began a full-fledged retreat that within minutes bordered on a rout. Outnumbered and nearly surrounded, Kenly did the only thing he could, which was to order his men to fall back as quickly as possible. They streamed down off the bench toward the river with the Confederate forces in hot pursuit. The Southern batteries had not been needed after all. In fact, they had not been called on to fire a single shot.

The Union retreat had come so fast that neither Ashby nor Flournoy had been able to get into position to cut them off. The Federals streamed across the railroad bridge, the last stragglers pausing just long enough to set it on fire before continuing to flee. Will reined in before he reached the bridge and watched as flames leaped up from the wooden trestle. The Shenandoah was too wide and deep here to be forded easily, so it looked as if the Northerners might get away.

But Flournoy's cavalry, sweeping in from the north after their flanking movement had failed to trap the Yankees, pressed on. Will watched as the cavalrymen put their horses into the river. The riders held their pistols and rifles high out of the water as the horses began to swim. Within minutes, the cavalry had crossed the river without the loss of a single man. Dripping wet, they resumed their pursuit of the retreating Federals. Seeing movement to the south, on the other side of the river, Will took out his field glasses and looked in that direction. He spotted another column of gray-uniformed horsemen and recognized it as Ashby's unit, closing in from that direction. They must have forded the river somewhere to the south, Will realized.

He and his infantry company were stuck on this side of the Shenandoah, however. An effort was being made to put out the fire on the bridge. Even as the flames were snuffed out, Will spotted more black smoke rising into the sky to the west. That must be the second bridge, he speculated. The Yankees probably set fire to it as they retreated, too.

Eventually, the blaze on the first bridge was extinguished, but enough damage had been done so that the Confederate soldiers had to cross it almost single-file. That slowed them down considerably, and it took a long time for Jackson to get all his men across the river. Once there, however, they set off after the Yankees. Will had heard a lot of gunfire in the distance and figured that at least some of the Confederate cavalry had already caught up to them.

The infantrymen were beginning to grow tired after several hours of fighting and more hours of waiting to get across the Shenandoah. Jackson and his officers, including Will, pushed them on, however. Within a short time, it became apparent that more efforts would not be needed from them today. Jackson's forces caught up with Flournoy's cavalry and discovered that Flournoy had captured nearly all of the fleeing Federals. Only a few had managed to get away. The cavalrymen had herded hundreds of prisoners into a large field near the village of Cedarville.

Jackson was immensely pleased with the outcome of the day's battle, Will could tell when the general gathered his officers to announce his next move. He expected it to be an attack on Strasburg, where Banks was concentrating the rest of his force, but Jackson had something else in mind.

"Winchester is the key," Jackson announced as he pointed on the map to the town some thirty miles to the north of their current position. "Banks will not try to defend Strasburg. I expect that as soon as he receives word of the defeat here today, he will set out for Winchester. The hills just southwest of there are where he will make his stand."

Will didn't know how Jackson could be so sure about that, but the general had been right so far about what the Federals would do.

"So now it becomes a race, gentlemen," the general continued. "Banks will likely reach Winchester first, but we must press him so that he does not have adequate time to prepare for our arrival. Tell your men to get a good night's sleep tonight, because tomorrow night they will probably be marching."

The meeting broke up shortly after that. As Will and Yancy walked back toward their companies, Yancy noted, "The general loves harrying the Yankees, doesn't he?"

"So far he's been pretty good at it," Will commented. "We beat them at McDowell and now at Front Royal. The Yankees have to be pretty worried about what he's doing up here."

"If we can run them completely out of the Shenandoah Valley, we ought to move on Washington itself," declared Yancy. "That would get McClellan off the peninsula in a hurry, I'll wager."

Will nodded, frowning in thought. He had been so busy keeping up with Jackson's lightning-like moves here in the

Valley that he hadn't given much thought to what might be going on elsewhere in the war. The troops had heard that the Confederacy had suffered a big defeat somewhere out in Tennessee, at a place called Shiloh, and they knew McClellan had advanced up the Virginia Peninsula past Yorktown and Williamsburg and was moving on toward Richmond. From the sound of things, Jackson's little army here in the Shenandoah was the only Confederate force that had been licking the Yankees in recent days.

Will realized all they could do was to keep it up and hope for the best. Because it was possible, he thought, that sooner or later the survival of the entire Confederacy might come down to them . . .

Chapter Eleven

TRUE TO HIS WORD, Jackson hurried his men toward Winchester early the next morning. In the predawn gloom, Will rode to the head of his company and led them to their place in the column that was marching up the turnpike. As the sky grew lighter, he looked back over his shoulder at them and saw the weariness on their bearded faces. A night's sleep had helped them regain some of their strength after the previous day's march and battle, but they were still tired. No one complained, though. They marched on, their rifles shouldered, ready to do whatever their commanders asked of them.

With men like these opposing them, Will thought proudly, how could the Yankees even hope to win?

During the morning, he saw companies of cavalry leaving the column and galloping off and returning later. The horsemen were monitoring the progress of the Union flight toward Winchester, Will realized. At midday, gunshots rattled in the distance. The cavalry must have engaged the enemy.

Riders came racing in a short time later to report to Jackson, and a short time after that, new orders were passed along the column. The Southerners were veering toward the route being followed by the Federals. Will didn't see how they could have gotten ahead of Banks, but he followed the command and sent his men to the northwest with the others.

The crackle of gunfire continued, and soon the sounds grew closer. Will knew that excitement and anticipation were sweeping through the men, because he felt those same sensations himself. The spring was back in their step as they marched; they had forgotten that they were still tired from the efforts of the previous day.

The gunshots were loud by the time the Confederate column reached a wooded ridge, pushed through the trees, and came out at the top of a hill that sloped down to the Valley turnpike that ran from Strasburg to Winchester. Will reined in as he saw the scene playing out before him.

The Confederate cavalry had caught a large Union wagon train rolling along the road. The riders were dashing back and forth, their pistols cracking, as they tried to keep the Yankees pinned down. Will saw that many of the leaders of the teams pulling the wagons had been shot, stalling the wagons where they were. A small Federal infantry force had evidently been traveling with the wagon train as a guard detail, and they had taken cover behind the canvas-covered vehicles and were throwing potshots at the swarming Rebel cavalrymen.

It was instantly clear to Will what needed to be done. The horsemen had been strong enough to stop the wagon train but lacked the numbers to overwhelm the Yankee defenders and capture it. It came as no surprise to him when the infantry was ordered to move down the hillside and join the fight.

Whooping and hollering, the gray tide rolled down the slope. Will left his saber in its scabbard. The men didn't need him waving it around to goad them on. They were attacking strongly without any prodding. He drew his pistol instead and galloped down the hill.

Minié balls whined around him. Will knew he should have been frightened about charging into that hail of lead, but he discovered to his surprise that he wasn't. He had been through enough battles so that everything about it was familiar to him: the zing of bullets around his ears, the acrid bite of powder smoke in his nose, the hammering of his heartbeat. He was excited, yes, but not scared. As he neared the line of wagons on the road, he focused his attention on the Union soldiers crouched behind them and began looking for a target.

Suddenly, his hat was plucked off his head. He knew without thinking about it that a bullet had come within inches of blasting his brains out. That made him angry, and he aimed his horse straight for the gap between two of the wagons.

Will held his fire until he was almost on top of the wagons. A Yankee soldier darted into the opening, lifting his rifle to his shoulder as he aimed at the onrushing Confederate captain. Will fired instinctively, using the skills that had come to him naturally the first time he ever picked up a revolver. The Colt Navy bucked in his hand, and the .36 slug slammed into the man's chest. The soldier went over backward as if he had been jerked down by a giant hand. Will rode right over the body, fired a shot to the right, then twisted in the saddle and snapped off another shot to the left. He hauled on the reins, wheeling the dun around. Another Yankee was running at him, bayonet outthrust. Will shot him in the head, turning away as the man sprawled limply on the ground. He fired twice more into the knot of blue-clad infantry behind the wagons, then the hammer fell on an empty chamber as Will cocked the Colt and pressed the trigger again.

There was no time to reload. He holstered the gun and reached for his saber, but before he could grasp it, something slammed into him from the side. The horse jumped skittishly, and Will felt himself slipping out of the saddle. He kicked his feet free from the stirrups even as he struggled against the man who had just leaped up and tackled him. Both Will and the Northerner slammed hard into the packed earth of the road.

Will rolled to the side, trying to throw the Yankee off him. The man had a tight grip, though, and Will's arms were pinned to his sides. The Federal tried to butt Will in the face. Will jerked his head to the side, so that the man only scraped his ear.

Lying there side by side, Will had a good look at the Yankee's face. The man had a ginger-colored beard, freckles across his nose, and light brown eyes. The lips under the beard were drawn back in a grimace of hate, and the eyes burned with the need to kill. Will wondered later if he had looked as fearsome as his oppenent at that particular moment.

The man's eyes widened with pain as Will brought up a knee and slammed it into his groin. That loosened the man's grip enough so that Will was able to get a hand free. He drove his fist into the soldier's face, pulping the Yankee's nose. The man yelped. Will got his hand around his throat and hung on grimly, forcing him over and back.

Will rolled again, putting himself on top and the Yankee on the bottom. He had his other hand free now, and it joined the grip on the man's throat. Will squeezed hard, digging in with his thumbs, and he heard a grotesque gurgle as the Federal's windpipe collapsed. The soldier bucked and heaved frenziedly, futilely trying to draw air into his lungs, but Will hung on tightly for a moment longer, until all the life had run out of the suddenly glassy eyes.

Gasping for breath, Will flung himself upright. He reached for his saber, found that it was still in its scabbard, and dragged the blade free. Nearby, a young Confederate private was fighting with a much larger Yankee. Their bayonets rang and struck sparks against each other as the two men engaged in a crude fencing match. Will stepped up and drove his sword into the Northerner's back, feeling the blade grate against bone before he ripped it free again. The Federal screamed and fell forward, collapsing on the ground at the feet of the Confederate private.

The young man began, "Thanks, Cap—," then grunted as his head jerked back and a round black hole appeared in the center of his forehead. His knees unhinged and he folded up, dropping onto his face so that Will could see that most of the back of his head was gone, exploded outward by the minié ball that had burst through his brain.

Will spun away, slashing at the legs of a Yankee who was running past him. The man yelled and staggered, then fell, blood spurting from a severed artery in his thigh. Will was growing numb now. He moved toward the wagons, stumbling a little. A burly figure in gray appeared beside him, clutched his arm. "We got 'em on the run, Cap'n!" Darcy Bennett shouted. "They ain't goin' far, though."

Will turned and looked and saw that Darcy was right. Some of the Yankees were fleeing while others were throwing down their weapons and surrendering. The wagon train had been over-run and surrounded by the Confederate troops. Will raised a gore-splashed hand and rubbed it wearily across his face, not caring that the gesture left streaks of red behind. The drumbeat of his pulse slowed slightly. The battle was coming to an end.

"Get the men together and gather up all the prisoners you can," he told Darcy. He saw smoke rising from some of the wagons. "And get those fires put out, if you can. There are bound to be supplies in the wagons that we can use."

"Yes sir." Darcy started to move away to follow the orders, then hesitated. "You all right, Cap'n?"

Will nodded. "Fine. I'm not hurt."

Darcy sketched a salute and went on about his business. The gunfire had died away to only an occasional report. Will leaned over and cleaned the blade of his saber on a tuft of grass growing beside the road, then straightened. He sheathed the saber and started looking for his horse, stepping over sprawled corpses as he did so.

This was bloody work, he thought, damned bloody work, and he wished, not for the first time, that it had never come to this.

IN THE heat of battle, Will had not noticed that there was a vil-lage close by the place where the Union wagon train had been captured. The settlement was called Newtown, and Will tried to make his mind recall the details of the maps he had studied during the meetings with Jackson. Newtown was south of Kernstown and Winchester, he remembered. The Confederate army had been through here before, had marched along this very road, in fact, on the way to the battle at Kernstown. So much of this campaign was covering familiar ground.

He found his horse but not his hat. The headgear would have had a bullet hole in it anyway, he told himself, and it would have been trampled in the charge. Bareheaded, he mounted up and rode toward the front of the wagon train. Jackson and the other officers were gathering there.

"As soon as the prisoners and the captured supplies have been started south, we'll push on toward Winchester," Jackson was saying as Will rode up. The general glanced at him, then looked again and observed, "My word, but you're a gruesome sight, Captain."

"Thankfully, it's not my blood," Will clarified. He brought his horse to a halt next to where Yancy Lattimer stood and swung down from the saddle. Yancy reached over and took the dun's reins.

"I'll hang on to your horse, Will," he said. "You look pretty tuckered out."

Will nodded his thanks, then turned his attention back to the general, who was visibly proud of the victory.

"The Yankees are on the run, and they're running without most of their supplies now," Jackson noted. "If we can drive them from Winchester, they'll have no choice but to flee across the Potomac, out of Virginia entirely."

"In that case, General Shields will surely be recalled from his advance on Richmond," one of the other officers commented.

The general nodded emphatically and waved the arm he was holding upright. "Exactly, Colonel. Bit by bit, we are draining the Yankees' strength away from them. I daresay McClellan himself may well be paralyzed upon the peninsula, unsure as to whether our efforts may land us on the front lawn of the White House!"

As the meeting broke up, dead horses and mules were being unhitched from the teams and dragged out of the road, so that the wagons could be turned around and started south. The prisoners were herded in that direction as well, several hundred dispirited Federals who would likely spend the rest of the war in a Southern prison camp. Only a few men were needed to guard them. After catching their breath, the rest of Jackson's force moved out again, this time following the road straight toward Winchester.

The Stonewall Brigade, including the Thirty-third Virginia, was in the lead this time. Still bareheaded, Will rode at the head of his company, which, Darcy reported to him, had lost only two men during the battle, with several more wounded.

Late in the afternoon, Kernstown came into view ahead of the column. Will looked to his right and saw the ridge topped by the stone fence where Jackson's forces had opposed those of Union Generals Shields and Banks. That day had ended in a Confederate retreat, but now the Yankees were gone from Kernstown. In fact, the town was practically empty when the soldiers marched through it, following the Valley turnpike on toward Winchester.

They hadn't gone far when shots rang out ahead. The Federals must have left pockets of men along the route of their retreat to slow up Jackson's pursuit, thought Will. The column ground to a halt. Will turned in the saddle and called to Darcy, "Skirmishers forward, Sergeant!"

A handful of men trotted ahead of the main body of troops. When bullets began kicking up dust around their feet, they left the road and scurried for cover in the fields bordering it. Will saw smoke drifting from a clump of trees ahead of them and knew the Yankees were holed up in there. The skirmishers worked their way toward the trees, returning the fire, taking turns covering each other's advance as they dashed ahead. It took awhile, but the Confederates finally reached the trees, and then there were a few minutes of fierce gunfire and hoarse shouting. The noises of combat gradually ceased, and one of the Southern skirmishers stepped out of the trees and motioned the column ahead. Will rode forward cautiously, just in case the signal was premature.

It wasn't. The nest of Federals had been cleaned out, and the road was clear again—momentarily. Less than a half-hour later, though, right after sunset, more shots rang out, and again the skirmishers went forward to drive the Union resistance back.

That was the beginning of a long, frustrating night for the Confederate army under Gen. Thomas J. Jackson. The general intended for the men to march all night, but their progress was slowed dramatically by a series of ambushes set up by the Federals left behind to cover the retreat. Each time the shooting started, the main body of the army was forced to halt until the way had been cleared again. During one of the pauses, Will heard Darcy Bennett mutter, "Them Yankees are like damn' pesky gnats, buzzin' around our heads and makin' us stop to swat at 'em."

That was exactly what was happening, Will realized. In his homespun manner, Darcy had put his finger on the heart of the situation.

The march toward Winchester was a slow, stop-and-start affair, but gradually the distance to the town diminished as the night wore on. Will caught himself dozing in the saddle a time or two and jerked himself upright. If his men could not sleep, neither was he going to.

By dawn, the roofs of the buildings in Winchester could be seen in the distance. Between the Confederate position and the town, however, were a series of ridges west of the turnpike, running at right angles to the road. As the advance came to another halt, Will lifted his field glasses to his eyes and studied the ridges. He saw Union artillery batteries atop the second one and counted six cannon arrayed with the barrels pointed toward the Confederates. Yankee troops blocked the turnpike itself, and to the east of the road were two more artillery batteries, along with more troops. Jackson had harried and pressed the Federals all the way to Winchester, but they had still managed to put together a formidable-looking defense in a very short time.

Gunfire began to rattle to Will's right as the Confederate troops who had spread out east of the turnpike began to push forward again, engaging the Yankee pickets. The shooting was only sporadic, but the sounds of battle served as a goad to the other forces gathered here. Union artillery began bombarding the Southern troops. Some of the Confederate cannon had once again caught up with the army and tried to return the fire, but there were too few of them to have much effect on the Federals' barrage.

As grapeshot burst and solid rounds wailed overhead, Will wondered when the order to charge would come. Surely Jackson wouldn't let them just sit here while the Union artillery carved them up!

The wait was not a long one. "Stonewall Brigade, forward!" came a shout from one of the generals, and with a yell, the soldiers launched into a run. They were headed for the ridges where the Yankee cannon were located.

Will rode back and forth along the line of the attack, firing his pistol over the heads of the men in his company. The Federals atop the first ridge didn't put up much of a fight before turning and running for the second ridge, and Will saw that none of his men had gone down in the attack. He followed them closely up the slope to the crest, then watched them plunge down the far side of the ridge, still yelling their lungs out. None of the Union cannon were up here, Will knew. They were all on the ridges farther back.

He used his field glasses again, training the lenses on the top of the second ridge. It was thick with blue-clad figures. The resistance was going to be stiffer this time, a lot stiffer, he thought grimly. Through the glasses, he saw smoke puff out from the line of Union soldiers atop the ridge as they fired their first volley.

The shots came as the Confederate troops reached the bottom of the second ridge and started up. Several men fell. The only thing that kept the casualties from being worse was the difficulty of aiming downhill. Southern marksmanship uphill wasn't much better, however. Like so many of these engagements, this one was going to come down to hand-to-hand fighting.

Will tucked the field glasses back in their pouch on the saddle and drew his pistol again as he sent the dun down the slope. His men were surging gallantly up the next hill, and he wasn't going to let them go into battle alone. Some officers always hung back as far in the rear as they could, claiming that they accomplished more for the cause of the Confederacy by directing the engagements from long range. Most of them were probably even sincere in that belief, Will thought. But he could never be that kind of officer, playing it safe while the men under his command risked their lives.

He let out a whoop as his horse reached the bottom of the slope and started up the second ridge. He had already caught up to the rear ranks of his company, and as his men saw their captain right there among them, they surged forward even stronger, determined not to let Will down. He felt a swell of pride as he saw their reaction.

The Confederates continued struggling up the ridge. The front lines of the attack reached the top of the slope but were thrown back. Some of the men were retreating down the hill when Will reached them and bellowed, "Up, boys, up!" They turned and drove toward the crest again.

As Will came within pistol range, he began firing slowly and methodically, making sure he had a target each time before he pressed the trigger. He saw several of the Yankees go down under his fire. When the weapon was empty, he holstered it and drew his saber, but there was to be no close, bloody blade work for him this time. The Confederate infantry reached the top of the ridge again and swarmed over it, and this time the Federals were unable to repulse the attack. Gradually, all along the line of the ridge, the Southern forces began to take control.

As he reached the top of the slope, Will reined in and leaned forward in the saddle. From this vantage point, he could see how the battle was progressing. To the east of the turnpike, troops under General Ewell had pressed forward, forcing the Yankees back. The Union artillery batteries near the road had been captured, Will noted, and the cannon had been turned around and were being fired by Rebel gunners toward the retreating Federals. To the west, past the point where the ridges petered out, more Confederate brigades were advancing, flanking the Northerners. The point of strongest resistance had been right here on the ridge, Will realized, and that was broken now, too. The Yankees were falling back toward the town as quickly as they could, and the Southerners were also pressing on toward Winchester. Beyond the ridges was an open field, and the Federals put up no fight at all as they retreated across it.

Will ordered his men on, and by the time they reached Winchester at midmorning, the fleeing Yankees had come and gone. Clearly, no effort was going to be made by the Union forces to regroup and defend the town. Winchester was solidly in Confederate hands, along with all the supplies abandoned there by the Federals.

Jackson, however, was not satisfied, Will learned a short while later. His men barely had time to catch their breath when new orders arrived. The army was going to push on after the Yankees as they fled toward the Potomac. By noon, the Southern soldiers were marching again, this time leaving Winchester and heading toward Harpers Ferry.

The river through the valley of the Shenandoah grew narrower as it neared the point where it flowed into the Potomac. Harpers Ferry was there, surrounded by steep hills. Across the Potomac lay Maryland. A Confederate thrust across the river would place Jackson's army north of Washington City, within a relatively short march of the Federal capital. As Will rode alongside the exhausted but still game men of his company, he wondered just how far Jackson was going to push this campaign.

He found out over the next couple of days. The general led his men all the way to Harpers Ferry and occupied the town, capturing straggling bands of Yankees as they advanced. Over two thousand prisoners were sent back south, but by the time the army reached the Potomac, the rest of the Union forces had successfully crossed the river into Maryland. Instead of pursuing them, Jackson spent two days moving his forces around, marching them back and forth so that it would appear to any Federal observers across the river that their numbers were larger than they actually were. Then, on the third day, Jackson began pulling his troops back slowly, heading south again from Harpers Ferry.

Will found himself riding alongside Yancy Lattimer as the worn-out army resumed its march. "It was a bluff, wasn't it?" Will mused. "The general said all along that he wanted to make it look like we were going to attack Washington, so that the Yankees wouldn't know what to do."

"From what I've heard, it worked," Yancy noted with a grin. "The scouts say that McDowell is moving west with the men that McClellan had wanted to be sent to the peninsula, and Frémont's heading east toward us, so he can't go help McClellan, either. We've got the Yankees so worried they don't know if we're coming or going."

Will nodded. "I'm not sure how long we can keep it up, though. The boys are pretty tired."

"Jackson's foot cavalry," Yancy said. "That's what they're calling us, I hear. Nobody has ever moved infantry around as fast as old Stonewall has in this campaign. I don't think any of my former instructors at the Point would have believed it was even possible."

Will had rustled up another hat to replace the one he'd lost at Newtown. He took it off now and sleeved sweat from his forehead. This was May 30, he realized, and the sun was warm, almost hot. The spring rains finally seemed to be over, and the roads had dried out quickly. Now instead of fighting to pull free from mud, the feet of the marching men raised clouds of dust.

The army was on the move again, and movement was the main element of Jackson's strategy, Will thought. But Union forces were converging on them from east and west, and the time would soon come when the Confederates would have to turn and make a fight of it once again.

Chapter Twelve

ON THE VIRGINIA PENINSULA, the Confederate retreat from Yorktown had resulted in a battle at Williamsburg, as Union forces momentarily caught up to the Southern army. Although the Confederates put up a stout defense at Fort Magruder, the most prominent of the line of redoubts that had been built just south of Williamsburg, they took heavy losses of over fifteen hundred men and were forced to continue their pilgrimage toward Richmond.

Mac heard about the battle when General Stuart and his men rode to Eltham's Landing the next day to rejoin the cavalry units under the command of Col. Fitzhugh Lee. Stuart was elated to hear that Lee and his men had rebuffed the attempt by the Yankees to use the York River to flank their foes. From there, the reunited cavalry once again served as the rear guard for the Confederate retreat toward Richmond.

MAC HAD been to Richmond plenty of times before, but he had never seen the city like it was now. The place reminded him of a madhouse as he and the other cavalrymen rode through the streets. The sidewalks were crowded with worried-looking people, and the cavalry mounts had trouble making their way through the throngs of wagons, many of them piled high with household goods. Mac realized after a short time that Richmond's citizens were evacuating the city, no doubt out of fear that it would be falling to the Federals any day now.

"O ye of little faith," muttered Fitz Lee as he rode alongside Mac. "They believe the capital is doomed."

"The scouts say McClellan has over a hundred thousand men," Mac pointed out. "And he's coming this way."

"Slowly," Lee corrected.

"Steadily." Mac had grown to know the colonel well enough to speak to him without an abundance of formality. Just as a precaution, though, in case Lee decided to take offense at being argued with, Mac added, "sir."

Instead, the colonel grinned, "I can't deny that. But perhaps we'll come up with some way to slow him down."

The cavalry detail continued to make its way toward the capitol. Most of the men were in camp just outside Richmond, a camp Stuart had christened Quien Sabe, a Spanish phrase meaning "Who knows?" That was pretty appropriate, Mac thought, because nobody knew how things were going to turn out. All that was certain was that the massive Union army was only a few dozen miles away.

Stuart, Fitz Lee, and some of the other cavalry officers were on their way to a meeting at the capitol with Gens. Robert E. Lee, Joseph E. Johnston, and their staff officers. The defense of Richmond was going to take some planning, Mac knew, and he felt privileged that he was going to be allowed to observe the meeting as Colonel Lee's aide.

He couldn't blame the citizens for being worried. Rumors were flying. It was known that President Davis had sent his family to Raleigh, North Carolina, where they would be safer, and supposedly all the other politicians in the city had already sent their families to some place of refuge or were about to. The leaders themselves were rumored to be making preparations to flee before the Yankees got here. The government would take up residence somewhere else if it had to. To that end, the gold in the treasury was being crated up so that it could be gotten out of Richmond in a hurry.

With everyone in authority acting like the city was on the verge of capture, naturally the rest of the people felt like that was the case, too. Hence the heavily loaded wagons, Mac thought. Some folks might call the exodus a case of rats deserting a sinking ship. Mac figured it was more like getting out while the getting was good.

The group of cavalry officers and their aides reached the capitol, dismounted, and turned their horses over to enlisted men who had been detailed to the task of caring for the animals. Mac followed Stuart and Lee up the steps and into the building. A lieutenant met the group and ushered them into a large chamber where Davis, Lee, Johnston, and several other officers were waiting. There were a number of civilians in the room, too, seated around a long table, and it took Mac a moment to recognize some of them from newspaper illustrations he had seen. He realized they were the president's cabinet, and he knew this meeting was destined to be even more grave than he had anticipated.

President Davis said to the newcomers, "Thank you for joining us, gentlemen. Please be seated. I trust you didn't have too much difficulty making your way through the . . . hubbub outside."

"The city appears to be very frightened, Mr. President," Stuart said as he and Lee took their seats.

Davis inclined his head in agreement. "Indeed." He turned to the white-haired, white-bearded, distinguished-looking man on his left. "General Lee, have you considered the question that I posed to you earlier?"

"Yes, Mr. President," replied Robert E. Lee. He looked around the table for a moment at the other men, then went on, "I believe the best line of defense, should we be forced to withdraw from Richmond, would be along the Staunton River, southwest of here."

Davis nodded. "Thank you, General. I know it must be painful to contemplate such a possibility, but with the loss of the *Virginia* and the presence of Union gunboats so close to us, we must take into account every alternative."

Mac had heard of the calamity that had befallen the Confederate ironclad *Virginia*. After the Yankees had been unable to prevent the gunboat from controlling the area around Hampton Roads and sealing off the James River, they had tried a different tack, capturing the *Virginia*'s home port of Norfolk instead. With no place to go and unwilling to allow the Federals to ultimately capture the ironclad, the captain of the *Virginia* had decided to scuttle the ship. The explosion had sent the proud vessel to the bottom of the bay.

That loss had opened the way for Union gunboats to steam up the James River toward Richmond. There were conflicting reports about just how close the gunboats were to the capital, but it was certain they were near enough to pose a distinct threat on fairly short notice.

General Lee was silent for a long moment following the president's statement about considering every possibility. His impassive face showed nothing of what he was thinking. So Mac was surprised when the general spoke up again, louder and more emphatic than before.

"Richmond must not be given up," he declared. "Richmond shall *not* be given up!"

Davis and his cabinet seemed taken aback by this response from the president's military adviser. A murmur went around the table. Mac glanced at Fitz Lee and saw that the colonel was gazing at his uncle in admiration, as was Stuart. Lee, despite his staid appearance, had something in common with these dashing cavalry officers, Mac decided.

President Davis leaned forward. "How do you propose to stop the Federal gunboats from threatening us, General?" he asked.

"I have already ordered a force of men under the command of Col. Custis Lee to reinforce the defenses at Drewry's Bluff, Mr. President," Lee replied. "I believe we can stop the Yankee gunboats there."

Custis Lee was the general's son and one of Fitz Lee's cousins, Mac recalled. But he was unfamiliar with Drewry's Bluff.

"How far from here is that, General?" asked one of the cabinet members.

"Eight miles downstream, sir," Lee replied.

Davis frowned again. "Then, if this defense fails, the Federal gunboats will be here very shortly thereafter and will be able to shell the city."

"The defense will not fail, Mr. President."

For a long moment, no one said anything. Then Davis sighed. "Very well. We shall put our trust in you, General. Continue with your plans."

"Yes sir," Lee replied with a crisp nod.

The meeting adjourned shortly after that, and Fitz Lee went to speak with his uncle. While the colonel was doing that, Stuart turned to Mac and asked, "Do you think Fitz would be willing to spare you for an errand, Corporal Brannon?"

The question took Mac by surprise. "I suppose you'd have to ask him, sir." Then he was bold enough to add, "What did you have in mind, General?"

"I want someone at Drewry's Bluff to act as an observer, someone who can gallop back here immediately to bring word of our success or failure. Would you be interested, Corporal? That stallion of yours is one of the fastest animals in these parts, I'd say."

"Yes sir, he is," Mac agreed. "But as for the rest of it, you'd have to ask the colonel."

Fitz Lee sauntered over to join them in time to hear Mac's statement. "Ask the colonel what?" he wanted to know.

"I'd like for Corporal Brannon to ride down to Drewry's Bluff and act as an observer for us," Stuart repeated to Lee. "What do you say, Fitz?"

With a grin, Lee replied, "I say I'd rather go in his place so I could watch the action, but I suppose I'm needed here. Of course it's all right."

Mac felt a surge of excitement. "Thank you, sir. Would you happen to know how I should find the place?"

"Just follow the James River downstream," Stuart told him. "You can't miss it. It's a sharp bend in the river, and there's a high bluff on the south bank. That's where Custis will be gathering his defenses."

Fitz Lee clapped Mac on the shoulder. "Start as soon as you can," he said. "And come back as soon as you can when it's over. I don't want to spare you any longer than I have to."

"Yes sir."

Mac hurried out of the capitol and retrieved his horse. He had supplies and a full canteen hung on the saddle, so there was no need to return to Quien Sabe before leaving on this mission. He rode over to the James River and began following the stream as it wound its way through Richmond.

Once he'd left the city behind him, Mac urged the silver gray stallion into a ground-eating trot. He sensed that the horse wanted to run, but he held it back, knowing that he might need the stallion's speed and strength even more if the defense of Drewry's Bluff failed and he had to carry the word back to the Richmond leaders that the Yankee gunboats were unstoppable and their arrival was imminent.

Here in this beautiful countryside, bursting with the new life of spring, it was hard to believe that a war was raging. Mac wished, not for the first time, that the Federals had just stayed where they belonged and let the Southerners work things out for themselves. In the long run, things could have been settled peacefully; he was certain of that.

But that was not to be, he told himself, and longing for it was not going to help anything.

He thought instead about General Stuart and Colonel Lee and the easygoing friendship between the two men. As a general, Stuart could have simply ordered him to go to Drewry's Bluff, and Lee would have had no choice except to go along with his superior officer's command. But instead, Stuart had done Lee the courtesy of asking him if Mac could act as an observer at the bluff. There was something special about these men, Mac sensed, but it wasn't just Stuart and Lee. It was the entire cavalry. They were different from the rest of the army, a class of men that hearkened back to the knights of old.

He was proud to be one of them.

———◦◦◦———

DREWRY'S BLUFF was just where he had been told it would be. It rose in a fairly gentle slope some two hundred feet high overlooking a sharp, almost ninety-degree bend in the James River. There were open fields on both sides of the river, which was 120 yards wide at this point, and trees and brush lined the banks. At the bottom of the slope, men were digging trenches, Mac saw as he rode past them toward the crest. No one challenged him until he reached the top, where several heavy cannon were being wrestled into position. A guard stepped out toward him, rifle ready, and called, "Wait a minute, Corporal. Where do you think you're going?"

"I need to speak to Colonel Lee," replied Mac as he reined in. Both Stuart and Fitz Lee had told him to report to the colonel when he got there. He went on, "I was sent here by General Stuart to act as an observer and courier."

The sentry relaxed a little and jerked his chin toward a nearby tent. "The colonel's over there."

"Thanks," Mac nodded as he urged the stallion into motion again.

He rode over to the tent and found an officer standing there talking to several others. The resemblance to General Lee was easy to see, Mac noted. Col. Custis Lee had the same erect bearing and closely trimmed beard, although his was dark instead of white.

The colonel swung around toward Mac, who dismounted and saluted. "Corporal Brannon reporting, sir," Mac said.

Lee returned the salute. "At ease, Corporal. What unit are you with, and why are you here?"

"I was sent by General Stuart, sir, to act as an observer to your defense of the bluff."

Lee nodded. "I see. And if the Yankees get past us, you're to gallop back to Richmond as quickly as possible, I take it?"

The colonel also had his father's quick mind, Mac decided. "Yes sir, that's correct." Then he added, "I normally serve as aide to Col. Fitzhugh Lee, but he released me for this mission."

A smile spread over Custis Lee's face. "I'll wager Fitz wanted to come down here himself, didn't he?"

"Yes sir, he did," admitted Mac.

Lee reached for his hat, which was sitting on a three-legged stool. "If you're to act as an observer, I suppose I'd best show you what we're doing to get ready for the Yankees. Come along, Corporal."

Mac walked alongside the colonel to the edge of the bluff. He counted six cannon positioned so they could cover the river below. Three of them were Columbiads, veritable behemoths; the other three were slightly smaller but quite lethal-looking.

Lee slapped the iron barrel of one of the Columbiads and predicted, "We'll give the Yankees a warm welcome with these lads when they come calling. That is, if they ever get this far. Look downstream there." He pointed.

Mac looked where the colonel was indicating and saw several boats in the water. A huge splash went up as a bulky shape was pushed off one of the boats into the river.

"We're filling cribs with rocks and sinking them," Lee went on. "With any luck, some of them will gouge holes in the hulls of the gunboats. We've also scuttled some old boats down there. That should slow them down, if nothing else." The colonel pointed to the trenches being dug at the foot of the bluff. "Our best sharpshooters will be stationed down there."

"Rifle fire against gunboats, sir?" Mac knew he sounded skeptical, but he couldn't help it. Some of the Yankee gunboats would probably be ironclads, and the rifle fire would bounce harmlessly off their armored plates.

Lee smiled. "I said we'd be using sharpshooters, Corporal. A gunboat, even an ironclad, can't be steered blindly. If my men can put their shots through the viewing ports, they'll make things rather interesting for the Yankee helmsmen, don't you think?"

"Yes sir," Mac agreed. Now that he thought about it, he knew Lee was right. It would take some mighty good shooting to hit those small slits in the gunboats' armor, but it could be done. His brother Titus could shoot that well, Mac thought.

"And after the first several men are picked off, the Yankees will think twice about venturing out to fire any of their deck guns," Lee continued. His voice was confident, "We'll stop them."

Mac hoped he was right. If the gunboats made it past here, the Yankees might be able to capture Richmond before McClellan ever got there.

For the rest of the afternoon, Lee was busy, striding from place to place to check on the progress of the work being done. Mac stayed with him for the most part and was impressed with both Lee's control of the situation and the hard work being done by the soldiers. As night settled down over the Virginia countryside, rain began to fall, but the men continued their preparations for the Federals without slowing down.

Mac was invited to share a tent with several other officers' aides, and once he had made sure that the stallion had been tended to, he accepted the shelter gratefully, glad to be able to get out of the rain. He dozed a little during the night, but he was restless, knowing that the next day would likely bring another battle. All the reports indicated that the gunboats weren't far downstream. Although they would have tied up for the night, it wouldn't take them long to cover the rest of the distance in the morning.

The rain stopped during the night, and the next day dawned almost clear again. Only a few clouds floated in the sky. After a quick breakfast from his pack and a cup of coffee, Mac noticed thin columns of smoke rising downstream and knew they came from the approaching vessels.

An air of tense anticipation hung over Drewry's Bluff. Sandbags had been piled in front of the trenches, and the riflemen waited behind them. The crews manning the artillery batteries were ready, too. Time seemed to stretch out and drag by endlessly, but finally, more than an hour after dawn, the first of the Yankee gunboats appeared.

It was an ironclad, Mac noted, the first of the armored vessels he had actually seen. He knew next to nothing about boats, but even to his inexperienced eye, the ironclad looked slow and awkward. Its armor appeared formidable, though, and it was bristling with guns.

From the corner of his eye, Mac saw another vessel approaching from upstream. It was a wooden gunboat, and it flew a Confederate flag. Lee, who was standing nearby, noted Mac's interest and explained, "That's the *Patrick Henry*. One of ours. We plan to hit them from the river, too, as well as from up here."

To Mac, the *Patrick Henry* didn't look like much of a match for the bigger and heavier—and more heavily armed—Federal ironclad. As he watched, a second ironclad came into view, following the first one, and behind the second were several wooden gunboats. They hung back, out of range of the cannon atop the bluff. Only the first ironclad came on boldly, as if daring the gunners to open fire on it.

A few moments later, that was exactly what happened. With a roar so loud it felt as if giant fists had boxed Mac's ears, the shelling began. He winced and narrowed his eyes in response to the thunderous sound, and he saw the ironclad shudder and jerk as two of the shells slammed into its deck. The vessel steamed on, however, seemingly undeterred.

The riflemen in the trenches opened up, raking the decks of the ironclad with a withering fire that prevented any Union sailors from venturing out, just as Lee had predicted. The barrage from the cannon continued. Water spouted high into the air as the shells that missed fell into the river instead.

The ironclad's guns began to fire, lobbing shells up the bluff toward the Confederate batteries. Dirt was thrown up as the rounds struck the hillside and exploded, leaving ugly craters. By now Mac was growing a little more accustomed to the barrage, but he had to wonder if his hearing would ever be the same again.

The long-range duel wore on through the morning. Several Confederate gunners were killed when a shell from the ironclad burst close to them. The Yankee vessel had suffered considerable damage but was still in the fight. The second ironclad steamed closer, but in fact it was too close to the riverbank. Its guns could not be elevated high enough to aim them at the top of the bluff. Lee pointed that fact out to Mac, then said, "They'll pull back now, just watch."

The withdrawal began a few minutes later. Unable to take a part in the battle, the second ironclad retreated downriver, being peppered as it went by the rifle fire from the trenches.

The *Patrick Henry* entered the fight then, striking at the Yankee ironclad while the armored vessel was still exchanging cannon fire with the batteries atop the bluff. The aim of the gunners on the wooden vessel was true. Several shells slammed into the ironclad, and a moment later, dark smoke began to bellow from it. Cheers of triumph went up from the Southerners on top of the bluff.

"We've set her on fire!" Lee shouted. "The Yankees have no choice now except to turn and run!"

Ponderously, the burning ironclad began to swing around. Its guns fell silent. The other ironclad and the wooden boats were already withdrawing downstream with all the speed they could muster. The first ironclad followed them, being hurried on its way by some parting shots from the Confederate batteries.

Lee turned to Mac with a grin. "Well, it looks as if you'll be carrying good news back to Richmond, Corporal. Tell my father and President Davis that they don't have to worry about those Yankee gunboats anymore."

"Yes sir," Mac responded. His ears were still ringing from the noise, but he managed a smile, too. The Yankee sailors had planned to cripple the Confederacy with a quick thrust aimed at its heart, but they had failed and been turned back.

Mac's smile faded as he saddled up the stallion, said good-bye to Colonel Lee, and started up the road to Richmond. The Yankee gunboats had been thwarted, true enough, he thought . . .

But a short distance down the peninsula, Gen. George B. McClellan still waited with a hundred thousand men.

And they would not be turned back so easily, Mac knew.

Chapter Thirteen

TITUS RAN A HAND over his hair, smoothing it down as best he could, then used the same hand to lift the heavy brass knocker and rap it sharply against the front door of Mountain Laurel. He was wearing his best Sunday-go-to-meetin' clothes, and he had his broad-brimmed, flat-crowned brown hat clasped in his other hand.

He was about to knock again when the door swung open. An elderly, white-haired black man in servant's livery stood there. "Hello, Elijah," Titus said.

"Massa Titus," the servant replied. "What can I do fo' you?"

"I'm here to see Miss Polly."

Elijah frowned. "Don't recollect her sayin' nothin' about expectin' any callers today . . ."

"She's not expecting me, but I'd like to see her anyway. Would you tell her I'm here?" Titus asked. He kept a pleasant smile on his face, but inside he was having to curb his impatience. It had taken him a long time to work up the courage to ride over here again, and he didn't want to waste the opportunity.

Before Elijah could say anything else, several men rode up to the front of the mansion. Titus heard the hoofbeats of their horses and looked over his shoulder. One of them was Duncan Ebersole himself. The other men with him included two of his overseers. Two of the men who had beaten him on the night of the dance, Titus recalled bitterly.

Ebersole reined in and looked at Titus in surprise. He was wearing a sweat-stained linsey-woolsey shirt, whipcord trousers, and high-topped boots. A patina of dust lay on his black hat. Obviously, Ebersole had been out to the fields.

"Hello, Brannon," he said without dismounting. "Something I can do for you? Ye look like ye're ready for church."

"No sir," replied Titus. "I just came to pay a visit to Miss Polly."

Ebersole's eyes narrowed. "I don't recall ye askin' permission to call on my daughter. If ye had, it would ha' been denied."

Titus took a deep breath, controlling his anger with an effort. "Mr. Ebersole, if you'll just give me a chance—"

Ebersole grunted as he swung down from the saddle. "Don't get me wrong, Brannon," he said as he turned back toward Titus. "Ye and yer family are good neighbors, and I appreciate the help ye gave me awhile back with those soldiers. But I'll speak plainly: you ain't the sort o' man I want to be callin' on my daughter."

Titus couldn't restrain his temper any longer. It flared up as he said, "But you'd be damned glad to see me and my rifle if there were Yankees breathing down your neck, wouldn't you?"

"Shut your mouth, Brannon," growled one of the overseers. "You can't go around talkin' to Mr. Ebersole like that."

Ebersole raised a hand toward the overseer. "No, 'tis all right, Wickham. Maybe the young fellow has a point. There aren't many men around these parts who can shoot the way he can. And it'll be up to us to protect our land and our families when the damned Yankees come. We can't expect much help from the militia."

Sensing a slight softening in Ebersole's stance, Titus said quickly, "You can count on me, Mr. Ebersole. I'd do just about anything to help protect Polly."

Ebersole turned to the overseers. "Go on wi' those chores I gave ye."

"You don't want us to throw this gent off the plantation first?" proposed the one who was glaring at Titus.

"No, I don't." Ebersole came up onto the porch and put a hand on Titus's shoulder. "Come on inside wi' me, lad, an' we'll have a talk."

Titus thought the overseers turned their horses and rode away rather reluctantly, and he figured they would have liked to hand him another walloping. They would have liked to have tried, he thought. Even with odds of two to one, they wouldn't have found it easy.

Ebersole steered him into the house, through the magnificent foyer, and down a hall to a dark, book-lined room dominated by a massive desk in its center. Casually, Ebersole dropped his hat on the desk, then turned to face Titus.

"We've had our differences in the past, lad, but perhaps th' time has come to put that aside. I'd like to offer ye a job."

"A job?" Titus repeated, taken completely by surprise. "What sort of job?"

Ebersole leaned a hip against the corner of the desk and folded his arms across his chest. "Now that th' army's gone, 'tis no secret that the Yankees will be comin' through here sooner or later. Like a plague o' locusts they'll be, burnin' and stealin' and ruinin' everything in their path." Ebersole leaned forward and a new intensity came into his voice. "But I don't intend to let them have Mountain Laurel. I can't protect the whole plantation, but by God, I can protect this house!" He settled back again. "I've got my slaves diggin' rifle pits in a perimeter around the house. I plan to put the best sharpshooters I can find into those pits, and when the Yankees come, they'll have a damned hot surprise waitin' for 'em."

"You want me to be one of your sharpshooters?" Titus asked.

"Aye. In fact, I'd like to see ye take charge of 'em all."

Titus frowned as he considered Ebersole's offer. If he headed up the defense of Mountain Laurel, that would mean he would get to see a great deal of Polly, and when the time came, he would be defending her as well.

But he also had a responsibility to his family, and to the land that the Brannons had been farming for many years. When the Yankees came sweeping through Culpeper County—like a plague of locusts, as Ebersole had said—how could Titus desert his own family and home to come over here and fight for Mountain Laurel? He couldn't just leave his mother and Henry and Cordelia to fend for themselves.

But maybe there was yet another alternative, he thought.

"Do I have to give you an answer right now?" he asked Ebersole as he struggled to work out all the ideas in his head.

"Well . . . I suppose not. But don't be too long makin' up yer mind, lad. The Devil only knows when those Yankees will come, and I got to be ready for 'em when they do."

"I'll let you know as soon as I can," Titus promised. "Now, do you think I could see Polly for a moment?"

Ebersole didn't look like he thought much of that idea, but after a couple of seconds he nodded. "All right. Go on down th' hall to the parlor. I'll have Elijah tell her you're waitin' for her."

Titus and Ebersole left the library and went in opposite directions. Titus knew where the parlor was, and he was waiting there a few minutes later when Polly swept into the room, as beautiful as ever in a blue dress with an embroidered neckline that revealed the upper swells of her full breasts.

"Titus!" she greeted him. "I didn't know you were here until Elijah just came and told me. I hope I didn't keep you waiting too long."

"No, I had a good talk with your father while I was waiting," Titus said.

Polly looked worried about that, as well she might have considering that she knew how her father felt about Titus. "There was no . . . trouble, was there?"

"Of course not. Your father and I see eye-to-eye on more things than you might think." That was stretching the truth a little—probably the only thing he and Ebersole agreed on was their hatred of the Yankees, thought Titus—but he didn't care. He didn't want Polly worrying unnecessarily.

"Well, I'm glad to hear that, I suppose." She gestured toward a divan. "Why don't we sit down?"

Titus perched on the front edge of the divan. He wasn't completely comfortable sitting on fancy pieces of furniture.

But he was close enough to Polly as she sat down beside him that he was able to reach out and take her left hand in both of his. It was a bold move, but she didn't jerk her hand away or even flinch. Her hand was warm and smooth and soft, and she returned the pressure when he gently squeezed her fingers.

He swallowed and began, "You know how I feel about you, Polly, how I've felt about you for a long time."

She smiled. "My, you are being forward today, aren't you, Mr. Brannon?"

Titus plunged ahead. "Remember that night in your garden, when your father had that party?"

"I . . . remember."

He didn't know if her hesitation was caused by the memory of the kiss they had shared or the violence that had followed it. He hurried on, "You felt the same thing I did when I kissed you. I know you did. There's something between us, Polly, something too strong for us to deny—"

She shook her head. "Hush, Titus, hush. Don't say these things."

"I have to," he insisted. "I have to because there's no telling how much time we have left to us, what with the war and everything." His grip tightened on her hand. "I know I ought to court you properly, Polly. You deserve that, Lord knows you do. But since things are the way they are, I . . . I reckon the only thing I can say is . . ." Titus swallowed hard, and then the words came out of him in a rush. "Polly, will you marry me?"

She gasped and drew back, eyes widening in shock, as from the doorway of the parlor came a loud crash. Titus jerked his head around and saw the elderly slave Elijah standing there, a silver tray and the ruins of a pitcher of lemonade at his feet. "Massa . . . Massa Duncan sent me to fetch y'all somethin' to drink . . . ," the old man choked out, and then he turned on his heel and ran down the hall with a spryness belying his age.

Polly had gone pale, but at least she was more composed than Elijah had been. She looked intently at Titus and said, "You want me to marry you?"

"I love you, Polly." It was easier to say now, he discovered. "I've loved you for years. I'd be the happiest man on the face of the earth if you'd agree to be my wife."

"They say you drink quite a bit."

"I haven't touched a drop for more than two weeks." In fact, he hadn't had a drink since he had helped Ebersole run off the scavenging Confederate troops. There had been some bad times during that period when he'd craved whiskey so badly that he thought he would die. But some inner voice had told him that he had used up most of his chances to get what he wanted out of life, and what he wanted much more than a drink was Polly Ebersole. So he had stayed sober, and he was sober now.

"I believe you," Polly said softly. "But . . . but marriage . . . I just don't know . . . ."

Titus leaned closer to her. "You know that old man ran to get your pa. He'll be here any minute, more'n likely."

"Yes, I'm sure he will." Polly clasped Titus's hands with her other hand, so that all four of them were entwined. "Yes, I'll marry you, Titus. I'll be honored to be your wife."

Then she kissed him, and the same dizzying sensations that Titus had experienced in the garden came over him again. The world seemed to spin madly around him, and his only lifeline to reality was the soft sweet warmth of Polly's mouth.

Titus couldn't have said how long the kiss lasted, but he was certain that it wasn't long enough. Heavy footsteps made Polly pull away from him, and both of them turned toward the door of the parlor as Duncan Ebersole loomed up there, his face dark with anger. "What's this about a marriage?" he boomed.

Polly's face was more ashen than ever as she said, "Titus has asked me to marry him, and I said yes."

Ebersole flushed even more as his angry gaze swung toward Titus. "Brannon, what's the meaning o' this?" he demanded.

Titus came to his feet. "Beggin' your pardon, Mr. Ebersole, I know I should have asked you for Polly's hand first, but something just sort of . . . sort of came over me. I'm truly sorry if I offended you, and I'm askin' you now . . . may I have your daughter's hand in marriage, sir?"

"I told ye not half an hour agone that ye weren't a proper suitor for Polly!"

"That's not for you to say," she objected.

"The hell it isn't! I'm yer father, dinna ye forget that fact, lass. Ye do what *I* say!"

Polly stood, too, and caught hold of Titus's hand as she stepped closer to him. "I want to marry Titus," she said simply. "I suppose you can stop me, but if you do, I'll never forgive you."

With his chest heaving, Ebersole stood there staring at the two of them for a long moment without saying anything. Finally, he asked, "Are ye sure about this, Polly?"

"I'm certain," she declared. "I know what I want, Father. I want to be Titus's wife."

Just hearing her say things like that almost made Titus pass out with joy. She wanted him just as much as he wanted her. After all this time, he could barely believe it.

Ebersole drew the back of his hand across his mouth, then glanced at Titus. "Get out."

"I won't—"

"Go back to the library," snapped Ebersole. "I want to talk to my daughter alone."

Titus looked at Polly, his expression questioning. She nodded. "It's all right, Titus. Go ahead. I'll see you in a few minutes."

Grudgingly, he let go of her hand and moved slowly toward the door of the parlor. "I'll be right down the hall," he said. "If you need me, just give a holler—"

"My God, do ye think my own flesh and blood has anything to fear from me?" Ebersole growled disgustedly. "Go on wi' ye."

Titus went, but he looked back over his shoulder at Polly as he left the parlor. She smiled at him, a rather weak smile but a smile nonetheless, and he felt his spirits lift again.

Polly had promised herself to him, and now nothing could ever come between them.

———◦◦◦◦———

"WHAT DO ye want?" Ebersole asked when Titus was gone. "Whate'er it is, if 'tis in my power, I'll give it to ye."

"I want to be married to Titus Brannon," Polly said simply.

Ebersole waved a hand. "Och, don't tell me that! Ye've always been a perverse creature, willin' to do anything to cross me . . ."

With her lip trembling slightly, Polly sighed, "I've always done everything you asked of me, Father. Everything."

Ebersole's eyes met hers for a moment, then he had to turn away. He stalked back and forth across the parlor floor. "I just want the best for ye," he muttered. "That's all I've ever wanted."

"Then let me marry Titus."

Ebersole made a sound of disgust low in his throat, then stated, "I offered him a job, ye know."

Clearly, Polly was surprised. "A job?" she repeated. "Titus didn't say anything about that."

"He's got an eagle's eye when it comes to shootin'. I asked him to be one o' my sharpshooters when the Yankees come."

"You want him to help defend Mountain Laurel?"

"I know a good fightin' man when I see one," declared Ebersole, "even though I may not like him."

"Don't you think he would fight even harder if he knew he was defending his wife's home?"

Ebersole frowned. "Do ye think so? I was afraid he'd want to take ye away from here and make ye live on that farm o' his."

Polly came closer to him, smiling now as she lifted a hand and touched her father's cheek. "Do you really think I'd ever leave you and Mountain Laurel? I've always been here for you, Father. I'll always be here for you."

Ebersole began to breathe heavily again. "Aye, that ye have been. But why do ye want to marry that lout?"

"I want something of my own," Polly explained. "I want a wedding and a husband. But nothing really has to change."

"Nothing?" Ebersole asked in a whisper.

Polly shook her head.

⋘•◦•⋙

TITUS LOOKED up sharply, a part of him ready to fight if need be, as the library door opened and Polly came in. She was smiling, and that made Titus dare to hope.

"Father has agreed that we can be married," she said.

"You . . . you mean it?"

She nodded.

Titus let out a whoop of sheer joy and ran to her, grabbing her up in his arms so that her feet left the floor as he whirled her around and around. She laughed and started pounding her fist against his chest. "Stop it!" she cried. "Stop it, you fool! I'm getting dizzy!"

"I'm dizzy with love," Titus exclaimed. But he stopped turning around and kissed her instead, feeling the soft warmth of her body molding against his.

When they broke the kiss, Polly said, "There will be a lot of planning to do, and the sooner we get started the better."

Titus nodded. "The sooner the better," he agreed, but he wasn't thinking just about the wedding arrangements. His head was full of visions of how it would be when they were truly married, the way husbands and wives were supposed to be, and he felt himself growing aroused. He stepped back a little so that Polly wouldn't feel his reaction and think he was some sort of crude backwoodsman. Forcing his mind to practical matters, he reflected, "I'll have to get a cabin built for us on the farm. I reckon Henry'll help me, so it shouldn't take too long."

"A cabin? Why will we need a cabin?"

"Well . . . to live in."

She put a hand on his chest. "Don't be silly. We'll live right here at Mountain Laurel. There's plenty of room. I'm sure my father will insist that we stay."

Titus stiffened. He had never considered the possibility that Polly might want to stay here. He had figured that by marrying her and moving her to the Brannon farm, he could protect both Polly and the rest of his family when the Yankees came. He didn't care much for the idea of them trying to make a life together here, under Duncan Ebersole's roof.

"I don't know . . . ," he began dubiously.

Polly came up on her toes and kissed him again. "It'll be all right, Titus. You'll see. I know you think you and my father won't get along, but everything will work out."

"I just don't know."

An icy glitter came into her blue eyes. "I thought you said you loved me. You said you'd be the happiest man on the face of the earth if I was your wife."

"That's true. I do love you," Titus insisted.

"Then give me a chance to prove to you that I'm right. After we're married, we'll come here to Mountain Laurel to live."

Titus felt himself nodding, even though a voice in the back of his brain screamed that he was making a huge mistake. "We'll live here at Mountain Laurel," he heard himself promising.

Polly came into his arms again. "And we'll be so happy together," she murmured. She rested her head against his chest, and the scent of her hair filled his senses as he put his arms around her.

Well, he told himself, at least they could give it a try until the Yankees came. His arms tightened around her at that grim reminder of what the future might hold. Once the Yankees came to Culpeper County, everything might be different . . .

Chapter Fourteen

FRUSTRATED BY THE LACK of reinforcements, George B. McClellan continued moving his army closer and closer to Richmond, but its progress was slow. McClellan had expected some forty thousand more troops under the command of Gen. Irvin McDowell to join his forces, but instead of sending McDowell to the peninsula, Lincoln ordered him to northern Virginia, where he was to cross the Blue Ridge Mountains into the Shenandoah Valley and attempt to catch Stonewall Jackson between his forces and those commanded by Gen. John Charles Frémont. It was Lincoln's hope that McDowell and Frémont would crush Jackson and end his threat once and for all.

That left McClellan to push on alone, grinding out the miles over muddy roads and across swollen streams. But day by day, he was coming closer to his goal.

———————

MAC HAD never seen such a downpour in his life. Rain fell from leaden skies in solid sheets. The downpour was so heavy that he didn't see the man riding toward him until the horse was almost on top of him. Mac put up a hand to grab the bridle and yelled, "Whoa!"

The rider reined in and shouted, "Mac? That you?"

Mac recognized both the booming tone and the massive shape of Corporal Hagen. For all his size, the big man was a good scout, able to move quietly and blend into his surroundings. He swung down from his saddle and faced Mac, rain dripping in a steady stream from the brim of his cap, which was wrinkling and softening from being soaked.

"The general sent me to watch for you," Mac called over the downpour. "Said he wanted to see you as soon as you got back." He put a hand on Hagen's arm and led the corporal toward the tent where Jeb Stuart and the other cavalry officers were waiting.

It was a relief to step inside, even though the ground was still muddy underfoot. Several lamps illuminated the inside of the tent; it was only late afternoon, but the heavy overcast made it almost as dark as night. General Stuart and Col. Fitzhugh Lee looked up as Mac and Hagen came in.

"Good to see you, Corporal," Stuart offered as he stepped over to clap a hand on Hagen's arm. "What news do you have for us?"

"Gen'ral McClellan's a damn fool," Hagen reported bluntly. "He's split his army, got two divisions south o' the Chicka-hominy whilst the other three divisions are still north of the river. An' the Chickahominy's risin' by the minute. By tonight, won't anybody be able to get 'crost it."

Stuart frowned, and Mac wondered if the general didn't like the disrespectful way Hagen had referred to McClellan. McClellan might be a Yankee, but he was also a general. Still, enlisted men had been saying worse things about officers—sometimes even their own—ever since there had been armies, Mac supposed.

"Well done, Corporal," Stuart said. "We'll let General Johnston know the situation. Why don't you go get something to eat? I'd tell you to change into some dry clothes, but I doubt that such a thing could be found tonight."

"Don't reckon a little water'll hurt me," rumbled Hagen. "Leastways it never did when I was a boy and my ma made me take a bath once a year."

After Hagen had left, Lee turned to Mac. "Can you take the report to General Johnston?"

Without hesitation, Mac nodded. "Yes sir. Two divisions south of the Chickahominy, three north of it."

"That's right. Unless I miss my guess, General Johnston will decide to attack those two divisions while they're isolated."

Stuart nodded in agreement. "A tactically sound move. McClellan really shouldn't have divided his army."

Mac left the tent and found a horse, leaving the stallion with some of the other mounts under a canopy of tree branches that did little to keep them from getting wet. The stallion hated mud, Mac knew, so he chose another horse, a thickly built chestnut that was good in conditions such as this. He saddled up and rode out toward Richmond, less than a mile away.

During the past week, McClellan's forces had drawn so close to Richmond that their campfires were visible from the roofs of the taller buildings in town. There had been a couple of small battles, one near Savage's Station and the other not far from Hanover Court House, in which the soldiers had clashed briefly then withdrawn. A mingled sense of fear and anticipation hung over the town. The terrified chaos of a few weeks earlier had faded, probably because many of those who were most afraid had already fled Richmond. The government was still in place, however, and Mac knew that a feeling of stubbornness had set in among Davis and his cabinet. Richmond was the capital of the Confederacy, and they weren't going to leave unless it became absolutely necessary.

The darkness was thick by now, but Mac was able to find his way to Johnston's headquarters. A guard stopped him, but when Mac produced his orders stating that he had news from Stuart, the sentry passed him into the building that had been taken over by the general and his staff. Mac reported first to a lieutenant, and a few minutes later, the Confederate commander came down a narrow set of stairs from an upper floor. His collar was unbuttoned and weariness was etched on his face. Mac saluted, all too aware that water was dripping from his clothes onto the rug in the foyer.

"What news do you have for me, Corporal?" asked Johnston.

Mac repeated the information almost like a litany: two Federal divisions south of the Chickahominy, three to the north. Johnston nodded and pressed, "What about the river?"

"By now it's too swollen to cross," Mac told him. "That's what our scout said, and I believe him."

Johnston grunted. "So must General Stuart, or he wouldn't have sent you here to me tonight." The general straightened his back and fastened his collar. "Very well, Corporal. Go back to your general and tell him that you delivered your message as ordered."

"Is there anything else you'd like me to tell him, General?" asked Mac. *Such as what you're planning to do about this*, he thought.

Johnston shook his head. "No, there's no return message. Dismissed."

Mac saluted and left the house. He thought the rain had slacked up a little, but that might have been his imagination. For once, he didn't want the rain to stop. If it did, the river might go down enough for McClellan either to withdraw those two divisions or to reinforce them. Neither alternative would be good for the Confederate cause. Better to leave those Yankee troops sitting there like the tempting target they were, because Johnston was sure to attack them. Mac was no military strategist, but even he could see that this was too good an opportunity to pass up.

They had retreated all the way up the peninsula, Mac told himself as he rode through the rainy night, but now the time had finally come for the Confederacy to strike back.

———————

BY THE next morning, the rain had stopped, but the sky was still thick with gray clouds. Every time the weather cleared and it appeared the spring rains were over, they came back again after a few days, Mac thought as he placed his saddle on the stallion. The horse might not be fond of the mud, but Mac wasn't going to go into battle on any other mount.

The orders had come early this morning, before dawn. The Confederates would advance toward the Union troops south of the Chickahominy and engage them in the vicinity of Seven

Pines, a small settlement where the Williamsburg road and Nine Mile Road intersected. The area was heavily wooded, which would cut down on the ability of the cavalry to take part in the battle, but Stuart planned to be there anyway.

Mac mounted up and rode over to join Lee at the head of his troops. The colonel nodded and said, "Ready to go, Mac?"

"Yes sir. And I'm glad it stopped raining, at least for a while."

Fitz Lee grinned. "Makes it easier to see the enemy, eh?"

"I'm just tired of being soaked all the time."

"It's a soldier's lot in life to be either too hot or too cold, too wet or too dusty. But we tolerate the inconveniences because they allow us to take part in the great events that shape the destiny of mankind."

Mac just nodded. He didn't particularly share the colonel's high-flown attitude. He wasn't here to shape destiny. He just wanted the Yankees to go away and leave the South alone.

A short time later, Stuart arrived, and the cavalry joined Longstreet's division. Stuart had linked himself to Longstreet's troops during the battle of Williamsburg, which Mac had missed because he was at Eltham's Landing. Clearly, Stuart intended to repeat the pattern of that conflict. Mac just hoped that this clash turned out differently, since the Southerners had been forced to retreat at Williamsburg, with considerable loss of life.

Longstreet's division began marching east along the Williamsburg road with Stuart's cavalry bringing up the rear. They had not been on the move for long, however, when Mac became aware of a commotion behind them. He looked back over his shoulder and saw more gray-clad troops on the road where there should not have been any. A lieutenant on horseback galloped alongside the soldiers and passed them, catching up a few minutes later with the cavalry.

"What are you doing here?" the lieutenant demanded angrily. "Who's in charge?"

Stuart reined in and noted quietly, "You'd better pay more attention to rank, young fellow."

The lieutenant paled as he realized he had been shouting at a general and several colonels. He straightened and snapped a crisp salute. "Begging the general's pardon, sir. I was agitated because this is the road that General Huger's division was to take to the front."

Stuart frowned. "There's been some misunderstanding. Those are General Longstreet's men up ahead, and they're on their way to the battle."

"Again, begging your pardon, General, but I believe General Longstreet was supposed to be north of here."

"Come with me, Lieutenant," Stuart ordered with a shake of his head. "We'll speak to General Longstreet and get to the bottom of this." He turned to Lee. "Fitz, keep the men moving."

Lee acknowledged, and Stuart and the lieutenant galloped off toward the front of the Confederate advance.

Mac looked at Lee and asked, "Do you think someone made a mistake, Colonel?"

"It's possible," Lee replied. "Communication between various parts of the army is one of the most difficult—and most important—things about fighting a battle, Mac. Best remember that."

"Yes sir, I will."

The advance continued, with the other division impatiently bringing up the rear behind Longstreet's troops. As the morning passed, Mac listened for the sounds of gunfire in the distance but didn't hear anything. Finally, near midday, Stuart came back to rejoin the cavalry.

His face was set in tight lines under his thick beard. "We are in the wrong place," he said quietly to Lee and the other officers. "Longstreet will have to call a halt and move his men off the road so that Huger can pass us."

"That'll slow things down considerably," Lee pointed out.

"The attack has already been delayed several hours. Couriers have been galloping like madmen trying to get everything straightened out. I'm told that General Johnston is livid."

Mac remained silent as the discussion went on around him, but he took in all the details of the botched attack. Luckily for the Confederate forces, the river was still too high for the Union soldiers to cross, so they could not retreat or get reinforcements. But there was no way of knowing exactly how long that situation would last, Mac thought. If they weren't careful, this opportunity was going to slip away from them.

As Stuart had indicated, Longstreet's division came to a halt and then moved off the Williamsburg road. Huger's division marched rapidly past them, disappearing around a bend in the road, cut off from view by the thick trees. The infantry under Longstreet once again took up the march.

It was difficult to judge the hour since the sky was so overcast, but Mac estimated it was about an hour after noon when rifle fire suddenly rattled in the distance. The sound made the Confederate soldiers, infantry and cavalry alike, surge forward. Obviously, the battle had been joined, and no one wanted to miss it.

"Blast it, we should have been in the forefront of that attack," Stuart complained. "I need someone to find out what's going on." He looked around, and his gaze fell on Mac.

Without hesitation, Mac volunteered, "I'll go, General."

"General," Fitz Lee teased, "you're always commandeering my aide."

Stuart smiled and pointed out, "You heard Corporal Brannon volunteer, Colonel."

Lee waved a hand at Mac. "All right, go on. But steer clear of the actual fighting. We need you to get back safely with your report."

"I want Corporal Hagen to go with you, Brannon," added Stuart. "That way you two can look out for each other." He turned in the saddle and motioned the giant Hagen forward. When Hagen had joined them, Stuart ordered, "You and Corporal Brannon are riding ahead as scouts, Hagen. Bring us word of the battle."

200 • *James Reasoner*

"Yes sir, Gen'ral." Hagen looked at Mac and grinned, but the expression didn't make his face look any less fierce. "Let's go kill us some Yankees."

As the two corporals urged their mounts into motion, Mac pointed out, "The general said we were supposed to act as scouts, not join the battle."

"Yeah, but if any Yankees shoot at us, I'm plannin' on shootin' back at 'em."

Mac couldn't argue with that. He just shrugged and rode on.

The Williamsburg road made a long, gentle curve through a thick stand of woods. Trees pressed in closely on both sides of the path, so that the two riders could see only what was directly ahead of them. The hooves of their horses clattered on the planks of a bridge that spanned a small creek. Up ahead about a quarter of a mile, Mac could see that the trees gave way to a stretch of open, grassy ground on both sides of the road.

The firing was louder now, and Mac could smell the remnants of powder smoke lingering in the heavy, damp air. He and Hagen reached the edge of the trees, and Mac could not help but rein in when he saw the scene spread out before them. Horror made his jaw tighten.

The road ran through the middle of the open ground, and to the left of it the Yankees had constructed a barrier of felled trees with the broken branches pointed toward the Confederate advance. The barrier stretched off to the north for several hundred yards, but the road and the area to its south were still open. Most of the Confederate attack had been able to follow that route and avoid the trees. Most—but not all.

Men were impaled on those sharp branches, some hanging limply from them in death, others still screaming and trying feebly to pull themselves free. Other bodies, some in blue uniforms and some in gray, sprawled among the trunks of the trees.

If the Yankees had had time to erect a similar barrier on the south side of the road, it might have stopped the Confederate attack. As it was, the majority of the Southern troops had been able to sweep on past. Mac saw the remains of a camp on the far side of the barrier and knew that was where the Yankees had spent the previous night. Now the tents were knocked down and trampled in the mud, the ashes of the campfires scattered. Clearly, the Union forces had been knocked back from their positions and made to retreat. Roughly half a mile away, Mac could see the battle still going on, surging waves of blue and gray seen only dimly through the clouds of smoke that hung over the conflict. The roar of artillery and rifle fire filled the air as well, along with something else, something that sounded more animal than human. After a moment Mac recognized it as the grim harmony of thousands of struggling soldiers as they fought and died.

Mac's hands held tightly to the stallion's reins. This was the first large-scale battle he had witnessed. He looked to the north and saw that the fighting had spread in that direction, too, into another stretch of woods that lay between the Williamsburg road and the Richmond and York River Railroad. The front was at least two miles long, and Mac recalled a mention of more Confederate troops coming down from the northwest along Nine Mile Road. Those forces must have engaged the Yankees, too.

"Dadgum, that looks like a mighty fine scrap!" Hagen exclaimed from beside him. "Reckon we can get in on it?"

Mac shook his head. "We're just here to gather information." He tried to force his mind to regard what he was seeing dispassionately. "Come on." Turning the stallion off the road to the north, he put the horse into a trot across the open field. Corporal Hagen followed, somewhat reluctantly.

The two men skirted the makeshift barrier of the fallen trees and reached the edge of the woods. They followed the tree line in a looping course that took them to the northeast, keeping the woods on their left and the open ground to their right. Mac halted from time to time to study the situation with his field glasses. He saw that the Northerners had constructed another, larger barrier about half a mile beyond the first one, but it had not stopped the Confederate attack, either. The Southern troops were steadily driving the Federal forces back toward the village of Seven Pines, which Mac could barely see in the distance.

The trees closed in so that Mac and Hagen were forced to make their way through them as they moved closer to the northern fringes of the battle. After a few minutes, they began to see wounded and dead men from both sides lying on the ground under the canopy of branches. They came to a Confederate aid station in a small clearing where a couple of doctors in shirtsleeves were tending to the wounded. The men's shirts had once been white. Now they were gray and heavily stained with sweat and blood and gore.

Mac reined in and saluted one of the medicos who glanced up at him. The insignia on the man's hat indicated he was a colonel. He didn't return the salute, just growled, "What do you want, Corporal?"

"We're scouts from General Stuart's cavalry, sir," Mac informed him. "We're trying to determine the situation so that we can report back to the general."

The doctor had a face like a bulldog. The sleeves of his shirt were red to the elbows. He grimaced and growled, "It's the same as always—damned bloody." Then, sighing, he went on, "But I reckon that won't do you any good with your general, so I'll tell you what I know. We've pushed the Yankees back to Seven Pines on the right of our advance and up to a place called Fair Oaks Station on the left. They're retreating all across the front, or so I've heard. But that doesn't mean they'll keep running. Now, I've got to get back to my butchering."

Mac suppressed a shudder that went through him and turned to Hagen. "Let's ride on back to the general. I think we know enough now."

Hagen still looked disappointed that they hadn't gotten in any of the action, but he turned his horse and followed Mac.

They rode as quickly as they could back along the path they had followed, and when they reached the Williamsburg road again, they found that Longstreet's forces had moved up to the edge of the open ground.

It took a few minutes to locate Stuart. Once they had, Mac passed along the information they had gathered, and Stuart nodded and rode off to confer with Longstreet. Lee reined his horse closer to Mac's and said, "You look a little green around the gills, Mac. How bad was it?"

"Bad enough, sir," Mac answered quietly.

"You saw men die at Eltham's Landing," Lee pointed out.

"Never so many," murmured Mac with a shake of his head. "Never so many."

Lee's voice hardened. "That's what war is about, Corporal. Whether we live or die is up to a power much greater than ourselves."

"Yes sir," Mac managed to say.

Stuart returned a short time later to say that Longstreet was sending his men forward to reinforce the Confederate divisions that were still engaging the Yankees.

"We're moving up to Fair Oaks to see what the situation is there," continued Stuart. He looked at Mac. "Corporal, you've been over the ground before, at least part of the way. Is there a road that will take us up there?"

Mac frowned and forced himself to remember the details of the terrain he had seen earlier in the day. He and Hagen had made their way through the trees, but he had noticed a small road, little more than a trail, actually, that had angled northward from the open battlefield.

"There's a road that must intersect Nine Mile Road somewhere north of here," Mac said. "That goes right to Fair Oaks, doesn't it?"

"Indeed it does," Stuart agreed. "I recall that from the maps. Very well, gentlemen . . ." The general turned his horse. "Let's ride!"

Chapter Fifteen

JEB STUART WAS NOT the only officer who had decided to move toward Fair Oaks. When the cavalry reached the trail that cut through the woods toward Nine Mile Road, they found that one of Longstreet's brigades, commanded by Gen. Richard H. Anderson, had already fought its way up the path and divided the Yankees who were trying to form a defensive line in the trees. Stuart signaled his men to halt. The path was narrow and clogged with infantry troops. There was no way the cavalry could get through. Stuart's horse pranced back and forth impatiently, as if sensing its master's frustration.

Mac and Colonel Lee were a short distance behind the general. Lee glared around at the trees. "Blast these woods! The cavalry can't operate efficiently in terrain such as this."

"Maybe we should pull back," Mac suggested.

Lee shook his head. "The general wants to see what's going on. I suppose we'll just have to wait until the way is clear."

That meant sitting there as the afternoon wore on and listening to the roar of artillery and the crackle of rifle fire. Late in the day the sounds of battle intensified from the north, and Mac knew the clash around Fair Oaks Station must have gotten worse.

News of the battle began to filter back from the front. Stuart stopped a courier who came galloping down the path through the woods, and Mac was able to overhear the soldier's breathless report. Confederate thrusts had sliced through the Union lines at several points, dividing the Yankees in their efforts to form a defensive line but also leaving the Confederate forces vulnerable to counterattacks along both flanks. Johnston himself had led a large Confederate force down from the north along Nine Mile Road toward Fair Oaks, only to encounter unexpectedly stiff resistance when they got there.

That accounted for the surge in the firing they had heard earlier, Mac thought. Despite the resistance, Johnston had been on the verge of overwhelming the Northerners when, from somewhere, Federal reinforcements had arrived.

The courier wiped the back of his hand across his mouth and said, "Nobody knows how, but the Yankees got some men across the Chickahominy some way, General. All the bridges must not have washed out in the flood after all."

"How do things stand now?" Stuart asked.

"When I left, the fightin' was still hot and heavy, sir. We're pushin' 'em back, but it's mighty slow work."

Stuart nodded. "Where are you bound with this news?"

"Supposed to take it to General Longstreet, sir. I don't reckon I know what he can do about it, though. Looks like he's got his hands full down here."

That was true, Mac decided. If the battle had not developed so that it had to be fought on two fronts, at both Seven Pines and Fair Oaks, the Confederate forces could have linked up and possibly destroyed the two Union divisions. As it was, though, everything had been delayed long enough for the Federals to bring in reinforcements.

The courier went on his way, and Stuart, making up his mind, waved his men forward. The sounds of fighting had diminished up ahead on the trail, and the general obviously still wanted to reach Fair Oaks before nightfall.

The horses trotted along the muddy road, the line of cavalrymen stretching out lengthily because no more than two or three could ride abreast. Mac was near the front of the column, right behind Colonel Lee. Several times as they rode through the gathering dusk, snipers fired at them from the concealment of the thick growth. The shots were always returned, but the riders had no way of knowing if their bullets hit any of the Union riflemen. Bodies littered the trail, and although Mac knew the callousness with which they were ridden over was necessary, it still sickened him.

After half a mile, the trail met Nine Mile Road, which was wider and more firmly packed, but still muddy and also strewn with corpses. The battle had moved on from this point, so that Stuart and his men were able to ride unmolested to Fair Oaks. Artillery and rifle fire still sounded clearly from the east, however.

Fair Oaks consisted of a small depot, where Nine Mile Road crossed the railroad tracks, and several farmhouses. Seeing a great many horses at one of them, Stuart rode toward the house with Lee and Mac. As they came to a halt, two men stepped out. Even in the gathering shadows, Mac recognized the president and General Lee.

Stuart came to attention and saluted, as did his men. "President Davis," he said. "I didn't expect to find you and General Lee here."

Lee returned the salute. "At ease, General. The president and I rode out here to see how the battle is coming along. We have arrived only to find unfortunate news, however."

"I thought the battle was going well, General, from what I've been able to gather."

Lee inclined his head toward the door of the farmhouse. "I was speaking of General Johnston's injuries."

This was the first any of them had heard of Johnston's being wounded. As the cavalrymen dismounted, Stuart said, "I was unaware of the situation, General. What happened?"

"As I understand it, General Johnston was checking the disposition of the troops a short time ago when he was struck in the shoulder by a musket ball. No sooner had that happened than a fragment from a bursting shell also struck him in the chest."

"Is he alive?" asked Stuart.

Lee nodded. "Yes, but his injuries are quite serious."

"Then who is in command of the army?"

Davis answered that question. "I have just placed General Lee in overall command of our forces, General."

Stuart and Lee looked at each other for a second, then Stuart nodded.

"General Smith is still in command in the field," Lee explained, referring to Gustavus W. Smith, who had been Johnston's second in command. "We seem to be at something of a stalemate with the Federal forces here at Fair Oaks. How have we fared at Seven Pines?"

"The Yankees have been pushed well back to the east of the crossroads," Stuart reported. "They must have formed three defensive lines during the day, but they've had to abandon each of them in turn."

"Very good." Lee looked up at the now fully dark sky. "More hostilities will have to wait until tomorrow. The men are exhausted and must rest."

"We'll make our camp here, then, and be ready for whatever tomorrow brings." Stuart turned to his men and issued the orders.

Mac gave the stallion some of his meager supply of grain and picketed the horse where it could crop some grass growing in tufts from the mud. After holding off all day, a light drizzle began to fall as the men were making camp. In the dampness it was almost impossible to get a fire going, so they had cold rations for supper. The guns had finally fallen silent with the coming of night, but the woods all around were haunted by the cries of wounded and dying men.

Mac hunkered on his heels with his back against the trunk of a tree and gnawed on a piece of stale pone even though he wasn't really hungry. As he grew wetter from the rain, he looked up and saw that the top of the tree against which he leaned had been blown away by artillery fire. Slowly, he moved to another tree, seeking a drier place to spend what promised to be a long night.

MAC JERKED awake to the sound of gunfire. During the night he had slumped down at the base of the tree and slept in the mud. Despite the fact that it was June 1, the nightlong drizzle had chilled him, and his stiff muscles protested painfully as he hauled himself to his feet and looked around for the source of the firing.

The fighting wasn't close by, he realized, but it was near enough that the sounds of the struggle had roused everyone in the cavalry camp. Troopers were rushing around, catching their horses and throwing saddles on their backs. Mac spotted Col. Fitzhugh Lee striding through the confusion, calling orders to mount up.

Mac hurried over to where he had left the stallion picketed. The horse was still there. Mac got the blanket and saddle on the stallion, who turned its head and gave him a baleful look. "Don't blame me," Mac told the animal. "I can't help it if it's raining."

The stallion snorted, its nostrils flaring. Mac understood its disgust as well as if the horse had spoken in English. He had always been that way, able to communicate better with animals than most people could. They seemed to understand him, and he certainly understood them.

When the cinch was tightened, Mac untied the picket rope and swung up into the saddle, tugging his campaign cap down tighter on his head. He joined Colonel Lee, who had also mounted one of the horses.

Mac could tell now that the firing was coming from the east, along the railroad tracks. Fitz Lee grinned at him in the early morning light and observed, "Sounds like the Yankees didn't waste any time in putting up a fight."

"Did we attack again this morning?" asked Mac.

Lee nodded. "General Stuart has informed me that Generals Smith and Longstreet talked it over during the night and decided to launch a two-pronged attack to push the Yankees north of the railroad and farther east of Seven Pines. I imagine that's what we're hearing now."

"What are we supposed to do?"

"Well, as you might expect, the general wants to go take a look and see if there's any fighting we can get in on. In fact, I believe he's ready to go right now."

Stuart cantered up on his horse, and Mac wondered fleetingly how he managed to keep the ostrich plume on his hat looking so dashing in this damp weather. Stuart smiled at them, called, "Good morning, gentlemen," to his troops, and then waved them forward, taking the lead himself.

They started riding on the northern side of the tracks, but they had gone less than a quarter of a mile when bullets suddenly sang overhead and a cannon roared somewhere nearby. It was light enough now for Mac to see men in blue uniforms running toward them, and he realized that the Yankees were launching a counterattack. Either that, or the Confederate attack had not even gotten started before the Yankees struck first. At any rate, they were in trouble.

Stuart motioned to his right and shouted over his shoulder, "Across the tracks!" His cavalrymen responded instantly, veering their horses down the shallow embankment to the roadbed where the tracks ran. They thundered across and up the embankment on the other side. To the south, the woods came up almost to the tracks. In a matter of moments, the cavalry was among the trees. They had to slow down, but at least now they had some shelter from the Yankee bullets.

The riders splashed across a shallow creek and twisted their way through the undergrowth until they reached Nine Mile Road. They followed it until the sound of heavy firing was loud to their left. Mac sniffed the air and grimaced. Powder smoke and blood. Once a man had smelled enough of either of them, he never forgot what they were like.

An officer on horseback galloped up. He was hatless, and his left arm hung limply in a bloodstained sleeve. He reined in with some difficulty and called to Stuart, "What unit is this? Where's Longstreet?"

"I'm General Stuart. What do you have to report, Major?"

The major sat on his horse for a moment, breathing heavily, then said, "I'm from General Mahone's brigade. We're taking heavy losses between here and the railroad. The Yankees came across early this morning. General Longstreet was supposed to send more men, but we haven't seen them."

Stuart shook his head. "I don't know where your reinforcements are, Major. We're on our way to the battle from Fair Oaks. You say the Yankees attacked first?"

"Yes sir," the major replied. He was pale, and Mac thought he might pass out and fall off his horse at any moment. "I've got to find those reinforcements and make sure they get to the front."

Stuart turned and said to Lee, "Fitz, you and your men go with the major and help him find General Longstreet."

Lee looked angry. "But General, if the fighting is up ahead—"

"Then General Mahone needs those reinforcements," Stuart cut in. "See that he gets them."

"Yes sir," Lee answered tautly. He wheeled his horse and motioned for his men to do likewise. The wounded major accompanied them.

They rode to the south, on the lookout for Longstreet's forces coming toward them. After making their way through the woods for nearly half a mile without sighting any reinforcements, Lee drew his mount to a halt.

"Where are they?" he asked, without really expecting an answer. "If the attack was to come this morning, our troops should already be moving toward the front."

"Maybe all the brigades didn't start at the same time," Mac suggested.

Lee looked at him with a frown. "Or perhaps someone didn't understand the orders. Longstreet may be just sitting down there waiting." He glanced over his shoulder in the direction Stuart had taken when the cavalry split up. The firing was still heavy that way. "No telling what Beauty has run into," Lee muttered.

Mac could tell that the colonel was considering disobeying Stuart's order and rushing back to the front. The major must have seen that, too, because he said, "I'm going on to find General Longstreet, Colonel, as I was told to do."

Lee stiffened in his saddle. "And I was told to see that you accomplished your mission, Major, so that is what I intend to do." He waved the cavalrymen on again.

Mac tried not to heave a sigh of relief. He would have done as Lee commanded unquestioningly, even if that meant disregarding Stuart's orders, but he wouldn't have liked it. For one thing, he was afraid such insubordination on the part of the colonel would have ruined the long-time friendship between Lee and Stuart.

The riders pushed on through the woods, only to halt a few minutes later when they encountered Confederate troops fleeing through the trees from their left. The men were running wildly, in a total rout. One of them yelled at the cavalrymen, "Get the hell out of here! The Yankees are right behind us!"

Lee leaned down from the saddle and grabbed the collar of one of the men, jerking him to a halt. "Hold on, soldier! What unit are you from?"

"The . . . the Fifth Virginia, sir," the breathless trooper panted.

"General Armistead's battalion?"

The soldier nodded. "Yes sir."

"What about the attack?"

"What attack?" the soldier asked, a note of hysteria creeping into his voice. "The Yankees jumped us before we even got started!"

That confirmed the fears they had all had, thought Mac. Somehow, the Northerners had seized the advantage, even though they had been beaten back consistently the day before. The fresh troops that McClellan had gotten across the Chickahominy late in the afternoon must have swung the balance to the side of the Federals.

"Is the retreat widespread?" Lee questioned the soldier he had stopped.

"Hell, it's all the way across the front!" The trooper was trembling now and casting apprehensive glances over his shoulder in the direction he had come from. The firing from that direction was growing louder almost by the minute. Cannon began to crash somewhere nearby.

Lee let go of the soldier's collar and motioned him on. The man broke into a run without looking back again. Lee turned toward the wounded major and said bleakly, "It looks as if General Mahone isn't going to get his reinforcements, Major. And it seems that it wouldn't matter even if he did."

"I think you're right, Colonel. Still, I have to try to locate General Longstreet, as I was commanded to do."

Lee nodded. "Yes, and we were told to go with you, so that's what we'll do. But I think it would be wise to alter our course a bit, so to speak. I believe we'll find the general farther toward the rear than we first anticipated."

Mac heard a note of bitterness in Lee's voice. It could be he blamed Longstreet for not acting more quickly to reinforce the units on the front line when the Yankee counterattack came. Mac could see where such hesitation—if that was indeed what had happened—could prove fatal in a battle.

Bullets began to whip through the tree branches. Lee called to his men, "Follow me!" and turned to send his horse plunging through the woods. Mac and the other troopers followed. A few minutes later they crossed Nine Mile Road, but instead of turning onto it, Lee waved them into the woods on the far side. The road would have taken them across the front of the Union advance, and right now they wanted to put as much distance between themselves and the Federals as possible.

Mac was riding beside Lee, and the colonel said to him, "By God, I hate this! I'd rather turn and fight them, but in these trees, we wouldn't be able to maneuver."

"We should be getting to some open ground soon," Mac observed.

True to that prediction, they broke out of the forest less than five minutes later. In the distance, they could see the Williamsburg road, two houses, and a line of earthworks behind which were Confederate riflemen and artillery batteries. They were well west of Seven Pines now, Mac estimated, and the fortifications were evidence that the Southern forces were setting up a defensive line and had lost almost all the previous day's gains.

The cavalry galloped around the earthworks, and Lee led them to a makeshift command post, where he reined in and saluted an officer who stood there. Mac didn't recognize him, but Lee said, "General Hill, sir. Colonel Lee and his men, at your disposal."

Hill nodded grumpily. "Colonel. I fear I have no tasks suitable for you save that of functioning as our rear guard."

"We're pulling back, sir?"

"To our positions near Richmond, yes. Those are our orders."

"Sir, have you seen General Stuart?"

Hill shook his head. "No, Colonel, I have not. Is he supposed to be in this vicinity?"

"He was going to attempt to link up with General Mahone, I believe."

"Then he has likely been routed, too," Hill said.

Lee looked as if he wanted to challenge the very idea that Jeb Stuart could ever be routed, but he controlled his thoughts. "It would be our honor to help protect the retreat, sir."

That must have cost him some effort, Mac thought. To a man such as Fitz Lee, there was never any honor in retreat.

But as the day went on and the defensive line moved ever backward, Lee and his men did their best to cover the Confederate soldiers who were pulling back to Richmond. They dashed back and forth along the Williamsburg road, harassing any attempt by the Yankees to catch up. At midday, Stuart and the rest of the cavalry joined them, and Lee was pleased to see his friend and commander again.

"Well, our thrust against the Yankees was a success, Fitz," Stuart declared after the two men had shaken hands. "We dealt them a hard blow. Their losses were considerable."

Mac, riding behind the two men, frowned. He didn't see how Stuart could consider what had happened over the past two days a Confederate victory. True, they had gained a great deal of ground the first day, but they had lost it all today. And the goal had been to destroy those two Union divisions while they were isolated south of the Chickahominy. As far as Mac could see, that effort had been a failure.

"We've shown them that we can fight," Stuart went on.

That was true enough, Mac supposed. But surely, after Manassas and all the other battles that had taken place, the Yankees knew that their Southern opponents could fight.

The question now, Mac thought grimly, was whether or not they could ever win.

Chapter Sixteen

WILL BRANNON WOKE TO the sound of singing. It was a hymn, he realized a moment later, a hymn that he was very familiar with from all the times he had sung it in the Baptist church at Culpeper. He sat up, rolled his shoulders to ease the stiffness in his neck, and looked around.

The morning sun was bright. There had been a few more rain showers during the first week of June, but for the most part the weather had been glorious in the Shenandoah Valley, so much so that Will had slept outside the night before instead of in his tent.

A grin stretched across his face as he walked over to one of the campfires and accepted a cup of coffee from a private with a nod of thanks. He felt a swell of pride as he listened to the singing. How these men could find the energy to sing after all they had been through was beyond him, but he was glad that they could.

Since the battle at Winchester and the foray up toward Harpers Ferry, Jackson had driven his troops mercilessly, marching them south at a pace that would have killed some men. Even burdened with prisoners and wagons full of captured supplies, Jackson's army had made amazing strides, covering sometimes close to thirty miles in a day's time. With Union forces looming to both east and west, the forced march had enabled the Confederates to slip away from the two enemy armies. Now they were camped near the village of Cross Keys, a short distance behind the front lines established by forces under the command of Gen. Richard S. Ewell.

Capt. Yancy Lattimer came walking up to the campfire and nodded to Will. "Morning," he said. "Sleep well?"

"Like a baby," Will replied dryly. "It was almost too quiet, though."

"I know what you mean. By the time this war is over, I'll probably need the sound of cannon to soothe me to sleep."

It would be all right with him, thought Will, if he never heard an artillery barrage again. Or a volley of fire from thousands of rifles at once. He was used to the sounds of battle, but he wouldn't miss them if they were gone forever.

Yancy inclined his head away from the fire, and he and Will strolled a short distance away so that they would be out of earshot of the enlisted men. "The scouts say that Frémont is close by to the west," Yancy said quietly. "He'll probably move against our positions today."

Will nodded. "I wouldn't be surprised. He's got to be upset that we slipped out of the trap he and McDowell tried to set for us."

"General Jackson says we'll support Ewell's lines, but he's counting on Ewell to drive the Yankees back."

"He's in a good place to do it," Will noted.

Late the previous afternoon, Will had ridden up to the front lines of the Confederate position so that he could see for himself what the situation was. He knew that Ewell had placed his men along a ridge overlooking a large area of open field where the Federals would have little or no cover. Ewell's artillery batteries were in the center of the line, ready to lay down a heavy fire across the field when the Federals started forward. Unless the Federals' numbers were larger than what the Confederate scouts had reported, Will didn't think it would be possible for Frémont to win this engagement.

Frémont would have to try, though. Jackson's exploits up and down the Valley had to have the Yankees in a tizzy. They didn't know where he would strike next, and even though he was moving away from Washington at the moment, they couldn't be certain that he no longer represented a threat to the Union capital. At an officers meeting the night before, Will had heard that Shields was moving back down from the north with his men in an attempt to catch up to Jackson.

That had not been all the news to arrive in the Confederate camp. Word had also come that Turner Ashby, the commander of Jackson's cavalry, had been killed the day before in a skirmish with some of Frémont's advance guard. Ashby had been struck in the chest by a bullet and killed instantly, and the news of his death had shaken Jackson considerably. The general had ordered that the body of his friend and trusted subordinate be taken to the state university in Charlottesville and buried there, since Ashby's hometown of Fauquier City was now under the control of Union forces.

Will expected Jackson to recover quickly from the news of Ashby's death, even though Ashby's loss as a commander was significant. A few minutes later, as he was finishing his coffee and chatting with Yancy, he saw the general striding through the camp. Jackson seemed quite animated, pausing several times to exchange comments with the enlisted men around the fires. He spotted Will and Yancy and came toward them.

"Good morning, gentlemen," he greeted them. "Are you ready to cross swords with the enemy today?"

"Of course," Yancy answered without hesitation.

"I reckon," Will spoke more laconically.

"Not that we should be required to do so," Jackson went on. "I fully expect that General Ewell's batteries will be more than sufficient to repel General Frémont's advance. And once General Frémont has been stymied, we shall turn our attention to General Shields."

Shields represented a threat, all right, thought Will. Gen. Irvin McDowell was sitting off to the east with a sizable force, but he didn't seem to be going anywhere. Shields, however, was closing in on the Confederate army from the north, following the Shenandoah River down the Valley. Jackson had seen to it, however, that Shields was prevented from linking up with Frémont by having all the bridges along Shields's route burned. That way Jackson could deal with each of the Union generals individually.

A rumble like thunder sounded in the distance, but the sky was clear overhead. Jackson swung in that direction and exclaimed, "Ah, the battle commences!" He looked back at Will and Yancy. "Best see to your troops, gentlemen."

The officers weren't the only ones who had heard the cannonfire. The soldiers were already putting out their fires, picking up their rifles, and getting ready to move out if necessary. Will threw a brief wave of farewell at Yancy, then strode over to make sure the men of his company were doing as they were supposed to. He saw to his satisfaction that Sgt. Darcy Bennett was already forming them into ranks.

Will picked up his hat, which he had left under the tree where he'd slept, then found his horse. One of the hostlers had already put the saddle on the dun. Will swung onto the horse and rode back to his company.

He waited there, time stretching out interminably, as an intense artillery duel took place a mile or two away. A few shells burst closer than that, and after each explosion, the troopers in the ranks looked at each other. They didn't mind fighting, but they didn't like the idea of just standing there while a barrage came closer and closer.

Neither did Will. He fingered the hilt of his sword and wished Jackson would give the order to move forward. Such an order didn't come, however. So Will and the other men were forced to wait, and as they did so, the tension among them grew.

Finally, past midday, a courier came by and passed the word that the company commanders were wanted forward. Will rode up to join the other officers and found them congregated with Gen. Charles Winder, the field commander of the Stonewall Brigade. Winder was something of a martinet and was not well liked by either the officers or the enlisted men, but so far during the Shenandoah Valley campaign, he had proven to be an effective commander.

"At General Jackson's order, we are withdrawing to Port Republic," announced Winder. The settlement of Port Republic, on the south fork of the Shenandoah River, was only a short distance away.

A few mutters of discontent came from the officers, but Winder silenced them with an icy glare. He continued, "General Ewell's forces are dealing successfully with the enemy at Cross Keys. We shall be prepared to meet them at Port Republic if necessary."

That was pretty likely, Will decided. Shields had closed the gap between his forces and those of the Confederates, and the Union general had to be still smarting from the spankings Jackson had given him twice before. Shields would want revenge, and he wouldn't stop until he caught up to Jackson and had one more crack at him.

They had their orders. Will rode back to his company and directed Darcy to turn them around and start them marching down the road to Port Republic.

EVEN THOUGH the heavy rains had been over for several days, the Shenandoah River was still running high and fast in most places. This was true at Port Republic, where the south fork joined the main stream of the river. The bridge here had been burned, but upon arrival, Jackson decided that he wanted his men on the other side. To accomplish that as quickly as possible, the general hit on the audacious idea of driving wagons into the river and placing thick planks across them to form a crude bridge. He supervised this effort personally, even though the work lasted well into the night.

Watching the makeshift bridge take shape, Will thought it was just like the general. Jackson seldom did what anyone expected of him, which was probably why he had been able to elude the Yankees pursuing him for more than a month, hitting them where and when he wanted to and defeating them at every turn. Jackson's forces had won every battle in this campaign except the one at Kernstown, and even in defeat that engagement had served its purpose. Jackson had announced that day to the Federals that they would ignore him at their own peril.

Also during the evening, reports had come in concerning the battle at Cross Keys. The artillery batteries of General Ewell had indeed wreaked havoc on Frémont's advance, and instead of fighting merely a defensive battle, the Confederate right side had actually forged ahead, inflicting heavy losses on the Yankees and throwing them back. With the Confederates now entrenched on his left flank, Frémont had been paralyzed. He had broken off the fight and retreated, giving the Southerners yet another victory.

In the early morning, most of Ewell's men arrived in Port Republic, having left behind only a small force at Cross Keys to keep Frémont in check. With his forces bolstered by Ewell's arrival, Jackson was ready to strike the first blow instead of waiting for it to fall. He ordered the Stonewall Brigade to advance across the bridge of wagons and along a road that led through rolling farmland. Scouts had already galloped back to Jackson's headquarters with the news that the Yankees under Shields were closing in on the same farm.

As the Thirty-third Virginia reached the bridge, Will dismounted and led his horse across it, not fully trusting the planks. His men followed him, and once they had made it to the east side of the river without incident, they formed into their regular ranks once more and joined the column marching up the road.

Will rode alongside them, and when he glanced at Darcy, he saw a huge grin on the burly sergeant's face. Darcy was spoiling for a fight. They all were, himself included, Will realized. They had gone for over a week now without seeing any combat, and they were more than ready for another tussle with the Federals.

Once again, Will felt a surge of pride go through him, just as he had the previous morning when he had wakened to hear the men singing a hymn. They were magnificent fighters, each and every one of them.

They reached the farm and started across it, and suddenly from up ahead came a rattle of rifle fire. A volley ripped out from the top of a slight rise. Will heard the whipcrack of bullets passing close by his head. Near him, some of his men grunted or cried out in pain and stumbled. A couple of them fell.

The pride Will had felt a moment earlier turned into anger. He ripped his saber from its sheath and yelled, "At 'em, boys! Charge! Charge!"

Goading the dun into a run, Will galloped forward. An answering volley came from the Confederate troops as they moved ahead, following Will and the other officers. But then more shots came from the rise, and more men fell. The charge faltered and seemed in danger of coming apart. Will reined in and shouted encouragement at the men, but he had a horrible feeling that the attack was on the verge of collapsing before it even got started.

Then, suddenly, another figure on horseback was behind the men, bellowing commands and waving his arm. Gen. Thomas J. Jackson was in the thick of the fight, urging his men on personally. Will saw the general and thought that although the late General Bee might not have meant it too kindly when he referred to Jackson as "Stonewall," there was a great deal of truth to the nickname. Jackson was not going to allow his men to be defeated if there was anything he could do to prevent it.

Will wheeled his horse around toward the front and kicked it into a run again. He saw a spurt of smoke and flame from up ahead on his left and heard the roar of a cannon. The shell whistled by overhead as Will turned his mount toward a Union artillery battery at the top of a small hill.

Rebel yells sounded behind him. He glanced back and saw Darcy and the other men of his company following him. They went up the hill like a gray wave with him at its crest. Yankee infantrymen assigned to guard the cannon and its crew fired frantically down into the Confederate charge. Will felt something pluck at his shirt sleeve, and a second later, something cut one of the reins he held gathered in his left hand. The dun was running gallantly, though, and the loss of one rein meant nothing. Will guided the horse with his knees as much as he did the reins, anyway.

Will reached the top of the hill only seconds before his men swarmed the battery after him. He slashed back and forth with the saber as several Yankees lunged at him. Darcy and the other men struggled hand-to-hand with the Union defenders. Will dropped the reins completely, switched the saber to his left hand, and pulled his pistol with his right.

From the corner of his eye he saw one of the Federal gunners swinging a long pole at him. It was one of the poles they used to swab out the barrel of the cannon after each shot, so it had cotton wrapped around its end. That wouldn't stop the pole itself from cracking open his skull if it hit him, Will knew. He ducked, leaning forward over the neck of the horse, and let the pole pass over his head. While the Yankee who had swung it was off balance, Will smacked the flat of his saber across the man's temple, stunning him and dropping him to the ground.

The dun twisted around as Will's knees clamped on its flanks. He saw a knot of blue-clad Federals running toward the gun emplacement, obviously bent on reinforcing the men who were trying to defend it against the Confederates. Will emptied his pistol into them and saw several of the men stumble and go down. There was no time to reload, so he jammed the gun back in the holster and drove the dun forward into the charging Yankees, hacking at them with the saber.

The dun trampled one man, and Will cut down two more. He felt a heavy blow against his right side and reeled in the saddle for a second, then caught himself. He thought that one of the Northerners had slammed a rifle butt into him. Wincing in pain, he clamped his right arm down against the area of the blow and realized that it was wet. He had been wounded.

Someone grabbed his left leg and tried to pull him off the horse. Will slashed at the man's face and felt the edge of the blade grate across bone. The Yankee fell back, blood sheeting down over his features. Will turned the dun and saw Darcy Bennett and the other men of the company polishing off the last of the Federals around the cannon. He heeled the horse toward them.

Darcy saw Will coming and sprang to catch him as a wave of dizziness finally sent him plummeting out of the saddle. Will felt Darcy's strong arms close around him and hold him upright. "Cap'n! You're hit!" Darcy cried.

Will didn't think the wound was too bad. His right side was going numb, but he could still use his arm and his head seemed clear. He felt extremely weak, nevertheless he ordered, "Get that cannon turned around so we can use it on the Yankees!"

"You need some tendin' to," Darcy protested.

"The cannon!" Will insisted.

"Yes sir!" Darcy turned his head and bellowed, "Turn this damn cannon around!"

Will saw a wooden crate sitting on the ground and pulled free from Darcy's grip so that he could lower himself on it. Darcy had better things to do than stand around and hold him up. Will managed to get his saber back in its scabbard, then fumbled out his pistol and began awkwardly reloading it. His right arm worked, but not well. Still, he managed to get fresh rounds loaded in all the chambers and then gripped the Colt in his left hand. He wasn't as good with that hand, but he could still generally hit what he was aiming at.

From where he was sitting, he could see across the river to where another part of the battle was going on. Those were probably Frémont's men over there, he thought, pushing down from Cross Keys, slowed but not stopped by the men General Ewell had left behind. And on this side of the river, the

230 • *James Reasoner*

Stonewall Brigade had its hands full with the Yankees under Shields. Will pondered that Jackson's audacity had backfired. This might be the day that their side finally came up short.

"Here they come again!" Darcy yelled, and when Will looked toward the north, he saw a fresh wave of Union soldiers bearing down on them. Darcy had gotten the cannon turned around, however, and even though the men of Will's company weren't artillerymen, they knew how to load and fire the thing. The cannon roared and bucked on its carriage, and the shell burst in the middle of the Yankee charge. A volley from the Confederate rifles did even more damage and slowed the Federals long enough for the cannon to be reloaded. It thundered once more.

Will came to his feet and lifted the pistol in his left hand. He fired, pausing deliberately between each shot to cock and aim, and saw a couple of the Yankees go down.

That was the last thing he saw, because the brightness of the day suddenly turned dark, and though he felt himself falling to the side, he was unconscious by the time he hit the ground.

WILL BECAME aware of a rocking motion underneath him. It felt almost like he was on a boat, but he knew that was impossible. As pain welled up inside him, along with awareness, he realized that he was in the back of a wagon.

Something jostled his arm. He opened his eyes, turned his head despite the extra pain that caused, and saw the pale, haggard features of a man who was either dead or unconscious. Will hoped it was the latter. He hoped he hadn't been pitched in the back of a wagon with a bunch of corpses.

A groan came from the man beside him, putting that fear to rest. He was in an ambulance wagon. He tried to lift his head, but a hand on his shoulder gently pressed him back.

"You just rest easy, Cap'n." The rumbling voice belonged to Darcy Bennett.

"Darcy," rasped Will. "Wh . . . where's the company?"

"Don't you worry, Cap'n. They're all fine." A grim note entered Darcy's voice as he added, "Them that made it through the fightin'."

"Did we . . . beat the Yankees?"

"Damn right. It was a mite chancy there for a while, but then General Taylor's Louisiana boys come up and give us a hand. We sent them Yanks runnin' back north."

Will closed his eyes and heaved a deep sigh, grimacing at the twinge that caused in his side. He realized now that the tightness he felt around his middle was bandages.

"How bad was I hit?" he asked as he looked up at Darcy again.

"Not too bad. The bullet just sort of dug a hunk of meat outta your side. Didn't hit nothin' inside, the sawbones said. You just passed out 'cause you lost so much blood. The doc poured half a bottle of perfectly good whiskey over it and wrapped you up, said to keep you quiet for a few days and you'd be fine. Where we're goin', I reckon you'll have a chance to rest up for a little while, at least."

"Where . . . are we . . . going?" Will asked. He was suddenly feeling tired again, and he could hardly keep his eyes open.

"To the closest railroad station, first of all," he heard Darcy say as his eyelids dropped closed. "And then, accordin' to ol' Stonewall, we're goin' to Richmond."

Chapter Seventeen

G ENTLEMEN, IN TEN MINUTES every man must be in his saddle!"

Mac heard the words, spoken in the loud, clear voice of Gen. Jeb Stuart, but for a moment his groggy brain refused to comprehend them. He pulled himself into a sitting position on his cot and shook his head, trying to clear away the cobwebs.

Stuart stood at the entrance of the tent, holding back the canvas flap with one gauntleted hand. Around Mac, officers were scrambling out of their bedding and reaching for their clothes and boots. Fitzhugh Lee, who had the cot next to Mac's, muttered under his breath, and Mac understood only the words, ". . . Beauty . . . up to something . . ."

Mac had an idea what it might be, too, but only a hunch. Several days earlier, after Stuart's cavalry had reestablished their camp known as Quien Sabe, Stuart had vanished on some mysterious errand accompanied only by a new aide of his, a Prussian mercenary with the unlikely name of Heros Von Borcke. A giant of a man, almost as large as the fierce Corporal Hagen, he had joined the Confederate cause as much for the thrill of being in the war as for the money he was being paid. Stuart and Von Borcke had been gone for a couple of days, and upon his return, the general immediately summoned John S. Mosby, his chief scout. Mosby, a lantern-jawed Virginian who had been a lawyer before the war, had vanished for two days after that meeting. Mac had observed all this, and it was his theory that Stuart had been conducting some sort of reconnaissance with Von Borcke. Then the general had sent Mosby on an even more extensive scouting expedition. Stuart must have uncovered something interesting about the Yankees, and Mosby had confirmed it. Otherwise, Mac thought as he tugged on his trousers and then stomped his feet down into his boots,

Stuart wouldn't be rousting his officers out of bed in the middle of the night.

One of the men in the tent had lit a lantern, and in its glow, Fitz Lee looked over and grinned. "I hope you're ready to ride, Mac. I have a feeling we're going to be covering some ground."

"Yes sir, Colonel," Mac said. "I've got that same feeling."

IN LESS than the ten minutes Stuart had demanded, several hundred of his cavalrymen were in their saddles. Mac's brain was still a little fuzzy as he swung onto the stallion and followed Lee to the head of the formation that was gathering. In the light of several torches, he saw that the other Colonel Lee, Rooney Lee, Fitz's cousin, was also on hand and at the head of the horsemen he commanded. Stuart was resplendent in his colorful uniform and plumed hat, and his horse was pacing back and forth as if impatient to be away. As the riders formed themselves into a lengthy column, one of Stuart's adjutants hurried up to him on foot and asked, "General, how long are you going to be away?"

Stuart looked down at the man and announced in a voice loud enough for all the men near him to hear, "It may be years, and it may be forever." Then he snatched his hat off his head, waved it in the air, and sent his mount prancing forward.

There should have been a brass band playing, Mac thought.

The cavalry moved out, following the general through Richmond and onto the Brooke turnpike, which ran north from the city. They moved steadily, but not at an overly fast pace. By the time dawn began to lighten the sky to the east, they had covered only a few miles. As daylight spread over the countryside, more cavalry units that had been stationed north of Richmond began to join the column, adding to its ranks until it was nearly half a mile long.

Mac heard several of the men around him talking about how they must be on their way to the Shenandoah Valley to reinforce Gen. Stonewall Jackson. Word of Jackson's exploits in the Valley had reached Richmond frequently, and the eccentric but dashing general had become one of the Confederacy's heroes. Mac had wondered several times about Will and hoped that he was still all right. From the sound of it, Jackson's army had been fighting the Yankees almost every day.

Mac edged the stallion up alongside Fitz Lee's horse and asked, "What do you think, Colonel? Are we on our way to the Shenandoah?"

"General Stuart has let no one in on his plans but himself," replied Lee. "But it's certainly beginning to look like it."

That possibility seemed even more likely when during the afternoon, as the column reached a wide place in the road called Yellow Tavern, Stuart led them off the turnpike and headed northwest. That direction would take them straight toward the Blue Ridge Mountains and the Shenandoah Valley beyond.

His earlier speculations had been incorrect, Mac told himself. He had been sure their mission had something to do with the Union force under McClellan that was massed just south and east of Richmond. But he didn't mind being proven wrong. If they were on their way to the Shenandoah, then there was at least a chance that he would run into Will up there.

However, when the column had continued in that direction for only a few miles, Stuart abruptly turned back to the north, then to the northeast. Murmurs of puzzlement could be heard from the men, but Stuart ignored them, continuing to lead the column as if they were part of a parade.

By nightfall, they were actually heading east, and by the time the riders dismounted and began making camp near a farmhouse, everyone had realized that they were not on their way to join Stonewall Jackson. Instead, they were very near Union-held territory.

Mac unsaddled the stallion and began rubbing down the horse. He was tired, having been in the saddle for nearly seventeen hours except for a few short stops to rest the horses, but he was in the habit of seeing to his mount's welfare before his own. He heard footsteps behind him but didn't turn around, even when the steps came to a stop.

"Good Lord, that's the finest-looking horse I've ever seen," an unfamiliar voice blurted out.

Mac glanced over his shoulder. He saw an officer standing there, a major whose hat sported a plume similar to the one worn by Stuart. The major's plume was not quite so long or so magnificent, however.

"Thank you, sir."

"Where did you get that animal, Corporal?"

"I caught him on my family's farm over near Culpeper, sir. Before that, he was wild."

"And you tamed him?"

"I reckon you could say that. At least he sort of tolerates me riding him." Mac patted the stallion's shoulder affectionately.

"What will you take for him?"

The unexpected question make Mac glance around in surprise. "Take for him?" he repeated. "You mean sell him?"

"Of course," the major retorted with a tone of impatience. "What's your price?"

Mac shook his head. "I have no price. My horse isn't for sale."

The major snorted. "Nonsense. An animal such as that should be ridden by an officer, not an enlisted man. That's a gentleman's horse."

Mac's jaw tightened. He made an effort to keep his tone civil as he said, "Begging your pardon, Major, but this horse is going to be ridden by a corporal."

The officer stepped closer. He was a little shorter than Mac, thick-bodied without being heavy. Side whiskers came down almost to the point of his chin, but otherwise he was clean shaven. "Perhaps I should just commandeer the animal," he said. "That's my right as your superior."

Mac wasn't sure about that. He had enlisted in the Confederate army, but that didn't mean his horse had become army property. He was about to point that out when Colonel Lee strolled up and said, "Hello, Jason. I see you're admiring my aide-de-camp's horse."

The major stiffened. He turned to Lee and gave him a curt nod. "Yes, Colonel. That's quite a fine horse."

"I agree completely, and I'm sure Mac does, too. Doubtless you two have not been introduced properly. Major Trahearne, this is Cpl. Mac Brannon."

Mac made himself salute. "Major."

Trahearne grunted and returned the salute. Then he turned to Lee. "Good evening, Colonel."

"Good evening, Major." Lee stood there until Trahearne had walked away, his back like a ramrod.

"Thank you, sir," Mac said quietly when the major was out of earshot.

"When I saw him talking to you, I suspected there might be some trouble," Lee explained, still looking after Trahearne in the gathering dusk. "He wanted your horse, didn't he?"

"How did you know that?"

Lee shook his head. "Jason Trahearne was at West Point with the general and me. He never saw anything beautiful in his life without wanting it for himself. And if it isn't offered, he does his best to take it."

"He wanted the stallion," Mac confirmed. "He said he had the right to take it if he chose to, since he's my superior."

Lee swung around to face Mac. "Jason is a major, while I'm a colonel. And I say that horse belongs to you, Mac. I want my aide mounted on the best animal possible. If Major Trahearne gives you any more trouble, tell him to come see me."

"Thank you, sir."

The colonel chuckled. "Don't think I'm being entirely altruistic. I had my eye on a certain young woman once, and then Jason saw her . . . Ah, well, no need to go into ancient history, is there? Good night, Mac."

"Good night, sir."

Mac was grateful for Lee's intervention, but he wasn't convinced the matter was over. Maj. Jason Trahearne had not struck him as a man who gave up easily when he wanted something.

As if it wasn't enough that he had to watch out for tens of thousands of Yankees, Mac thought, now he had to keep an eye on a man who was supposed to be on the same side he was.

THE NEXT morning, the column of cavalry continued east. As they neared Hanover Court House, a messenger galloped up to Stuart. Mac was close enough to hear the man's report. He had been sent back to the column by Mosby, who had been scouting up ahead. Mosby had spotted a group of Union cavalry, but although he had only a few men with him, the Yankees had turned and fled.

"They knew a bigger force had to be coming up behind him," Stuart said. He turned to Colonel Lee. "Fitz, take your men and try to cut them off so they don't spread the word of our coming."

"Yes sir," Lee responded briskly, then turned in his saddle and called, "First Virginia, follow me!"

Mac was at the colonel's heels as they galloped toward Hanover Court House. Lee veered to the right to swing around the settlement in an attempt to intercept the flight of the Union cavalry. His men thundered behind him.

A line of trees loomed in front of them. Lee led the way into the woods. The trees would slow down the cavalry somewhat, but he seemed confident they would still be able to catch up to the Yankees.

Suddenly, water began to splash around the legs of the horses. Lee exclaimed in surprise and reined in, and right behind him, Mac followed suit. So did all the other men who had penetrated the woods. As Mac felt soft mud sucking at the hooves of the stallion, he realized that the trees had hidden a swamp.

"Back!" Lee called to his men. "Back out of here!"

As the horses struggled out of the muck, the dash to cut off the Yankees' flight came to a halt. Furious, Lee led his men up and down the edge of the swamp, casting back and forth for a way through, but it extended too far. Finally, Lee reined in and said disgustedly, "We've given them too much time. We'll never get in front of them now." He waved his men into motion and added dispiritedly, "Back to the column."

When the First Virginia rejoined the main body of the cavalry a short time later, they found themselves no longer in the lead. That place had been taken by Rooney Lee's Ninth Virginia. Stuart rode back along the column to greet Fitz Lee by asking, "What luck, Colonel?"

"None at all, sir," Lee replied, still angered by the turn of events. "We encountered a swamp that was too large for us to get around, and the Yankees made their escape."

Stuart shrugged philosophically. "Well, they were bound to notice us sooner or later. This won't prevent us from carrying out our mission."

Mac expected Colonel Lee to inquire just what that mission was, but Stuart didn't give him the chance. Instead, the general wheeled his horse around and galloped back to the head of the column.

During the day the Confederate cavalry encountered several small groups of Union infantry that had been sent out to form a rough picket line. Each time, the Yankees put up what little resistance they could, but they were quickly overwhelmed by the far greater numbers of Stuart's column. Thus the series of skirmishes barely slowed down the cavalry's progress. Riding in the middle of the column, Mac heard the shooting up ahead but took no part in the brief combats. By the time the First Virginia reached the sites, the Yankee pickets had all been either killed or captured.

The column reached a wide creek and clattered across the bridge that spanned it. A mile farther on, woods abruptly closed in on both sides of the road. Mac looked at the thickly grown trees and felt a sense of uneasiness. The cavalry wouldn't have much room to maneuver while they were making their way through this stretch of ground.

Mac's worries proved justified a few moments later when a line of mounted blue-clad figures appeared in the road at the crest of a small hill. The advancing Confederate column halted momentarily, but only until orders could be passed back from Stuart at the front: "Form fours! Draw sabers! Charge!"

Mac drew his pistol as he sent the stallion pounding forward along with the other horsemen. Shots rang out ahead. Mac held his fire; there was nothing for him to shoot at.

Suddenly, through the mass of men ahead of him, he caught a glimpse of the Union cavalry turning and running. Stuart's force had been too much for them. Some of the Yankees fled along the road, while others abandoned their horses and disappeared into the woods.

The short, victorious fight had not been without cost for the Confederates, however. Mac saw several men gathered around a fallen form in the road. The front of the man's coat was stained heavily with blood, and Mac decided he must be dead. He was a captain, but Mac didn't know him.

Stuart rode back from the front and removed his hat when he saw the dead man. To one of the officers gathered around the body, the general said, "There are several plantations near here, John. Take your brother to one of them, and I'm sure he'll be given a decent burial."

"Thank you, General," the grieving officer choked out. "As soon as I've tended to that, I'll rejoin you."

Stuart nodded. "Of course. I never expected less of you."

Mac and Lee and the rest of the First Virginia rode on past as the captain's corpse was lifted onto his horse. They moved rapidly, and Mac didn't look back. There was nothing more that could be done for the dead man.

A short time later, they left the trees behind and came upon a Union cavalry camp that was mostly deserted. The

Yankees had left quickly, but a few of them were still there. They surrendered, rather than putting up a fight.

Lee looked intently at the prisoners, then exclaimed, "I know some of those men!" Prodding his horse closer, Mac heard Lee ask, "Was this the Fifth Cavalry?"

"Yes sir," the man replied, then added, "Lieutenant."

Lee drew himself up in surprise. "You know me?"

"I had the honor of serving under you, Lieutenant," the man said. Then his voice turned ugly as he added, "Before you turned traitor!"

Mac saw Lee turn pale with anger. "I did *not* turn traitor to the Union," Lee snapped. "The Union turned traitor to me and to all my brethren in the South!"

That pretty much summed it up, Mac thought, and at that moment, he was proud of Col. Fitzhugh Lee, both as a commanding officer and as a friend.

DURING THE halt at the Yankee camp, Stuart finally called his officers around him and revealed the goal of this expedition.

"Information I received from Mr. Mosby indicated that the right wing of General McClellan's army is largely unprotected," he began. "You've seen for yourself that that assessment is correct. This information may well be vital to our cause, gentlemen, so I propose to get it back to General Lee in Richmond by the best way possible."

One of the officers spoke up. "If we retrace our steps, General, we may find the Yankees waiting for us."

"Indeed," Stuart replied with a smile. "That is why I propose to ride entirely around the Federal forces."

That announcement brought exclamations of surprise then smiles of admiration for the audacious plan. Rooney Lee stated, "I'm all for it, General." His cousin Fitz nodded his agreement.

Mac tried not to frown. Ride all the way around the Federals? That would put them far behind enemy lines. But it might be equally dangerous to try to go back the way they had come, he supposed. At any rate, the matter wasn't open for discussion. Stuart had said they were riding around the enemy, so they were riding around the enemy.

The column pushed on quickly, again with Mosby and a few companions going ahead to scout. When Mac saw something that looked like ships' masts sticking up over the tops of some trees, he thought for a moment he had lost his mind. But then he realized that the road they were following curved close to the Pamunkey River, and word came from the scouts that the ships were Union supply ships.

This was too good an opportunity for Stuart to pass up. Cavalrymen raced down to the river carrying torches and tossed them onto the tied-up ships before the few Yankee guards knew what was happening. Faced with a far superior force, they had no choice but to scramble ashore, surrender, and watch their ships burn.

Later in the afternoon, as the column approached Tunstall's Station, on the Richmond and York River Railroad, another group of Union cavalry appeared. They didn't put up a fight, however, but fled before the Confederate advance, leaving behind a small detachment of infantry to try to hold the depot. That effort was doomed to failure, as Stuart's men rolled relentlessly over the Yankee troopers.

Mac still had not fired his pistol today. He was holstering it because the fighting seemed to be over when he suddenly heard a voice nearby yell, "Damned Rebel!" A gun roared close behind him.

Even as the blast of the rifle sounded in Mac's ears, the stallion was moving, leaping aside with a twist of its body that almost threw Mac from the saddle. The stallion whirled around and reared up, its hooves lashing out at the Yankee soldier who had emerged from the concealment of a ramshackle shed and almost shot Mac point-blank in the back. One of the stallion's hooves connected with the soldier's head and sent him flying backward to land in a tumbled heap. Mac tasted bile in his throat as he saw how misshapen the Yankee's skull was after the stallion had kicked him. The man was dead.

Mac told himself not to waste any sympathy on the Yankee. The man had tried to kill him, only to wind up losing his own life because the stallion had reacted to the threat with almost supernatural speed. In fact, Mac thought, how in blazes had the horse known what was about to happen?

Mac felt an eerie shiver go through him. He rubbed the stallion's neck and murmured, "Ghost horse. Shouldn't be surprised at anything you do."

The stallion tossed its head but didn't look back at Mac.

"We'll keep each other alive," Mac whispered.

Feeling eyes on him, he turned his head. One of the storage buildings next to the station had already been set on fire. Stuart intended to take what supplies he could and destroy the rest. Sitting on horseback between Mac and the burning building was a solid figure in the uniform of a major. Even lit from behind by the flames, Mac recognized Maj. Jason Trahearne.

Had Trahearne seen what had happened? It seemed likely, Mac decided. And having seen how the stallion reacted to a threat, Trahearne might want the horse even more.

That would never happen, Mac told himself. From the beginning, he and the stallion had shared a bond that would not be broken.

Trahearne turned away.

"Come on," Mac said to his mount. "There's still work to do."

As darkness fell and the sky was lit by the leaping flames of the burning Tunstall's Station, the cavalry rode on, deeper into the night, deeper into the territory held by the enemy.

Chapter Eighteen

THE COLUMN PUSHED ON during the night with Stuart riding up and down the long line of men to make sure that everyone was in place and that there were no stragglers. No one knew if the Yankees were pursuing them, or if so, how close they might be. But it seemed likely that an enemy force would come up behind the Confederate cavalry sooner or later.

At Talleysville, the men and horses rested for a short time. The scouts had located a cache of supplies including several crates of bottles of champagne and more crates that held food probably bound for some Yankee officers' mess, since it was better than the fare usually furnished to enlisted men. The crates were broken open, leading to a veritable feast for the tired, hungry cavalrymen.

Mac took a couple of swallows from one of the bottles of champagne, then passed it on to Corporal Hagen, who tilted it up to his mouth and didn't lower it until all the contents had gurgled down his throat. Never much of a drinking man, Mac turned his attention to the sausage, crackers, and molasses he had liberated from one of the supply crates.

In the middle of the night, with some of the men groaning from overstuffed bellies and others swaying slightly in their saddles from the effects of the champagne, Stuart's expedition set forth again, leaving Talleysville behind.

At dawn the column reached the Chickahominy River. It was running high and fast, like most of the streams in the area, but one of the men who had lived in these parts before the war said that he knew of a place they could ford it. He rode on ahead with Rooney Lee to locate it.

When Stuart and the rest of the column reached the so-called ford, they found Rooney Lee and his men felling trees in an attempt to make a bridge. Lee approached Stuart and reported, "I'm sorry, General. We can't cross here. The current is too swift. I swam my horse across and back and nearly drowned both times."

Stuart smiled. "So you risked your life proving that it was too dangerous to cross. Somehow, I am not surprised at your audacity, Colonel."

Several trees fell with a crash and a splash, but when Stuart, both Colonels Lee, Mac, and the others gathered at the head of the column turned to look, they saw that the trees were not long enough to span the stream. The waters of the Chickahominy merely caught them and swept them downstream.

Stuart frowned and began to stroke his full beard, a sign that he was thinking furiously. Mac could understand why the general was concerned: there could well be a howling mob of vengeance-seeking Yankees coming up fast behind them, and with the river in front of them, they would be trapped. Somehow, they had to get across the Chickahominy.

"Gen'ral?" inquired the man who had first suggested this ford. Stuart turned to him.

The trooper pointed downstream with his thumb. "There's what's left of an old bridge down yonder a ways. Maybe we could fix it good enough so's we could cross, anyway."

Stuart nodded and said briskly, "Show me." He turned and called over his shoulder, "Hagen, you come, too."

Lee and Mac trailed behind Stuart, the guide, and the massive corporal. After a few minutes, they reached the old bridge. All the planking was gone, but some of the piers were still in place, as were the abutments at each end of the structure. Stuart and Hagen studied what was left of the bridge in the growing light from the rising sun. The general asked, "You've built bridges before, Corporal. What do you think? Can we get this one in shape to be crossed?"

Perhaps in unconscious imitation of the general, Hagen ran his fingers through his tangled beard. "Maybe," he rumbled. "We'd need lumber."

"There's an abandoned cotton warehouse near here," the guide drawled.

"I reckon that'd do," Hagen acknowledged. "Give me some men and a few hours, Gen'ral, and we ought to have us a bridge."

"You can have as many men as you need, Corporal," Stuart directed with a smile, "but I'm afraid the amount of time allowed us is up to our Northern friends."

Mac knew what Stuart meant. There was no telling when the Yankees might catch up to them. But since there was no other way across the river, they had no choice but to try to repair the bridge.

The column moved quickly to the site, and while a small number of cavalrymen remained on guard against the approach of Union forces, the rest went to work tearing down the old warehouse and carrying the planks to the ruined bridge. By the middle of the morning, Mac's tunic was soaked with sweat as he helped haul the long, thick, heavy planks. The bridge was beginning to take shape, growing slowly out from the northern bank of the Chickahominy and stretching toward the southern shore. Hagen and another man who had bridge-building experience supervised the work. Stuart stretched out under a tree on the riverbank and ate some of the food they had brought from Talleysville. Mac saw him and shook his head, not knowing how the general could manage to look like he was on a picnic when they were in such a race against time, with either capture or death as the probable stakes.

Shortly after noon the bridge was substantially completed. It had no sides, and there were places where it sagged precariously, but Stuart rode across to test it and pronounced it ready. He took off his plumed hat and waved it in a circle over his head, signaling the column to move out.

It took almost an hour for all the men to cross to the other side of the Chickahominy. Then Stuart joined Hagen at the foot of the bridge. "I'm sorry, Corporal, but you know what must be done now."

"Yes sir, I reckon I do," Hagen answered. He took a glass bottle from his saddlebags. "Found this in that old warehouse and figured it'd help matters along."

Mac watched as the corporal strode out onto the bridge. When he was about a fourth of the way across, he lifted the bottle and slammed it down against the planks, shattering it and splashing a liquid over the floor of the bridge. He squatted and began striking sparks with steel and flint. The liquid blazed up with a whoosh of flame.

Hagen ran from the burning bridge as the flames spread quickly behind him. As he reached the riverbank, someone in the column called out, "Look over yonder!"

At the far side of the river, Mac saw a troop of Union cavalry galloping toward the stream. Hagen mounted his horse, still moving unhurriedly, and Stuart said, "Well, gentlemen, shall we go?"

The column turned and began to ride away from the Chickahominy. On the other side of the river, the frustrated Yankees reached the stream and began firing as the Confederates disappeared into the trees. Only a few shots sounded, and none of the bullets came close. Mac glanced back and saw that the bridge was fully ablaze. No one was going to catch them from behind now.

NOR, AS it turned out, were they going to face any threat from the front. After resting on a plantation near Charles City Court House, where they were made welcome by the owners, the column prepared to move again that evening. Now, however, Col. Fitzhugh Lee was in command. Stuart had departed earlier, taking only two men with him, for a quick dash to Richmond. Lee's orders were to proceed more slowly and cautiously, in the hope that if Stuart was intercepted by the

Yankees, at least some of the men would get back to the Confederate capital with the information regarding the Union right flank.

On Sunday, June 15, 1862, Lee led the cavalry into Richmond, having encountered no more Yankees on their ride. They quickly discovered that Stuart had also reached the capital safely and had already conferred with Gen. Robert E. Lee concerning plans to take advantage of the Yankees' failure to adequately protect their flank.

As they dismounted, Fitz Lee turned to his aide with a grin and said, "Think about it, Mac. We left Richmond just three days ago, and in that time we've ridden a hundred miles, all the way around McClellan's forces. There may never be such a ride again. I'd say we're now part of history."

"Maybe so, sir," Mac agreed. "But I reckon right now I'm more interested in something to eat and a few hours of sleep than I am in history."

Lee laughed and clapped a hand on his shoulder. "I imagine most of the men feel exactly the same way. And if anyone has ever earned such a respite, it's you gallant cavalrymen."

THE RESPITE turned into an interval that lasted almost two weeks. Even though McClellan possessed the advantage in manpower and artillery, the little Union general seemed content to inch forward toward Richmond. Stuart spent the time visiting with his wife and children, who had come to the capital, while his men continued to patrol the area between Richmond and the Union lines, keeping track of McClellan's snail-like advance.

Mac knew from conversations he had overheard between Fitz Lee and the other officers that the forces commanded by Jackson were supposedly on their way to Richmond from the Shenandoah Valley. At the beginning of Stuart's already famous ride around McClellan, the feeling had been that the cavalry was on the way to the Shenandoah to reinforce Jackson. In fact, the opposite was true. Jackson was coming to Richmond and had a vital part to play in the campaign against the Northerners being planned by Robert E. Lee.

And if Jackson was coming, that meant Will was, too, Mac thought—if his brother was still alive.

On June 25 orders came for the cavalry to get ready to ride. As he saddled the stallion, Mac sensed that something important was about to happen. He patted the horse and murmured, "We stay together, you and me. I won't let anything happen to you."

Stuart's horsemen left Richmond in the afternoon and rode to the vicinity of Ashland, camping for the night near the settlement. Jackson's army, which had crossed the Blue Ridge by train and then marched to their current position, was supposed to be somewhere nearby. Mac felt his anticipation growing at the thought that he might soon see Will again.

Will was going to be surprised when he found out that his younger brother had joined the cavalry. And not just surprised, thought Mac, but probably a little angry, too. Mac had promised Will that he would stay on the farm and see to the family, but surely Will would understand that as the war had grown, so had the need for men to fight it.

The next morning, the cavalry reached Totopotomoy Creek, expecting to cross the stream on a bridge. Instead, they found that the bridge had been damaged by a group of Federals who had also dug in there. Stuart's men swept forward, quickly overrunning the Union defenders, and once again found themselves facing the chore of bridge-building. This span was not in as bad a shape as the one over the Chickahominy had been, so it was quickly repaired and the cavalry moved on in search of Jackson.

Riding near the head of the column with Lee, just behind Stuart, Mac saw a haze of dust in the air up ahead. Stuart noticed the dust, too, and galloped forward. Fitz Lee threw a grin at Mac and followed the general, so Mac came along, too.

They reached a crossroad, and as Mac reined in and looked down the road to the west, he saw a sight he would never forget: thousands of motley-uniformed soldiers marching along briskly despite the fatigue evident on their bearded, dust-streaked faces. Stonewall Jackson's famed "foot cavalry" had arrived.

Mac looked eagerly along the line of men, searching for the familiar face of his brother. There were so many, though, that Mac had trouble picking out individuals. A few yards away, Stuart was talking to an officer on horseback. Mac glanced in that direction then looked again as he recognized the black-bearded Jackson, despite the man's rather disreputable, sweat-stained uniform and battered fatigue cap.

It was a meeting of famous men, and Mac might have watched it with more interest if he had not been trying to spot Will. As it was he kept his attention focused on the marching men, studying them through the dust and haze.

He was about to despair of ever seeing Will again when one of the troopers called out to him, "Hey! Ain't you Mac Brannon from Culpeper County?"

Mac swung around and looked at the man, a burly, bearded sergeant who seemed vaguely familiar somehow. "Are you from Culpeper County?" he asked the sergeant.

"Damn right." The sergeant stepped out of the ranks and came over to him. Raising a heavily muscled arm, he pointed. "Your brother's over yonder."

Mac saw an officer on the other side of the wide column of marching men. Under the broad brim of the gray felt hat were the somewhat rawboned features of Will Brannon. Mac let out a whoop of excitement and shouted, "Will!"

Will must not have heard him over the tramp of thousands of feet. Mac worried for a second that Will would ride on and never even know how close he had been to his brother. Lifting his hands to his mouth, Mac cupped them and called again, "Will!"

This time, Will reined in sharply and twisted around in his saddle, looking across the column to see who was calling to him.

For a second, he couldn't locate Mac, but then his eyes went to the figure mounted on a big silver gray horse. Mac waved a hand over his head, and the eyes of the two oldest Brannon brothers met across the heads of the marching troopers.

"Mac?" Will shouted, sounding as if he were unable to believe what he was seeing. Then he turned his horse, waited for a gap in the column of soldiers, and started riding across toward Mac.

The sergeant said, "I best catch on up with the rest of the comp'ny. Good to see you again, Mr. Brannon."

Mac looked down at the man. "I'm sorry, I can't recall your name . . ."

"Darcy Bennett," the sergeant replied. He held out his right hand. "I'm one o' the sergeants in your brother's comp'ny."

"Will's in command of an entire company?"

Darcy grinned. "Best damned cap'n in the whole blamed Confederate army. See you, Mr. Brannon." He turned and walked quickly up the line of men to rejoin the troops he had left.

By that time, Will had almost reached Mac. He prodded his horse on until he was able to move the dun alongside Mac's stallion. "Mac!" he exclaimed as he leaned over in the saddle to throw an arm around Mac's shoulders and pound his brother on the back with his other hand. "What in blazes are you doing here?"

"Getting ready to fight the Yankees, same as you," Mac replied as he returned his brother's embrace. Suddenly, he heard Will take a sharp breath and flinch, and he drew back quickly. "What's wrong? Are you hurt?"

Will shook his head. "Got a pretty deep bullet crease during a skirmish at Port Republic a few weeks ago. Nothing to worry about. It's already healed up, but it's still a mite tender." He looked his brother up and down, taking in not only Mac's uniform but also the mount he was riding. "So you finally caught that horse," he noted. "But what are you doing in the army?" Will's expression darkened. "You said you'd stay on the farm and see to the family."

"Titus and Henry are there and tending to things just fine."

"How do you know that? Have you heard from them?"

"Well, no," admitted Mac. "But nobody in the family is real big on writing letters except Cordelia, and anyway I've been moving around so much with the cavalry that I don't know if a letter could have caught up to me."

That wasn't entirely true, Mac thought. Except for a few patrols, they had been in camp at Quien Sabe for a couple of weeks. Any letters for him would have found him there.

And he had to admit, too, that the silence from home worried him some. What he wanted to believe was that everybody was just too busy to write, but he couldn't know that for certain.

"What in the world made you sign up?" Will wanted to know.

"Same thing as you—" Mac began.

"Not the Fogartys again? Damn it—"

Mac held up his hands to stop Will. "No, none of the Fogarty kin have bothered anybody. I just had to get into the war and help send the Yankees packing. You felt the same way."

"Reckon I did," Will affirmed with a slow nod. "But you gave your word."

"All right, if you want to be stubborn about it, I suppose I did," Mac acknowledged, beginning to grow impatient. "But I'm here now, Will, and there's not a thing either of us can do about it. I'm just glad to see you again."

A grin broke out abruptly on Will's face. "So am I, blast it." He put out his hand, and Mac took it without hesitation, gripping it firmly.

"There's plenty to talk about," Will went on, "but I reckon we've both got things to do."

Mac nodded. "I'm part of General Stuart's cavalry, and I saw him talking to General Jackson awhile ago. They must be hatching something."

"Maybe we'd better go find out."

That sounded like a good idea to Mac. Side by side, he and Will rode toward the front of the column.

Mac and the rest of Stuart's cavalry had passed through this area during their ride around the Union army, so he was familiar with the landscape. He saw several places he recognized during the time it took to ride to the front of the long column. Once he and Will got there, they found the two generals riding alongside each other. Stuart and Jackson were a striking contrast in almost every respect, except for the intelligence and determination in their gazes.

Fitz Lee was with the generals, and when Mac rode up, he said, "There you are! I was afraid we were going to have to leave without you, Mac."

"Sorry, sir. I was talking to my brother." Mac inclined his head toward Will. "This is Capt. Will Brannon, Colonel."

"Colonel," Will echoed as he raised his hand in salute.

Lee returned the salute, then took off his gauntlet and shook hands with him. "I'm pleased to meet you, Captain. Did your brother tell you that he's been serving as my aide-de-camp and doing an excellent job of it?"

"No sir, but we haven't gotten around to swapping yarns yet. I'm not surprised Mac's worked out. He's always been able to do just about anything if he put his mind to it." Will nodded at the stallion. "Like catching this horse of his."

"Yes, I've heard about that. Quite impressive."

Jackson called over to them, "Captain Brannon, did I hear correctly? You're related to one of these dashing cavaliers of General Stuart's?"

"Yes sir," Will replied. "This is my brother Mac. Corporal Brannon."

"Sir," Mac responded crisply as he saluted Jackson.

"Excellent," Jackson said. "You've solved the question of which of my officers I shall send with Colonel Lee's men to function as my liaison while they scout out our route and cover our flank. I take it you'll have no objection to accompanying them?"

Will glanced at Mac, and the brothers grinned at each other. Will answered, "No sir, no objection at all. But my company—"

"The estimable Sergeant Bennett and his fellow sergeants will keep them moving, never fear," declared Jackson.

"Then I'd be honored to go with the cavalry, sir."

Stuart turned to Lee. "You'll lead the column, Fitz. You may encounter some Federal pickets. If you do, I trust you shall use your best judgment in dealing with them. However, if you come across any larger forces, send a galloper back immediately."

"Yes sir," replied Lee. He turned in the saddle and motioned his men forward. Mac called out the order for the First Virginia Cavalry to advance. The riders moved ahead at a brisk trot that would soon leave Jackson's marching soldiers far behind them.

At their head, Mac and Will rode with Lee. After more than a year apart, the Brannon brothers were together again and it felt good, Mac thought. It felt mighty good.

Chapter Nineteen

WILL HAD BEEN SURPRISED to see his brother but not to discover that Mac had captured the big silver gray stallion and even tamed it enough to ride. That stallion had been Mac's obsession. If anybody in the world could have trapped the wild horse and gentled it, it was Mac Brannon.

It wasn't like Mac, though, to have enlisted in the army. Mac had always been the gentlest of the Brannon brothers, the slowest to anger, the least likely to wind up in a fight. Will had believed that Mac had inherited less of their father's fiery temper. And yet he was here, a member of Stuart's cavalry and evidently a veteran of several battles.

But Mac wasn't fighting out of anger, Will realized as he looked over at his brother. Mac had joined up out of a sense of duty and responsibility, and that *was* like him. He wanted to defend his homeland. Will couldn't fault him for that.

He wished, though, that he knew things were all right back on the farm . . .

The First Virginia Cavalry spread out in front of Jackson's men and along their left flank. Lee himself took the point, accompanied by Mac, Will, and several other officers. They were trotting their horses along the road when gunfire suddenly broke out on their left. Will didn't hear any bullets passing close by, but when he looked at a line of trees in that direction, he saw smoke floating up from them. Yankee riflemen had to be hidden in the growth.

Fitz Lee twisted in his saddle and drew his saber, sweeping it toward the trees and shouting, "Charge!" A group of men veered their horses off the road and thundered across the field. Another, more ragged volley came from the trees. The quick response of the Confederates meant that not all of the Federals had had time to reload after their initial volley. Nor had they

264 • *James Reasoner*

chosen a good spot for their ambush. The trees grew too far apart to keep the cavalrymen from riding between them. In a matter of moments, the horse soldiers were among the trees, hacking with their sabers and firing their pistols.

Although he was not a cavalryman, Will was used to going into combat on horseback, so he was able to keep up with his brother and Lee's men. As he rode into the woods, one of the Northerners loomed out of the underbrush, thrusting a bayonet at him. Will managed to turn the deadly blade aside with the barrel of his pistol. As the man stumbled, Will shot him at close range, so close that sparks from the muzzle of the pistol set the soldier's jacket to smoldering. The bullet drove into the man's chest and dumped him backward into a limp sprawl. He was either mortally wounded or dead.

Will wheeled the dun around, looking for Mac. He spotted him several yards away, firing into a tangle of brush, probably used as cover by several Union soldiers. Will stiffened as he saw a man stand up to Mac's left, just behind him, and draw a bead on him. Mac didn't notice him. Will tried to shout a warning, realizing to his horror that it might be too late.

The Yankee fired, but even as smoke and flame geysered from the barrel of his rifle, Mac's horse leaped aside, moving so quickly it was little more than a blur. Mac swayed in the saddle, almost thrown by the unexpected leap. The shot missed him though, and Will drew a bead of his own on the rifleman and squeezed off a shot. The Federal crumpled to the ground.

Mac regained his balance, threw a glance at Will, and nodded his thanks.

He ought to be thanking that horse of his, thought Will. The stallion had saved Mac's life by spotting the danger in time and realizing the threat the man represented.

Will didn't have time to ponder how that was possible. His hands were full with helping the cavalry polish off the rest of the Yankee skirmishers. A few dropped their rifles and fled, a few were captured, but most were killed or wounded.

Lee detailed some men to tend to the prisoners, then waved the rest of his troops back to the road. Will and Mac fell in alongside the colonel again as Lee resumed the ride. This was their job, sweeping away whatever Union opposition might be lurking in the way of Jackson's advance.

As they moved on to the east, they encountered more Federal pickets during the afternoon. Will and Mac were in on some of the fighting and heard the reports Lee received on the other skirmishes. The Yankees seemed more interested in slowing down Jackson than in stopping him. Bridges were burned, roads were blocked with felled trees, and more ambushes took place.

Around the middle of the afternoon, Will and Mac were still riding at the head of the column with Lee when they all heard the rumble of artillery followed by the lighter sound of rifle fire. With a frown, Will twisted in his saddle and asked, "Am I crazy, or is that coming from *behind* us?"

The sounds of battle were indeed coming from the southwest. The two brothers exchanged worried glances. The noises grew louder. Quite a battle was being fought down there.

"Colonel . . . ?" Mac inquired tentatively to Lee.

Lee looked every bit as concerned as the other men. He reined his mount to a halt and frowned darkly. "Our orders are to proceed to the east and deal with the Yankees we find there, and that is what I intend to do."

Will had never met Fitz Lee until today, but he figured that was the last thing the colonel really wanted to do. Lee wanted to be in on that fighting, wherever it was and whoever it involved. Will couldn't blame him for that, because he was experiencing the same feelings himself.

Suddenly Lee's expression cleared somewhat. "We will proceed as ordered," he said, "but that doesn't preclude me from sending a rider to gather information from the other parts of the field."

"I'll go," Mac volunteered immediately.

Lee smiled. "Somehow, I thought perhaps you might, Corporal." He looked at Will. "What about you, Captain Brannon?"

Will wasn't officially under Lee's command, but Lee *was* a superior officer. Will replied, "I'd like to go, too, Colonel. I think General Jackson would want to know the situation."

"I expect you're right about that." Lee nodded. "Go on, both of you. But be careful, and get back to us as quickly as you can after you find out what's going on."

"Yes sir," Mac said, and Will echoed the response.

They turned—Mac on the silver gray stallion and Will on the rangy lineback dun he had ridden away from the family farm near Culpeper over a year earlier—and started back along the column. As they passed one of the officers, Will noticed the look the man was giving his brother. It was hostile enough to make Will frown.

"Who was that major back there?" he asked when they were past the man. "Sort of a blocky fella with long side whiskers."

"Maj. Jason Trahearne," replied Mac, and Will heard the taut dislike in his brother's voice. "The major thinks a mere corporal shouldn't be riding a horse like mine."

"Oh," Will said. "I reckon he thinks it'd be better if that stallion belonged to an officer . . . say, him."

"That's right."

"You'd best watch out for that one, Mac," Will advised. "I don't think I'd like to go into battle with him anywhere close behind me."

Mac nodded. "I don't intend to. I've been trying to keep an eye on him. And Colonel Lee made it clear to him that the stallion is mine."

"Be careful anyway." In his days as sheriff, Will had run into plenty of men like Major Trahearne, men who didn't think the rule of law applied to them. Sometimes he'd been forced to point out the flaws in their logic with the barrel of a gun.

They moved west along the road, listening to the cannon and the rifles until it seemed that the firing was coming from due south of them. Then they rode farther west, circling around to come at the battle from that direction, figuring that would put them behind Confederate lines. They sure didn't want to get turned around and wind up behind the Federal lines, thought Will.

After cutting cross-country for a short distance, they came to a road that ran northeast. Mac studied it for a moment, then said, "I think this is the road that runs up to Mechanicsville."

"From the sound of the fighting, that's the way we need to go," Will commented. He pointed. "And look at the road."

Seeing the signs left behind on the road by the passage of thousands of men and hundreds of wagons and caissons didn't require a tracker as skilled as their brother Titus. Obviously, a large force had moved along here earlier in the day, heading toward Mechanicsville.

"Let's go," Mac decided, prodding the stallion forward.

They moved at a fast trot along the road. In less than half an hour, they saw the roofs of buildings ahead, clustered in some trees, and knew they had reached Mechanicsville. The town itself seemed peaceful; the firing was coming from beyond the settlement.

The two rode into town and saw that appearances had been somewhat deceptive. No actual combat was going on in the streets, but the signs of fighting were everywhere in the form of wounded soldiers. Some were sitting up, others were stretched out in the road, but all wore the crimson stains of wounds received in combat. Will pointed grimly at a hastily erected hospital tent, and he heard his brother catch his breath at the sight of a bloody pile of amputated arms and legs just outside the entrance. As they watched, another arm, severed above the elbow, came sailing out of the opening and landed on the pile.

"My God," breathed Mac.

Will had seen things as bad as this before, so he wasn't as shocked by it as his brother was. But he knew he would never grow numb to the horror, and he felt a ball of sickness rolling around in his stomach. He looked away from the grisly sight and muttered, "We'd better find an officer."

A few minutes later, they spotted a major sitting in the back of an open wagon with his legs stretched out in front of him. He was cradling his left arm, and the way it hung loosely in the bloodstained uniform sleeve told Will that it had probably been broken by a bullet. The man's face was pale, and as they reined in next to the wagon, he looked up at them with dark, pain-haunted eyes.

"What do you want?" he croaked. "Who are you men?"

Will didn't bother saluting. He said, "I'm Captain Brannon from the Thirty-third Virginia. What's going on here?" He didn't introduce Mac because if there was any trouble, he wanted to take it on himself.

"What's going on here?" repeated the major. His voice rose shrilly as he continued, "We're attacking the Yankees at Beaver Dam Creek, just like we're supposed to! Where the hell is Jackson?"

"Up on the left flank," Will replied.

"My God! He's not even in position yet?" The major slumped against the back of the wagon seat and groaned. "Doesn't he know he's supposed to be supporting us?"

"Begging your pardon, Major, but what outfit are you from?"

"I'm part of General Hill's command. A. P. Hill. We're getting cut to ribbons up there. There's a bluff just on the other side of the creek, and the Yankees have half a dozen batteries up there. They're blowing us to hell and back when we try to get across the field on this side of the creek."

"With all due respect, sir, it sounds to me like we ought to try to go around them."

"That's what Jackson was supposed to do!" blazed the major as he sat upright again. "But he's not here!" The wounded man subsided, wincing at the pain in his wounded arm. "He's not here . . ."

Will looked over at Mac for a second, then asked, "How many men do we have attacking?"

The major shook his head. "How many do we still have alive? That would be a better question." He paused, then went on, "We have a division in action—at least we did have. A lot of them must have been wiped out by now. I never heard anything like those Yankee guns. When they opened up on us, it was like a death knell . . ." He gave another little shake of his head as he realized he was drifting off into a horrified reverie. "There was a small Union force here in the town. We took them easily and pushed on to the east. Then we came to the field and the creek and the bluff, and the cannon started firing as we advanced. As far as I know, what's left of the division is still there, dying in the field . . ." His voice trailed off, and his eyes closed.

"Thank you, Major," Will said quietly.

The officer roused himself, his eyes not only opening but growing wider than normal. "Go tell Jackson. That's an order, Captain. Go tell Jackson what's going on here."

Will nodded. "I intend to." He looked at Mac and inclined his head. "Let's get out of here."

Without saying anything, Mac followed as Will turned his horse. Together, they left the wounded major behind and rode out of Mechanicsville.

———✧———

THE ROAR of the Union artillery didn't grow any quieter as Will and Mac made their way back the way they had come. They didn't retrace their path exactly, knowing that Jackson's forces would have moved on farther to the east. Instead they took what they hoped would be shortcuts that would bring them to their destination more quickly.

After they had been riding for a while, Mac broached what he knew might be a delicate subject. "From what that major was saying, it sounds like General Jackson isn't sure what his orders are."

Will didn't disagree. He just sighed and reflected, "I never knew the general to duck a fight. Even at Manassas, when he stayed on Henry House Hill instead of going down to help General Bee, there was a reason for it. And he proved to be right."

"Well, maybe he's got something else in mind," Mac suggested. "I suppose we'll find out when we get back."

It was late in the afternoon, with the sun touching the western horizon, when they located Jackson. To their surprise, as they trotted through a tiny crossroads settlement called Hundley's Corner, they spotted row after row of tents with small campfires in front of them. Unless their eyes were deceiving them, it appeared that Jackson had put his forces into bivouac for the night.

Will and Mac reined in and looked at each other, then each of them glanced back in the direction of the battle. Jackson was in position to turn the Federal flank and make a difference in the outcome, but not with all his men bedding down for the night.

Will lifted a hand to catch the attention of an officer walking past them. "Dr. Maguire," he inquired. "Where's General Jackson?"

Hunter Maguire, Jackson's chief surgeon, looked up and said, "The general has retired for the evening, Captain."

"Retired!" Will was unable to stop the exclamation from escaping. "But why?"

"The general has slept perhaps four hours out of the last four days, Captain." Maguire's disapproval of Will's attitude was evident in his tone of voice.

"We have to wake him up," insisted Will.

Maguire shook his head. "I fear it would take the Last Trump to rouse him now that he is sound asleep, and even that might not suffice. Whatever you have to report, Captain, will simply have to wait until the morning."

Will's jaw clenched tightly in frustration. He knew he wasn't going to get anywhere arguing with the doctor. Maguire knew Jackson as well as anyone in the command, and if he said that it would be impossible to awaken the general, then Will supposed that was true.

But how could they just make camp for the night, knowing that their fellow Confederates were in desperate trouble only a few miles away?

"I'm going to find General Stuart and Colonel Lee," Mac murmured quietly.

Will turned to his brother and nodded. "Yes, that's a good idea." He knew what Mac was thinking: maybe the cavalry could do something to turn the tide.

It was clear that the Stonewall Brigade and the other forces under Jackson's command were not going to be placed into battle tonight.

"Excuse me, sir," Mac said to Maguire. "Do you know where General Stuart's cavalry is this evening?"

"Establishing a picket line around the encampment, I believe," replied the doctor.

Mac saluted. "Thank you, sir." He turned the stallion to ride off, then paused and looked at Will. "Are you coming along?"

Will shook his head and waved Mac on. "You know the situation. You can report it as well as I can."

"All right," Mac affirmed reluctantly. He heeled the stallion into a trot.

Will was sorry to see his brother go. He had enjoyed spending the day with Mac. But right now, he was just too damned ashamed to face men such as Stuart and Lee. For the first time since he had joined the army, Will was not proud to be part of Stonewall Jackson's famous foot cavalry.

MAC RODE to the edge of the large encampment and began circling it, knowing that if the cavalry was riding picket duty he would come across someone sooner or later, probably sooner. He was right. Only a couple of minutes had passed before a rider loomed out of the gathering shadows of twilight and demanded, "Who's there?"

"Corporal Brannon," Mac responded, "looking for General Stuart or Colonel Lee."

The cavalryman pointed to the other side of the camp. "Our outfit's over there, Corporal. But Colonel Lee is riding picket if you want him. Should be about five hundred yards yonder." He pointed again, this time in the direction Mac had been going.

"Thanks," Mac said as he got the stallion moving again.

He was challenged by two more mounted sentries before he found Lee. In response to Lee's hail, he replied, "Corporal Brannon reporting, sir," Lee returned the salute and then urged his horse forward and shook hands with Mac.

"Good to have you back, Corporal. After listening to those guns all day, I didn't know how you had fared."

"We didn't see any fighting, sir. But we were close to the battle at Mechanicsville. Forces under Gen. A. P. Hill took the town and then moved on to attack the Yankees at Beaver Dam Creek." Mac's voice became more grim as he went on, "We haven't been successful in pushing them back beyond that."

In the gloom, Mac saw Lee wave a hand toward the southwest. "That's what's going on over there?" asked the colonel.

"Yes sir."

"And we're not part of it?" The disbelief and dismay were evident in Lee's voice.

"No sir. Jackson's—that is, General Jackson's—men have made camp for the night."

"Blast it! We ought to be in the thick of that fight."

Mac didn't say anything. He agreed with the colonel, but it wasn't the place of a lowly corporal to question the judgment of a general, especially one as famous as Stonewall Jackson.

After a moment, Lee asked, "Does General Jackson know about this?"

Mac shook his head. "No sir. When Will and I—when Captain Brannon and I returned, he talked to one of the general's medical officers who said the general had already gone to bed and couldn't be awakened. Captain Brannon will have to wait until tomorrow morning to make his report."

Lee was seething with impatience and frustration. "If we hit the Yankees from behind—" he began to speculate.

Another rider came up in time to hear Lee's words and interrupted by saying, "We're attached to General Jackson's command at the moment, Colonel. Or had you forgotten that?"

Mac and Lee both looked around, recognized the ostrich plume on the newcomer's hat, and brought their hands up in salute. "No sir, General," Lee said. "I hadn't forgotten."

Jeb Stuart returned the salute. "I'm confident, then, that you weren't considering disregarding those orders, Fitz. You're too good an officer for that, no matter how much you may want to be elsewhere at the moment."

"No sir. I intend to follow our orders."

"As do I," added Stuart. "But just so you know . . . you're not the only one who wants to answer the call of those guns."

"No sir," Lee said quietly. "I didn't figure that I was."

Stuart turned to Mac. "So tell me, Corporal, what did you find out today?"

Quickly, Mac repeated the information he and Will had learned about the battle at Mechanicsville and the stalling of the Confederate advance at Beaver Dam Creek. Stuart nodded in thought then suggested, "It's growing dark. Perhaps the fall of night will bring an end to the battle for today. And tomorrow may be an entirely different story."

"I hope so, General," Mac ventured.

"Go get some rest, Mac," Lee directed. "You're excused from picket duty tonight."

"I can do my part, sir," Mac protested.

"You already have, Corporal," Stuart observed as he looked off toward the southwest, where the sounds of battle were indeed dying away as darkness settled down. "You've done all you could."

Chapter Twenty

IF JUNE 26 HAD BEEN a frustrating, largely wasted day for the commands under Jackson and Stuart, June 27 showed every sign of being even worse.

After successfully defending Beaver Dam Creek all day, the Federals had withdrawn during the night, falling back to a second defensive line along Boatswain's Creek near Gaines's Mill. This news was brought early in the morning to a somewhat revived Jackson, whose orders were to move up on the Confederate left. After a hurried breakfast, Jackson's men broke camp and began marching in what they hoped was the right direction.

The maps that had been provided for Jackson were none too reliable, however, and the mostly flat, marshy terrain north of the Chickahominy provided few landmarks. Hours passed with the army on the move, but they seemed no closer to the actual battle than when they had started.

Stuart's cavalry was still on Jackson's left flank as Mac rode along next to Lee. He hadn't seen Will this morning and wished he had had a chance to speak to his brother again before they went into battle. As morning turned into afternoon, Mac began to wonder if they would ever even reach the battle. The morning had been fairly quiet, broken only by the sporadic rattle of rifle fire in the distance, but around two o'clock the roar of artillery began to be heard once again.

They reached a command post, and as officers congregated there, Mac spotted the tall, impressive figure of Robert E. Lee stepping out of a tent. Jackson and Stuart joined Lee along with several other officers, among them Fitz and Rooney Lee. The reunion between the general and his son and nephew was brief but seemed to be heartfelt. Then Lee turned his attention to the matter at hand. Sitting on horseback in the circle of cavalrymen that surrounded the command post, Mac was able to hear most of the discussion.

"General Hill and his men have endeavored gallantly to cross Boatswain's Creek," General Lee explained, "but so far Porter's men have held them back."

Gen. Fitz John Porter was one of the Federal commanders, Mac recalled.

"General Longstreet is in position to reinforce General Hill on the right," continued Lee. "I have ordered him to delay his attack until you are in position to reinforce General Hill's left, General Jackson."

Jackson nodded briskly. "This affair shall hang in suspense no longer, General," he asserted. "We shall sweep the field with our bayonets."

That was easy to say, Mac thought, but maybe too late in coming. He knew perhaps he wasn't being fair to Jackson, but a lot of men had died yesterday and earlier today. Some of them might not have if Jackson had handled things differently.

Lee gave Jackson precise directions for the location of his attack, then shook hands around the circle of officers. "God-speed," he wished them.

As Jackson began arranging his column for the attack, Stuart waved the cavalry to the left, the same position they had occupied since being attached to Jackson's command. When the army began to move again, they trotted forward, holding their mounts back so that they wouldn't outstrip the pace of the infantry. The horses were impatient and so were the men riding them. The tension of the past two days had brought them all to the point that they were more than ready to get into action, even though it meant some of them would die.

Mac felt it himself, an eagerness to get to it and have it done with. Anything was better than this seemingly endless delay, he thought.

Off to the cavalry's right, the infantry under Jackson pushed forward. Suddenly, cannon began to roar, sending whistling shells overhead. Stuart looked around, grinning under his beard, and raised his voice to call over the tumult of the barrage, "Now the Yankee orchestra begins to play!"

If that was the case, Mac didn't care for the music.

Neither did the men on whom the projectiles were falling. The solid cannonballs swept soldiers down before them with devastating force, while the explosive shells burst open and spread their deadly clusters of grapeshot and scrap metal in an even wider circle of destruction. Although Mac was watching from a distance, he was close enough to see men blown apart, and the sight of arms and legs detached from their bodies and spinning through the air made him clench his jaw and swallow hard as bile tried to come up his throat.

Several shells came even closer overhead, causing some of Stuart's officers to duck instinctively. Stuart, however, sat upright on his charger, tall in the saddle, completely in his element in this rain of death and destruction. At the moment, there was nothing for Stuart and his cavalry to do, but that didn't stop him from watching avidly as the battle progressed.

Out here on the flank, though, it was impossible to see what was happening in the center of the advance. Mac sat tensely on the stallion and wondered if Will was all right.

THE LINE of battle stretched in a northeasterly curving arc along Boatswain's Creek for more than two miles, all the way to the headwaters of the creek. Jackson, on the Confederate left, was not in position to launch his attack until late afternoon, but once he was there, his men surged forward relentlessly. At the other end of the line, Longstreet's forces pushed ahead at the same time, and in the center, the Texas Brigade under John Bell Hood spearheaded the strongest Confederate thrust of all, the blow designed to break the back of the Federal resistance.

Will was only vaguely aware of the general plan of attack. He knew where his company of the Thirty-third Virginia was supposed to be, and when the order to advance was passed along the line, he sent them forward down a slight incline toward a broad, swampy valley where Boatswain's Creek had its origins. Will followed just behind the charging infantrymen, guiding the dun with his knees while he held his saber in his left hand and his pistol in the right. Rifle shots rang out from the trees and brush scattered through the swamp, and Will saw some of his men stumble and fall. Lead whined past his ear. He had learned to ignore such distractions during battle, to keep all his attention centered on his immediate goal, which at this moment was to take his men into those trees and clear out any Federals in the way.

Muddy water splashed around the hooves of the horses and the boots of the infantry soldiers as they charged forward. The smell of the fetid water was thick in the air, along with the acrid bite of powder smoke. Will fired his pistol, aiming at the muzzle flashes of the Federals' rifles. Then his men were in the trees and he was right behind them. He saw a Union soldier lunging at him from the left, bayonet lowered so that it could be thrust up into the belly of the horse. Will chopped down with the saber, slashing diagonally across the man's face. The soldier screamed and fell back, dropping his rifle and clapping his hands to his ruined face before he stumbled and fell.

A gun roared close by, and Will felt a bullet tug at his sleeve. "Damned Rebel!" someone shouted. Will twisted in the saddle and saw a Union officer riding at him, pistol leveled for a second shot. Will ducked as flame and smoke spouted from the barrel of the gun. He didn't know if the shot went over his head or missed in some other direction, but he was sure he hadn't been hit. Then the officer was on him, practically ramming his horse into Will's mount, and Will lifted his saber to drive the blade into the Yankee's side.

The officer cried out in pain as Will's steel pierced his vitals. He sagged in the saddle, and Will ripped the saber free before the man could fall off the horse and take the saber with him. The officer's mount shied away, and its rider tumbled off, one foot still caught in a stirrup. The last Will saw of the Yankee, the man's corpse was being dragged behind the running horse as the animal stampeded away.

The fighting in the trees at the headwaters of the creek continued as dusk fell. The gathering shadows made the orange glow of muzzle flashes seem even more garish and made it harder to tell friend from foe. Will and his company pushed on slowly, their only goal to reach the far side of the marsh and stumble up onto solid ground once more. That would mean they had driven the Federals back onto the south side of the creek.

Will reloaded and emptied the Colt Navy until he had no more ammunition, and then he kept fighting with the saber. The steel had a slick coating of blood on it now. Blood was everywhere, in fact, its bright copper smell mingling with the odors of rotted vegetation and burned powder. Will's side and leg ached from their old wounds, but he ignored the pain, just as he ignored the revulsion and horror he felt at the carnage around him.

Night fell, and darkness closed in as the Confederate soldiers finally reached the edge of the swamp. Will drove his horse up the slope, feeling the solid ground under its hooves. Without that, his numbed senses might not have realized that the troops had achieved their goal. They had broken the Union line.

So HAD Longstreet on the right and Hill in the center. With the Federal defensive line collapsing all along its length, the Yankees had no choice but to fall back in a quick retreat. If the Confederate forces had not been exhausted by two days of fighting, the Union retreat might well have become a bloody rout, but McClellan was able to withdraw his troops without much more damage.

The battles of Mechanicsville and Gaines's Mill shook the normally cautious McClellan to his core. The losses suffered by the Union on these vast, bloody battlefields made up McClellan's mind for him. Unable to get the visions of the carnage he had witnessed out of his head, the Federal commander ordered what he called a strategic withdrawal.

Behind his back, some of his less sympathetic officers began referring to the retreat as the "Great Skedaddle." To the Confederates, once it became obvious from their scouts' reports what was happening, it seemed that McClellan was running like a whipped dog with his tail between his legs.

Stuart's cavalry spent a couple of days seeking out the Federal supply lines along the Pamunkey River in hopes of disrupting them, but they discovered that the Northerners had already abandoned their positions in the area. For a time, the plantation known as White House, the ancestral home of the Lee family, had served as McClellan's headquarters. As Stuart and his men rode up to the once-grand plantation house, they saw to their dismay that it had been torched as the Federals fled, leaving only a smoking pile of rubble. Mac felt a surge of sympathy as he looked over at Rooney Lee, who had grown up here. Tears were rolling down the young officer's cheeks, but other than that, his face was set in stony, tightly controlled lines. Fitz Lee, who had often visited here as a boy, was also visibly moved by the wanton destruction.

The Southern horsemen spent the night at White House, resting both horses and men. The next morning, leaving a small force behind to guard the plantation, Stuart set out again. Somehow, the war seemed to have gotten away from him. Judging by the intent look on the general's face, Mac knew Stuart wanted to get in on any fighting that was left before McClellan completed his retreat.

Farther south, the officers and men under Jackson's command were growing equally frustrated. The general had spent a day rebuilding a bridge while, only a few miles away, a small

Confederate force had caught up with the rear guard of McClellan's retreating army. Outnumbered, the Southerners had not attacked but had waited instead for Jackson to join them. Unfortunately, this did not happen because Jackson's men were busy with their reconstruction task. With this opportunity for battle lost, the rest of the day passed in relative quiet for Jackson's command.

In the meantime, the Confederate forces gathering near a farm that belonged to a family named Frayser had grown too impatient to continue waiting for Jackson. Launching an attack, the troops under Generals Longstreet and D. H. Hill had found fierce opposition from the Yankees in the woods that bordered the farm. Back and forth, the two armies slugged bloodily at each other until finally, as night fell, the Federals withdrew again. But they had achieved their goal, which was the chance for McClellan to move his retreating Army of the Potomac farther to the south, toward the James River.

Will awoke on the morning of July 1 not knowing what had happened at Frayser's farm the day before, but he quickly became aware of the events as he and the other officers attended a brief conference with Jackson. "We must push on and find General Lee," the general declared, and the orders went out to break camp quickly and prepare to march south.

As Will left Jackson's tent, he was unable to keep a note of frustration out of his voice as he turned to Yancy Lattimer. "Do you think we'll actually stumble across the war today?"

Yancy grinned. "I expect we will. We're not that far from the James now, and McClellan has to be somewhere between us and the river."

The men moved out briskly, heading south toward White Oak Swamp. The swamp itself slowed them down somewhat, but they encountered no Union opposition as they tramped through the mud and shallow water. Emerging from the swamp near the settlement of Glendale, they found Robert E. Lee waiting there with a sizable number of troops. The

Frayser farm was nearby. Jackson had finally arrived at the scene of battle—a day late.

Lee and Jackson conferred, surrounded by their officers and staff. "I believe we can still catch General McClellan," Lee said. "I expect him to mount a defense at Malvern Hill, just north of the James."

Will had never been to Malvern Hill and didn't know the terrain, but if Lee was right, he would no doubt become familiar with it soon enough. The meeting concluded, and Jackson took the lead this time, moving the Stonewall Brigade to the front of the column.

At midmorning, Will spotted some sort of height rising in the distance. It was more of a plateau than a hill, with its flat top extending more than a thousand yards in every direction. As the army drew closer, Will estimated that the plateau was not over a hundred feet tall, but that was plenty high enough to give anyone up there a commanding view of the approaches to it. And a commanding field of fire as well, thought Will with a worried frown.

He left Darcy Bennett to keep the company moving and rode over to fall in alongside Yancy Lattimer. "Do you reckon that's Malvern Hill in the distance?" Will asked the aristocratic young captain as he pointed to the flat-topped elevation.

"I wouldn't be at all surprised," replied Yancy. "If the Yankees are dug in on top of that plateau, it won't be easy to root them out."

A low-pitched rumble sounded in the distance. Both Will and Yancy raised their heads and peered toward the plateau. They heard a whistling noise.

"Damn it!" grated Will. He yelled across at his men, "Get your heads down, blast it!"

The warning came just in time. Artillery shells burst on the road ahead, sending canister and grapeshot screaming through the front ranks of the advancing Confederates. Will wheeled the dun and galloped back toward his company. He could see that some of his men were down, writhing in pain from the wounds they had received.

The woods were thick along the sides of the road. Will waved toward them and shouted, "Into the trees! Darcy, get them into the trees!"

"Yes sir, Cap'n!" Darcy called in return. He bellowed at the troops, "Get off the road! Skedaddle, you sons o' bitches!"

The soldiers broke ranks and ran for the woods as more shells rained down around them. The smells of smoke and dust bit at Will's nose. He kept a tight rein on the dun and drove his men toward the relative safety of the trees. For a second, he twisted in the saddle and glanced over his shoulder, looking for any sign that Yancy had made it to safety. He couldn't see his friend anywhere.

There was no time to worry about Yancy. Will had to see to his own men. The ones who weren't hurt were carrying the wounded men to safety, leaving behind those who were beyond help. Will dashed up and down the road until everyone was in the woods, then he rode into the trees after them, the last member of the company to leave the field of battle.

He saw that most of the men were hunkering behind the thick trunks of the trees. A few were directing futile rifle fire toward the distant crest of the plateau. Cannon could reach that far; most rifles could not. Will swung down from the saddle and joined Darcy Bennett behind one of the trees.

"Them Yankees got a warm welcome for us, looks like," Darcy commented with a grin. He held his rifle ready but wasn't firing. Darcy didn't waste powder and shot.

"Did you get a look at that plateau?" asked Will. "The ground to the east and west looks too rugged for us to launch an attack from either side."

"Straight ahead," Darcy asserted with a grim nod. "That's the only way we can go, Cap'n."

As it turned out, however, the Stonewall Brigade wasn't going anywhere. Seeing how the Union artillery batteries had opened up on the front of the Confederate column, General Lee had ordered that the rest of the army abandon the road as quickly as possible and move up through the woods to establish a line of attack. By the middle of the day his army had accomplished that, stretching into an arc facing Malvern Hill and as long as the plateau. Some of the Confederate artillery had been moved into position to return the barrages, too, but most of the cannon were still bogged down in the swampy ground to the north.

Lee met with his generals again, and when Jackson returned to his men, he brought news that none of them liked. They were to remain in reserve while other divisions would lead the attack on the broad plateau.

Will was seething inside as he moved up to where he could watch the battle through his field glasses. Yancy, who had come through the initial attack without a scratch, joined him, carrying a collapsing telescope. Waves of Confederate soldiers surged toward the hill. The roar of the Federal guns seemed never to stop, and as hundreds of shells exploded in the charging ranks of soldiers, Will had to look away.

Yancy had lowered his telescope, too. "My God," he muttered. "They're cutting us to ribbons."

"We can't take that hill," Will sighed. "It's impossible."

"Nothing's impossible for us Southerners," Yancy responded hollowly. "Didn't you know that?"

Yancy desperately wanted to believe that, Will thought, but the evidence to the contrary was before their eyes as the afternoon wore on and more and more Confederates died in the charges hurled against Malvern Hill. Southern cannoneers managed to get a few pieces of artillery to the top of a nearby hill that was roughly the same height as the plateau, and the fire they directed toward the Yankees from there blunted the Federal barrage a bit. It wasn't enough to do the attackers any real good, however; dozens more cannon would have been needed for that.

Late in the day, the orders came for Jackson's men to move up and reinforce the Confederate left. As far as Will was concerned, the order had come too late.

And yet, he thought, if they had gone into battle earlier, chances were they would have died just that much sooner. Even though he was running, McClellan had found the perfect place to defend his retreat. Malvern Hill proved unassailable.

Darkness fell as Jackson was moving into position, but new orders came down the line before the attack could be launched. The battle was over. The Confederates were pulling back. Slowly, the sound of rifle fire died away, although most of the Yankee batteries continued their roaring blast for a while.

McClellan had gotten away. That knowledge was bitter but inescapable. Harrison's Landing was close by on the James River, and while the Confederate army under Lee had been occupied with the assault on Malvern Hill, most of the Union army had reached the river and established a large camp on its northern bank. The Southerners might have forged over Malvern Hill and tried to push McClellan into the James, but their losses had been too heavy; the battles of the Seven Days had been too costly and exhausting in every sense of the word.

But as Will sat that night in the Confederate camp almost in the shadow of Malvern Hill and sipped a cup of coffee, he knew that the costly campaign had not been for nothing. A week earlier, McClellan had been on Richmond's doorstep, ready to lay siege to the Confederate capital and ultimately capture it. Instead of sitting back and waiting, however, Lee had ordered the defenders to go out and meet the enemy head-on. The battles at Mechanicsville and Gaines's Mill, along Beaver Dam Creek and Boatswain's Creek, had caught the Federals by surprise, at least to a certain extent, and they had been forced to turn tail and run. Despite the Union army's superiority in both manpower and firepower, the Confederates had sent them packing.

The same thoughts must have been going through Yancy Lattimer's mind, because as he strolled over to the campfire holding a coffee cup of his own, he hunkered on his heels next to the flames and announced, "Well, we saved Richmond."

Will nodded. "I reckon so—for now."

Chapter Twenty-one

TITUS HAD NEVER BEEN so frightened in his life. Not even when he'd been twelve years old and run smack-dab into what was probably one of the last bears in the area while he was out hunting one day. That bear had reared up on its hind legs, looking as big as a mountain, and let out a roar that seemed to shake the very ground underneath Titus's feet. Then it had charged him, moving much faster than anything that big and awkward-looking had any right to move. Nearly every part of his brain had screamed at him to turn and run, but far back in the recesses of his mind, a cool, calm voice had told him that to do so would just get him killed. So he had listened to that voice and lifted the old flintlock rifle that had been his father's and carefully lined up his shot before squeezing the trigger and putting a heavy lead ball right through the bear's left eye and into its brain. It had taken a few more yards for the bear to realize it was dead, but luckily it had collapsed before it reached Titus. In fact, the bear had still been a good six feet away when it plowed nose-first into the ground. He had been scared then, Titus reminded himself, but he had come through it just fine. There was no reason to think he wouldn't survive today just as well.

Besides, it wasn't as if he hadn't had a few weeks to get used to the idea of getting married.

Henry came up behind him and slapped him on the shoulder as Titus studied his reflection in the mirror. "You look plenty handsome, big brother," Henry commented with a grin. "I reckon if Polly hasn't figured out by now how crazy she is to be getting hitched to you, she won't run away screaming when she gets a look at you."

Titus felt a flash of anger and started to turn toward Henry with a frown, but then he realized that his brother was just joking. Titus forced a smile of his own and answered, "I hope not."

291

He had been waiting for something to go wrong ever since Polly had agreed to marry him, and he wasn't totally convinced yet that everything would be all right, even though the wedding was only a couple of hours away.

He couldn't fault the arrangements. Duncan Ebersole had insisted that the wedding be held at Mountain Laurel, and to keep from offending Abigail Brannon, he had agreed to have Benjamin Spanner, the new Baptist minister, perform the ceremony instead of the local Congregationalist preacher. After his initial hostility when he'd learned that Titus and Polly were engaged, he had been civil and at times almost friendly toward Titus. No doubt part of that was because he was relying on Titus to help him defend the plantation against the Yankees when they came. No one in the area was thinking in terms of *if* anymore. The Union invasion was only a matter of time.

So while Polly had been taking care of the wedding plans, Titus and Ebersole had been busy supervising the construction of Mountain Laurel's defenses. Earthworks had been dug to command all the main approaches to the plantation, and Titus had selected the trees in which riflemen should be hidden. Crude bombs had been made from gunpowder, nails, and earthenware jugs. They would be ready for the Yankees, Titus told himself.

Of course, deep down he knew that there was no possibility a few dozen men could prevent the Union army from occupying the plantation if that was what they wanted to do. His hope was that he and his companions could make the effort so costly to the Yankees that they would move on without taking the time or trouble to root out Mountain Laurel's defenders. That was their only real chance.

He turned away from the mirror to find Henry struggling to tie a string tie around his neck. "Let me give you a hand with that," Titus offered impatiently. "We ain't got all day."

Cordelia came into the bedroom while Titus was fussing with Henry's tie. She watched for a moment, then set aside a small package she was carrying and intervened, "Here, let me. Men's fingers are just naturally clumsy."

How would she know that, Titus wondered, when no man had ever touched her? Sure as blazes, that milksop Nathan Hatcher didn't have the gumption to even kiss her on the cheek, let alone anything else.

Cordelia looked mighty nice, though. Titus had to admit that much. She wore a bright yellow dress and bonnet, and her dark red hair looked like molten copper. Titus and Henry were in their Sunday best, sober black suits and boiled white shirts. Titus had shaved and combed the tangles out of his long hair, and he thought he looked presentable enough to get married.

Cordelia finished with Henry's tie, then turned to Titus. "I have something for you," she said. She picked up the package she had put down and unwrapped it to reveal a beautiful red rose. She pinned it on Titus's lapel, ignoring the frown on his face.

"I didn't figure on wearing no flower."

"It's lovely," Cordelia stated as she stepped back. "Besides, you need a spot of color in that outfit, otherwise people would think you were on your way to a funeral. Weddings are supposed to be happy occasions."

Maybe so, thought Titus. They were damned sure scary, he knew that.

Abigail appeared in the doorway. She was dressed in a dark gray suit and matching hat. "We'd best be getting started," she urged. "Wouldn't want you to be late for your own wedding."

"I reckon not, Ma." Titus reached for his hat, which was lying on the bed next to Henry's.

His mother had been just about as opposed to this marriage as Ebersole was at first, Titus recalled. She didn't care much for the Ebersole family, thinking that Duncan was a heathen Scotsman and a Congregationalist and knowing also that he liked to take a drink. In addition, he was one of the richest men in the county, if not the richest, and Abigail had a fundamentalist's dour distrust of wealth. It was easier for a camel to pass through the eye of a needle, she liked to quote Scripture, than for a rich man to enter the kingdom of heaven.

Titus had never understood how having money was supposed to make a man more likely to be a sinner. More temptations, maybe. All he knew was that he wouldn't mind seeing what it was like to be rich. That wasn't why he was marrying Polly, of course. He was certain of that. He was marrying her because he loved her, and because she loved him.

The family went downstairs and left the house, climbing into the buggy that Henry had hitched up earlier. Titus and Abigail sat up front, Henry and Cordelia in the back. Titus flicked the reins and got the pair of horses moving.

He hadn't broached the subject of where the newlyweds were going to live after the wedding. The rest of the family probably thought it was a little odd that he hadn't started building a cabin somewhere on the farm for him and Polly. He supposed they thought he was going to bring his new bride back here to the farmhouse. Henry could move into the room that had been shared by Will and Mac before they went off to war.

Abigail wouldn't like it when he announced he was going to live at Mountain Laurel, Titus knew. She would just have to understand that he wasn't abandoning his family. He could ride over every day and help Henry with the chores. He would probably be even more help after he was married than he was now, he told himself. He wouldn't be spending most of his days either drunk or hungover. A fella would just naturally work harder when he was happily married and was going home to a beautiful wife every evening, he told himself. The only thing he really had to worry about was the Yankees . . .

It was a beautiful summer day, warm with only a few clouds in the sky. Titus drove the buggy briskly toward Mountain Laurel, and as they approached the plantation and then turned into the long, tree-lined lane leading to the big house, he saw other people arriving in buggies and wagons and on horseback.

The wedding of Duncan Ebersole's only child would be well attended. No one in the county wanted to incur his displeasure. There would have been a bigger crowd before the war, though, mused Titus. Most of the men had gone off to join the army, and some of the women and children who had been left behind had gone to live with relatives in other parts of the state or even in other states until the war was over.

Still, as he drew the buggy to a halt near the mansion's portico, he saw several dozen people waiting around for the ceremony to get underway. Most of them greeted him cordially as he helped Abigail out of the buggy and then took her arm to escort her into the house. The real friendliness was reserved for Abigail and Cordelia and Henry, Titus noted. That was because of his reputation for carousing, he supposed.

Let them look down on him because he liked to take a drink, he thought. No matter what they thought of him, he, Titus Brannon, was marrying the beautiful daughter of the richest man in Culpeper County. Let any of them do better than that if they could.

Elijah, the white-haired slave, was waiting in the open doorway. He smiled at the Brannons and said to Abigail, "Welcome to Mountain Laurel, Miz Brannon. Massa Duncan done tol' me to show you folks right to the parlor. The preacher's already waitin' there."

"Thank you, Elijah," Abigail responded politely.

"You surely do look mighty gracious today, Miz Brannon," Elijah went on as he ushered them into the house. "An' you as pretty as a picture, Miss Cordelia."

"Why, thank you, Elijah," Cordelia said, smiling.

"And Massa Titus, you an' Massa Henry are just plumb handsome—"

"Where's Polly?" Titus cut in, weary of the slave's flattery. Abigail gave him a quick look of disapproval at his brusqueness, but he didn't care at the moment. All he wanted to know was where his wife-to-be was.

Elijah had been a slave too long to take offense at any white man's tone of voice. He replied easily, "She upstairs gettin' ready, Massa Titus. But you can't see her. No sir, it be bad luck for the groom to see the bride 'fore the weddin'."

Titus nodded. He had waited a long time for Polly, and for most of that time he'd had no reasonable expectation that they would ever be together. He could wait a little while longer.

The Reverend Benjamin Spanner turned to greet them as they came into the parlor. The minister, bluff and hearty in a dark suit, shook hands with Titus and Henry and Cordelia, then took Abigail's hand in both of his, the long, blunt fingers closing firmly around hers. "Mrs. Brannon, it's always a pleasure to see you. I look forward to the services every Sunday morning because I know you'll be there in the congregation looking up at me in the pulpit."

"Where else would a God-fearing woman be on Sunday morning except in church?" Abigail responded. She looked a little surprised that Spanner was clasping her hand so enthusiastically, but Titus noticed that she didn't pull it away. In fact . . . good Lord, was that a blush on his mother's face?

Couldn't be, he decided. Abigail hadn't taken an interest in any man since the death of John Brannon. On the other hand, if she was going to start, then a big, rugged, hellfire-and-brimstone-shouting preacher like Benjamin Spanner might be just the sort to get her stirred up.

Titus gave a little shake of his head. He had better things to think about than something as far-fetched as that.

Like the fact that right upstairs was the woman who would soon be his wife.

———

THE DOOR opened softly behind Polly. She knew without looking around who had come into the room. She sat at her dressing table in her dazzlingly white wedding gown and didn't look up until she felt his hands drop onto her shoulders. Then she lifted her eyes to the mirror and met her father's intense gaze as he stood behind her.

"Ye're lovely," rasped Ebersole. "Just like yer mother."

"Yes," Polly replied hollowly. "You've told me before how much I look like her."

"Girl, I . . . I can't tell ye how much I . . . I'm sorry . . ."

He wasn't the least bit sorry, thought Polly. He wasn't sorry for anything he had ever done. He just wasn't the sort of man to feel guilt. But she didn't want to argue with him now, not on her wedding day, with Titus probably downstairs by now waiting for her. So she summoned up a smile from somewhere deep inside her and lifted a hand to pat one of his hands where it lay on her shoulder.

"It's all right," she lied. "It's all right, Father."

Ebersole took a deep breath, drawing himself up straighter. "Elijah tells me the boy's here wi' his family, and all the guests are here, too. No need in puttin' this off."

Polly stood up and reached behind her to grasp her veil, which was made of the finest, most delicate lace. This dress had been her mother's wedding gown. It was appropriate she was being married in it, she thought. She arranged the veil in front of her face, then took the arm her father held out to her. Together, they walked out of the room and started downstairs.

THE WEDDING was to be in the great ballroom of Mountain Laurel. Chairs for the guests had been brought in and placed on the polished hardwood floor. Later, after the ceremony, slaves would clear them away so that there could be dancing. Despite the fact that it was the middle of the day, all the candles in the crystal chandeliers had been lit. The air was fragrant with the scent of the hundreds of flowers that had been brought into the room. A bower of sorts, covered with white blooms, had been erected at the front of the room. That was where Titus and Polly would stand before the minister and say their vows.

Cordelia clutched a bouquet of flowers that one of the maids had handed her. She was going to stand up with Polly, even though the two of them had never been close. They weren't even friends, Cordelia thought. But she had agreed to Polly's request that she be a member of the wedding party, since she didn't want to do anything to ruin the day for Titus.

Henry was serving as Titus's best man. Abigail sat on one of the chairs in the front row. Titus stood there waiting, rocking back and forth slightly on his heels. Cordelia couldn't blame him for being impatient. He was about to achieve a goal that no one other than himself had ever believed he could achieve. It might not be the best thing for him—Cordelia still couldn't bring herself to believe that Polly was the best choice as a wife—but she was the one he wanted. Cordelia told herself she ought to be happy for her brother. She managed to smile. She was going to be happy if it killed her, she told herself.

Then, familiar notes sounded from the harpsichord as one of the ladies from town began to play the wedding march. Everyone in the ballroom stood up and turned to look as the bride entered the back of the room on her father's arm. Ebersole began to escort Polly up the aisle that had been left between the chairs.

Titus looked like somebody had just poleaxed him, thought Cordelia. *Close your mouth, big brother,* she thought. He wouldn't want to stand there with his jaw hanging open.

Henry touched him on the arm. Titus swallowed hard and straightened, composing himself slightly. He was still a little walleyed, but he no longer looked as if he were about to bolt like a wild horse, like that stallion of Mac's.

Ebersole brought Polly down the aisle and stood with her next to Titus. Reverend Spanner stepped up, motioned for the guests to sit down, cleared his throat, and began the ceremony, saying, "Dearly beloved," and continuing with all the usual words. Cordelia heard them but didn't really pay attention to them. After a moment, Ebersole gave the bride away and stepped back to take his seat, also in the front row but on the opposite side from Abigail.

Cordelia felt someone watching her, and that was odd because during a wedding, all eyes were supposed to be on the bride and groom. She turned her head just enough to glance out at the guests, and in the rear of the ballroom she spotted a familiar figure standing just inside the door. Nathan Hatcher had his hat in his hands and was turning it over nervously. What was he doing here? Cordelia asked herself, but then she supposed Duncan Ebersole had invited him. Practically the whole county had been invited, except for no-accounts like the Paynter boys and Israel Quinn and the rest of the Fogarty bunch. She was a little surprised that Nathan had come to the wedding, though. She hadn't seen him since the day they had argued in town.

The ceremony didn't take long. After what seemed like just a few moments, Spanner concluded, "By the power vested in me by the everlasting grace of God, I now pronounce you man and wife." He leaned forward a little and added to Titus, "You can kiss her now, son."

Titus lifted Polly's veil back over her head, then gently placed his arms on her shoulders and leaned forward to kiss her. Cordelia felt a pang of emotion as she watched. She wished the two of them all the happiness in the world. She truly did.

Titus broke the kiss, stepped back, and grinned broadly as he turned and took Polly's arm to lead her out of the ballroom. The guests applauded, and Henry let out a whoop that drew looks of disapproval from both Abigail Brannon and Duncan Ebersole. That was probably the only thing they would ever agree on, thought Cordelia, except for the fact that the Yankees were a bunch of godless rascals who needed to be sent back where they had come from.

For a while after that, everything was a whirl. The guests gathered around Titus and Polly to congratulate them and wish them well. While that was going on, the servants cleared the ballroom of the chairs and brought food and drink in, placing the bowls and platters and pitchers on long tables set up against one wall where they would be out of the way. Several men went to their wagons and buggies and got their fiddles, so that they would be ready to provide the music.

Elijah brought three glasses on a silver tray to Ebersole, Polly, and Titus. As Ebersole raised his, he said in a loud, commanding voice, "Here's to my lovely daughter and her new husband! Health and good fortune and long life!"

Quite a few of the guests had drinks already. They echoed Ebersole's toast. He threw down the liquor quickly, as did Titus. Polly merely sipped her drink.

None of the other Brannons had glasses, and Abigail looked none too pleased with the idea of Titus drinking. But she didn't say anything, and Cordelia knew her mother was making an effort not to let her beliefs spoil things for Titus.

Bows began to scrape on fiddle strings, and the guests poured back into the ballroom to begin dancing. Cordelia was drifting in that direction when someone put a hand on her arm and stopped her. She looked over and saw without any real surprise that it was Nathan Hatcher.

"Hello, Nathan," she said coolly. "I didn't really expect to see you here today."

"Judge Darden insisted that I come," replied Nathan. "I suppose he didn't want to offend Mr. Ebersole. They're thick as thieves."

Cordelia glanced toward Ebersole and saw that the heavy, florid-faced attorney who was Nathan's employer was indeed talking to the plantation owner.

"But I wanted to come anyway," Nathan went on, "because I wanted to talk to you."

"I'm sure I don't know what we might have to talk about." Cordelia hadn't told anyone what Nathan had revealed to her about being a Union sympathizer. It was too shameful a secret for her to expose. But given the feeling in the county about him, there were probably some whispers going around already about his failure to enlist in the army.

"Listen, Cordelia," Nathan appealed urgently. "You and I have been friends for a long time. I'd like to talk to you somewhere in private. I think you owe me that much."

"*I* owe you?" Cordelia struggled to keep her anger in check.

"You're the one who kissed me and made me think that you liked me."

"Hush up about that!" Cordelia hissed. She glanced around. No one seemed to have overheard them over the music and the dancing and the talking. "All right, I'll listen to what you have to say. But that's all I'll promise."

"That's enough," Nathan said quietly.

Cordelia wasn't familiar with the plantation house, but she found a sitting room that opened off the ballroom. Nathan pulled the door closed behind them, then turned to face her.

Her emotions were running riot inside her. Anger, remembered shame at the brazen way she had kissed him, resentment, and an unaccountable tenderness that she couldn't keep from feeling when she looked at him all surged through her. She didn't feel the least bit calm, but she managed to sound that way as she asked, "What do you want, Nathan?"

He moved a step closer and looked like he wanted to reach out and take her hand, but if so, he controlled the impulse. "I wanted to tell you that I've decided to leave Culpeper."

"Going north to join your Yankee friends?" She couldn't stop the words.

"I don't *have* any Yankee friends. I don't even know anybody who doesn't live either here or in Richmond. But I can't just stay here where people hate me because I don't believe the same way they do."

"Afraid they're going to tar and feather you, like they threatened?"

"Maybe I am," Nathan conceded. "Or maybe I'm just tired of banging my head against a stone wall." He stopped, gave a dry, humorless laugh. "Stone wall. Your brother Will knows all about those, doesn't he? Isn't he with Jackson?"

"He is," Cordelia confirmed. "He's defending our homeland. Your homeland, too, Nathan."

Nathan's voice was hollow as he said, "I'll have to remember to thank him . . . if there's time before he kills me."

"Kills you?" she exclaimed. "Why in the world would—oh, my God." Her heart seemed to stop as realization hit her. "You're going to join the Yankee army!"

"That's one way to prove to myself—and to the others—that I'm not a coward." This time Nathan couldn't stop himself. He reached out and closed his hand around her arm. "I'm not afraid to die, but I won't die for a cause I don't believe in. So . . . I'll die for one that I do."

"Nathan . . ." Cordelia's head was spinning. She didn't know what to do, where to turn. "Don't go. Don't leave town. Don't throw your life away." She pulled her arm free, but instead of stepping back, she moved closer to him and placed her arms so around his neck. "We . . . we can figure things out."

"Th—there's nothing to fig—"

She kissed him. Cordelia felt tears running down her cheeks as her lips found his and pressed desperately against them.

After a moment, Nathan pushed her away, not roughly but firmly. "I'll probably hate myself for this," he said, his voice thick with emotion, "but it's too late, Cordelia. Too late for both of us."

He turned away and reached for the doorknob. Cordelia sank down on a divan, unable to stand any longer, and choked out, "Nathan."

He paused for a heartbeat but didn't turn back to her. Then he opened the door, slipped out into the ballroom, and closed the door behind him.

She sat there for a long time. Even through the door, she could hear the happy, raucous strains of the fiddle music.

Chapter Twenty-two

As HE LEANED ON THE handles of the plow, Henry shaded his eyes and peered into the distance, to the southeast, toward Culpeper. As he watched the cloud of dust grow larger and larger, he felt apprehension growing inside him.

"Titus!" he called. "Look at that!"

They had been working in the fields all morning, preparing ground that had already been harvested once this season for a fall planting. The August sun beat down hotly, plastering the shirts of both men to their backs with sweat. Titus sleeved more beads of sweat off his forehead as he turned toward Henry. "What are you talkin' abou—"

He stopped short as he saw the brown cloud. A lot of feet and hooves would be required to kick up that much dust. Hundreds . . . no, thousands, maybe even tens of thousands.

An army.

And it was moving toward Culpeper from the north.

"Get back to the house," Titus tautly ordered his brother. "Make sure all the guns are loaded. Stay there with Ma and Cordelia."

"Where are you going?" Henry demanded.

"I've got to get to Mountain Laurel and warn them."

Henry had figured that would be his brother's response. Ever since Titus's marriage a couple of weeks earlier, Titus had lived at the plantation, coming to the Brannon farm only to help out with the chores. Henry had little doubt where Titus's concerns lay, but he couldn't stop himself from saying, "Damn it, you ought to be here, too, Titus. This is your home, not that blasted plantation."

Titus shot him a hurried look. "Polly's there," was all he said as he broke into a run toward the horse tethered at the edge of the field.

And Polly was all that mattered to him, Henry thought bitterly. The rest of the family knew that or should have known by now.

Titus jerked the reins of his mount loose, swung into the saddle, and galloped off toward the south, toward Mountain Laurel. Without bothering to watch his brother go, Henry quickly unhitched the mule from the plow and left it where it was, leading the mule back toward the barn. When he got there a few minutes later, he called out, "Ma! Cordelia!"

The two women came out of the house, drawn by the sound of urgency in Henry's voice. Abigail was wiping her hands on her apron. "What is it?" she asked.

"Looks like the Yankees are moving toward Culpeper. Titus and I saw the dust."

Cordelia lifted both hands to her mouth, but Abigail just looked grim and not at all surprised. "Where's your brother?"

"Gone to Mountain Laurel."

Abigail nodded. Clearly she had expected that answer. She had been furious when Titus had declared after the wedding that he would be living at the Ebersole plantation, but she had known there was nothing she could do to talk sense into his head. He was too swept away by the idea of being married to that girl and living in the middle of all that luxury. But when they had gotten home, she had predicted, "'Pride goeth before a fall.' Titus will learn."

Henry didn't really care how proud his brother was. As he led the mule into the barn and put it in one of the stalls, he just wished Titus were here because Titus was the best shot with a rifle in the whole county. If the Yankees came . . .

He stopped short and lifted his hands. When he looked down at them, they were trembling. He clenched them both into fists, and that helped the shaking a little without stopping it completely. If the Yankees came, what could they do, really? Even if Titus hadn't run off to Mountain Laurel, it would still be four people against an entire army. How could they fight that?

The answer was simple. They couldn't.

If the Yankees came, it would be the end of the Brannons' world.

———◆◆◆———

TITUS HURRIED to the place he already thought of as home, even though he had lived there only a couple of weeks. As he galloped through the fields, he shouted to the workers he passed, "Yankees! Yankees comin'!" The slaves just looked up at him stolidly, but Ebersole's overseers were plenty excited. They started herding the slaves back toward their quarters near the plantation house and the other main buildings.

Duncan Ebersole must have heard the hoofbeats of Titus's horse and sensed the urgency in its gait. He was waiting on the porch of the big house when Titus pulled his mount to a halt and practically threw himself to the ground. "Ha' they come at last?" asked Ebersole.

Titus was out of breath, but he managed to nod and after a moment was able to say, "Henry and I saw the dust cloud. Looked like thousands of them movin' down the Warrenton turnpike. We'd best get all the riflemen ready."

"Aye. See to it, lad, just as we planned."

Titus hesitated then added, "I'd like to go back to the farm."

Ebersole looked at him sharply. "Back to th' farm?" he repeated. "Your ma's farm?"

"That's right."

"I thought we were agreed ye would help defend Mountain Laurel."

"I will," Titus replied, "but there's time to get my mother and my brother and my sister and bring them back here. They'll be safer here."

Polly came out onto the front porch in time to hear Titus's words. She intervened, "Go get them, Titus, but hurry back here."

"Wait just a damned minute!" exclaimed Ebersole. "The lad is yer husband, girl. His place is here, defendin' ye."

Polly ignored her father. "How far away are the Yankees?"

"Hard to say," he replied with a shrug. "Several miles, at least."

Polly turned toward Ebersole. "I don't know anything about armies—" she began.

"That's right, ye don't."

"But I don't think they can move very fast," she went on stubbornly. "Titus will have plenty of time to get back. At least he came to warn us."

Ebersole threw his hands up in defeat. "All right. Fetch whoever ye want. But be quick about it. While yer gone, I'll be gettin' the boys in place to fight off them Yankees."

Titus nodded and mounted up again. "I'll be back," he promised. He wheeled the horse, which was still tired from the run to the plantation from the Brannon farm, and kicked it into a gallop that carried him back down the tree-lined lane in front of the house.

———

HENRY CLIMBED into the hayloft of the barn and opened the small door at the end so that he could peer out toward Culpeper. The dust cloud was closer to where he knew the town to be, but it wasn't moving very fast. Henry cradled a rifle in his hands as he watched.

He spotted the figure on horseback approaching rapidly. It turned off the road onto the dirt lane that led up to the farmhouse, and he recognized Titus. Quickly, Henry went to the hayloft ladder and climbed down.

Titus reached the house just as Henry was emerging from the barn. Henry called out, "I didn't expect to see you again so soon."

Abigail and Cordelia came out of the house. Cordelia had a shotgun in her hands, but Abigail was unarmed. She fixed Titus with a steady glare and demanded, "What do you want?"

Titus didn't dismount. He merely leaned forward a little in the saddle and said, "Come to Mountain Laurel with me."

Abigail sniffed. "This is my home. I don't figure on being run off of it by some godless horde of Yankees."

"Damn it, Ma—"

"You know better than to use profanity in front of me, Titus Brannon!"

Titus controlled his frustration and impatience with a visible effort, then urged, "You'll be safer at Mountain Laurel. All of you will. I know that Mr. Ebersole has told some of the other farmers in the area that they can come there for shelter if the Yankees show up."

"Of course he has," snapped Abigail, "so he can put them to work defending his plantation while the Yankees plunder the farms they've abandoned." She shook her head. "Well, I'll not go. This has been my home for forty years, and I won't leave it."

Henry turned his head and looked toward Culpeper, and then he said, "It looks like you won't have to, Ma."

"What are you talking about?" Titus asked.

Henry pointed. "See how the dust is moving on toward town? It's not coming this way. I think the Yankees just want to control the railroad. They'll probably occupy the town but not bother the country around it too much."

Titus gave a snort of disdain. "When'd you learn so much about how armies operate, little brother?"

"I read the newspapers when we can get our hands on any," Henry said, "and I listen to people talk, too. War's about who controls the supply lines, like the Orange and Alexandria."

Titus frowned. Clearly, he wasn't accustomed to hearing such talk come from Henry. Henry wasn't really used to it himself. He hadn't given a great deal of thought to the tactics of the war; what he was saying just sounded like common sense to him.

Titus turned back to Abigail. "I still wish you'd come back to Mountain Laurel with me."

She shook her head. "We're staying right here."

"Suit yourself." Titus lifted his reins. "I've got to get back."

"Good luck," Henry called as Titus turned the horse to ride away. Henry might not agree with what Titus was doing, but he was still his brother, after all.

When Titus was gone, Henry climbed back into the hayloft. He watched as the cloud of dust that marked the progress of the Union army enveloped the point on the landscape where he knew Culpeper lay. The Yankees were in the town now. Henry listened intently for the sound of gunfire, but he couldn't hear any. Of course, rifle fire might not carry this far, but the noise of artillery would. He took it as a good sign that no cannon were being fired.

Along toward dusk, another lone rider approached the farm. Henry stayed in the hayloft with his rifle trained on the horseman until he got close enough so that Henry recognized Michael Davis, the storekeeper. Davis didn't represent any sort of threat, so Henry climbed down to meet him.

"Hello, Henry," Davis greeted him wearily. "I reckon you've figured out what happened today, otherwise you wouldn't have been up in the hayloft with a rifle."

"You saw me up there?" Henry was a bit chagrined that his perch had been discovered so easily.

Davis took off his dusty hat and knocked it against his leg. "Just happened to notice you."

"Mr. Davis," Abigail called from the porch. "How are you?"

"Dispossessed, ma'am," Davis replied with an ironic smile. "The Yankees have taken over the town, lock, stock, and barrel, including my store. Not that there was much to take over there."

"Was anyone hurt?" Cordelia asked. She had come out onto the porch behind her mother.

Davis shook his head. "Nobody fired a shot. Wasn't any point in it. We couldn't fight General Pope and his whole blasted army."

"General Pope," Henry said. "He's the one the Yankees called back from out west somewhere, ain't he?"

"Yep. I heard him givin' a speech before I snuck out of town and came here. Said he was occupyin' Culpeper in the name of the United States and the Army of Virginia. He claims he doesn't want to cause trouble for any civilians, but his men have the right to take whatever they want and if anybody gives them a fight, they'll hold the whole town to blame."

"They're thieves!" Abigail burst out. "Nothing but low-down, contemptible thieves."

"Yes ma'am," agreed Davis. "I reckon you're right."

"What are you going to do, Mr. Davis?" Henry asked.

"Thought I'd head on south, maybe see about joinin' up with ol' Stonewall Jackson. I'm not much of a fighter, but I couldn't just sit there in town and watch those Yankees parade around like they own the place." Davis settled his hat back on his head. In the fading light, his face was all harsh planes and angles, showing his weariness, but his eyes burned with a peculiar light. "They've come too far," he asserted. "Yes sir. Too far."

"Why don't you have some supper with us before you ride on?" suggested Abigail.

Davis shook his head. "No, ma'am, though I thank you for the offer." He glanced around at the farm buildings. "With any luck, those Yankees won't come out here, at least not for a while. When they do, they'll want your cows and chickens and hogs and any grain you've got stored up. If you give it all to 'em, they likely won't hurt anybody."

"Give what we've worked so hard for to the Yankees?" Abigail sounded as if she could not force herself to even contemplate that possibility.

Davis wiped the back of his hand across his mouth. "It's a hard thing, I know. But you folks want to come through all this alive, and that's the way to do it."

"What about you?" Henry challenged. "You're not staying to cooperate with them."

"I don't have anything left to lose. Good luck, folks." Davis turned his horse and rode away into the gathering shadows.

Abigail folded her arms and glowered after him. "Mr. Davis is a good man," she said, "but he doesn't understand. We can't give in to the Yankees. We just can't."

Henry knew his mother meant every word she said. But if the Yankees did show up at the farm, what else could they do except cooperate?

The answer to that was simple, he thought. They could all die.

————

THE COMMANDERS of the Confederate army were as aware as the citizens of Culpeper County that Pope was moving down the line of the Orange and Alexandria Railroad, capturing each station as he came to it. And after sitting in their huge encampment at Harrisonburg on the James River for a month, some of the troops under McClellan were beginning to move again, too. During the meetings between Robert E. Lee and the generals of his army, the feeling was evident that McClellan would eventually withdraw completely from the Virginia Peninsula and move to join forces with Pope in the northern part of the state. After turning back the Union threat to Richmond from the southeast, the Confederacy might easily find itself facing a similar menace to the capital from the northwest.

Unless the army acted quickly to counter it . . .

————

WILL FELT the pangs of familiarity as he rode alongside his company through the Virginia countryside. It was the morning of August 9, a hot morning with a clear, brassy sky overhead, and the Stonewall Brigade, along with the rest of the forces under the command of Jackson, had left Gordonsville a short time earlier, marching north toward Orange Court House and, beyond it, Culpeper.

Home, Will thought.

He gazed toward the northwest, and it seemed almost as if he ought be able to see past the rolling hills of the Piedmont all the way to the Brannon farm. Knowing that he was only a few hours' ride from there gnawed at his insides. With a feeling bordering on desperation, he wanted to know how everyone was: his mother and Cordelia and Titus and Henry. He knew Mac was all right; he'd seen him several times during the past month in Richmond. Stuart's cavalry had carried out a few patrols and raids, but Mac hadn't seen any serious action since the battles of the Seven Days that had turned back McClellan's army. Will wondered, too, if any more letters had arrived from Cory. He would have welcomed any news about his wandering brother, far to the west.

Any thoughts of visiting the farm would have to wait, however. Will knew that. For one thing, the Yankees controlled that part of the state now. Confederate scouts had brought back reports of how the Union soldiers had taken over all the towns along the railroad. From what he had heard, though, Will believed that the Yankees hadn't been ravaging the rest of the countryside too badly. The occupation had been, by and large, a peaceful one where civilians were concerned.

Will was thankful for that. But it might all change once the Yankees met some serious opposition. And that was just what Jackson and his men were going to give them.

The heat continued to climb as the men marched on past Orange Court House toward Culpeper. Will's uniform was soggy with sweat, and he felt like he couldn't get his breath. The only good thing about the heat, he thought, was that his old wounds ached less when it was hot than when it was cold and damp.

Not long after midday, cannon fire erupted up ahead somewhere. The men kept moving, marching steadily toward the sound of the barrage, until a courier came galloping back along the line. "Move to the high ground!" the man shouted as he rode past. He waved toward a low ridge to the east. "Move to the high ground!"

Will swung his men in the direction of the ridge. He knew that it was called Cedar Mountain because of the trees that grew on it. It was hardly a mountain, though. Still, the ridge commanded a better field of fire than the road did. Quickly, the Confederate troops moved toward the slope.

As more orders arrived by courier, Will spread his men out along the side of the ridge to cover the advance of the artillery. The heavy cannon were hauled up the slope by their mule teams as the infantry laid down a withering fire toward the Federal batteries north of Cedar Mountain. In less than an hour, the Confederate guns were emplaced atop the ridge and began returning the Federal fire. The long-distance artillery duel was fierce, so fierce that even though he wasn't all that close to the cannon, their constant roar began to make Will's ears ache.

He was glad when the Stonewall Brigade was shifted to the Confederate left, away from Cedar Mountain and the tumult of the shelling. During the afternoon, the troops were positioned in a long line that stretched westward from the ridge across the turnpike and then across a newly cut wheatfield to a stand of thick woods. Will and his men were at the far left of the line, and around four o'clock the order came for them to move forward.

Will drew his saber and shouted, "Charge!" and his company of the Thirty-third Virginia surged forward. Suddenly, from the woods to their left, rifle fire ripped out. Will had been able to see the blue coats of the enemy up ahead, but this flank attack took him completely by surprise. No one had told him that the Yankees were in the woods, too. Lead whined around him as he twisted in the saddle and hauled his horse's nose to the left. No one had ordered him to take the woods, but to charge straight ahead while that fire was coming in from the side would be suicidal. "Darcy!" Will shouted to Sergeant Bennett. "Follow me!"

"You heard the cap'n!" Darcy bellowed to the rest of the company. "Let's go!" He let out a blood-curdling Rebel yell.

As he leaned forward over the dun's neck, Will sheathed his saber and drew his pistol instead. He dashed into the woods, sweeping the gun from left to right and emptying its chambers. He didn't know if any of the shots hit anything, but the woods were so full of Yankees that some of them must have.

The dun leaped over a deadfall and came crashing down in a knot of Yankee soldiers. One of them was trampled beneath the horse's hooves, and Will caved in the skull of another with the butt of the empty pistol. He jammed the gun back in its holster and reached for his saber again, but before he could draw the blade, one of the soldiers caught hold of the horse's harness and hauled down as hard as he could.

The dun stumbled and fell. Instinctively, Will kicked his booted feet free of the stirrups and rolled out of the saddle. He lost his hat as he landed with a hard jolt on the ground. Rolling again, he came up on one knee and slid the saber out of its sheath in time to thrust it into the belly of a Yankee who was charging at him. The man's momentum carried him on into Will, and the impact bowled him over.

Will struggled to his feet. He found that he had managed to hold on to the saber. A fallen pistol was at his feet. He bent and scooped it up, hoping that it wasn't empty, and fired it three times into the mass of Federals before the hammer clicked on an empty chamber.

Still yelling like fiends, Darcy and the rest of the company burst into the woods. Their arrival turned the attention of the Northerners away from Will. He used his saber to hack out a path through the press of blue-clad soldiers and found himself standing shoulder to shoulder with Darcy. They probably looked like a savage pair, Will thought fleetingly, splattered with blood as they were and with faces grimy from powder smoke.

Union reinforcements poured into the woods. Will didn't know where they were coming from and didn't care. All that mattered was that his men were outnumbered. They were fighting valiantly, but they couldn't stand up for long against odds such as these.

"Fall back!" he heard himself shouting. "Fall back!"

Battling every step of the way, the Confederates gradually relinquished the woods and broke back into the open ground of the wheatfield. The Yankees came after them, doing some howling and shrieking of their own. Bullets buzzed around Will's head like bees as he tried to keep the retreat orderly.

There was no chance to do that. The men broke and ran. For the first time in their illustrious existence, the Stonewall Brigade was being routed.

In the distance, nearly a mile away to the east, a thick haze of artillery smoke hung over the ridge called Cedar Mountain. Will saw that and knew the big guns were probably holding their own in the battle. Much of the rest of the Confederate line had encountered heavy resistance from the Federals, but it was holding, too. Here on the left, however, where the Yankees had somehow flanked them, the Southerners' line was on the verge of complete collapse.

"Rally, damn it!" Will shouted at his men. "Rally up!" He threw aside the empty gun in his hand and plucked another weapon from the ground next to the mangled corpse of a Confederate lieutenant. Will braced his feet and fired toward the onrushing Northerners. He saw two of them spill to the ground.

Suddenly, Darcy was beside him, firing a rifle. Another Yankee fell. Darcy dropped the gun, snatched up another and fired again. Will reached for another fallen weapon and emptied it. Another man joined him and Darcy, then another and another. Scavenging from the fallen dead, Federal and Confederate alike, Will and his companions made their stand.

From behind them came the rattle of more gunfire. Will threw a glance over his shoulder and saw thousands of gray-and butternut-uniformed figures surging toward the lonely bastion he and Darcy and a few others had formed. Reinforcements were on the way, and leading them, Will saw, was Jackson himself.

The tide of Southerners swept forward around Will and the others. The Union troops put up a stiff fight, but they were forced back steadily. The fighting moved back into the woods, but this time it was the Confederates who outnumbered their foe.

Left behind, Will turned and started walking toward the edge of the wheatfield. His legs felt like rubber, but he didn't realize he was swaying and nearly falling until Darcy put an arm around his shoulders to brace him. "Come on, Cap'n'," said the burly sergeant. "Whyn't we find a place to sit down for a spell?"

That sounded good to Will. Damned good, in fact. He was bleeding from a score of minor wounds, and his uniform was ripped and tattered. Darcy wasn't any better off.

But both of them were better off than the hundreds of men who lay sprawled in the wheatfield and in the woods, dead or dying from their wounds.

They found what was left of an old wagon overturned on the edge of the field and sat down on it gratefully. A few minutes later, Yancy Lattimer rode by, reining in abruptly when he saw them. "Will!" Yancy exclaimed. "Are you all right?"

"Reckon I'll live," Will replied tiredly. "We were in the thick of it for a while."

Yancy nodded. He had come through the battle unhurt. "We've got them on the run now. I expect they'll pull back all the way to Culpeper." He hesitated, realizing what he had just said. "Good Lord. That's your home, isn't it?"

Will stared into the distance to the north and nodded bleakly. The Federals had been on the brink of victory here today, but then they had taken a licking. They wouldn't be in a very good mood when they got back to Culpeper.

Will hoped that in winning this battle, he and his comrades hadn't doomed his family.

Chapter Twenty-three

BOTH GENERALS IN COMMAND of the forces at the battle of Cedar Mountain, Jackson for the Confederacy and Pope for the Union, claimed to have won the day, but in truth the victory belonged more to Jackson. The Federals, who had been advancing steadily down the Orange and Alexandria toward its crucial junction with the Virginia Central Railroad at Gordonsville, found their thrust blunted. Even worse, they were forced to retreat and massed their forces in the area between Culpeper and Brandy Station.

Because of the continuing threat that McClellan's Army of the Potomac might withdraw from the peninsula and join forces with Pope's Army of Virginia, Robert E. Lee knew that he could not allow the Federals to catch their balance. In a typically bold move, he shifted even more of his troops north of Richmond, leaving the Confederacy's capital city only lightly defended. Together, the forces under Jackson and Longstreet would move north, then split so that Jackson could feint around Pope and make the Union general pull back to thwart a potential attack on the Northern capital. Then, after joining forces again, Jackson and Longstreet would be in position either to crush Pope or force him completely out of Virginia.

That was the plan. In order for it to have the best chance of working, however, Pope's communications and supply line from the north had to be disrupted. That job, requiring both boldness and speed, fell to the men best equipped to carry it out: the cavalry under the command of Stuart.

MAC RODE north but no longer as a colonel's aide. Fitz Lee had been promoted to brigadier general, and he commanded one-third of Stuart's forces. The other two brigades were under the command of the South Carolinian, Gen. Wade Hampton, and another Virginian, Gen. Beverly Robertson. For the mission on which they were now embarked, Hampton's brigade had been left behind at Mitchell's Ford on the Rapidan River. The rest of Stuart's men were bound for the rear of the Federal lines, where it was hoped that no one would be expecting them.

A few days earlier, some of Stuart's cavalry had clashed with Yankee horsemen at Brandy Station, north of Culpeper. Mac had not been with them, but he had heard the yarns about how the battle had been fought at close quarters with sabers. Heros Von Borcke, Stuart's gigantic Prussian aide, claimed to have lopped off the head of a Union soldier with one swing of his blade. Mac didn't know whether that was true or not, but he did know that the Northerners had retreated even farther up the rail line toward Manassas.

And he knew, too, that he was close to home.

One of the hardest things he had ever done was not to head for the farm to see how his family was doing. He knew the Federals had occupied Culpeper County for the past several weeks, but there were no reports of widespread destruction. Mac held out the hope that his family and the Brannon farm had not been disturbed.

He had talked to Will briefly while Stuart, Fitz Lee, Hampton, and Robertson were conferring with Jackson a few days earlier. Will had no news from home, either, and like Mac, he had been struggling with the desire to visit. Both of them were needed with their units, though, because things were beginning to happen quickly now. Will had told Mac about the fighting at Cedar Mountain, and Mac had shuddered to think that his brother had to endure such. Things were likely to get worse before they got better, though.

The sky began to darken with clouds as the cavalry approached Warrenton. Ever since leaving on this mission, the horsemen had taken back roads and cut across country at times, skirting the Union forces that lay to the east. Now, as they rode into Warrenton, Fitz Lee said to Mac, "I wouldn't be surprised if we find some Yankees here."

Mac thought the general sounded as if he would be disappointed if there weren't any Union forces here to oppose him.

As the cavalry rode into the settlement, no blue uniforms were anywhere to be seen. Instead, civilians flocked into the street and greeted the horsemen with shouts of welcome. Lee reined in his mount impatiently and asked one of the townsmen, "Where are the Yankees?"

"Been and gone!" the man replied enthusiastically. "They were here a few days ago, but we ain't seen hide nor hair of 'em since."

Stuart rode up in time to hear the man's statement. He reined in and leaned forward in the saddle to ask, "Do you know where they went?"

The townsman looked up at Stuart with awe, recognizing the dashing cavalry leader. "No sir, not for certain," he managed to say after a moment. "But they was headed east toward the railroad when they left."

"So shall we be," said Stuart. "Catlett's Station is in that direction, isn't it, Fitz?"

Lee nodded. "Yes sir."

"We'll find Yankees there, or my name's not Jeb Stuart!"

A cheer went up from the crowd in the street at Stuart's bold prediction. The bold cavalier swept off his plumed hat—a new one, since he had lost the old one a few days earlier—and bowed to the citizens of Warrenton. The cheers grew louder, and Mac couldn't help but grin at the way Stuart was playing up to the crowd. If Stuart had not been such a skilled officer, he might have been regarded as a vainglorious popinjay. But he could back up his theatrics with results and had demonstrated so on numerous occasions. That made him a hero.

After a brief rest, the cavalry rode out of Warrenton, heading east now. Not long after their departure, the clouds grew even thicker, and thunder rumbled in the distance. "We're going to get wet," Lee predicted to Mac.

"Yes sir, it looks like it," Mac agreed, and a moment after that, the first fat raindrop hit him in the face.

The rain was sporadic but heavy when it fell. The closer they came to Catlett's Station, the harder the rain. As overcast as the sky was, night fell early, and it was a dark night indeed, lit only by flickers of lightning.

Mac could barely see Stuart when the general held up a hand to bring the column to a halt. The riders lurched to an awkward stop, and Stuart motioned several of them forward. Lee leaned toward Mac and murmured into his ear, "The general must sense that there are Federal pickets ahead. We must be close to Catlett's Station by now."

Lee walked his horse forward, and Mac followed closely. Stuart put out a hand to stop them. "I know what you're up to, Fitz," Stuart said. "I'll not risk one of my brigadiers on a scouting mission."

Lee shifted impatiently in the saddle. "But, sir—"

"Rest easy, Fitz. There'll be action aplenty before this night is over."

A short time later, the men Stuart had sent ahead returned, driving several prisoners ahead of them on foot. In the flashes of lightning, Mac could see the Yankee pickets who had been set upon and captured quietly by the cavalrymen.

Sullenly, the prisoners refused to answer any of Stuart's questions. "Take them on to the rear," he ordered. While that was being done, the cavalry started forward again, riding slowly and cautiously. They were at least ten miles behind enemy lines, and quite probably surrounded by thousands of Union troops.

Mac stiffened in his saddle as he suddenly heard someone singing in a deep, rich voice. Stuart motioned for a halt, and a moment later, a figure came walking along the road, a man singing to himself and not even noticing the cavalry blocking his way until he had practically run into Stuart's horse. Then he jumped back with a frightened hiss of breath.

"Easy, my friend," Stuart reassured him. "I know you, don't I? You sang for me once in my camp at Qui Vive."

The man snatched a battered old hat off his head as a flash of lightning revealed he was a slave. "Gen'ral Stuart?" he asked in amazement as he peered up at the riders. More than a little fear was etched on his face, too.

"Hello, Bodie. That's your name, isn't it?"

"Yessuh. Lawd, I never thought to see you again, Gen'ral, suh. What're you doin' up here?"

"This is Catlett's Station?"

"Yessuh."

"The Yankees are here?"

Bodie nodded. "I been workin' for one o' Gen'ral Pope's officers. They made me work for 'em, Gen'ral. I never wanted to."

Stuart reached down from the saddle and patted the man on the shoulder. "I know that, Bodie. Can you tell us the layout of the camp?"

"Do better'n that," Bodie boasted with a wide grin. "I can show you Gen'ral Pope's headquarters and ever'thin' else."

Mac felt his pulse begin to race. This simple raid on the Union supply line might turn out to be much more important if they could capture Pope himself.

That hope was dashed as Bodie went on, "The gen'ral, he ain't here right now—but the paymaster is."

"Interesting," murmured Stuart. "Lead on, old friend."

The horses moved at a walk, any sounds they made being swallowed up by the rain and the thunder. The large Yankee camp around them seemed to be asleep. Mac was able to spot a few tents with lamps glowing yellowly inside them, but no one was out and about. Everyone was staying out of the rain.

They reached the railroad tracks and followed them a short distance, then a large, two-story frame building loomed out of the darkness on the left. That was the station building itself, Mac figured. On the other side of the tracks, directly opposite the depot, was a large warehouse.

Stuart turned in his saddle and called for the buglers to be sent forward. "Pass the word, gentlemen," he directed his officers. "On my signal, we give the Yankees a taste of havoc."

Mac slipped his pistol from its holster and waited tensely. A moment or two dragged by, and then suddenly the buglers sounded the clear tones of the call to attack. On the heels of the signal to charge came the shouts of the cavalrymen as they surged forward.

Mac sent the stallion galloping straight ahead. Stuart and Lee were bound for the depot, and Mac was right behind them. The rest of the column spread out, some of the men racing through the rows of tents and firing at the startled Federals who came scrambling out of the canvas shelters, others making for the warehouse and the line of supply wagons parked outside it, while still others threw ropes over the telegraph wires on the poles beside the railroad tracks and began hauling them down. It was chaos, but controlled chaos.

Shots blasted from inside the warehouse as Union soldiers posted on guard duty there tried to mount a resistance. Mac threw a glance over his shoulder and saw several of the cavalrymen jumping their horses onto the platform that ran along the front of the warehouse. They emptied their pistols into the darkness, aiming for the muzzle flashes of the sentries' guns.

From the corner of his eye, as lightning flashed again, Mac saw several men come scrambling around the corner of the depot. They had rifles in their hands, and they stopped short to lift the weapons and try to draw a bead on Stuart and Lee. They hesitated, waiting for another lightning flash, and that gave Mac the chance to twist in the saddle and fire his pistol toward them. He eared back the hammer and squeezed off another shot, then another. A staccato of gunfire came from close behind him as more of Stuart's men reacted to the threat to their leader. The Yankees were thrown back against the side of the building, riddled with bullets.

Stuart swung down from his horse and charged into the station, saber in hand. Lee, Mac, and several other men hurried in behind him. They found the general standing over a balding, rather mild-looking Union colonel who had his hands raised in surrender. He was sitting at a desk, and behind him were more than a dozen heavy trunks that probably had been delivered to Catlett's Station by train earlier in the day. Several of the trunks were open, and Mac saw stacks of greenbacks and canvas pouches that might be full of coins.

"Gentlemen," Stuart said with a grin, "this fine fellow has decided that he wishes to make a generous contribution to our noble cause."

"You . . . you can't do this!" the Yankee paymaster gulped. "There's over half a million dollars here!"

"Thank you for that bit of information," Stuart replied, still grinning. "Gentlemen, let's find some wagons to carry this booty."

While several of the men left on that errand, Mac stepped to the doorway and looked out at the rainy night. The warehouse was on fire now, as were some of the wagons. Other wagons were quickly claimed to carry the captured money. The tents had been trampled and scattered by the charge, and the startled, demoralized Federals, many of them unable to get to their weapons, had fled into the countryside. Stuart and his men had indeed wreaked a great deal of havoc in a very short period of time.

Stuart sent a patrol north with orders to destroy the railroad bridge over Cedar Run. The men returned a short time later to report failure. The wood was too wet to burn, they explained, and Union riflemen on the far side of the trestle had peppered them with fire when they tried to chop through it with axes. Stuart nodded, clearly disappointed but unwilling to risk any more men in a futile effort.

"Gather up whatever you're taking, men, and let's be away from here," he ordered. He was twirling a hat on his finger, Mac noticed, a Union general's hat, to be precise. Noticing that Mac was watching him, Stuart smiled. "According to our friend Bodie, this hat belongs to General Pope himself. A fair trade for the one I lost, don't you think?"

"Yes sir," Mac agreed. He didn't really care about hats. He just thought they ought to get out of here and head back to their own lines as quickly as they could.

That was what Stuart and his cavalry did, riding away from the burning station with a fortune in cash and supplies. Most of the Union prisoners had escaped in the confusion, but that was all right. The object had been to threaten Pope's rear and destroy his communications and supply lines. Not much damage had been done to the railroad, but all the telegraph lines were down, and it would take time to restring them.

Maybe by the time the wires were up again, Mac thought as he rode with the others, Robert E. Lee would have another surprise for the Yankees.

———

PROBABLY THE most valuable item captured in the raid on Catlett's Station was not the Federal payroll but the dispatch book discovered among the plunder. It belonged to Pope himself. When it had been delivered to the Confederate commander, he read grim news in it: McClellan's army was indeed planning to join forces with Pope. Some of the Union divisions that had been forced back down the peninsula earlier in the summer were in fact about to do that very thing. If Lee's plan was going to work, it had to be put into operation quickly.

That was why, in the predawn hours of August 25, Will found himself moving hurriedly north along with the rest of Jackson's men.

Jackson, closemouthed as always, had not shared Lee's plan with his staff, so Will had no idea what their destination was. All he knew was that Jackson's foot cavalry was on the move again, traveling light.

Will heard someone riding up alongside him in the darkness and turned to see a slender form on horseback. Yancy Lattimer's voice said, "It's back across the Blue Ridge to the Shenandoah for us, I'm thinking."

Will shook his head. "I don't know. The Yankees have most of their men on this side of the Blue Ridge now."

"They won't once they decide we're bound for Washington again."

Will shrugged. Yancy might be right. This march might be another feint designed to make the Yankees think their capital was threatened. That had worked before to split the Union forces; it might again.

But when they reached the town of Salem later in the day and turned east instead of west along the Manassas Gap Railroad, everyone realized they weren't on their way to the Valley after all.

Will knew what lay in this direction: Manassas Junction and the huge Federal supply depot that the Federals had built there. They had flanked Pope, Will realized, and now they were poised to strike at his rear.

Jackson drove the men as never before, riding back and forth along the lengthy column and calling to the troops, "Close up, boys, close up!" The soldiers responded with grim eagerness and determination. Will knew that there had been some questions about Jackson's effectiveness in the relatively close quarters of the Seven Days' battles around Richmond. At long-range strikes such as this, however, the men of Jackson's command had no equal. They could march and march and march and then fight better than anyone else on either side in this war.

Following the railroad, on August 26 the column moved through Thoroughfare Gap in the Bull Run Mountains and found the pass undefended by the Northerners. Will could barely believe their good fortune. Pope had missed a bet by not sending men to close off the gap, and Jackson was ready to take full advantage of the Union general's mistake. On August 27 Jackson's men moved quickly across the flat terrain around Manassas. They closed in on the supply depot at the junction, with the Federals seemingly having no warning that they were coming.

The Southerners reached the Orange and Alexandria Railroad a few miles south of Manassas, and Jackson ordered the men to start tearing up the tracks. Before they could do so, Will heard the whistle of a locomotive in the distance. He called out to Darcy, "No time for that now! Fell some trees and throw them on the tracks!"

Axes rang out as they bit into the tree trunks. Several cedars crashed to the ground, and soldiers gathered around to lift them and place them on the railroad tracks. Will lifted himself in his stirrups and peered down the tracks to the south as the men grunted and strained with the effort to erect the makeshift blockade. Will spotted smoke and knew it came from the locomotive's stack.

"Here it comes!" he shouted. "Get ready!"

That Yankee engineer must be shocked as hell, Will thought with a grin as the train rumbled closer and closer. The cars behind the locomotive were likely empty, on their way to be refilled with supplies at Manassas. Will thought that the engineer might bring the train to a stop and try to back up when he spotted the barricade and the thousands of Confederates on both sides of the tracks, but the man was braver than that. The whistle screeched again, and more smoke billowed from the stack. The engineer had opened up the throttle all the way, Will realized.

Bullets pinged off the steel sides of the cab as the locomotive plunged ahead. The engineer was crouched down, out of the direct line of fire, although he was still in danger from ricochets. Will waved his arm at his men and ordered, "Get back! Get away from the tracks!"

With a grinding crash, the locomotive's cowcatcher struck the barrier of fallen trees. The train was going so fast that the trees were flung aside like matchsticks. Troopers had to dive frantically out of the way to avoid being crushed by them. In frustration, Will sent a couple of pistol shots after the train as it roared past, but he knew it wouldn't do any good.

The Federals at Manassas would have warning now that the enemy was only a few miles south of them.

Jackson realized that just as well as Will did, and he delegated some of his men to continue their efforts to tear up the tracks while the rest of his forces went north. Will heard later that the next empty supply train to come along had been derailed, sending the locomotive plunging violently into a gully and dragging the cars after it.

As for Manassas Junction, it was only lightly defended despite the vast amount of supplies housed there, and those Union soldiers trying to do so as Jackson approached decided on the better part of valor and abandoned the depot.

The Southerners swarmed over the supplies. Exhausted from the long march, poorly fed, they were like children, laughing hilariously as they feasted on the food originally meant for Union soldiers. Jackson didn't attempt to hold them back from their plunder. His only concession to discipline was an immediate order to pour out all the liquor. Full bellies were a welcome change for his men, but he didn't want them drunk, not this far behind enemy lines.

That evening, as flames leaped high from the warehouses—torched after the soldiers had cleaned them out as much as possible—Will sat on a log and gnawed gratefully on a turkey leg. Yancy strolled over to join him, followed by the young slave, Roman.

"A veritable Dionysian feast, don't you think?" asked Yancy as he waved a turkey leg of his own in the air. From the sound of his voice, he had managed to get his hands on some of the spirits before they were all dumped.

332 • *James Reasoner*

"Don't reckon I know what that means."

"Dionysius, the Greek god of wine and good food," Yancy clarified.

"Don't know the fella. But I'm glad to see the boys getting to eat their fill for a change."

Yancy settled down on the log beside Will, and Roman hunkered on his heels next to the two officers. The garish red light from the flames lit all three faces.

"I wonder what Jackson has in mind now," mused Yancy.

"We'll find out when he tells us, not before."

"We wouldn't be here in the enemy's rear, though, unless we were going to do more than loot some supplies."

Will nodded slowly. He thought Yancy was right. Jackson, and probably General Lee, too, had something else in mind, something that would knock the stuffing right out of the Yankees if it worked.

But in the meantime, Will was content to sit and eat and watch the flames. He tore off another hunk of the turkey leg with his teeth and began to chew.

Chapter Twenty-four

JACKSON'S MEN THOROUGHLY ENJOYED their time at Manassas Junction as they looted the Union supplies and filled their packs for the march to wherever their commander would lead them next. They did not have long to wait. During the night, orders came to leave the Federal supply depot, which was now nothing more than a square mile of smoldering rubble. By now, Pope would have been told what had happened, and indeed, Confederate scouts reported that the Union army was on the move, abandoning their positions around Culpeper and Brandy Station and pulling back north toward Manassas.

Robert E. Lee was on his way to the area with Longstreet's divisions, following the same route Jackson had taken through Thoroughfare Gap in the Bull Run Mountains. Jackson's job was to keep Pope occupied until Lee and Longstreet could arrive on the field. In order to do this, he chose to establish a defensive line that would block any thrust the Federals made in the direction of the mountains. After splitting his forces into three sections and sending them by different routes in hopes of confusing the Northerners even more, Jackson ordered them to regroup at Stony Ridge, a long, rocky embankment that lived up to its name. The ridge paralleled the Warrenton turnpike, and just below it was the graded and leveled roadbed of a railroad. The tracks had never been laid because the building project had been abandoned, but the roadbed made the Confederate position that much stronger because of the extra cover it provided.

Will Brannon sat on his dun horse on the ridge and watched as the thousands of troops in Jackson's army packed themselves onto the roadbed below. There were so many of them that it appeared they could barely move. They had spent the previous night resting under the trees on the ridge and enjoying the food from the full packs they had carried away from Manassas Junction. Now reports had come that Union troops were in the area, and the Southerners were getting ready to fight again.

Will's eyes scanned the men of his company. Darcy had them in good order, which came as no surprise. In the Shenandoah campaign, in the Seven Days' fighting, and in the clashes since, Darcy had proven himself to be an exemplary sergeant. Will counted himself lucky to have such a man serving with him, although back in his days as the sheriff of Culpeper County, he never would have dreamed that the roistering, brawling farmer would turn into such a fine soldier.

But he had never figured that he himself would make much of a soldier, either, Will thought with a chuckle. War did strange things to a man. Some responded well, and others didn't. Will looked toward the southeast. He had a good view of the rolling countryside where the battle of Manassas had taken place a little over a year earlier. He saw Henry House Hill in the distance, where Jackson had made his stand and earned the name Stonewall. That was where it had all begun, for Jackson, for Will, for Darcy Bennett, for Yancy Lattimer, and for so many others . . .

Will's head lifted as he heard the tramp of marching feet in the distance. A large group of men was coming along the turnpike from the east. Will looked along the line of the ridge and saw the Confederate troops getting prepared for battle. Several batteries of cannon had been brought up to the edge of the ridge and were loaded and ready to fire. All that was left was for the Federals to show up.

A few minutes later, they did just that, marching into view on the turnpike. *Damn fools,* Will thought as he saw their casual attitude. They hadn't even sent any scouts or skirmishers ahead to see if it was safe to come through here, and they were about to find out what a bad mistake that had been.

The gunners waited impatiently by their cannon until the Union column was stretched out along the turnpike. Then the order came to fire. Lanyards were tugged hard, igniting the friction triggers, and the big guns roared out their destructive message. Will watched grimly as the shells exploded among the startled Northerners. He didn't care for the long-range slaughter of artillery barrages, but he had to admit they were effective, especially when the enemy wasn't expecting an attack.

Over the thunder of the cannon, Will shouted, "Fire!" to his men, and a lethal volley of rifle fire swept down from the roadbed. The Federals were confused, dying where they stood, cut down by a foe they hadn't even known was there.

Several Confederate companies charged down from the ridge, no doubt hoping to take advantage of the chaos gripping the Yankees and utterly destroy them. Before the charge could reach the turnpike, however, some of the Union officers rallied their men, and the shouting Southerners were met with stiffer resistance than they had expected. They came to a stop about seventy-five yards from the Federals and began laying down a fierce fire. The Yankees returned the fire, and men fell on both sides.

Will's expression grew more bleak as he watched what was happening. The battle quickly turned into a stalemate, with the two sides standing a short distance apart and blazing away at each other. Whenever a soldier fell, fatally wounded, another stepped forward to take his place. Will had never seen anything like it. Men were dying by the hundreds, perhaps even the thousands, and yet neither side charged the other. The carnage was so great that Will was almost glad when the haze of powder smoke over the field grew too thick for him to see all that was happening.

The surreal duel continued until darkness fell, and then both Union and Confederate forces pulled back. The Southerners retreated up the slope to Stony Ridge, while the Federals turned and marched raggedly back the way they had come. Will hadn't fired a shot all day, but still he was drained by what had happened. His men had remained on the roadbed during the battle, being held in reserve, so their losses were few. Overall, though, Jackson had lost a great many men. The burial details would be busy all night.

———◦❈◦———

WILL KNELT and sipped from a cup of hot coffee. The night had finally passed, horrible as always because of the moans and cries of wounded men lying on the battlefield, and morning had broken, bringing with it some relief as the last of the wounded were carried behind the lines on both sides to field hospitals.

Darcy Bennett hunkered close by, gnawing on some hardtack. He glanced up and noted, "There's your brother yonder, Cap'n."

Will looked and saw Mac riding into the Confederate camp atop Stony Ridge with the rest of Stuart's cavalry. Will hadn't seen him since before the battle the day before, and he wasn't sure the cavalry had even been involved. He stood up and strode toward Mac, raising a hand in greeting. Mac swung down from the stallion's back and turned toward Will as Stuart, Lee, and the other cavalry officers began to confer with Jackson.

The Brannon brothers embraced quickly, then Will said, "I see you came through it all right yesterday."

Mac nodded. "My company wasn't in the thick of it. We were lucky." He thought of the way the men had fallen during the battle. "A lot of men weren't."

Wearily, Mac rubbed a hand over his face. He had always been thinner than Will, but now his features were drawn. "We skirmished with Yankee patrols between here and Thoroughfare Gap all day yesterday and most of the night. But General Lee and General Longstreet got through all right. Some of the Yankees got around us and managed to plug the gap for a while, but they didn't slow things down for long."

"So Longstreet's still on his way to join us?"

Keeping his voice low and quiet, Mac carefully whispered, "He's going to come up on the right flank and turn the corner on the Union left when Pope hits General Jackson today. At least, that's what the generals think."

Will knew Mac's information came from discussions overheard in his capacity as Lee's aide. Maybe it wasn't proper military procedure for him to pass along what he knew, but Will was glad to hear it anyway.

"It's sure that Pope will attack today?"

"He's in position to," Mac confirmed. "I can't believe he won't."

"McClellan didn't, when he was sitting there just a few miles out of Richmond," Will pointed out.

"Pope's not McClellan. General Stuart says he'll come, and I believe the general."

So did Will. In the battle the day before, Jackson had thrown down the gauntlet. Pope had little choice but to pick it up.

MAC AND the rest of the cavalry rode out a short time later. Their orders were to locate Longstreet and inform him and Lee of Jackson's situation on Stony Ridge.

By the middle of the day they had done so, meeting Longstreet's men as they marched east from the Bull Run Mountains. Lee, Longstreet, and Stuart met by the side of the road, and Mac sat nearby with Fitz Lee while the three commanders sorted out their options. Then Stuart approached them.

"Fitz, I want you to hurry back to Jackson and deploy your men as he sees fit," ordered Stuart.

"What about you, General?" Lee asked.

"The rest of us are going to guard General Longstreet's right flank as he advances toward the battle." Stuart smiled. "So you see, Fitz, I'm doing you a favor. I'm sending you where there is likely to be the most glory."

And the most danger, thought Mac, because it was Jackson's job to keep the Yankees busy until Longstreet was in position to hit their flank.

Lee nodded without hesitation and snapped a salute. "We're on our way, General," he said, then wheeled his horse and put the spurs to it. Mac followed.

Lee's brigade immediately started back toward Stony Ridge. Despite their hurry, it was the middle of the afternoon before they neared the battlefield, and for quite some time they had been able to hear the roar of artillery and the rattle of rifle fire in the distance. Will was in the middle of that somewhere, Mac thought, and he was glad he was going back to join his brother, even though they might not be together during the fight.

A short time later, Fitz Lee and his horsemen galloped up to Jackson's command post back of the ridge. Jackson came out to meet them, looking rumpled as usual, and Lee saluted. "Compliments of General Stuart, General Lee, and General Longstreet, sir. They are on their way and ask that you endeavor to hold your position."

"We shall do more than endeavor, sir," replied Jackson. "We shall succeed!"

Seeing the fire in Jackson's eyes and hearing the determination in his voice, Mac didn't doubt for a second that old Stonewall was right.

Jackson told Lee to reinforce the far left of the Confederate line. They did so, riding along the back side of the ridge until they reached the spot where it ended, sloping down to a junction of two roads. A small church stood near the intersection, empty and abandoned now. Services might be held in it again someday—if it survived the battle.

At Lee's command, the cavalrymen dismounted. In front of them along the road was a line of Confederate infantry engaged in heavy fighting. Mac spotted movement to his left and looked to see more Union troops charging in an attempt to turn the Confederate corner.

Fitz Lee saw the Northerners at the same time and called out an order. The men who had rifles lifted them and fired, sending an unexpected volley into the forefront of the Federal charge. As the Yankees in the lead stumbled and went down, the Confederates on horseback rushed down the hill on foot, firing rifles and pistols as they came.

Mac emptied his pistol into the blue-clad wave, which broke before the charge. Instead of engaging the Southerners in hand-to-hand combat, the Union troopers turned and retreated back the way they had come. Whoops of triumph went up from the infantrymen who had nearly fallen victim to the Federals' flanking movement. Fitz Lee's men joined in the shouts.

Mac stopped to reload his pistol. From where he was, he could see all the way along the line of the ridge, and what he saw was awe-inspiring in a terrible way. Thousands of Union soldiers were hurling themselves at the ridge and the railroad embankment just below it, and the Southerners under Jackson were beating them back with equal determination.

Cannon roared on both sides, from behind the advancing Federals and from above on the crest of the ridge. The shells crisscrossed in the air above the battlefield, whistling their songs of death through the air and then exploding as they plunged back to earth.

Below the artillery barrage, wave after wave of Union troops charged toward the slope. Many of them fell long before they got there, cut down by the withering fire from Jackson's men, but others took their place, trampling over the bodies of their fallen comrades as they continued the charge. Each time one of the Yankee color-bearers was hit and started to fall, another man would snatch the flag before the colors could hit the ground. As Mac watched, he couldn't help but feel grudging admiration for the soldiers. The Northerners had profaned the Constitution with their arrogant, illegal invasion of the South, but most of them were not lacking in courage.

With his pistol reloaded, Mac fired into the Union ranks again. He reloaded the weapon several times as the battle continued. Gradually, this far left segment of the Confederate line began to waver. Some of Jackson's companies began to pull back, retreating up the slope toward the ridge. Mac noticed the subtle pullback and realized that if Lee's men weren't careful, they were going to find themselves alone and ahead of the line, isolated in the middle of the advancing Federals.

Lee noticed the same thing and waved his saber over his head, shouting, "To the church! Fall back to the church!"

The cavalrymen hurried toward the small wood-and-stone structure. Mac glanced up at the stand of trees where he had left the stallion. He hated to abandon the horse, but there was no time to fetch it now. He would just have to hope that the Yankees would not overrun this end of the ridge.

Suddenly, in the distance to the south, the firing intensified. When Mac looked, he saw a dust cloud billowing into the air that could have only come from a large attacking force. Longstreet was sweeping in on the Union left, just as planned. Mac reached the corner of the church, leaned against it, and fired back at the closest Federals. He grinned wearily as he saw the blue-uniformed troops start to peel back. Pope would need all the men he could get on the other side of the battlefield as he tried to deal with Longstreet's smashing blow.

Within an hour, it was obvious that the strategy concocted by Lee, Longstreet, and Jackson had worked. The Northerners were pulling back all across the line of battle, collapsing on their flanks and concentrating their defense in the center. They had been forced south of the turnpike by a Confederate force that was no longer fighting a defensive battle but an offensive one instead. From his position atop the ridge, where the cavalry had regrouped and mounted their horses again, Mac could see that the ragged edges of the Union right were starting to fray even more as men broke and ran. The whole Federal army began to shift to the east.

"Mac!"

Mac twisted in the saddle as the familiar voice called his name, and to his immense relief, he saw Will riding toward him, a big grin on his powder-grimed face. Mac looked over his brother's uniform for fresh bloodstains but didn't see any. It appeared that Will had survived the battle unhurt.

Will confirmed that a moment later as he came up beside his brother and gripped his hand. "I was hoping you'd come through all right," Will said.

"What about your men?" asked Mac.

Will's expression became solemn. "We lost some. There was never any chance we wouldn't. The Yankees threw everything they had at us. But we held on until Longstreet was ready to hit them."

Mac nodded. "I saw some of it from up here. We've got them on the run."

Will rested his hands on the pommel of his saddle and leaned forward. "It's mighty odd," he mused, a contemplative look on his face. "Last summer, the positions were mighty near backward from what they were today. Today the Yankees made their stand on Henry House Hill, just like we did under Jackson." The grin reappeared on his face. "It all came out the same in the end, though. The Yankees turned tail and ran."

"What are you going to do now?" As he asked the question, Mac noticed that many of Jackson's men were on their feet, gathering their gear as if they were getting ready to march.

"We're heading east to try to get around the Yankees and cut off their line of retreat on the other side of Centreville," Will replied. "If we don't, Pope will likely run all the way back to Washington City."

"I'm not sure that would be such a bad thing," Mac noted.

"No, but if we can get ahead of them, maybe we can destroy the entire army in Virginia."

Mac couldn't argue with that strategy. He stuck out his hand. "Good luck."

"Thanks," Will said as they shook again. "Any idea what you'll be doing?"

Mac had learned a thing or two about military tactics during his time with Stuart and Lee. "I reckon we'll be harassing the Yankees' rear guard while they're retreating."

"Move 'em along toward us," Will said, then with a wave of farewell, he urged his horse into a trot that carried him away from the battlefield.

"I hope you're ready for them," Mac said, even though his brother could no longer hear him.

———————

As it turned out, neither the weather nor the Yankees cooperated in Jackson's venture. Jackson crossed Bull Run at Sudley Ford, but a heavy rain during the night slowed him down and made progress almost impossible the next day, August 31. After slogging along roads that were little more than swamps, the Confederate foot cavalry bedded down for the night, not only soaking wet but also hungry because their supply wagons were unable to catch up with them because of the rain.

The next day was little better, but in the afternoon, Jackson, unable to get ahead of Pope's army and intercept it, was at least able to catch up with them. Unfortunately, so did more rain, and a driving thunderstorm struck just as the two sides clashed near an old mansion called Chantilly.

Will had never experienced a harder downpour in his life. The rain slashed and lashed at the troops, making it difficult to get their rifles to fire. The Federals were forted up in some trees fronted by an open field. Repeated charges finally succeeded in the Southerners' reaching the trees, but once they were there, the fighting turned hand to hand in the worst way against the determined Northerners.

On this day, Will was riding a different horse, a sturdy chestnut, because his dun had been exhausted by the two-day-long chase through the mud and rain. He led his company across the field and into the woods, and as he entered the stand of trees he felt the horse lurch violently underneath him. The animal's front legs crumpled, and Will realized the horse had been hit. He threw himself to the side before the animal could roll over on him and pin him as it fell. Will came up covered with mud from his roll on the ground. He didn't bother pulling his gun because he knew it was likely to be fouled. Instead he jerked his saber from its scabbard and waded into the fight, hacking to the right and the left as he found himself almost surrounded by Yankees.

Something slammed into his left shoulder blade from behind. Will felt himself falling forward but could not catch his balance, could not stop himself from sprawling once more in the mud. His whole left side was numb. He knew that either he had been shot or one of the Federals had smashed a rifle butt against him. There was no time to check and see if he was bleeding. He rolled over, thankful that he still had control of his right arm, and saw a boot coming at his face. He twisted his head to the side and thrust up with his saber. The attacker who had just tried to stomp his skull screamed as the blade ripped into his groin.

Will tore his saber free, then through the driving rain he saw Darcy Bennett shoulder the dying Yankee aside. Darcy reached down and grabbed Will's arm. He hauled Will to his feet as if he weighed hardly anything. "You all right, Cap'n?" Darcy called over the steady roar of the rain and the shouts of struggling men.

"Maybe hit . . . in the back," gasped Will.

Darcy checked quickly, then reported, "Your coat ain't torn, Cap'n. I reckon you just got hit hard."

Will nodded and the feeling started to come back to his left arm and side. They ached badly, but not like the sharp, fiery pain of a bullet wound.

Darcy spun around as a Union soldier came at him. He bayoneted the man in the belly, then pushed him aside. He threw a grin over his shoulder as he called to Will, "I guess I better go kill me some more Yankees!"

Yes, Will supposed, that was why they were here.

———◦◦◦———

JACKSON WAS unable to stop the Union retreat as he had hoped. The battle of Chantilly ended in a stalemate as the Federal troops continued their withdrawal toward Washington and the Confederates were unable to pursue due to the weather and their losses. Despite that, the campaign to drive Pope from Virginia was an unqualified success.

Less than two months earlier, Richmond had been on the verge of being captured by the Yankees. Since then, in a series of daring moves, the Confederate army under Robert E. Lee had not only saved the capital from McClellan, it had also delivered a staggering blow to any Union hopes of taking Richmond from the north. By not sitting back and waiting but by going on the offensive, the Southerners had won the most important series of battles in the war thus far.

But the war was far from over, and Lee, flush with success, decided it would be foolish not to press his hard-won advantage.

Across the Potomac River lay Maryland, ripe for an invasion.

Chapter Twenty-five

LAUGHTER RANG THROUGH THE camp of Union Gen. Joseph "Fighting Joe" Hooker's First Corps, which was near Brookeville, Maryland. From the sound of the merriment, an observer never would have guessed that less than a week earlier, these soldiers had been running for their lives after their humiliating defeat at the battle of Second Manassas. Since that time, however, they had been able to retreat to safety across the Potomac River and begin regrouping their shattered brigades. Pope, who had ignored the threat that Longstreet represented to his flank, had been transferred to Minnesota, far away from the fighting, and full command of the Union army had been restored to George B. McClellan, who was a favorite of the troops.

Even more important to the Union soldiers, they had full bellies, relatively dry places to sleep, and plenty of camp followers who had come from Washington to cook meals, wash laundry, and tend to any other needs the demoralized troops might have. Within days the men were feeling much better about themselves, and they were almost looking forward to the next clash with the Confederates.

One of the officers in charge of picket duty at the First Corps camp was in his tent, taking his ease with a young woman from Washington, when he heard his name being called. "Lieutenant Baxter! Got us a spy out here!" The lieutenant sat up hurriedly from his cot and reached for his uniform trousers.

When he emerged from the tent a few moments later, tucking in his shirt as he pushed aside the entrance flap, he still looked disheveled but not too much like he had just been enjoying a romp in the middle of the afternoon. At least he hoped not. Two of his men were standing there with a slender civilian between them. Each soldier held one of the man's arms, and he looked like he was in pain from the tightness of their grips.

Baxter ran his fingers through his hair and then smoothed down his thick, luxurious mustache. "What have we here?" he inquired.

"We caught this Rebel spy trying to sneak through the lines, Major," replied one of the sentries. "You want us to go ahead and shoot him or should we hang him instead?"

Before Baxter could answer, the man burst out in unmistakably southern tones, "Damn it, I told you I'm not a spy! I want to enlist!"

Baxter frowned. "A Rebel? And you want to join the Union army?" He shook his head. "What sort of fools do you take us for, Reb? Do you know how many spies we've caught who tried to tell us the exact same story?" Baxter jerked a thumb toward the woods. "He's not in uniform. Shoot him."

The civilian was aghast. As the soldiers started to drag him away, he called out, "I'm telling the truth! I just want to fight for the side I believe in!"

Baxter snorted. "You expect me to believe that?" He started to turn away, only to come up short against a figure in a crisp blue uniform. Baxter recognized him as a captain of scouts.

"You don't believe that a Southerner could want to fight for the Union?" asked Captain Pryor. His soft drawl revealed his own southern origins. In Pryor's case, he was from the Rio Grande country in Texas.

"Yes sir, I'm sure there are some loyal Southerners, but this man—" Baxter gestured toward the civilian. The sentries had stopped dragging him away when the captain intervened. "This man is clearly a spy—"

Pryor turned toward the civilian and motioned for the troopers to let him go. "What's your name, son?"

The young man straightened his coat. "Nathan Hatcher, sir."

"Where are you from?"

"Culpeper, Virginia."

"And yet you want to fight for the Union?"

Without hesitation, Nathan nodded. "I think the Confederacy is wrong, sir. I don't believe in slavery, and I don't want to fight for it."

"Some say this war's about other things besides just slavery," Pryor pointed out.

"Yes sir, I know. But whatever it's about, I don't want to see the Union dissolved. That has to be wrong."

Pryor nodded. "I reckon a lot of folks feel the same way. Come along, Mr. Hatcher. We'll go talk to the colonel." He glanced at Baxter. "If that's all right with the lieutenant here. After all, it was his men who brought you in."

Baxter wasn't going to argue with Pryor. He saluted and said, "Of course, sir."

Pryor led the young Rebel away, and Baxter watched them go with slitted eyes. He didn't like the way Pryor had butted in, but there was nothing he could do about it.

Except remember the damned Texan—and that young man Pryor had taken under his wing.

GEN. ROBERT E. LEE'S strategy of aggression had worked during the Seven Days and again at Second Manassas. Now, knowing that a successful invasion of Union territory would not only demoralize the Federals but also increase the chances of the Confederacy's receiving recognition and aid from the European powers, Lee's army moved north across the Potomac into the rolling farmland of Maryland.

Not all of the troops went with Lee, however. Once again, the Confederate commander had thrown the dice and split his army, risking an all-out attack by McClellan in order to achieve his objectives in the North.

This was how Will Brannon came to find himself standing on a rocky height overlooking the junction of the Potomac and

Shenandoah Rivers and the village of Harpers Ferry nestled between the streams.

Cannon roared thunderously all around him as he observed the barrage that was pounding the Union supply depot. Just like at Manassas, General Lee had sent Stonewall Jackson to capture a Federal stronghold in preparation for a larger attack. Jackson and his brigades had marched directly here and taken advantage of the high ground that surrounded Harpers Ferry. The Federals, to their dismay, had failed to occupy those heights, so Jackson had moved in quickly and placed his batteries there in position to send shell after shell raining down on the Northerners.

The barrage had been going on for only a short time, but already Will felt confident of victory. The Union garrison had put up almost no resistance. At the bottom of the valley like that, there wasn't much they could do against the barrage.

Yancy Lattimer moved up alongside Will, trailed as usual by Roman. "It won't be long now," Yancy predicted. "The Yankees can't hold out."

"Nope," Will agreed, raising his voice to be heard above the roar of the big guns. Behind the two young officers were the companies they commanded, but it was beginning to appear that the infantry would not be needed to win this victory. Jackson was going to do it with artillery alone.

A few minutes later, Roman pointed and said, "Look, they're strikin' their colors."

It was true. The Stars and Stripes that flew over the armory where the Federals were headquartered was being lowered, and a moment after it was taken down, a white flag rose in its place. Jackson passed the order to cease firing, turned to his assembled officers, and announced, "Gentlemen, the town is ours. Let us go down and take it."

Quickly, the Confederates did just that. They swarmed down from the hills and accepted the surrender from the commander of the Union outpost. Once everything was secure,

Jackson again called his officers together and announced that they would be heading back to rejoin Lee as soon as possible.

"General Hill will remain here at Harpers Ferry for a short time to handle the disposition of the captured supplies and the parole of prisoners," Jackson went on. "General, come as quickly as you can once you have completed your tasks."

Gen. Ambrose Powell Hill nodded. He was small in stature but a fiery commander, given to wearing bright red shirts into battle that made him more visible and inspiring to his men but also more of a target to the enemy. Will knew that Hill would carry out his orders but would also be anxious to march north toward the action.

"The rest of us must be off," continued Jackson, "because I fear that General Lee may find himself in a perilous position indeed if General McClellan ever bestirs himself to move."

UNKNOWN TO General Lee or anyone else in the Confederate command, they were in more danger than they realized. Lee had laid out his battle plans in a document he had entitled Special Order No. 191. This detailed how the Confederate forces would be divided, with Jackson going south to Harpers Ferry. Somehow a copy of it, wrapped around three cigars, had been dropped accidentally in a field near Frederick, Maryland, as the Confederate army moved through there. Arriving in the area later, a pair of Yankee soldiers picked up the cigars, realized that the paper wrapped around them was some sort of important document, and took it to their commanders. Within an hour, this copy of Special Order No. 191 was in the hands of McClellan.

The Federal commander had just been handed the key to smashing, once and for all, the Army of Northern Virginia. Already weakened by weeks of fighting, wretched undernourishment, and lack of proper equipment—especially shoes—the Southern forces were in poor shape to be launching an invasion.

Now, divided as they were, if McClellan pushed forward immediately he could drive his troops between Lee and Jackson, then
destroy each in turn with his larger, fresher army.

Even presented with this gift, McClellan reacted in his
usual cautious way. Lee's forces were gathered to the west of a
long ridge known as South Mountain, which was breached by
only three gaps. After discovering Lee's plans, McClellan still
waited for eighteen hours before starting his men in motion
toward those gaps.

On the far side of South Mountain, Lee marshaled his
command around the settlement of Sharpsburg. Antietam
Creek lay between the Confederates and South Mountain;
behind the Confederates, blocking any speedy retreat, was the
Potomac River itself. Unwittingly, Lee had placed his soldiers
in the jaws of a trap, and now all he could do was try to prevent it from closing.

The South Mountain gaps were crucial. McClellan had to
be stopped or at least slowed down there, or the invasion of
Maryland would be shattered almost before it began.

MAC PEERED over the barrel of the rifle he had picked up,
along with a bandolier of ammunition, from beside the body
of a dead Confederate soldier a short time earlier. Every time
he aimed a rifle, Mac was reminded of his brother Titus. If
Titus were here at Crampton's Gap, no doubt he would be
more effective with his fire. But Mac was doing the best he
could. He squeezed the trigger and sent another shot toward
the Yankees who were struggling to advance through the gap.

Stuart and the cavalry had ridden up to Crampton's Gap,
the southernmost of the openings through South Mountain,
earlier in the afternoon. In this rugged, rocky, heavily wooded
terrain, there was no place for cavalry charges, so Stuart and his
men, who had been riding back and forth between the gaps all
day, had dismounted to help rally the defenders, who were

becoming disorganized and demoralized by the ever-increasing numerical superiority of the enemy. The Northerners kept pouring into the gap, and it was all the Southerners could do to prevent them from breaching the ridge.

Mac was crouched behind a stone fence that meandered along the southern side of the gap, just west of the narrowest part of the passage. With him were several cavalrymen from Lee's brigade and a number of soldiers from the command of Gen. Lafayette McLaws, who had been ordered to hold Crampton's Gap. Mac ducked below the top of the fence as he reloaded the rifle, then came up in a crouch and slid the barrel of the weapon over the fence.

Before he could fire, a sharp whine split the air and some-thing smashed into the rifle, ripping it out of his hands. The impact of the blow shivered up Mac's arms as he fell backward. Alternating waves of pain and numbness went through him.

After a moment, the sensation began to subside, and he looked around for the rifle. It had fallen beside him. He picked it up with aching hands and saw that the barrel was bent and the breech smashed. A Yankee bullet had done that, Mac realized, and then ricocheted off before it could hit him. The bullet could have just as easily continued on and struck him, too. He had come that close to death.

The sound of hoofbeats made him look up. Fitz Lee was riding toward the fence and leading the silver gray stallion. "Mac," he called as he reined in. "We have new orders."

Mac gave a little shake of his head to clear away the cob-webs of his close brush with death, then scrambled to his feet. Staying low, he hurried over to take the stallion's reins from Lee and then swing up into the saddle. Both men prodded their mounts into a gallop that carried them out of the gap, away from the fighting.

"Report," ordered Lee when the two men had come down from the western slopes of the ridge. Lee had sent Mac to the gap to observe the state of the Confederate defenses.

Mac shook his head. "We'll never hold the gap, General," he said bluntly. "The Yankees have too many men. The terrain favors us, but not enough to make up for that."

Lee nodded slowly. "I thought the same thing, and so does General Stuart. He's ridden to tell General Lee that General Jackson is on his way back from Harpers Ferry. If we can keep the Yankees on the other side of South Mountain long enough for Stonewall to get back, we may have a fighting chance."

Mac had known that Jackson went south to capture Harpers Ferry, but he hadn't heard any word of how the assault on the Federal supply depot there had gone. "Was General Jackson successful at Harpers Ferry, sir?" he asked now.

"Very much so," Lee replied with another nod. "He overwhelmed the Yankees there with an artillery bombardment and didn't even have to use his infantry. Your brother is with him, isn't he?"

"Yes sir." Mac knew that Will had come through the battle of Second Manassas without any injuries, and now he was confident that Will had survived Jackson's latest foray against Harpers Ferry, too.

"I expect you'll be seeing him again soon," Lee went on. "We're going to follow General Stuart back across Antietam Creek and join General Lee's forces there."

And that was where Will was bound for, too, thought Mac. He was glad the cavalry was moving west. It was inevitable that the Federals would soon come pouring through the gaps in South Mountain and equally inevitable that they would fall upon the Confederate forces near Sharpsburg. When the battle came, he and his brother might not be together, Mac told himself, but at least they would be on the same battlefield, fighting for their homeland.

WILL YAWNED and tried to ignore the growling of his stomach. His men had been living on corn and apples for the past two weeks, ever since the Confederate army had moved across the Potomac into Maryland, and while as an officer Will had access to fare that was more nourishing than that, he chose not to take advantage of that. If it was good enough for the men he fought beside, it was good enough for him. So he was making do on the same meager diet these days.

But Lord, he would have almost killed for a cup of coffee this morning!

It was Wednesday, Will thought as he watched the sun rise over the high ground of South Mountain to the east, on the far side of the creek. He couldn't come up with the date right away, but after a moment he recalled that it was September 17. At least, he thought that was right. In the army, it was easy to lose track of such things.

Will and his company were camped in some woods just west of the Hagerstown turnpike. Nearby, Yancy Lattimer's company had also spent the night in the woods and was now waking up, just as Will's men were doing. From where he stood, Will could peer through the trees and across the road into the cornfield that bordered the turnpike to the east. Beyond the cornfield were more woods.

Some of the corn had been harvested before the war came to Maryland, but many of the ears were still on the stalks, snug in their husks, waiting to be picked. For a moment as he stood there looking at the field, a longing came over Will. He wished he was back home in the cornfield on the Brannon farm, work-ing alongside Mac and Titus and Cory and Henry. He wished Cory hadn't been so restless, and that the Yankees hadn't been so damned stubborn and self-righteous, and that all of the Brannon brothers were still together instead of scattered to hell and gone. What he wouldn't have given right now to feel the sun hot on his back as he toiled in the fields with his brothers, to hear his sister's voice as she called out to them and brought them a bucket of cool water to drink, to see his mother's face, stern though it usually was . . .

The tramp of marching feet came to Will's ears from the north. He reached for his hat and called to Darcy Bennett, "Get the men ready to move out, Sergeant."

It was just past seven o'clock in the morning.

"MY GOD, would you look at that?"

Gen. Fitz Lee's voice made Mac glance up. The cavalry-men sat on their horses on Nicodemus Hill, west of the Hagerstown turnpike and overlooking the road. Maj. John Pelham's artillery batteries, which were attached to Stuart's cavalry and were sometimes known as "horse artillery," were here. While Lee and some of his men watched from the hill, the rest of Stuart's forces deployed to the southwest, waiting in the Confederate rear to go wherever they were needed.

Mac looked where Lee was pointing. What he saw made him feel hollow inside. Wave after wave of blue-clad figures were marching down the turnpike, so many of them that their ranks spread out for several hundred yards on each side of the road. Mac swept his eyes in an arc from north to south and saw similar advances occurring all along the Confederate line, although nowhere did the attack appear so strongly concentrated as here on the Confederate left.

They had known it was coming, Mac told himself, but still it was an awe-inspiring thing to see. The Union army under McClellan vastly outnumbered the invasion force under Lee, but Mac knew that the Confederates had a chance. Their delaying tactics at South Mountain had won enough time for Jackson to bring his men back from Harpers Ferry, except for the forces he left behind with A. P. Hill. The Federals would be facing an army that was together, rather than split apart as it had been mere days earlier.

But there were so many soldiers, so many . . .

The cannon began to roar, sending shot and shell down on the advancing Federals. Below Nicodemus Hill, rifle fire crackled in the early morning air. Clouds of smoke slowly spread across the valley along Antietam Creek.

And Mac sat on the hilltop and watched, thrilled and appalled at the same time.

NATHAN HATCHER'S pulse thundered in his head. He lifted a hand and tugged at his collar. The thick wool of his tunic made his neck itch. But that was the least of his problems. When his company reached the woods up ahead, he planned to find a bush and retch. Otherwise he would disgrace himself in front of the other men, these strangers who were now his comrades despite the fact that they were from the North and he was from the South. Despite his being a Virginian by birth, he now wore Union blue.

And he was starting to wonder just how much of a favor Captain Pryor had done him. Maybe it would have been better if those sentries had shot him on that first morning when he crossed the Federal lines.

It wasn't very far to the woods now, he told himself. Surely he could step out of ranks long enough to throw up without getting into trouble with his sergeant. He wasn't sure why he felt so nauseated this morning. It wasn't just fear. Of course he was fearful; there were Rebels up ahead somewhere, everyone said, and before the morning was over, he and the rest of Hooker's men would probably run into them. But despite the fact that everyone back home had considered him a weakling and a coward, Nathan knew he wasn't afraid to fight. He wasn't even afraid to die, as long as it was in a noble cause.

But he was still sick to his stomach, no matter what was causing it, and he wished they would reach the trees.

A dull boom sounded in the distance, and a shrill whistle came from overhead. Men who had been in battle before cried out and threw themselves to the ground. Nathan stopped in his tracks and stood rooted to the spot, lifting his head to look up into the air. Something was coming at him from the direction of a hill to the west of the road.

Then the entire world seemed to explode in a brilliant flash of light and the loudest noise Nathan had ever heard in his life.

Chapter Twenty-six

WILL DIDN'T BOTHER SADDLING the dun. As he moved to the edge of the woods and looked north at the tide of Union soldiers rolling closer and closer, he knew that this battle would be fought on foot. He pulled his pistol and waved his company forward, and at that moment the artillery on Nicodemus Hill opened fire. Several shells burst in the middle of the Union advance, obliterating some of the troopers and sending the others who were nearby leaping for cover. The assault jolted the Federals forward, however, and they charged toward the woods and the cornfield with a roar welling from their throats.

"Fire!" Will shouted, and a volley rippled along the Confederate line at the edge of the woods. The lead scythed through the Northerners but barely slowed them down. Will glanced at his men and saw that they were anxious to close with the enemy. They wanted to rush out there and meet the Federals head-on. But there was cover here in the woods, and Will wanted to preserve that slender advantage as long as he could. "Steady, boys!" he called as his men reloaded. "Wait for them to come to us . . . Fire!"

Again bullets tore through the approaching blue wave. They began to return the fire. Shots sizzled through the trees, knocking leaves from branches and thudding into trunks. A few men cried out and fell. Will glanced at the cornfield to his right and saw the hail of bullets cutting through the growth, knocking ears of corn from their stalks, and making the plants sway as if a wind were blowing over them.

It was a wind of death, thought Will, and that was all he had time to think before the Federals were upon them.

He emptied his pistol at almost point-blank range as the leading edge of the Union attack reached the trees. Around him, the men of his company could hold back no longer. With Rebel yells sounding from their mouths, they leaped forward, firing their rifles, thrusting with the bayonets, slashing with rifle butts. The two sides came together with an audible crash. Grunts of exertion mingled with shrieks of pain. Men who tripped and fell were trampled ruthlessly underfoot by friend and foe alike.

Will pulled his saber from its scabbard. His training in its use had been rudimentary at best, but he knew how to hack back and forth with the blade. As he fought, his senses alternated between a heightened awareness and a dull numbness. There were moments that were crystal clear, etched in his memory for the rest of his life: the open, shouting mouth of a Union soldier lunging at him, the bitter stench of powder smoke in his nose, the burning pain of a bullet that grazed his left shoulder and tore his uniform but left only a red mark on his flesh. At other times he seemed surrounded by a fog that pressed in on him so that the figures around him were blurry and the sounds of battle only a distant din. But always he fought, striking out at anyone in a blue uniform.

Something brushed his face, and he realized it was a corn tassel. He had stumbled into the field without knowing it. All around him the plants were falling, some of the stalks cut down by flying bullets, others toppled by the bodies of men as they fell wounded, dead, and dying. Green was splashed with crimson and then crushed into the earth. Will thrust his saber into the side of a Federal soldier, tore it free, shoved the man aside, and turned to look for another foe.

He saw Yancy Lattimer twenty yards away from him, trying to rally some of the men, and in one of those vivid moments that would haunt Will, he saw flesh and bone and blood explode from Yancy's right knee as a bullet shattered it. His friend twisted and started to fall, his mouth opening wide in a scream. Will leaped toward him, trying to go to his friend's aid, but before he could reach Yancy one of the Union attackers smashed into him from the side, knocking him off his feet. Will landed underneath the man, who struggled to get his hands around his neck to choke the life out of him.

Will was able to gasp in part of a breath before the man's hands closed around his throat. He had dropped his saber when he fell, and he started to slap around on the ground next to him, searching for it. As he stared up at the man looming above him, Will saw past the Federal's head to the top of several corn stalks standing out in stark contrast against the sky. Will's fingers touched the hilt of his saber.

He grabbed it and thrust it into his assailant's side, not realizing until he jerked it out and struck again that the blade was broken so that it was only a foot long. That was enough, though, as the jagged end of the saber penetrated the man's heart. He gasped, died, and fell to the ground. Will rolled over, pushed himself to his knees, and looked toward where he had last seen Yancy.

The aristocratic young captain still had his pistol in his hand. Despite the agony he had to be in, he continued to fire at the Federals around him. Behind Yancy, Will saw one of the blue-clad soldiers preparing to thrust his bayonet into Yancy's unsuspecting back. Will looked around desperately for a gun. He knew he couldn't reach Yancy in time to stop the man from killing him.

Someone crashed into the Northerner from behind, reaching over his shoulder to grab the rifle and jerk the bayonet to the side. Will saw a dark face over the soldier's shoulder. Roman looped an arm around the trooper's neck and hauled back hard. With all the hellish noise on the battlefield, Will couldn't hear the crack of the man's spine, but he knew from the way he went limp that Roman had broken his neck.

Will stumbled toward them as Roman flung the dead Federal aside and bent to help Yancy. He got an arm around his master and started to lift him, and then Will was there on the other side, helping him. Yancy muttered something and then his head fell forward as they brought him upright. His face was ashen. He had only passed out from the pain of his wound, Will told himself. He wasn't dead.

"Let's get him back into the trees!" Will shouted to Roman. He was surprised to see the slave here on the battlefield, even though he knew that Roman had never been far from Yancy's side. The two of them had grown up together, Will recalled Yancy saying. There had never been any question that Roman would go off to war with his master, but until now he had never been in the thick of the fighting.

If Yancy survived, he would have Roman to thank for it, Will thought. But at the moment, the odds of survival seemed pretty slim for all of them.

"I got him!" Roman said. "You go on, Mr. Will."

"You're sure?"

Roman nodded. As Will stepped back, Roman began dragging the unconscious Yancy toward the trees.

There wouldn't be much solace there, Will realized. The fighting spread from the woods across the turnpike and through the cornfield into the far woods. Everywhere he looked, soldiers in blue and gray and butternut struggled. Artillery shells fell, killing men indiscriminately and leaving smoking craters and grisly remains. Will swayed for a second, almost overcome by the horror of it, then steeled himself and wiped the back of his free hand across his mouth. He lifted his broken saber, looked at it, then tossed it aside and bent to snatch up a fallen rifle instead. The rifle was unloaded, but he could still use the bayonet . . .

He glanced toward the trees, but Yancy and Roman were gone. With a hoarse yell, Will turned and threw himself back into the battle.

———◦◦◦◦———

THE FIGHTING in the cornfield between the two stands of trees was fierce, but it was not the only battle taking place that day.

Farther south, along a winding country lane that had been worn down by use until it was below the level of the surrounding fields, Confederate troops under Gen. D. H. Hill used the sunken road as a natural defensive line when another section of the Union army attacked. They drove the Northerners back at first, but then some misunderstood orders caused some of the defenders to try to retreat. That led to more of the Confederates falling back, and suddenly the Federals were able to swarm over the road, firing down into it and ruthlessly cutting down the fleeing men who tried to scramble up the other side. Bodies fell, only to tumble back down the slope and form a gruesome pile at the bottom. It was a slaughter, pure and simple, and the new name given to the road by a civilian who looked at it the day after the battle was all too appropriate: Bloody Lane.

Meanwhile, on the Confederate right at the far southern end of the conflict, Union troops under the command of Gen. Ambrose Burnside were ordered forward to capture a stone bridge that arched across the waters of Antietam Creek. Burnside was slow to follow that command from McClellan, however, and Southern defenders along the western bank of the creek were able to drive back Burnside's tentative assaults. The Federals might have been able to wade across the creek without using the bridge, but Burnside stayed stubbornly focused on his objective, even though he was hesitant to commit enough troops to actually capture the bridge. Finally, after midday, the Northerners were able to break the back of the Southerners' defense and take the bridge, allowing their troops to pour across the creek and threaten the right flank of the Confederate line.

With the Federals advancing on both flanks and the Confederate center at the sunken road broken, it seemed inevitable that the day was going to belong to the Union.

MAC REINED the stallion to a halt as he saw the men marching toward him along the road. They were coming at a quick pace, led by a red-bearded officer on horseback. Mac recognized him as A. P. Hill. He straightened and saluted as the general rode up to him.

"General Stuart's compliments, sir," said Mac. "He and General Lee sent me to see if you were coming yet."

"I'm here, aren't I?" snapped Hill. He nodded toward the northeast, where the battle continued. "And I take it the Yankees are over there?"

"Yes sir," Mac replied grimly. "General Lee—that is, Gen. Fitzhugh Lee—and I have been covering the field all day and keeping up with developments. A short time ago, we saw the Yankees push across Antietam Creek and turn our right flank."

"They did, did they?" flared Hill. "Well, we shall see about that!" He turned in his saddle and raised his voice in a shout. "There's plenty of fighting left for us, men! Let's get to it!"

An answering roar of eager voices came from Hill's troops. They surged forward, marching even quicker than before, and Mac reined the stallion to the side of the road to let them pass. He saw that many of them wore no shoes, and the blisters on their feet had broken and were bleeding, leaving red stains behind them in the dust of the road. But still they marched on, anxious to engage the enemy.

Mac hoped it would be in time. From everything he had seen this afternoon, the Confederate army was teetering on the brink of utter collapse.

THE TIMELY arrival of Hill's forces staved off total defeat. Storming in on Burnside's men who had just tramped across the bridge, Hill drove them back savagely, forcing them to retreat over the same span they had just spent hours and hundreds of lives to capture. Gen. Isaac Peace Rodman, one of the Yankee field commanders, was fatally wounded in the battle, and his death demoralized the surprised Federals that much more. They had had no idea they were about to be attacked so strongly. In a matter of minutes, they went from being poised to deliver the fatal blow to the Confederate army to fleeing for their lives.

Mac watched the fierce onslaught until he saw the Northerners scrambling back over the bridge, then turned the stallion and went in search of someone to report the news. Robert E. Lee's headquarters was in Sharpsburg, a short distance to the west, but Mac knew from Fitz Lee that the commander probably wasn't there. Robert E. Lee had been seen throughout the day riding close to the Confederate front line, directing the battle personally.

A short time later, Mac spotted several officers on horseback coming toward him along the Harpers Ferry road. He recognized the distinctive ostrich plume on Stuart's hat, and the white-bearded man next to him was Robert E. Lee. Fitz Lee was also with the group, and he spurred forward to greet Mac. "There you are!" Lee exclaimed. "Did you see any sign of General Hill?"

Mac saluted as the other two generals rode up. "Yes sir," he answered. "I spoke to General Hill and directed him toward the Yankees."

Stuart observed, "I suspect the general could have followed the smell of powder smoke and found the battle."

"Yes sir," Mac agreed. "We were taking a terrible beating. But General Hill was able to turn the Yankees back."

Lee nodded, his lined face grave with thought. "They will regroup on the other side of the creek, I suspect," he said. He looked toward the west, where the sun was lowering toward the horizon. Mac figured there was less than an hour of daylight left. Lee went on, "It has been a long and bloody day, gentlemen. Let's wait and see what the morning brings."

If anybody had any sense, thought Mac, morning would bring retreat. They were beaten. This ill-fated excursion had been turned back, and now they had no choice except to get across the Potomac and into Virginia as quickly as possible.

But then, he wasn't a general, he reminded himself. He was just a soldier. He didn't make the decisions, he just carried them out.

He knew, though, that nightfall couldn't come too soon to suit him. He was ready for this day . . . "this long and bloody day," as Lee had called it . . . to end.

———◦◦◦———

USING THE rifle to support himself, Will stumbled through the trees. The weapon's stock was broken, but he had used it to smash in the skulls of quite a few Federals before it had shattered. The bayonet still worked fine, though, as Will had proven numerous times throughout the ghastly, seemingly endless hours of battle. He had fought until his arms and legs were leaden and his brain was numbed beyond thought.

Now, the sun had slipped below the trees that bordered the road, and dusk was settling down. The bombardments on both sides had stopped, and the rifle fire was dying away, too. Not the cries of the wounded, however. Those were still going on, and Will knew they would last long into the night.

He just wanted to find Darcy and the rest of his company and see how badly they had fared in the battle. And Yancy, too; Will wanted to scour the field hospitals and see if Yancy and Roman had turned up. He staggered on, limping on a twisted ankle, an injury he couldn't recall happening.

"S—stop . . ."

The feeble voice made Will pause. He figured it was just one of the wounded calling out to him, begging for water or whiskey or any kind of release from the unimaginable pain, but then Will heard a sound he knew all too well: a rifle being cocked. He turned slowly and saw a blue-clad figure standing in the cornfield. A Union soldier, bloody and bedraggled. A Union soldier, pointing a rifle at him.

"You . . . you're my prisoner," he rasped. There was something odd about his voice. He didn't *sound* like a Yankee.

Will didn't care about that. He just stared at the young soldier for a moment, then started to laugh. The laughter rolled out of him, shaking him until he had to clutch his makeshift crutch more tightly to keep from losing his balance.

"Stop it!" the Federal demanded. "Stop that laughing, damn you! And drop that gun."

Will's laughter trailed away. "The rifle's busted," he said.

"I . . . I don't care. You're coming with me—"

"I'm not going anywhere with you," Will growled, and his voice was harsh with anger now. "Haven't you had enough, you stupid son of a bitch? We fought all day, and what'd it get us, either of us? Go home." He shook his head wearily and started to turn away. "Go home if you can."

"I . . . I can't," the man sobbed. "And if you don't stop, I . . . I'll shoot you."

"Go ahead," Will told him without turning around. "Right now, I just don't give a damn."

He limped away, while behind him, the young soldier let the barrel of the rifle sag toward the ground until he dropped the weapon. The soldier fell to his knees, covered his face with his hands, and cried.

There had been something familiar about that boy, Will thought, but he knew he was crazy for thinking such a thing. He didn't know any Union soldiers. He didn't *want* to know any Union soldiers. He just wanted to find someplace to sit down and rest for a while, and then he wanted to know if any of his friends were still alive.

In the cornfield, Nathan Hatcher lifted his tear-streaked face to the heavens and saw the stars beginning to come out. Their cold, clear, timeless brilliance mocked the carnage below.

Chapter Twenty-seven

THE NEXT MORNING, BOTH armies occupied roughly the same positions as they had the day before. The biggest difference was that some twenty-four thousand men who had been alive and relatively healthy before the battle were now dead or mortally wounded. The single bloodiest day in the war had come and gone.

An air of tension hung over the battlefield all day, but no new fighting erupted on September 18. Both sides were exhausted and seemed to have had enough of killing, at least for now.

———◦◦◦———

WILL PUSHED through the doorway of a large stone building. A few days earlier, it had been a barn on a farm just outside Sharpsburg. Now it was a field hospital where many of the Confederate wounded had been brought.

More like a charnel house, Will thought as he looked at the figures lying anywhere there was the least bit of space. Many were missing arms or legs or both. On his way into the building, Will had passed a large pile of severed arms and legs that had been tossed out after being removed from their former owners. The smell of rotting flesh filled the air along with the moans and low-voiced curses of the wounded. Uniforms had been replaced by yards of bloodstained bandages. This place was as close to hell as Will Brannon ever wanted to come.

A man in rolled-up shirtsleeves and covered with rust brown splatters looked at Will and growled, "What do you want? If you're not hurt, get out of here."

"I'm looking for somebody," Will told the man, whom he supposed was a doctor.

"If they're in here, you'd be better off not findin' 'em." The man jerked a thumb toward the door. "Go on, son."

Will was about to argue, but then he heard a familiar voice call softly, "Cap'n. Over here, Cap'n Will."

He looked into a shadowed corner of the barn and saw a man rising from the ground next to a blanket-shrouded shape. Will recognized Roman. The slave had a bandage around his forehead, but he didn't seem to be badly hurt. The man lying next to him, though . . .

Will ignored the doctor and stepped closer to Roman. "Yancy?" he whispered as he looked down at the man on the floor. To his relief, as his eyes adjusted to the gloom he saw that the blanket had not been drawn up over the man's face. Yancy was still alive. He had probably been drugged into a deep sleep.

Will put out his hand and Roman gripped it hard, neither of them caring at the moment about what color either of them might be. "Massa Yancy, he lost his leg," Roman said.

Will felt his heart sink, even though he had known ever since he'd seen the rifle ball strike Yancy's knee that such destruction could never be repaired. The doctor came up behind Will and stated, "Had to take the leg off halfway up the thigh. Only way to stop gangrene from setting in. 'Course, he'll get blood poisonin' and will probably die anyway—"

Will spun around to face him, and it was all he could do not to grab the lapels of the man's bloodstained shirt and shake him like a rat. "No," Will snapped. "He's not going to die."

The doctor pulled back a little, clearly startled by the tall, brawny captain who had just spoken to him so savagely. "We'll do all we can for him, of course," he stuttered. "Soon as we get back to Virginia, he'll be sent to a regular hospital, probably in Richmond."

"You see that he stays alive until then, you hear?"

The doctor swallowed. "Captain, we're not miracle workers. We just do the best we can."

Will took a deep breath and forced himself to nod. He knew he was being unreasonable. "Sorry, doctor. I reckon I've just seen too many good men die."

"We've all seen too much of that, Captain. But I promise you, we'll do everything we can for your friend."

Will nodded again, then turned back to Roman. He put a hand on the slave's shoulder. "Is there anything you need?"

Roman shook his head. "Naw, sir. Don't you worry. I'll stay with Massa Yancy all the time, be right with him until he gets home. I'll take good care of him."

"I know you will." Will felt like he was choking, so he just patted Roman's shoulder and turned to leave the field hospital. He couldn't stand it in there anymore. He moved as quickly as he could toward the door, weaving through the crowd of wounded men and being careful not to step on anyone.

As he entered the fresh air, he thought that the doctor was probably right: Yancy would get blood poisoning and die. Any kind of serious wound was usually fatal, even if it didn't kill right away. Will hoped fervently that when his time came, his end would be a quick and clean one. He could think of no worse fate than wasting away like Yancy was bound to do.

Darcy Bennett was sitting on a wagon tongue waiting for Will. He rose to his feet as he saw his captain emerge from the barn. "Did you find Cap'n Lattimer?" he asked.

Will nodded. "Yes, Yancy was in there, just like his sergeant told us. He's going to be sent back to a hospital. He lost his right leg above the knee."

Darcy shook his head in sympathy and said, "Hope he comes through it." It was clear from his voice that he didn't hold out any more hope for that outcome than Will did. "What about the rest of us?" Darcy went on. "You reckon we're goin' home?"

Will turned his head and gazed to the south, toward Virginia. "I hope so. There's nothing up here for us. Not now."

ON THE night of September 18, the Confederate army began withdrawing toward the Potomac River. Long lines of men straggled across the river at Boteler's Ford. Despite the day of rest they had just had, the soldiers were still exhausted, and many of them were nursing minor injuries. The more seriously wounded were taken across the ford in wagons. Those who were hurt too badly to travel at all had to be left behind in Maryland, in the hope that the Federals would take care of them.

Mac tried not to fall asleep in the saddle as he sat on the stallion and watched the ford from the top of a nearby rolling hill. Fitz Lee's cavalry brigade had been given the job of guarding the retreat. On the night of September 17, following the battle, and all during the next day, the cavalrymen had been patrolling the area, making sure that McClellan wasn't about to launch another blow at the bloodied, battered Confederate army. Mac wasn't sure how long he had gone without sleep, but he figured it had to be close to forty-eight hours.

Lee rode up the hill toward him, looking as weary as Mac himself was. Mac doubted if even Stuart could have managed to look dashing under the circumstances. Lee asked, "Any sign of the Yankees?"

Mac shook his head. "No sir. It looks like McClellan's going to let us go home."

"He's a fool." Lee laughed humorlessly. "But that foolish caution of his is probably the only reason we're not all dead or prisoners of the Yankees right about now. That's the only bit of luck we've had."

Mac wasn't used to hearing his commander sound so bitter and full of despair. They had all been so hopeful when they crossed this river the first time, he thought. The Federal forces had been on the run, and even though the Confederates had known that the Northerners outnumbered them, they had been convinced, almost to a man, that their string of victories would continue.

Instead, it had come to a bloody end in the farmland along Antietam Creek. The battle itself had been a draw, but it was the Army of Northern Virginia that was withdrawing from the field. The Northern newspapers would crow about it and call the battle a great victory for the Union. That was going to be a mighty bitter pill for the Confederacy to swallow.

"I saw your brother down there a few minutes ago," Lee said after a moment of silence. "His company just forded the river."

Mac nodded. He had seen Will briefly during the day, just long enough for the two of them to embrace and assure each other that they hadn't suffered any major wounds in the fighting. Mac had come through it without a scratch since he hadn't been involved in any of the actual combat. Will had a few scrapes and bruises and a twisted ankle, but that was all. Fortune had certainly smiled on the Brannon brothers.

"Why don't you go ride with him?" suggested Lee.

Mac looked at the general. "Are you sure, sir?"

"Go on."

Mac thanked him then heeled the stallion into a trot.

He had gone only a short distance when he felt someone watching him. Mac slowed and looked to his right. Twenty yards away, he saw a blocky figure on horseback that he instantly recognized as Maj. Jason Trahearne. The major was staring at him, and even though Mac couldn't make out the man's expression, he felt sure Trahearne still coveted the stallion. With everything that had been going on, Mac had almost forgotten about Trahearne, but clearly Trahearne had not forgotten about *him*.

Mac gave a little shake of his head and rode on. He had more important things to worry about now than some arrogant officer.

In the bright moonlight, Will's company wasn't that difficult to find. Mac spotted his brother's rangy figure on the dun horse and rode up alongside him. Will looked over and grinned, then asked, "What are you doing here?"

"General Lee said I could ride with you."

"Gen. Robert E. Lee?"

"Fitzhugh. The one I work for."

Will nodded in understanding. "Where will you be bound once we get back?"

"Don't know," Mac replied with a shake of his head. "Wherever the cavalry goes next, I suppose."

"If there's time . . . if we're anywhere near Culpeper . . . why don't we try to go home for a day or two? I . . . I'd really like to see everybody . . . again . . ."

His voice broke, and Mac was surprised to see tears coursing down Will's cheeks. In all his life, he couldn't recall a similar sight.

"I think that'd be a good idea," Mac said quietly. He swallowed hard and went on, "Looks like the sun's going to be coming up pretty soon."

They rode on to the south, the men of Will's company marching beside them.

———

ON SEPTEMBER 22, 1862, President Lincoln, after visiting with McClellan at the Antietam battlefield, returned to Washington and issued a preliminary Emancipation Proclamation. The idea of doing this had been in the president's head for a while, and this seemed to be the proper time since the North had claimed to have won a great victory.

The proclamation stated that, effective January 1, 1863, all slaves in the states then in rebellion would be, from that moment and forever after, free. Critics charged that the proclamation was only a political move, but to many it was a signal of a change in the North's war aims. It abandoned the idea of reclaiming the South for the sake of the Union alone and transformed it into a moral crusade for the rights of individuals.

But issuing a proclamation was one thing, and enforcing it was something entirely different, as Lincoln—and the rest of the divided nation—would find out.

———

THE CITIZENS of Culpeper County had heaved a huge collective sigh of relief as summer drew to a close and the devasta-

tion of war had come no closer than Manassas. A few skirmishes had taken place in the county while it had been under
Union occupation, and even now with the Federals gone,
times were hard, no doubt about that. But people still had
their land, and they were thankful for that.

Abigail Brannon was kneading bread dough in the kitchen
of the farmhouse when she heard the shouting outside. For a
few moments, the noise didn't fully penetrate her conscious-
ness. She was thinking about the sermon Benjamin Spanner
had preached the previous Sunday morning. His words had
been both eloquent and moving, as usual. She had been fond of
Reverend Crosley, but he hadn't been the preacher that
Benjamin was.

Nor had he been anywhere near as handsome . . .

Abigail frowned as that thought crossed her mind. It was
bad enough that she thought of the minister as Benjamin, rather
than Reverend Spanner, but he had insisted that she call him
by his given name, at least when they were talking privately.
And that was happening more and more often as he came to the
house to pray with her and discuss the Bible with her. She had
a keen mind for theology, he liked to say, and he never failed to
gain some new insight from their discussions.

Everything was entirely proper, of course. Cordelia was
often in the parlor with them as they talked. And both she and
Benjamin were long past the age at which such things as
romance mattered, Abigail told herself. They were merely
friends and fellow strugglers along the path to glory.

Still, at times she found herself thinking that Benjamin
Spanner had the most intense blue eyes she had ever seen.

She finally looked up from her work as she realized that someone was whooping exuberantly on her front porch. A second later
the front door flung open, and Cordelia came running through
the house, calling, "Mama! Mama, come quick!"

Abigail took her hands out of the bread dough and wiped
them on her apron, muttering, "Land's sake, what now?" She

went into the front room and found her daughter there, smiling from ear to ear.

Cordelia grabbed her hand and tugged her toward the front door. "Come on!" she cried.

"What is it?" asked Abigail. "Henry hasn't done something foolish again, has he?" Henry was always coming up with some prank or other. He had been like that ever since he was a child.

Abigail stepped onto the porch following Cordelia. To her left, she saw Henry and Titus, their clothes covered with dirt from their work in the fields as they got the fall planting in. That was where they should have been now, she thought, not lollygagging on the porch in the middle of the day.

Then the two tall figures standing to her right caught her eye, and beyond them in the yard between the house and the barn she saw two horses. She recognized them as the big, wild-looking stallion Mac had somehow tamed and the rangy dun with the dark stripe down its back that had always been Will's favorite mount. But the two men standing there on the porch, those two gaunt, haggard men in dusty ragged uniforms, they couldn't be . . . they just couldn't . . .

"Mama," Mac said. "I told you I'd be back. And look who I've brought with me."

Abigail's mouth was as dry as cotton, and her head was spinning. She looked at the taller of the two men, at the harsh planes and angles of his face, and saw the son she had expelled from the farm. The son she had disowned because of the violence that followed him and the trouble he had brought down on all of them. The son that she had told herself she could never forgive.

"Mac and I thought we'd pay you a visit while we can," Will said. "That is, if I'm welcome here."

"Welcome!" Cordelia blurted out. "Of course you're welcome. Isn't he, Mama?"

Abigail didn't say anything.

"Ma?" Titus prodded. Like Henry, he was clearly glad to see his older brothers.

"Ma, say something," Henry prompted.

The words wouldn't come out of Abigail's throat. Because of Will, Henry had nearly died when the Fogartys bushwhacked him. Will had the blood of other men on his hands, too.

And yet Abigail had prayed to God to watch over Will. She had tried to harden her heart, but he was still there, just as he had always been. He was her son, and nothing could change that.

"Ma . . . ," Will said, his voice almost a whisper.

So much had happened to him, Abigail thought. She could see it in his eyes. He had been through too much, seen too much death and pain and suffering. But there was still strength there, too, and Abigail liked to think that he had gotten that from her.

"We can both go if you want," Mac said softly.

"No." Abigail heard the word come from her mouth, and warmth flooded through her. She blinked her eyes, feeling the tears there. "Don't go. Either of you."

Then she stepped forward, reaching out, and embraced both of her oldest sons.